About the Author

Lexie Winston has been an astronaut, rock star, princess and time traveller. In her dreams. But none of the dreams have lived up to what becoming an author has been like. She gets to live in a world of pure imagination, and her heroines get to do the things she's always wished she could.

When not writing books, Lexie is a mother of two gorgeous teenagers and the wife to a patient and understanding man. They live in Western Australia and are lorded over by a black toy poodle. She loves camping, reading and if her iPad was stolen, her world would explode. (It has the kindle app on.)

And check out my website at lexiewinston.com

Also by Lexie Winston

The Collectors Division

(Reverse Harem Series)

Guardian

Guardian's Blood

Guardian Ascending

Arbor Vitae Coven

(Paranormal Romance Series)

Candy Conniptions

Dreamy Delights

Fangtastic Fireworks

Neighpalm Industries Collective

(Adult Bully Reverse Harem)

Abandoned Girl

Broken Girl

Tormented Girl

Wanted Girl

Cherished Girl

Seductive Sins Collection

(Reverse Harem Series)

Glorious Gluttony

Gangs, Guns, and Glory

Galaxy Circus

(Sci-Fi Reverse Harem Series)

Apprentice

Broken Promises

(Dark Poly Romance Series)

Secrets Kept

TORMENTED GIRL

LEXIE WINSTON

First published by Neighpalm Publishing in 2021

Broken Girl: Neighpalm Industries Collective

Mobi : 978-0-6489412-4-8
Print: 978-0-6489412-5-5

Cover design by Infinity Cover Designs
Edited by Inked Imagination

❀ Created with Vellum

made their way closer to me, forming some kind of protective barrier between me and whatever might come next. I can feel them all around me, each of them having more than enough presence that makes them impossible to ignore. Now that my adrenaline is gone, I'm starting to realize just how cold my soaked clothes are. Each drop that slides to the ground leaves a cool trail that has me shivering. As much as they're eyeing our surroundings, they must be keeping an eye on me as well since they all shuffle even closer, their warmth offering a small amount of comfort. That hits me with a startling moment of clarity. Who would've thought that I'd ever find their presence comforting? I mean, Kai, sure, but the others? Now's not really the time to contemplate my relationship or lack thereof with the Summers men, but it's more pleasant to think about than how closely Holden is tiptoeing alongside death.

Everyone seems lost in thought as we wait for the helicopter, and it's not much longer before the telltale thump of the blades can be heard. The noise grows louder and louder as it gets closer, and the four of us move out of the way, giving the helicopter plenty of room to land in the field. My hair whips around my face as it descends, and Kai wraps his arm around my shoulders, pulling me into his body to shield me from the flying debris the rotors are kicking up.

We watch in silence, knowing there's no use in

trying to yell above the noise as the door opens. Two paramedics jump out, one carrying a stretcher and the other a bag of supplies, their faces set in carefully neutral expressions despite the obvious emergency. Ducking their heads, they hurry toward the group surrounding Holden. With the sound echoing through my ears, I can't hear what they say, but Oliver, Thomas, and Dad move away, allowing them room to check him out. They make quick work of taking his vitals and bandaging the wound. From where I stand, it looks like the blood may have slowed, which is a good sign that it didn't hit anything vital.

Before I know it, they've maneuvered him onto the stretcher. Once they have him settled and secured, they say something else to Dad, and after a quick nod, the paramedics efficiently get Holden squared away in the helicopter. Dad turns to Oliver and Thomas, his mouth moving quickly and hands gesturing toward the rest of us. Oliver doesn't seem to be listening at all, his eyes focused on where Holden has been taken, but Thomas is alert enough for the both of them, returning Dad's hug then waving him off. Without a glance at the rest of us, Dad rushes to the helicopter, the pilot taking off as soon as the door is fully closed. Hiding my face in Kai's shirt, I don't turn back until it sounds like it's moving away.

Thomas starts to move toward us, turning back when he realizes that Oliver is still staring after the helicopter even though it's become no more than a speck on the horizon. He walks back to him, swings an arm around his shoulders, and guides him to the rest of us.

"Right, they're headed to the Cedars, and Dad told us to meet them there. Let's start walking back. Jacinta should have made it home by now, so it's only a matter of time before she gets to us. We'll send Josh back with the tack after we're all home."

"What did the paramedics say?" Declan demands.

"His vitals were strong, and they said they'll probably do a CT scan on his head when he gets there as the gunshot alone isn't enough for him to stay unconscious. He must have hit his head fairly hard when he came down on the jump. They're optimistic though, said we did the right thing by trying to slow the bleeding and getting him out of the water as quickly as we could."

Turning back to look at the five of them trailing after me, Tom still has his arm around a very pale-looking Oliver, his hands covered in Holden's blood. It's only now I notice that apart from me and Kai, none of the others are wearing helmets. Anger flows through my body, overruling the guilt that I feel, and I rush back toward them. They stop at my sudden movement, and I use the moment to my advantage. Pushing my hands against Declan's chest, I shove him, trying to channel all of my whirling negative energy into the motion. Shoving

Declan has very little success, which honestly sparks that anger even higher. "Why the fuck are none of you wearing helmets?" I shout, and they all jolt in surprise. Growling, I move to shove him again, but he grabs at my hands, his mouth tipped down in a scowl.

"Like, what the fuck? Do you think that all the money you have will save you from something like this? *I'm a big man, and I'm rich and hot and sexy, so I don't need to cover my head because I won't fall off of my horse!*" Lost in my rant, I barely notice that I've deepened my voice in what has to be a *terrible* impression of a man's voice. Even though they should be cowering right now, and they would be if they could feel the actual force of my rage, smirks start to twist their lips. Even Oliver looks less upset, and his eyes are gaining back some of their usual sparkle at my outburst.

"What?" I scream at them. "What the fuck are you all laughing at?" I try to escape Declan's hold, but he quickly twists me around so that my back is to his chest, my arms pinned to my sides.

"So which one of us do you think is hot and sexy?" he whispers not so quietly in my ear, and I hear the others chuckle. Stilling suddenly, I think back to what I just said and internally facepalm. Fuck my life.

I stamp on Declan's foot and pull myself out of his arms, stalking away. "None of you, you're all assholes." Stalking back along the fence line of the paddock, I find a fire break and assume Jacinta will bring the vehicle back this way. I walk like I have a firecracker up my ass, not wanting to address the question Declan asked. I don't want to lie to them, but I'm *definitely* not willing to admit that I find them all fucking sexy, bad attitudes excluded, especially as they seem to be going out of their way to be nicer.

"Oh, Harlow, don't be like that," Jaxon shouts, and even more chuckles follow behind me. A little smile crosses my mouth, thankful that I'm able to distract them from their worry for just a moment even though it's at my own expense, but silence quickly falls.

We walk on without further conversation, in a moment of respite that's just that—a moment. All of the guys have caught up with me, and Oliver is walking on his own now. Those little thoughts I've had recently are popping back into my mind. There's 100% something more here than grieving the potential loss of a sibling, but I don't know who's a safe bet to ask what I really want to know. Normally, I would just go directly to the source, but I don't want to upset him more than he is.

Thomas and Declan have fallen behind us as we've trudged along for the last ten minutes, the two of them having a quiet conversation. They seem to be arguing about something, and the way they continually increase the distance between us just a little too purposefully makes me think they're trying to keep it private. Finally, they stop arguing, and I hear the shuffle of them catching up to the rest of us before they settle next to me, the remaining tension speaking much louder than their silence.

Only another minute or two passes before I can't take the edge in the air. "What's the problem?" I question, and they exchange a look. I guess through whatever voodoo brother mind speak they have going on, Declan is nominated as the one to talk to me.

"Harlow, I really think that we should have Luke take the horses down to the movie set tomorrow," he suggests quietly. "Things are starting to escalate, and it feels like an unnecessary risk."

My gaze flicks between him and Thomas, taking in their worried eyes and accompanying frowns. "Have you guys noticed that the last three incidents haven't actually been aimed at me? Or the violent ones haven't been, at least." I tick off on my fingers. "It was Oliver's car that was damaged, Jacinta was the dummy that was shot at, and now it's Holden who actually has been shot."

Declan's eyes widen as he realizes I'm right, but Thomas looks less surprised, like he had already considered it too, and he gives me a nod of acknowledgment. "So far the only things aimed at me were the saddle, the photo of DS, and being pushed into the pool."

Jaxon, Kai, and Oliver have been quiet while we've been talking, but they've been paying attention. "But DS and Jenny were covered in blood too, and their actions against Jacinta, Oliver, and Holden show that they have the potential to be violent. I feel like it's just a matter of time before they escalate," Jaxon points out, and I have to give him that.

"It's almost like they can't make up their mind. Whether they want to hurt you or hurt one of us," Kai muses.

"But why? Why target you guys instead of me?" I'm so confused, but right now, I almost appreciate it. Trying to puzzle together any little part of this mystery is keeping my mind off of the worry for Holden as well as the guilt that this is somehow my fault, and it's doing a great job of smoothing over any boundaries that were still awkwardly in place between the Summers men and me. What'll happen when we're no longer distracted, who knows?

"Actually, that's a really good question. Maybe you were the original focus, but then we got onto their radar too. We've tried to keep it quiet that Jacinta was responsible for the billboard, but maybe it's gotten out. I mean, between **PR** staff and the original marketing people, someone must have said something to the wrong person. It's the only reason I can think to target any of us," Thomas suggests, but I shake my head.

"But why do anything to *me*? Offense mostly intended, but you guys are the assholes. I haven't done anything to anyone!" Needing to move, I start walking again until the others catch up.

"Well, you did suspect the stalker was Jacinta to begin with. We all did, and that could have been the stalker's big break to try and control you—where you were, who you were with. Maybe they capitalized on that and continued on in that vein to scare you off? But then that seems to suggest that whoever it is has insider information. Stuff that not everyone would know," Declan adds, and there's a light in his eyes that tells me he's ready to grab hold of this challenge. For whatever reason—anger over Holden, worry for Jacinta's life… worry for me?—he seems like he's not going to just let this go.

"Yes, but why change their tactics? Why aim at you guys now? It just doesn't feel right that there would be two separate agendas here, one to get rid of me and the other to punish you guys."

Before anyone can answer, the sound of a fast moving vehicle heading toward us draws everyone's attention. Coming down the track is Jacinta in a black truck that's kicking up a plume of dust behind it. She's driving it like she stole it, and I honestly didn't think the princess had it in her. She pulls past us and circles, coming back around before the window rolls down. "Jump in. Josh will come back for the gear later." There's not enough room for all of us, so I climb into the bed, Kai joining me, as Declan jumps into the front and Thomas, Jaxon, and Oliver squeeze into the back. As soon as we're all seated, Jacinta floors the gas, sending us flying back to the house.

The ride is bumpy, and I end up being jostled around, but Kai shuffles closer and wraps an arm around me, holding me tightly against him. Embraced in his warmth, I feel my body relax slightly, his familiar arms bringing comfort that I haven't previously felt.

"I can see you destroying your lip with worry," he says in my ear. "Tom said that Holden was stable, and the bullet wound, while concerning, wasn't the biggest issue. A bump on the head can be dangerous, but he's already being checked out, and he'll be okay. We're going to head straight to the hospital after we get home and change. Are you going to come with us?" His warm breath caresses my ear, and a tingle of desire flows through me, followed quickly by one of complete guilt. *Fuck, how can I be feeling horny when Holden has taken a bullet for me?*

I've been thinking about what's the safest choice for everyone, and I huff in defeat before telling him my plan. "I'm not sure I should be around any of you anymore. I think I'll take the horses to the movie set tomorrow with Luke's help and then put us both on a flight back home. Jenny and DS can follow as soon as I can arrange it. I can't risk whoever is doing this taking a shot at another one of you. Next time, his aim might be better." I shudder as the memory of the sound, the slow motion of Holden falling playing back through my mind.

Kai's arm tightens around my shoulder almost to the point of being uncomfortable. "Like fuck you are," he growls. "Declan will go with you tomorrow, and at no stage will you be left on your own. One of us will be with you until this asshole has been caught. Also, don't forget we're going to Hawaii on Friday. They won't be able to get to you there." He sounds hopeful, almost pleading, as he reminds me of the trip I'd agreed to go on.

My stomach sinks with the thought of disappointing him, but before I can argue my point, he shuffles me around and pulls me between his legs so my back is to his front. Now, he can talk to me easier despite the rush of the wind. His warmth sinks into me, and I lean back into him as his arms wind around my front, holding me like I'm the most precious thing in the world to him. I've never really felt this way before, never been held in this way that just says someone cares about me. Not by someone who wanted to get in my pants, anyway. It's weird but refreshingly nice at the same time. I only wish it wasn't happening in the midst of such a traumatic event.

"Please, Harlow. Don't let them run you off. Holden will be okay, and when he wakes up, I know he'll say the same thing. Plus, you had a point back there. We don't know what this person's real agenda is, and if they're out to get you and we're just a bonus, then you might be in more danger if you leave. Without us to draw some of their attention, who knows what would happen to you. Don't let them win by scaring you into leaving us behind. A Summers never backs down from a challenge, and that's all this is. Practically a speed bump on the road that's life. This person will be caught, and we'll think back to the time when it all happened and be grateful we stuck together."

His words hit a place deep inside of me, one that refused to feel full despite all the love the Bostons have always given me. Prickles cover my skin, whether from his words or just the warmth of his breath on my ear, or maybe from both. I have no idea why he affects me the way he does, but I do know that for the first time ever I feel wanted in a way that is more than just familial love. This is something that I have basically no experience with, and I get the feeling that I might desperately fail at managing any kind of romance, but I want it. I want it so badly I can taste it.

Just as I go to answer, my gaze registers that we're here. Jacinta screeches to a stop in front of the house, and everyone climbs out. Nana is waiting for us on the front steps, her hands wringing with worry.

"Hurry up and get changed. We'll take the helicopter. It will be here in ten minutes, and we have clearance to land on the roof of the hospital."

Thomas comes around and opens the tailgate, making it easier for me and Kai to climb down. He raises his eyebrows at the sight of Kai's arms wrapped around me, but he doesn't say anything nor does he look upset. I must have mistaken the heated looks that I had seen in his eye previously, and a pang of disappointment hits me before I shake it off. *Jesus, Harlow, stop being so greedy. Kai isn't enough for you? You've got to torment yourself by chasing after the other brothers too?*

He holds out a hand, and I untangle myself from Kai and move toward him, allowing him to help me down. His hand holds onto mine for just a moment longer than necessary, leaving me looking up at him in question until Kai follows after me, jumping down without assistance.

Once Kai is on his feet, Thomas suddenly lets go, and they both rush up the steps with the others while I hang back. It's only as Jacinta opens the door to go in that Nana's voice has them all pausing. "Well, Harlow, what are you waiting for? Get moving!" The siblings turn back to face me, and I blush under all the attention. I'd been hoping they'd all be so wrapped up in getting ready that they wouldn't notice I wasn't there. God knows they've never wanted me anywhere with them before.

"Ahh, I was just going to wait here, see if Josh and Luke needed help catching the horses. I would just be in the way at the hospital." Jacinta narrows her eyes and opens her mouth to say something, but Declan gets in first.

"Bullshit," he snaps, surprising me. Does he *actually* want me around? "I wouldn't want to risk anyone else getting hurt because of you." And there it is, asshole extraordinaire. My heart races at the thought that he blames me for what happened to Holden... even if it is true.

"What the fuck, man!" Kai exclaims, and Thomas adds in his own complaints.

"Seriously?" He sounds amazed. Declan frowns at them, and then it looks like he's thinking about what he just said. A moment later, he shakes his head, eyes wide.

"Fuck! No, sorry, that's not what I meant. I meant you shouldn't be on your own. It's not safe at the moment, and we don't want anyone else getting hurt, including you." My heart slows at his apology, my gaze moving to each of the siblings before landing on Nana. Despite the horrible reason for us all being gathered together right now, the woman has a small sly smile on her face. Deciding the conversation is over, Jaxon and Oliver both push past Jacinta and disappear through the door.

"Well, come on then," Jacinta insists. "Let's get moving. The quicker we're changed, the quicker we're in the air." My eyes meet hers, and they are a lot less icy than they normally are. I know that letting her ride our horse was maybe a tiny twig on an olive branch, and maybe with a bigger threat to occupy her mind, she'll finally put aside her feelings about me. I nod at her, earning a slight one in return before she disappears after the other two. Thank fuck. In the back of my mind, I'd been worrying that this would cause her to ramp up the dislike again, but it appears to be the opposite. She actually seems to have thawed a tiny bit. Maybe, just maybe, I'll end up an accepted member of this tight knit family. Maybe they could even learn to love me?

Chapter Two

Harlow

Despite everyone wearing a headset, the helicopter ride is uncomfortable, and the occasional attempt at conversation is tense and fraught with worry. We're passing over the city when Nana thinks of something and gasps.

"Has anyone thought to call Hope?" Everyone exchanges glances before shaking their heads. Oliver doesn't respond at all, his gaze blindly looking at something outside his window, Jacinta's hand clasped firmly in his. Every few minutes, someone peeks at Oliver with concern; his catatonic state is worrisome and so out of character for the man that I have gotten to know. Considering I have no idea about this secret that no one else seems surprised by, there's not much I can do about that. For now, I help in another way.

"I'll do it," I offer as the helicopter starts to descend. That'll give me an excuse to hang back a bit and allow them to take the lead. I mean, it's not like they're going to allow all of us to see him at once, is it? Not to mention that I meant what I said about being in the way. I'm still the outsider in this family, and the looping thought that this all has happened because of me won't let go. Plus, as head of the PR department, Hope really does need to know, not to mention she's Holden's best friend. For the latter reason alone, I'm sure she's going to freak out, and the rest of them don't need the added burden of sorting through her emotions on top of their own and Oliver's.

"Thank you." It's Jaxon who responds this time, grabbing my hand and squeezing it. It's all I've been able to do to not fidget for the whole flight. His thick thigh has been pushed up against mine, and that intoxicating scent I remember so well from the club has filled my senses, but I didn't want to show that it still affects me, so I gritted my teeth and kept still. But now the touch of his rough hands has the memories flooding back. The tingling trail that followed his fingers as he caressed my skin. The way he whispered dirty words into my ear, causing my panties to grow damp with my desire. A shiver shoots down my spine, and my nipples prickle at the memories. His hand in mine squeezes once more, and my eyes shoot to his. It takes all of my self-control to keep them from widening. If the barely there smirk on his lips has anything to say, I haven't hidden my reactions as well as I thought.

The helicopter lands with a thud, and the doors open to a man in a suit who helps Nana down, waiting for Poppy before he turns and escorts them to the elevator. The rest of us quickly follow behind, Thomas slamming the door shut behind him so that the helicopter can take off. Everyone's heads are down, and no words are exchanged until the elevator doors close behind us all. Though his eyes make the rounds to each of us, he addresses Nana and Poppy.

"Mr. and Mrs. Summers, I'm Levi Petesburg, the director of the board of the hospital. I'll show you down to the private waiting room I have your son in. Your grandson is still in surgery, and as soon as we know anything, his surgeon will be out to update you." His words are gentle, but I can tell he's the money man. There's not quite a *hungry* gleam in his eye, but he's slightly on edge, like he knows that this could be a big deal for the hospital. It's his job to smooth any ruffled feathers and make the hospital look good in front of Dad, Nana, and Poppy as a well-known and wealthy family who could certainly become thankful donors if all goes well.

I'd seen the type before when I attended one or two charity functions with the Bostons. I mean, there's nothing wrong with it, all businesses need to be able to function, but it comes across a little like a vulture circling a carcass. Although the others keep their poker faces firmly in place, Jacinta is as bad at it as I am, and she scowls at him in open disgust. I move over, turning to face her, and her eyebrows rise in surprise. "Settle, girl, he's just doing his job," I whisper out of the corner of my mouth. She huffs and starts to say something, but I continue. "Vultures have to scavenge to survive; it's in their nature." She blinks once, then twice before a snort of laughter escapes loudly enough to be heard despite the background music of the elevator and conversation that we've both tuned out.

Finally, the elevator comes to a stop and opens onto a bustling floor. That trademark scent of a hospital hits my nose, antiseptic with a layer of decay. As much as they try to hide it, nobody can avoid that lingering smell of impending death that all hospitals carry.

The suit hurries us past private rooms, dodging people clad in scrubs gathered around work stations. The bustle is loud after the quiet music of the elevator, and the incessant beep of monitors echoes through my ears, almost feeling like they're beeping in time with my heart. Surely, they can't be beeping that fast though.

After it seems like we've trekked through half the hospital, we stop at a room. The board member opens the door, ushering in Nana and Poppy and the siblings, but I hesitate in the hallway. He turns back with a slightly panicked expression, as though he's seeing dollar signs flying away right in front of his eyes, likely thinking he's lost a wealthy, distraught Summers somewhere in the halls rather than plain ol' me. Not caring that I almost gave the man a heart attack, I pull out my phone and wave it at him. "I need to make a quick call. Can I do that here?"

He frowns, showing his distaste at the question, but waves down the hall. I'm not really sure what his problem is, though it's possible I might not have spoken to Jacinta as quietly as I'd thought. "If you go down to the next waiting area, there's a balcony. You can go out there and use it. Even in our private rooms, we discourage the use of cell phones. These rooms are to provide privacy and comfort to our valued patients, not for socializing."

"Thank you." I smile pleasantly before tacking on *asshole* in my mind. I've only made it a few steps down the hall before I stop in my tracks, a sudden chilling thought hitting me. *Should I move away from the others?* But surely I'm safe here at the hospital. Deciding I am, if for no reason other than their security cameras and the hope that someone is actually monitoring them, I head in the direction he indicated, finding the waiting area and the glass doors that lead out to the balcony, but a disturbance up ahead at a nurses' station draws my attention.

"But I'm Mr. Summer's PA! He needs me, and you need to let me through. I demand it!" Unfortunately, I'm pretty sure I recognize that voice, right down to the toddleresque petulance in every word of the entitled "request." I wander closer, and sure enough, Cecelia is kicking up a stink, and the poor nurse she's harassing looks absolutely frazzled. Before I can slip away unnoticed, Cecelia spots me, her eyes lighting up with no effort made to disguise the hunger. *Speaking of vultures…* "Hannah, yoo hoo!" she calls, waving a manicured hand at me. I roll my eyes in disbelief that she doesn't even know my name. "Tell them who I am and get them to let me through."

Looking back toward the private room they're waiting in, I can see Jacinta and Declan watching from the doorway, the former's eyes narrowed with a blatant hatred that I haven't even seen aimed at me. On one hand, I could be a bitch and let her through… but on the other, I could avoid subjecting my dad to that torture on top of his worry for Holden. Not to mention the bitch just flagged me down as if I'm her servant. I will tolerate and forgive a lot for the Summers kids thanks to my love for Nana and Poppy and my desire to make a connection with Dad, but I owe Cecelia nothing.

Turning back toward the nurse, I shake my head and keep a straight face. "Sorry, I have no idea who she is. You may need to call security. The Summers family always has some crazy followers, but to prey on us during such a private family moment? This one might be unhinged." A small smile crosses the nurse's lips as she reaches for the phone, and the look Cecelia gives me is enough to strip paint. The shiver that runs down my spine tells me to be wary of the enemy I've just made, but it's not enough to dampen my satisfaction at knowing the parasite is being denied for today.

When I turn back, Jacinta is smirking and Declan inclines his head in a nod. Well, look at that, us behaving civilly to each other, who'd have guessed? I guess the enemy of my enemy truly is my friend.

I walk out the glass door onto the balcony and pull up Hope's number on my phone. It only rings twice which makes me think she had the phone in her hand.

"Hey, bitch, what's up with all the Summers bailing on their empire today? I haven't been able to get in touch with any of them, and usually they're all glued to their phones if they're not physically in the office." Her voice comes through cheery but a little frazzled.

"Hope, you need to get down to Cedars-Sinai. Holden's been in an accident." There's nothing to be gained from beating around the bush. I know she cares about him enough that it'll just piss her off if I spend time on bullshit when she could've been on her way to be with the family. The silence on the other end is deafening, but then I hear her heels clicking as she starts running.

"Hold the elevator! I'm on my way," she quickly replies before hanging up.

Looking out at the city beyond, it's the first chance I've really had to process what's happened. Just five minutes of quiet to deal with all the emotions flooding me and then I'll bottle it all down and join my family. And it's weird because that's how I see them all now. Albeit a dysfunctional one that still has *a lot* of amends to make, but a family nonetheless.

The worry hits me hard when I think about Holden and imagine all the things that could be wrong with him. I should stick to my plan and go home, but there's a selfish part inside of me, one that I've never indulged before, that says I want to stay and go to Hawaii with Kai. Of course, only if Holden is out of the woods. I can't imagine Kai being that keen to leave until we know he's going to be okay. But what if he isn't? Brain injuries are tricky. If Holden had been an animal, I'd have euthanized him by now; unfortunately, there's not a lot we can do for brain injuries in animals, and it'd be kinder to put them out of their misery. Thankfully, humans are more resilient, and there's so much more that can be done for him.

Tears trickle down my face, and a sob escapes before I can stop it. Bringing my hand up to my mouth, I cover it before anything else can escape. My entire life, I've really only had five people to care about: Chuck, Melinda, Max, Nana, and Poppy. Max's grandparents are more like stern acquaintances, and god knows my mom would never be a real example of what family is like. Now that I've had a taste of the Summers family, even though my most positive glimpses have been of how they treat each other, *not* me, I don't want to lose this. I don't know that I believe in Nana's crazy schemes, but I feel like there could be a lot for me to gain here if we make amends and move forward. My body shudders with emotion, but I know I need to pull myself together. Grabbing the hem of my shirt, I use it to wipe away my tears and take a big breath to collect myself before heading back inside.

Once there, instead of returning to the room, I go to the nurses' station I'd seen Cecelia at before. She's no longer there, but the poor nurse is. She looks up and smiles at me when I approach.

"Can I help you?" Despite being tired and probably half traumatized by Hurricane Cecelia, she's still got the perfect professional voice, albeit a little bit of wary.

"Long day?" I ask sympathetically.

"You have no idea." Actually, I'm sure I do, but I don't correct her. The woman just had to deal with Cecelia, and she saved me the trouble, so I'm not going to give her any more grief.

"I have a friend coming up soon; it's Holden Summers' best friend Hope. Can you please let her through when she does, so she can wait with us?"

The nurse writes Hope's name down on a piece of paper on her desk and gestures to an envelope.

"I found this on the desk after your other friend

was escorted out by security. I didn't see who dropped it; a patient had pressed their call button, so I was seeing to them. Can you give this to one of the Summers?"

The envelope has *Harlow Stubbs, Care of the Summers Family* written on it. I frown as she passes it to me. "That's actually me." A quick flip back and forth gives me zero clues, no return address or any identifying information on it, and my heart rate increases as I realize who this might be from.

Thanking the nurse, I turn and hurry back down the corridor to the private waiting room. I can't resist checking it out before I join the others, wanting to know just what I'm getting us into. With a quick slide of my finger under the flap, the envelope opens, revealing a note and a picture inside. The image is of Holden on the ground with Thomas beside him, his mouth set in a grim line as he tries to control the bleeding. The note says, *Next time, I won't miss.*

The door flings open, and Poppy sticks his head out, his frown easing when he sees me standing near the door. "Ah, there you are, Hally. I was wondering where you had gotten to. What have you got there?" He moves away so I can walk inside the room, and I can't put it off any longer. It's quite spacious, with a couple of big sofas, a coffee table, and a little kitchenette that has a coffee machine and a fridge. The walls are painted in a light mint green color. I guess it's supposed to be soothing, but

I'm still shocked about the note, so it does nothing to calm my now erratic heartbeat. Poppy must get impatient because he takes it out of my hand before I'm able to stop him.

"Fucking hell." The words rip from his mouth, and I flinch. I haven't heard Poppy use that kind of language before.Not even the time he got caught in the crossfire of a paintball fight Max and I had been having in the backyard. He did look pretty covered in neon yellow and pink paint. "Declan, call the detective in charge of Harlow's stalking case. We need to update him on what has happened, and now we also need to give him this as evidence before we send him out to the farm. I'm not feeling very optimistic, but maybe they'll be able to find some kind of evidence left behind."

Dad had been sitting on one of the sofas, his eyes crinkled with worry, when I walked in. But at Poppy's outburst, he jumps to his feet and storms over, snatching the envelope and its contents out of Poppy's hand. His eyes blaze with fury, and he whirls on me.

"Harlow, this is getting out of hand." There's no disguising the unconscious flinch that his quick movements and palpable anger trigger. Even though my mind knows that Dad wouldn't hurt me, my body remembers these clues as a sign of pain to come. "Oh, honey, no!" he blurts out immediately, holding up a hand like he's trying to calm a wounded animal. "I'm not blaming you, and I'm so sorry it came across like that." By the end of his sentence, Dad looks as wrecked as I'm feeling, his face pale and eyes wide. All I can do is close my eyes and take a breath, willing my body to calm down and reminding myself that I don't have to be on the defensive. When I've got my fight or flight instinct settled, I manage to give Dad a nod.

Declan moves over and takes the piece of paper out of Dad's hand before passing it to Thomas. It makes its way around all of the siblings before it gets to Nana, and the sob that leaves her mouth when she reads it has my heart breaking.

"I think it might be better if you returned home." Dad's eyes cloud with sadness as he slowly reaches out, grabs me, and pulls me against his chest, holding me tight. "Safer is what I mean. I wouldn't be able to live with myself if anything happened to you. We're just lucky that Holden was only shot through the shoulder."

I pull away from him. "Is he okay? Have you heard anything?"

"The doctors confirmed it was a through and through, and he's going to be fine. He may need some PT on his shoulder, but he was *very* lucky. They were worried about swelling on the brain from hitting his head, but the CT scan has cleared that. He's got a big lump and a bad concussion, but they're expecting him to wake up soon."

The wave of relief that flows through my body has me shuddering, and Dad gathers me close again. The affection and warmth I'm still getting from this man when I'm the one responsible for one of his other kids being shot is mindblowing and what finally breaks the dam holding back my emotions. I start to sob into his chest embarrassingly loudly, but he just croons to me, softly rubbing his hand up and down my back.

The room is silent while I have my breakdown, and I squirm self-consciously at the thought that everyone's watching. My mind races with information overload and panic, but the one thing it latches onto is that I think Dad is right. I know what Kai said earlier, and there's part of me that still thinks he has a valid point, but if even Dad is saying I should go… Maybe that's best? Finally, I pull away, wiping my face on the edge of my shirt.

"I'm going to call Chuck and tell him what's been going on and ask if he can arrange for a truck to come and get the horses. Then I'll call Alex and ask him to come and get me and take me back to the estate. I'll pack up my things, and once the truck comes tomorrow, I'll catch a flight home." My voice hitches at the end in disappointment. I can't believe it's all come to this.

I dealt with Jacinta's jealousy and survived her best effort to chase me off, kept a strong face despite the Summers men playing their weird game of hot and cold, and had a real family right outside my reach. Now I'm going to be chased away by some nameless asshole who's decided to make my life hell. By the time I get to that last thought, I'm starting to feel more anger than resignation. Why should I give all of this up? I want to see what my life with the Summers could become, damn it!

"Now, hang on a moment." Kai jumps up from next to Nana. "How do we know this will stop if she goes home? What if they follow her and she's on her own with nobody to protect her? Plus, maybe the stalker won't like her being around the Bostons any more than they like her being around us. We might be putting Chuck, Melinda, and Max in danger when we could've kept the problem central-ized here with us." My wannabe knight in shining armor, Kai's expression is so intense, you'd think one of them was revealed to be my stalker. He looks like he's ready to fight anyone and everyone who dares suggest I go home.

"If she stays here, we can assure someone is with her at all times." He looks at Jacinta. "You probably shouldn't go anywhere alone either. It was your likeness that had the bullet through its skull. You're obviously a target as well. In fact, maybe we should all go to Hawaii for the weekend. We all agreed that was a good strategy because it's a safe bet that the stalker doesn't have the same resources we do. Nothing that's happened changes that fact, so we should stick with that plan."

"I'm going to have to agree with Kai," Thomas adds. In fact, all the brothers are nodding their agreement, as is Nana, and holy crap, even Jacinta.

Before we can reach a final decision, the door opens and a doctor in blue scrubs walks in. "Holden has been moved to a private room if you would like to go in. We're just waiting for him to wake up. Normally, we limit how many can sit with patients, but it *is* a private room, and it's got plenty of seating, so you can all go in if you wish."

"Thank you," Dad says before he quickly follows the doctor. I let the others go in front of me. Maybe I can just slip out without anyone noticing.

Just when I think my plan has worked, a manicured hand lands on my arm. "Oh no, you don't. I know what's running through your mind. I won't let you slip away and get hurt, or worse, *dead*. You're not going to upset Dad like that because you think you're being all noble and shit. You're coming with us even if I have to get Oliver to use his handcuffs on you." Jacinta's mouth is pursed in the annoyance that seems to be a requirement when she's talking to me, but I can see worry in her eyes as she drags me out the door and after the others. "And don't think I don't know that you'd probably like being hand-cuffed by Oliver." She snorts in amusement like she can't help herself but quickly tries to hide it with a cough.

Damn it, why can't she just stay the vicious cold bitch she has been? I was just getting used to that version of Jacinta. I didn't like bitchy Jacinta, but at least she was predictable enough that I could work around her or just ignore her when I needed to.

The Jacinta who cares whether I'm dead or alive and almost teases me about my attraction to her brothers… *that* Jacinta is unpredictable and far more dangerous. "I thought you wanted to get rid of me."

She stops dead and turns, brows drawing down as she looks me in the eyes. "Not like this. *Never* like this. Humiliating you is one thing, but actually hurting someone, that's just unforgivable. I might not always do the nicest things, but I only do what I know I can live with in the end. *That* I would not be able to live with." Her eyes blaze with intensity before she rapidly blinks, calming some of that fire and looking at the ground like she needs a moment. Without another word, she starts dragging me down the corridor once more.

I've officially entered the Twilight Zone.

Jacinta

Harlow earned herself some points when she stopped Cecelia from getting through earlier. So when the doctor comes in and lets us know we can see Holden, I jump up just as quickly as everyone else, but then I stop. As much as I want to see my brother, to make sure he's okay with my own eyes, I wait. Because if Harlow is anything like me, and I'm suspecting more and more that she is, she'll try to do the noble sacrifice thing and disappear while everyone is distracted.

I could let her go and be happy that she's out of our lives, but with the stalker around, she'd probably end up hurt or dead. And that's not what I want. I would never want Dad to hurt like that. Before my last therapy appointment, my head had been whirling, and I had put a lot of thought into whether I deserved to die because of the horrible way I've treated Harlow. Now, I know that I deserve some humbling, and I need to apologize at some point even if it feels like that option will kill me. But if I don't deserve death when I've been such an awful bitch, then Harlow definitely doesn't deserve it. I don't know when I'll be able to say this out loud to anyone but *maybe* my therapist, but she hasn't actually done anything wrong.

All I really wanted was some distance. I didn't want my family life to be disrupted and thrown into chaos like it was when I let my mother get too close. Or every time one of my brothers trusted someone that betrayed them. I didn't want this new person shoved down our throats, but in reality that's not what's happened. In fact, the more I see her and the more I watch her, I think maybe, just maybe, I've made a horrible mistake.

"What is it about Harlow that scares you the most? Is it the worry she might replace you in the hearts of the ones you love? Or is it that she might actually be someone you *can learn to love?"* Ugh, damn her for making me think

about this. Dad would be pleased to know my therapist's exorbitant fees are worth it, but my life was so much easier when I could just hate the bitch.

I see the way my brothers look at her. *All* of my brothers, even Declan and Jaxon who usually stick by me through thick and thin. They try to hide it, but the attraction is real. Then Nana took me aside yesterday and had a very real and incredibly awkward conversation with me, woman to woman. Frankly, I deserve a goddamn medal for not jumping out of my seat and stomping out of the room. The fact that I didn't do either of those things speaks to just how loud of a wakeup call it's been to lose all the things I care about most: my dad and grandparents' respect and trust, my job, my smooth relationship with my brothers. *A chance with Alex and Shane…* Yeah, pushing that thought aside for now.

The crazy old woman seems to think that Harlow could be the key to their happiness—well, mine too. What if my brothers all shared the same woman? Think of how much easier their lives, and mine, would be if we could just put all our bets on one person who would never even think of straying because she'd get everything she needed from the six of them. And what better option than someone who was already meant to be family? Someone who needs no ulterior motive because the Summers legacy is already hers? According to Nana, there could be no stronger guarantee, no surer bet, than

Harlow being *the one* for my brothers. Not to mention, her theory of having a built-in friend for me, if not eventually a real sister, because Harlow and I would be on more even footing than any other woman in the guys' lives. While I've learned to love Hope, even she's not really family, and family trumps everything.

It really got me thinking. If I went along with things and got out of the way, I wouldn't have to vet six different women, nor would they have to worry about all six of them getting along. I mean, seriously, what are the odds that they find six women who would all fit in with the family and get along with one another? I'm exhausted just from thinking about that clusterfuck.

I also see the way she looks at my brothers. She tries to hide it, and she mostly succeeds, but occasionally, that attraction shines bright. And it's not just one of them. I see it when she looks at all of them, and it's not the same kind of thing that sparks in other women's eyes either. Other women look at my brothers, and I can practically see cartoon dollar signs rolling over their eyeballs. It doesn't matter which one they're looking at. To those gold diggers, my brothers are interchangeable, so any one will do. Now Harlow, she seems to look at them like they're individuals. But then it disappears, like she's fighting it. And I respect that. I respect her for not throwing herself at them.

"You need to slow down and ask yourself the hard ques-

tions, force yourself to think about what you really feel instead of hiding behind that surface anger."

Fuck, I *really* didn't want to like her. I really wanted to hate her, but I can't. I can't even fault her for finding friendship with Alex and Shane. I practically pushed her into their arms with the billboard stunt. Thank god Nana took pity on me and assured me that she knows their relationship with Harlow is platonic. I would have been sick with jealousy if it had been more. How she knew that's what was bothering me, I don't know. The damn woman is practically a witch; she knows things she shouldn't, always has.

Sure enough, as soon as everyone leaves, Harlow tries to slink off, but I quickly put a stop to that and drag her down to Holden's room.

Seeing my brother pale and unconscious is a huge kick in the teeth and really brings to light that my petty games and insecurities are small things in the great scheme of life. Maybe it's time to let go of some of the resentment and try, for the sake of everyone involved.

Letting go of her, I take a seat next to Oliver and put my arms around him, trying to comfort him. It can't be easy for him to see the love of his life in a coma. We all know about their previous relationship. Oliver didn't want to hide it and or feel ashamed about it, and he was quite defensive when he first came to us. None of us cared. Dad had already sat us down and explained their connection before they'd even arrived, but it was Holden that had decided he wasn't willing to risk his place in our family. No matter how many of us tried to assure him that it wasn't either/or—he and Oliver could have both our family *and* each other—Holden refused to trust it.

I'm hoping now they can finally put all this shit behind them and sort out their relationship once and for all. Maybe I'm not the only one who's seeing this situation as a huge wakeup call. I've got a feeling Oli won't be letting him get away with avoiding the subject anymore, and frankly, that conversation is long overdue.

Chapter Three

Harlow

The beeping of machines and that familiar sterile smell of almost death is stronger in Holden's room, and the shudder that courses through me as I look at his still, pale body has me almost sobbing uncontrollably again. Although I realistically know it's the smell of anti-septic and stale air that rarely moves, so much like all the surgical rooms I've worked in, it's still discon-certing to know someone I care about is in this kind of environment. My eyes shoot to his heart monitor where I can see a steady, strong rate, and his blood oxygen saturation is also good. My shoulders relax just minutely. These are all good signs.

Jacinta has already let me go, having claimed the seat next to Oliver and wrapped her arms around him as she softly whispers. Taking a seat next to Nana, my eyes don't leave the two of them as I try hard to listen in on what's being said. Nana sees where I'm looking and the curious crease to my brow, and she sighs before grabbing my hand and pulling me closer so she can whisper.

"When Brad was looking to adopt his last child, he decided that he should probably get an older child since the rest were teenagers already. Plus, what were the chances that some older teen would get adopted by anyone else? It was when he visited a group home that he came across Oliver and Holden. They were both sixteen and had been bounced around in foster care for years before ending up there together. At that point, they'd had enough nasty experiences and were old enough that they weren't likely to find a real home before they aged out of the system. When Brad met them, they'd already spent a year there. The boys had gravitated toward one another and become more than just friends."

Holy shit, is Nana saying what I think she's saying? That would explain all the tension and the guarded looks I was seeing earlier, but it still leaves me with more questions than answers. Like, what happened to break them up? Considering Nana's essentially pushing me to make a harem out of her grandsons, I can't imagine they'd be intolerant and try to break the boys up. Dad doesn't seem like the type either, but I guess I haven't had enough time to really see for sure.

"They were so intrinsically attached to one another, even at sixteen, that we all felt it would be detrimental if we separated them, so he adopted them both, knowing that their relationship was going to be very different compared to the relationships of the other kids." She sighs, sadness in her eyes when she looks between Oliver and Holden. "But then it all went haywire. Like I said, both boys had had horrible foster homes, and Holden was just so grateful to Brad that he was terrified of doing anything to rock the boat. Apparently, his bisexuality had been a trigger for his foster parents, and we learned that he'd been beaten, ridiculed, and essentially tormented by small-minded adults and foster siblings who made him feel that it was dangerous to be who he truly was."

My own eyes are wide at this point, looking between the two men. I care about what Nana's telling me, but not in the way that Oliver and Holden might think. It makes no difference to me who or how they love, so long as all parties are safe and happy. Instead, I'm feeling a little overwhelmed with the events of the day, now adding a weighty sense of empathy to the top of that emotional pile. Even though the Bostons' love and support helped fight back some of my mom's venom, I know what it feels like to be in a home that's not a home, to be around people who make you feel deficient. I was just lucky enough to have a safe space long before either Oliver or Holden did. Once again, I'm seeing bits and pieces of myself—who I am and who I could've been—in some of the Summers siblings, and it's a heavy experience.

Likely realizing I've gotten a bit lost in my head, Nana squeezes my hand, drawing my eyes and attention back to her before she continues whispering. "He made the decision to lock that part of himself away without any input from anyone else. It wasn't easy for anyone when he suddenly cut off his relationship with Oliver. The latter got mixed up with a bad crowd and was arrested. Poor thing had a new family, with more wealth and opportunities than he'd ever had before, but that wasn't enough to keep him from spiraling when the only solid support he'd ever had cut ties. It was then that I discovered his love of drawing and encouraged it; obviously, you've seen that that became a bit of a lifeline for him. Things between him and Holden were never the same. The worst thing is we wouldn't have cared if they had continued their relationship. We would have set boundaries, the same as we did for any of the other kids and their partners, but we would have supported them no matter what."

My mind whirls with the information Nana just imparted on me. That just shed a new light on so freaking much. When I was with Oliver at Neighpalm Ink, he'd implied that he had experimented, but this is *so* much more than I thought. My mind goes straight to the fucking gutter, ignoring the seriouness of the situation, and starts to picture

Oliver and Holden together. Even better, me, Oliver, and Holden together. I start to squirm with all the inappropriate thoughts, and it's Nana's voice that slams me back to reality. *#Awkward.* "It looks like Oliver is finally realizing how much Holden means to him. God only knows what kind of mess this is all about to be." She pats me on the arm before she gets up and walks over to the others, grabbing Oliver by the hand and pulling him into a hug. It's like Nana's touch makes the dam break, and he starts sobbing much like I did against Dad's chest.

"Jesus, anyone would think I was dying." The raspy voice grabs everyone's attention, and we all swing to face the bed. "I'm not, am I?" He sounds a little concerned, and from what I can see, his gaze is a little foggy still, blinking over and over as his eyes dart around the room like they're having trouble focusing. Everyone rushes over to him, which allows me the perfect opportunity to escape.

The door flies open as nurses and doctors respond to the emergency call button one of the others must have pressed. Slowly, I sneak out the door which has been left wide open and hurry down the corridor. I'll just catch a taxi to Shane and Alex's place. I can call Chuck on the way and start to get everything sorted out.

A set of heels on the vinyl floor has me looking up, and I find Hope rushing toward me. "Where is he? Is he okay?" She stops me from going any further, grabbing my arm with a steely grip that could rival Nana's and Jacinta's.

I smile and give her a quick hug. "Yes, he's okay. He just woke up, in fact. If you keep going down the hall, the open door with all the commotion is where you'll find them."

She squeezes me back, a grateful smile across her lips before rushing in the right direction. "Where are you going? Aren't you coming to see him?" she shouts back over her shoulder.

"I'm just going to find coffee for everyone." The lie flies out of my mouth before I can stop it, and I decide it's for the best.

"Okay, I'll see you when you come back." She doesn't even turn around, and I quickly reach the elevator to take me down to the ground floor. It's still there from when she got off, and with a wave of sadness, I climb in and hit the right button. The doors woosh closed, and I take the opportunity to lean my head back against the wall. I know I'm making the right decision. Or the right one to keep everyone safe even if it *is* currently breaking my heart. I can still get to know Dad over Skype or Facetime, and the man has an empire, for god's sake. He could be on a private plane and in Connecticut tomorrow if he wanted.

I grit my teeth in frustration and growl quietly, the sound thunderous in the empty elevator. What the fuck does the stalker want? They can't seem to make up their mind. Do they want to scare me? Or scare the Summers? Is the goal to isolate me and then do god knows what, or am I somehow a threat only if I'm with my new family?

Pulling out my phone, I do the sensible thing and send a text to Alex, letting him know what's going on. There's no point in not being cautious. I'm not going to be the stupid damsel in distress that doesn't take precautions. My phone starts to ring within seconds of me hitting send, but the elevator doors slide open when I reach the ground floor, and I put that thought on hold. I hurry out toward the exit in search of a cab, determined to get away before anyone can stop me, apologizing inside my head to everyone who is going to be upset once they realize I'm gone.

When an empty cab pulls up, I send a photo of the license plates and record the number of the taxi, sending that to Alex as well. My phone starts to ring again, Alex's name blazing across the screen, I continue to ignore it. He's only going to try and convince me that what I'm doing is stupid. And he may be right, but at this very second I feel that it's the best for all of us. At least now there's a trail of information to go on if something does happen to me between here and their place.

As I turn around and look back at the hospital before I climb into the cab, my eyes catch on the balcony I'd stood on earlier. Declan is there, watching me as I climb into the cab. I can't make out his expression from here, but he's certainly not doing anything to stop me, so that's as good as him agreeing, right? I almost lift my hand up to wave goodbye, but I stop myself at the last minute. No point in inviting trouble… any more than I already have.

I climb into the cab and give the driver Alex and Shane's address. I know they're not home because they flew to Louisiana with Jace, but they told me I was welcome to borrow one of their cars if I needed it. I'm going to use it to get back out to the Summers' estate and pack up my things, then I'll return it on the way to the airport. That way, I'll be in control of my own movements for a while. If I have to keep using cabs or Ubers, I'm going to try and be smart about it, but I definitely feel more comfortable being the one behind the wheel. Not knowing who my stalker is has raised too many questions about how close this person might be to me at any given time. The more I can be on my own and in control, the better.

With that decision made, I run through what else needs to be taken care of. I need to ask Josh to look after DS and Jenny until I can get a flight home for them. They may have to wait until Max is finished with the movie, but at least I know they'll be looked after while they're there. I want to also stick my head in on Princess and check on her for Declan. I'm sure he never thought he'd be away from her this long. It's the least I can do while I'm there, and I'll send him a text.

The hospital falls away behind me as traffic rushes by, and I pull out my phone to make a very difficult phone call.

Holden

As the words rasp out of my sore throat, my family swarms me, Nana and Jacinta's tears of relief drawing an arrow through my heart. All of them carefully give me hugs, Oliver's with a touch of desperation, and the feeling of his arms around me again, both familiar and also kind of strange, makes a thought hit me with startling clarity. Somehow, even though we haven't been intimate with each other in so long, there's still something about him that just feels like home. *I've been such a fucking idiot. What have I been doing all these years?*

"What happened? How did I get here?" I try to sit up, but shooting pain in my head and shoulder have me stopping instantly. Moving my head slowly, I look down and find my shoulder bandaged and my arm immobilized against my chest. *What the fuck?*

"What do you remember?" Dad asks gently, and I think carefully about the answer. My head is pounding, but I manage to remember we were all out riding. We had gotten to the water jump on the cross country course, and I remember it being my turn, but after that, nothing. Dad nods when I share that, so I'm guessing whatever happened to my head is probably responsible.

In a combined effort, my family tells me everything that happened after that. *Holy crap, I was shot.* My heart races as I realize how easily it could have been Harlow or Dad as they were both behind me.

Before I can press them about it further, the doctor comes in, moving them out of his way so he can do his checks. I'm trying to pay attention to his questions, I really am, but my eyes are looking for the one person who I haven't seen yet. Before I can mention it, Hope comes bustling into the room, tears streaming down her face, and I'm distracted. The sight of her is almost as meaningful as being in Oli's arms. I love my siblings, my dad, and my grandparents, but those two have a different yet still special place in my heart.

Finally, a few minutes later, Hope is settled and the doctor is done. While the hospital wants me to stay a bit for observation, the general consensus is that I'll be fine, thank god. The tension in the room drops, and it's like a huge sigh of relief escapes my family all at the same time. Once he leaves, I finally get a chance to ask the question.

"Where's Harlow?" Everyone looks around the room in surprise, like they hadn't even realized she was gone.

"Oh, she was going for coffee when I saw her

outside the room," Hope reassures me, not letting go of my hand, but my eyes are locked on Declan when he slips out of the room.

Nana paces and looks at Poppy and Dad. "On her own? She shouldn't be alone now! We don't know who could be waiting." Poppy wraps his arms around his wife while Dad pats her hand.

"Don't worry, Delcan's gone after her," he reassures her. He must have seen him slip out as well.

Jacinta snorts. "Yeah, bullshit, I bet she's gone. It's what I would do to keep you all safe." But I can tell by the way she bites her lip that she's as worried as everyone else. Nana's face pales even more and everyone scowls at Jacinta, but she shrugs unapologetically. "What? I'm coming to the realization that Harlow and I are more alike than I thought."

At this admission, everyone's eyebrows rise in shock, but then a pleased smile crosses Dad's face and he pulls Jacinta into a hug. "I'm so proud of you. Thank you." The look that crosses Jacinta's face is nothing short of awe-struck relief. I know the recent distance between her and Dad has been hard for her; she was always his little princess, and even though she fiercely loves all of her brothers, her connection with Dad is borderline sacred to her. Between him needing space from her to keep his cool and her godsend of a therapist, it looks like my sister is finally making some progress. *Thank god for all our sakes.*

Declan slips back into the room in the midst of

that warm moment, raising an eyebrow as he looks at all of us. "She's gone. I watched her hop into a cab and leave. I don't know for sure, but it's a good guess she's headed to Shane and Alex's to get a lift home. God knows she probably considers that place more comforting than our home."

"But they're not there." Nana frowns again. "They've escorted one of our new designers back home to help him pack up his things."

"Then I'm sure the estate is the next likely destination. I'll head over to the Neighpalm building and take the helicopter home. If she's not there, we'll worry about it then," Declan reassures Nana, and she seems to wilt, looking exhausted all at once. "Dad, why don't you and Poppy take Nana back to the hotel for the night? Holden is fine, and there's no point in you all hanging around." After a few minutes of back and forth, all parties have agreed, with Jacinta and Hope having been talked into a late supper with the three of them. The ladies are all looking a bit worn out, whereas my brothers and I are usually better at keeping up a poker face when we need to, Oliver being the definite exception in this case.

Blowing everyone's minds for the second time today, Jacinta refuses to leave the room until Declan promises to update her the moment he lays eyes on Harlow. That, even more than her earlier comment, reassures me that maybe we're finally going to see some progress there. Once Jacinta decides someone is worthy of her care, she loves hard, and we're just seeing the tip of the iceberg. When Jacinta's truly ready to let Harlow in, Harlow's going to need to prepare herself for a whole lot of sisterly affection in her life. *Whether she wants it or not.*

Once she's got her assurances, they all give me a kiss goodbye and head out the door, leaving behind just my brothers. Despite promising Nana that they wouldn't be far behind them, I know we're about to have one of our family meetings, regrettably lacking our usual joint and liquor.

I struggle to sit up in bed, and Oliver jumps up to give me a hand, his fingers lingering on my body after he gets me into a sitting position and his eyes telling me so many things. But I have something to say, and everyone needs to hear it, though I don't let go of Oliver's hand. I know the two of us need to have another conversation, but that can wait until we're on our own. While I'm finally feeling ready to talk to him about our complicated relationship, I'm not ready to have an audience for that talk.

"That conversation we had last night? The one about what Nana had to say... I'm all in. Life is too fucking short to worry about what anyone thinks, and Harlow is pretty much perfect for us, even with the attached stalker. I know that each and every one of you has had your own things with her, and I can see how attracted you are to her." I meet each of their eyes, and none of them deny it, though I can see both Thomas and Declan are still struggling with it a bit.

"Never before have the six of us been interested in the same woman, so surely that means something. The thought that all of that could have been taken away because of some psycho... That I might not have been able to experience love and be loved like Nana and Poppy have is one hell of a kick in the ass. I'm done denying myself things, and the minute I'm out of this bed, I am going to woo the shit out of Harlow." Oliver squeezes my hand in agreement. He's unusually quiet, but I know it's because he has things he wants to say to me.

"But what about Jacinta?" Jaxon sounds worried, but I don't think he needs to be.

"From what she's said in the last hour alone, she seems to be coming around to Harlow as well," Kai points out, looking smug as fuck. "We all know that's huge. If she's actually sharing those things with us in conversation, then it's got to have hit her hard on the inside. She wouldn't blurt out things like that by accident." The tiniest dart of jealousy strikes at me then, knowing that Kai's probably in the best situation with her out of all of us. He's been on team "give Harlow a chance" from the beginning, and he has a major head start since he's been the least of an asshole.

"Anyway, I just wanted to put that out there. I hope you'll all come around to the idea because I don't think it would work if we're not all in. We need to do this together, so think about it, okay?"

The talk moves away from that and back to who could be doing this, but we just don't know enough about Harlow's mom to make any guesses, so we're stuck waiting for Dec's PI to get us some info. Thomas said he's working an angle too, so it's a waiting game for now. It's never taken a Summers this long to get information; Dec's PI is usually reliable, so something has to be wrong there, but we've just had too much drama going on to stop and dig into it as much as we should have. Like right now, with Dec needing to find our runaway girl.

He leaves not much later, wanting to get back to the house to check on Harlow. As much as he seems to be uncomfortable, he's in. He just needs to admit it to himself. Thomas will be the hardest nut to crack, but we've got time. I think if he just spends more time around her, the decision will be made for him; she's just that kind of person.

The others trail after him until it's just me and Oliver left. He starts to say something, but I put a finger up to his lips. "I want this conversation, but I can barely keep my eyes open. Can we table it until tomorrow?" The relief in his eyes hits me in the gut, and I feel an incredible amount of shame. I have so much to make up for.

"Of course," he assures me, and those beautiful brown eyes framed by his black glasses and his warm hand in mine are the last things I see and feel as darkness surrounds me.

Harlow

I wasn't able to get a hold of Chuck, and it occurred to me once I got to Shane and Alex's and had put the address into the on-board navigation system, that it was probably too late to organize a truck for tomorrow anyway.

Once I finally get on the road, I realize how late it is; street lights are on, and the sun has almost set. There's only a slice of light left on the horizon. Thankfully, traffic has thinned, so it only takes me forty-five minutes to drive home. Shit, *home*! That really is what I consider it now, or one of them anyway. Chuck and Melinda's will always be home too.

As I drive along the highway, my mind is at war with my heart, not knowing which has more ground to stand on right now. The swirling emotions are too overwhelming, and I haven't felt like this in such a long time. Not since I was a teenager, dealing with all my mother's wishy washy bi-polar crap. Back then, I struggled to deal with things in a healthy way. I'm honestly not sure how many times my teenage nights ended with the last sip of a bottle. The night that Max and I were arrested for partying was the first big sign that I wasn't making the best choices, but it took a little while for Chuck and Melinda to realize that they needed to step in and put their foot down, insisting I start talking to a therapist.

By the time I'd gotten well into my freshman year of college, I'd calmed down on the drinking, but booty calls were still on the table. As I'd told Alex what feels like forever ago, I was too busy with my classes to get experience with *real* relationships, so hookups became my way to escape the stress and work out some of my tension. By far, I find the sex to be a healthier way to deal than the drinking, not to mention much more fun. In any case, with all the feelings whirling through me right now, I am desperate for an outlet. Unfortunately for me, my only options at the moment are battery operated.

I'm following the instructions of the recorded voice, my body on autopilot while my mind is otherwise occupied, when a helicopter flies low across my path. It scares the shit out of me, causing my foot to slam on the break a bit too abruptly for comfort, before it disappears into the distance. I couldn't make out any markings or numbers, so I cant't report them, but I fucking would have if I could.

As I pull up outside the stables once more, the Summers' truck is there and waiting for the horses to be loaded into it in the morning. Josh must have gotten it set up after they had dealt with all the saddles and tack we left behind in our dash to the hospital.

I pull the parking brake on the BMW and climb out, stretching. My bones are aching, and my soul is weary after the emotional wringer we've been through today. A hug from DS and Jenny is just what I need before heading inside to bed. Josh had messaged me earlier, assuring that all the horses were happy and safe back home, so I didn't need to worry about them.

Sliding open the door to the stables, a scream escapes when a man steps out of the shadows. He quickly dives toward me, slapping a hand over my mouth. "Fucking hell, Harlow, do you want to wake Josh and the other stablehand?" Declan's voice is low and growly in my ear, and he has me pinned to the wall, his body pressed up against mine. My heart beat slows once I realize who it is, but then I push him away, hissing at him.

"Good one, fuck knuckle, did you forget I have a stalker? You're lucky I didnt have a fucking gun in my hand to shoot you!"

I can't see his face clearly, but he runs his hands through his hair as he steps back. "Fuck, I'm sorry. I wasn't thinking." I turn around and reach out to flip the light switch, not sure how to deal with getting an apology from a Summers. Jacinta being nice? Holden being shot? The revelations about Oliver and Holden's relationship? And now an apology.

This day is trying to completely break my brain and drive me mad.

"Why were you sitting here in the dark, and how did you get here before me?"

"I didn't want to give you a chance to turn and run away, and the helicopter, of course." My temper fires up again with his answers.

"Was that you who buzzed me back on the road?" I growl at him. "You're fucking lucky I didnt have an accident!"

This time, he snorts, his expression lighting up a little. "That was you? That was just unlucky timing. I was pissed off and decided to take it out on an unsuspecting driver. It was stupid, but it did make me laugh. A little distraction from today. Look, I think we both know this day has been much longer than we all thought possible, and once I got up in the air, I realized I left Princess and her kittens alone much longer than expected, on top of everything else."

There's no apology in his tone, but he does seem to be owning up to his actions, and I know how much he loves his cat, so I honestly believe he'd be upset by that. Before I can chastise him any further, he crowds close to me once more. Obviously, he's realized that I'm over the fright. But now that I can see his eyes, I can tell he's pretty fucking pissed.

"Now, little girl, we need to have a chat. Did it not occur to you somewhere in that pea-sized brain of yours that once everyone realized you had disappeared, they would panic, thinking that maybe your stalker had gotten you? You didn't have a single thought for the people you left behind, just did what you wanted like the selfish bitch you are," he grinds out in his fury. A wave of guilt hits me, covering the anger that had been running hot moments before. "You're just lucky that I walked out onto the balcony to call the detective and saw you leave. They're all still worried, but not as much as they would be if we couldn't have found you." His hands are on my arms now, and he's practically shaking me. "Do you know what that would have done to Nana or Poppy or Dad? How can you be so fucking selfish?"

Before I can answer, he smashes his mouth down on mine and proceeds to punish me with his lips. Nipping at my lips and lashing me with his tongue, the kiss is full of heat and fury. I melt into his body and take every bit of punishment that he's giving me. Every bit of worry and concern leaks out of my brain until there's nothing left but a lust-filled fog that is being fueled by this man. Right now, I don't care that he hates me or that we're enemies. I'm diving head first into my old habit of letting sex push my feelings away, and there's no part of me that gives a single fuck.

Our mouths stay fused together while our hands fumble at each other's clothes. The sound as I slide the zipper of his jeans down echoes in my ears as he hikes my sun dress up and over my head. The groan that escapes his mouth when he sees I'm not wearing a bra spurs me on, and I try to shove his jeans down. His big hands come up and palm my breasts in our frenzy, and when he pinches at my nipple, it's my turn for a moan to escape. *Fuck, that feels good.* My panties are wet, and my core clenches in need as I shove my hand into his briefs, grasping his thick length in my hand and stroking it with a firm grip. He quivers against me as his knees threaten to buckle at the sensation, and a wicked grin crosses my mouth when he pulls away from me. He moves down my body, taking one of my nipples into his mouth as his hand pushes aside my panties and strokes a finger through my folds.

"You're so wet for me." Ragged breaths follow those words as I continue to stroke his cock, swiping my finger across the top to use the bead of precum to help with the slide. His finger moves to my clit, using the gathered juices to slide across it, causing my toes to curl.

Pulling his mouth away from my breast, he removes his finger and pulls my panties down, leaving me naked before his very eyes. Eyes that are still filled with anger and so much desire. *I do love a good anger fuck.*

He shoves his jeans down, his eyes not leaving mine, and lifts me, holding me against a stable wall. Wrapping my legs around his waist, I grab a handful of his hair and put my mouth to his ear.

"Fuck me like you hate me, Declan. I'm sure it won't be too hard."

He lines himself up to thrust into me, his tip nudging at my entrance, and my toes curl in anticipation of the burn, but before he can, a clattering sound outside the building has us both freezing.

"Fuck, did anyone else come home with you?" I whisper in his ear, the heat of the moment being replaced by fear.

Chapter Four

Harlow

Without answering, he quickly sets me down on my feet, pulling up his pants before picking up my clothes and throwing them at me. Grabbing a nearby pitchfork, he quietly moves to the doors, sliding out the gap. Logic dictates that I should let him, being the one who's armed, handle this, but I've never been one to let someone else handle things for me. Undeterred, I pull my clothes back on and follow after him, grabbing a shovel off the wall to use as a weapon.

I can only hope it was just an animal or something, but with my luck, I'm sure that's not it. When I get outside, he's standing next to the window that looks into the stable. Glancing down, I find a set of footprints in the garden bed beneath the window, and the pretty flowers that had been planted there are trodden and broken. Nearby, a set of trash cans are on their side and dented, almost like they've been kicked. *What the fuck?*

I come up next to him, peering through the window and feeling slightly disgusted, and a gasp leaves my mouth as it dawns on me that someone had been watching the two of us. They'd seen Declan strip me naked, his back to them but my bare body completely in view. Declan shifts, the movement bringing my attention to him as he pulls his phone from his pocket. His eyes meet mine, the desire completely gone, leaving behind a different kind of anger this time. One that's not directed at me. Taking the pitchfork from his hand, I return it and the shovel back inside as Declan holds a conversation with, I'm assuming, the detective in charge. One who had probably left not long ago.

When I get back to him, he's returning his phone to his pocket. "Give me the keys to the beemer, and I'll put it into Oliver's spot in the garage. I don't want anything to happen to it overnight." His demand is gruff, and when he looks at me, I see a hint of the disappointment I'm feeling, but that quickly disappears, becoming guilt.

Not wanting to start another fight, I hand over the keys and climb into the passenger seat. I'm not stupid! If this was a movie and I'd insisted on walking back to the house on my own, I'd end up kidnapped or dead. Why tempt fate to avoid an uncomfortable thirty-second trip?

The car ride is smooth and silent, but when we pull into the garage, he stops the car, locking all of the doors before I can get out. I look from the lock to Declan, and his eyes are clouded with indecision while he rubs at his stubbled jaw before sighing. It echoes loudly through the silence as he leans his head back against the headrest.

"Don't go, Harlow. Don't run away in some misguided attempt to save us or protect us. And don't listen to Dad. He's gone into protection mode, and to him, that means putting you out of the way of danger. Thomas and I think safety in numbers is a better idea, and the others tend to agree with me. You've got to deliver the horses. We'll do that, and you can use the time to think about what you want to do, and when we get back, we'll have a family meeting once Holden is home. Let's talk it out in a sensible manner, not making overly emotional decisions brought on by stress and guilt." I wince at what he's saying, knowing I can't really deny that all my decisions in the last few hours have been driven by exactly that. At least if I had followed through on what was about to happen in the barn, I would've enjoyed that bad decision.

I take a deep breath, willing myself to keep my words calm and even so that we can get through this conversation without having some kind of argument. He's being reasonable so far, albeit a little controlling, but I feel like taking charge is a bit of his default setting. "Okay. I wasn't able to speak to Chuck, and it's too late to organize a truck to deliver the horses tomorrow, so that's what I was planning to do anyway. I'm still not convinced that leaving isn't the best option, but I realize I'm now a part of this family, and I owe it to Dad to discuss it like you suggested." *See? I can be perfectly reasonable too.*

A minute passes as I wait for him to open the locks, but he doesn't. He sits there with his head back against the rest before blowing out another loud sigh and turning to me. The regret in his eyes is loud and clear, so I just hold up my hand, my chest aching with pain, and turn away from him.

When I was with Holden in the club, I felt so free. In the cover of all those moving bodies, Holden and I enjoying each other with no strings attached, I'd been able to just exist in that moment of pleasure, having a gorgeous man play with my body while letting myself be carried away by both his touch and the music. But Declan, he's an entirely different beast. Back in the barn, I wanted to bury everything negative beneath the ecstasy that I know Declan would have wrung from every part of my body. I wanted to let him take control, stealing away the burden of having to decide what to do with myself while he used me in the best way. Now, instead of helping me lock myself away from any pain, if only for a short while, he's adding to the cause of it. *Of course. Because fuck my life.*

"Don't. It's okay. I get it, okay? Let's just leave it at that." A moment later, the locks click, and I open the door, climbing out. Grabbing my bag, I hurry away to the soundtrack of him stomping much too closely behind me. I'm just about at the door to the house when my temper gets the better of me and I whirl on him. He stops where he is, surprise lighting his eyes as I stalk toward him.

"No, you know what? It's *not* okay. This emotional whiplash that you're all giving me is not okay. Especially you. Earlier today, you told me that it would always be Jacinta's side that you take, but then you ravish me! If that's not sending mixed fucking messages, I don't know what does."

I pace back and forth across the garage in front of him, anger only rising higher. "What is it with all of you? You think you can wind me up and get me all hot and bothered and then not follow through. Over and over again! You're all a bunch of teases." I stop and poke a finger into his well-formed pecs. "Stay away from me unless you're willing to follow through on your actions. I am *done* being a play-thing to you and your brothers. Fuck you and fuck all of them."

Wrenching open the door, I storm toward my wing of the house, leaving Declan in stunned silence behind me. On my way, I detour past the kitchen and grab an open bottle of wine out of the fridge. Mrs. Heyton goes to say something, but she must see the storm clouds on my face. Instead, she reaches into a cabinet and passes me a wine glass, her face wreathed with amusement. Grunting my thanks, I head to my room, a date with the bottom of this bottle and my vibrator on my mind. Today has been horrific, and I just need to lose myself for a while. What better way to do that than with alcohol and an orgasm? Even if it has to be a self-inflicted one.

First, though, I need to check on Princess and the kittens, but when I get to my wardrobe, I find they're not there. Declan must have moved them before he went out to wait for me by the stables. Putting my phone down after sending him a text to confirm, I pour myself a glass of wine and take it with me while I have the world's quickest shower. By the time I get back, there's a message saying that he set Princess up in his room so that she wouldn't bother me tonight. Well, that was kind of thoughtful, but I've got to say, I do miss my little bed buddy.

Switching off my phone, I dig around in my side drawer for the buddy I'm going to be using tonight then climb onto the bed. I set up my laptop, type Porn Hub into the search bar, and scroll through until I find a man fucking a woman against a wall. Closing my eyes and switching on my toy, I listen to them as my mind provides the visual of Declan and me back in the barn, throwing in all the details that I missed out on thanks to our interruption. His muscles rippling, head thrown back as he pounded his cock into my wet and wanting pussy.

My heels digging into his ass as my hands gripped his shoulders tight. It's not long before my orgasm is bursting out of me, and it's Declan's name that leaves my mouth in a moan of pleasure.

I'm up early the next morning with a slight headache sitting just behind my eyeballs. I chug my coffee like a junkie mainlining heroin just to shock my body into some semblance of enthusiasm. Only Mrs. Heyton is around to witness my walk of shame, thank god, and when I drop off my empty bottle and dirty glass, she informs me everyone had remained in town last night apart from Declan and myself. She also informed me, her lips twitching like she was fighting back a smile, that Declan was already up and had headed out to the stables a while ago.

"Fuck!" I slam down my coffee mug and grab my backpack, swinging it across my shoulders as I head through the back glass doors, across the patio area, and past the pool to the stables and the waiting horse truck. Scrambling around in my bag for my phone as I hurry is a little tricky, but I eventually get my hand on it and pull out the directions that Chuck had sent me a few days ago.

The movie is being filmed in Napa County. It's about a six-hour drive from where we are, and I'm more than a little afraid it's going to be awkward spending all that time with Declan. I'm not sure which of us is driving the truck, but I've brought my book just in case he does. I mean, what have we really got left to talk about?

Rushing across the grassy expanse between the house and the stables, I can hear the sounds of voices and clattering hooves as horses load into the truck.

When I round the corner, the truck's side load ramp is down, Josh leading Delilah up it. Standing behind him with a prancing Samson is Declan. Clad in jeans, a tight t-shirt, and work boots, it's the most casual I've seen him apart from his sweats. I can't deny it's a damn good look on the man. How he can look as smoking hot in casual clothes as he does in a suit is just beyond my comprehension this early in the morning.

Last night is a blur brought on by the wine and two self-administered orgasms. The sexual tension Declan had wrought on my body made it so the first one practically leapt out of me, but both things contributed to me sleeping better than I have since I arrived here in California. There's a good chance I may have overindulged, just slightly, on the wine though.

A throat clearing and Josh stepping between me and my view of Declan have me rousing out of my hangover stupor. Looking amused, he raises one eyebrow at me. Why does this man continue catching me checking out the Summers men?

"Looking a little rough this morning, Harlow." I'd thrown my hair up into a messy bun and put on a pair of old jeans and my favorite shirt that features an angry unicorn saying *I will cut you.* I'd stuffed my riding clothes in my backpack and have my boots in hand.

"Drank a little too much wine last night," I tell him, shrugging my shoulders before we both turn to watch Declan lead Samson onto the truck. Of course, the damn animal who'd usually be pitching a fit is as meek as a kitten, calmly walking on without any coaxing.

"They're all loaded now, Harlow," Josh tells me, and I lean over to give him a kiss on the cheek.

"Thank you so much, I'm sorry I'm running behind."

He smiles and waves me off. "No problem at all. It's the least I can do after everything that happened yesterday. I'm just glad Holden is going to be okay. The Bostons' horses followed the other animals back yesterday, and we gave them all a rub down and checked them over; none were worse for wear." The mention of *we* has me looking around.

"Where is Luke this morning? Is he coming with us? I wasn't able to get a hold of Chuck to ask him what he wanted with Luke. I'm assuming he's to go with the horses."

Josh frowns at me and shakes his head. "No, Luke left early this morning, said he had a flight to catch and to let you know."

"Huh?" I reply with surprise. "I just thought he'd go and help Max out. Four horses is a lot for one person to manage, especially if they've got her working as a stunt rider as well."

Just then Declan comes back out of the truck and catches the last of my words. "Max has been contracted for stunt riding, but unlike the last set she was on, the lead actress can ride, so it will only be the scenes they've deemed too dangerous for her to do. She'll have a lot more time than she had during the last one, but we do have horse handlers on set. It's quite an extensive cast, and these aren't the only four horses we'll be using. They're just the ones for the leads."

My eyes raise at that information, and he smirks quickly before it disappears into a neutral expression. "I looked into it when the horses first arrived."

It makes me smile that he knew I'd want the info, internally of course, because I can't let him think he's getting off so easily. It's unsurprising that Mr. Cool Control knows these things. It must have bugged the crap out of him when Dad questioned him and he didn't know the answers. I'm sure he went out of his way to correct that real quick.

My eyes scan his body, and unlike me, he looks well rested. I kind of resent the fact that our almost interaction didn't weigh on him the way it did me, but I guess after all of yesterday's drama, it would be easy to fall into an exhausted sleep.

"Have you heard anything about Holden this morning?"

"Yeah, I spoke to Dad. He said he's been trying to call you," Declan scolds, and I flinch. *Oops.*

"Fuck, my phone is off, and I forgot to turn it back on once I'd charged it." I put my boots down and scramble around in my backpack. Finding my phone, I quickly turn it on, and sure enough, it starts to beep with voicemail and message alerts.

"I assured him you were fine and that we were taking the horses today together. He was going to send one of the others back, but we'd have to wait, and we need to get moving if we want to make good time." While he's speaking, I close out my message app and throw my phone back into the bag, knowing I'll go through them all later.

"Holden is much better. His head and shoulder are sore, but landing in the water saved him from banging up his body too much. Now he's just grumpy because his shoulder hurts, and the pain kept waking him up every time he moved around in his sleep." I sigh with relief and smile at the thought of him being grumpy. I want to know what sleepy, rumpled, grumpy Holden looks like. I bet it's sexy.

My eyes meet Declan's green ones, and he must be able to see the heat in mine as his go from disinterested to smoldering and then back again. I think if I had blinked, I would have missed it. The thing is, he can hide it behind the Mr. Cool facade, but

I've got his number now, and I know how fucking hot he burns.

Now that I think about it, the journey could be interesting. I'm not about to let him go back to Mr. Cool now that I know what's deep down inside. I'm going to use the trip to poke and prod and find out all I can. Declan Summers isn't going to know what hit him.

The rumble of the truck starting has me jumping and breaking our staredown. Josh comes back around, leaving the truck running with the AC going so that the animals don't overheat. "The gear is all loaded, and you're set to go." He shakes Declan's hand and waves goodbye to me before disappearing back into the stables.

"Shall we?" Declan gestures to the truck, but before we can leave, I hear something.

"Wait, hang on, my lieblings." Mrs. Heyton walks briskly from the house, and when she gets in front of us, she's breathing heavily. "Goodness, I thought I would miss you! Here." She holds out a travel mug of coffee to each of us and has a bag hanging over her arm, which she hands to me as well. "I made you both sandwiches, and there are also more drinks in the bag, so you don't have to worry about finding parking for the truck. You can just stop at a rest area."

Declan leans in and gives her a kiss, showing that warmth in his eyes that he tends to reserve for only his family or Princess. "You spoil us," he teases, and she blushes. I follow that up with my own thanks, receiving a fond pat on the cheek in return.

"Make sure you look after this one," she says sternly to Declan. "Too many bad things have happened already. No more." His expression turns serious, and he nods.

"Don't worry, she'll be fine. I won't let her out of my sight."

She nods and turns away without another word, and we climb into the truck with our food haul.

I pull out my phone for the directions, but Declan already has them in the onboard navigation. As we hit the road, I can't help but bounce in my seat, a little excited, partly about heading toward the movie set and seeing Max again, and partly because I've got this man trapped for the next however many hours, and I'm excited about getting to know him. *If he'll let me.* I don't doubt he's going to make me work for the information, but I don't think he understands that once I set my mind to something, I won't give up until I achieve it.

Chapter Five

Declan

Climbing into the cab of the truck and closing the door, Harlow is already seated, her unique fragrance surrounding me. My dick perks up the minute that scent hits my nose, and my jeans are tight like they shouldn't be when you have a long drive. I rub a hand across my face in frustration.

"Are you okay?" Her low raspy voice only makes my dick pulse in excitement. I turn to face the cause of the current problem, and she's looking a little rough herself this morning, which makes me want to smile, but I don't.

It was the hardest thing ever to put her down just before I thrust into her warm heat, but her safety is worth more than a quick fuck. It was even harder not to take her in her friend's car when I parked it in the garage. I wanted to pull her into my arms and continue what we had started, but there is so much unresolved between us, and if I'm going to do this with her, I'm going to do it right. Even if I think that quick fuck would have been better than anything I'd had in a long time. Harlow really does feel like she could be the missing piece that we need. She's not going to let any of us get away with any of our shit, and she really doesn't give a crap who we are. I guess all the animosity in the beginning was probably a blessing. It opened her eyes to our flaws and showed her the truth, not just the media image of the Summers brothers. Now we need to work hard on making it all up to her and the other big issue.

I stand by what I've been saying—to my brothers, Harlow, and myself—and need to talk to Jacinta. We need to open her eyes to this being the best thing for all of us. We need her to see that Harlow could be the best thing to happen to our family since Dad adopted Oliver and Holden. Honestly, I think my brothers are a little over dramatic and not as observant of Jacinta as they think they are. I don't think winning her over will be too hard. Already, I can see the cracks in Jacinta's brittle veneer. She worries about Harlow's safety as much as any of us. She pretends to be tough, saying it's exactly what she would do, but I could tell by the way she bit her lip that she was worried. My little sister isn't as indifferent or as angry as she was at the beginning, or she *never* would've asked me to check in when I found Harlow. Jacinta doesn't waste time on people she doesn't care about. Ever. Not unless she's running them off, and wanting to make sure Harlow's okay? That shows that she just might be done running.

Harlow clears her throat, clueing me in to the fact that I've been staring at her this whole time. Her brow is wrinkled with worry lines, so I smile at her, making the strangely adorable lines jump in surprise. "Yeah, sorry. Just worried, got a lot going on in my mind, and I didn't sleep great last night."

"Join the club," she mumbles, tearing her gaze away from mine and digging around in that back-pack she carries everywhere before pulling out a battered paperback.

"You can read while on a car ride?" I ask her as I release the hand brake and the truck rolls forward. I start off slow as it's been a while since I drove the thing, but as we head down the driveway and out of the estate, I'm feeling solid with it again.

She looks down at the book in her lap. "Yeah, I've always been able to." She smiles back at me, and it feels like I've been punched in the junk. It's a wide genuine smile that I normally don't see because I'm being a complete ass to her, but it lights her face up in a way that's much more alluring than I can handle right now. "It made the bus journeys to and from college pass a lot quicker."

"You didn't have a car?" She laughs at my surprise.

"God, you sound like such a spoiled rich kid. Lots of people can't afford cars, Declan." I can feel my cheeks heat slightly at her response, but I don't want to turn this into a fight; she's got a bit of a point. "I did ride back and forth with Max, but I made use of the bus a lot too. Max had a life and partied a lot more than I did. Don't knock it until you try it. Not having to worry about anything during that ride was blissful."

I try to think about the last time I didn't have to worry about things, and I can't remember anything like that. Highschool maybe? Back then, it was parties, football, and girls. College was similar, but by then I was ready for whatever I needed to do to take my place in the Neighpalm empire. So I still partied, and I still fucked my fair share of girls, but my studies were important to me. I was also going into the offices and learning the ropes from Dad and Poppy, so there wasn't time for much else. I certainly had learned by then that women saw me as a commodity and not someone they could have a loving partnership with. It was all take, take, take, and none of them supported me for me.

Blowing out a deep breath, I decide to share a little about my life with her. Try and make her see I'm not really the spoiled rich kid she thinks I am. Although I'm not ready to dive head first into a romantic relationship with her, that doesn't mean we can't start laying the foundation. We've already got the physical chemistry, and she's got Princess' approval. If I want her to end up liking me for who I am, then that makes it obvious what I need to do: show her the real Declan who doesn't always have his head up his ass or his foot in his mouth.

"I lived in the dorms for the first year of college, but I couldn't have my cat with me and I missed my family. It's embarrassing to admit, but I didn't make it too far into my first year before I asked Dad to buy me a house close by. Thomas, Kai, and Holden all moved in when it was their time for college, but Oliver decided to live in the dorms, as did Jacinta and Jaxon when it was their turn. Of course, we all came home as often as possible, but it was the first time in our lives, since being adopted, that we'd been without Dad or Nana and Poppy around." I snort when I think back to the chaos of that time. I don't know if Mrs. Heyton would have died laughing or broken out into sobs if she saw some of the monstrosities that came out of that kitchen in the early days of being on our own. There's a reason that woman has the power to stop any of the Summers with a single word. We know we've got it good with her.

"To say we had quite a learning curve was an understatement, but I'm now proud to admit that I can cook and clean and do all those things that 'normal' people have to do. It also made me realize that I didn't want to be without my family.

Sure, Jax, Jacinta, and Oliver were near enough, but it just wasn't the same as having all of us at home. I don't know if it's because we're all a little… broken in our own ways, but I think I've never really felt completely at ease when my family is too far from me." I cringe slightly at the next memory but choose to share it with her anyway. I'm already putting myself out there more than I even expected to, but there's something about her that makes me feel like she'll be a good listener. Not to mention, it might help her understand why up until now we've been anti-relationships.

"As much as I love my family, there was a bit of a drawback… Dating became a nightmare. The girls we brought home wouldn't get along, and tensions were always high. We decided to keep our private lives exactly that, private, but it caused a rift in our once harmonious household. Eventually, we all just stopped dating and threw ourselves into the businesses and more temporary solutions. A never-ending parade of one night stands passed through that house, and it has continued like that for the most part since. Apart from Thomas' big mistake and Jaxon's latest, no one has ever been serious with anyone for longer than I can remember."

I fall silent, not sure what else I can say right now. I think that's why the idea of sharing Harlow is so appealing to everyone. We're all at the age where one night stands are just not what we want anymore. I know Kai especially wants a woman to spoil and love and to have a family with.

"Look, Declan, I appreciate you telling me all of this. I'm going to be honest, right now there's a lot to process, but I want you to know that I've heard everything, and as much as you guys might not have taken a chance to get to know me, I *do* want to learn more about what makes you all tick. Call me crazy or idealistic or stupidly optimistic, but I feel like maybe there'll be something about each of you that I could even like. Maybe we all have more in common that we could figure out if you all just get out of your own way. I don't know how much of myself I'm ready to share just now, but I think that if I ever get the chance that I should've had in the first place, well… who knows?" There's an almost sad smile on her face, and I regret that I've somehow put it there, but at least I'm trying. That's got to be worth something in the long run, right?

After her question, which I don't think either of us know how to answer, we both let the silence grow between us. Despite how the conversation ended, or maybe because I was actually honest and a little bit open with her, the silence is more comfortable than I would've expected. A little more time passes before I see her shoulders are totally relaxed. She's curled up into her seat as much as she can, her head stuck in a book. I take advantage of her distraction, studying her out of the corner of my eye as I try to make sure we also don't crash into something, and she almost manages to startle me when an unexpected giggle breaks the silence.

That's an opportunity that I just can't pass up. For the first time in a long time, I want this woman's attention on me. I want to know what she's thinking and what's bringing a smile to her face. "What are you reading?" She looks up in shock, and then her face flushes with embarrassment. "Come on, tell me about it. It's been a while since I read a good book, so I may have to borrow it after you're done."

This comment earns an even more extreme reaction. Her eyes just about bug out of her head before she slams it closed.

"Harlow," I growl at her, and this time her eyes heat with something other than embarrassment. Hmm, I like that reaction from her. "Tell me," I demand.

"Well, it's a paranormal romance book," she starts.

"What, like vampires or something?" I ask, and she looks surprised. "Harlow, I produce movies. I know what paranormal romance is."

"Oh yeah, I guess you would. Well, this one is shifters, wolf shifters to be specific, and, well, it's a...." Her last few words are mumbled, so I can't catch them.

"I'm sorry. What was that?" I push, unwilling to give it up now that I see how badly she doesn't want to answer. It's got to be something horribly smutty for her to be so shy about it.

She sighs her frustration before blurting out, "It's a reverse harem romance." I run the words through my head. *Reverse harem. So a harem is a man with lots of women...* And then my eyebrows jump when I figure out what the reverse of that is. Well, well, well, maybe Nana's idea won't be shot down as quickly as I had thought.

"Oh really?" She looks at me with trepidation like I'm going to judge her. "Does it have lots of hot sex in it? And is it just one woman with multiple male partners, or are there other females involved, or do any of the men have relationships?" I prod, and this time it's *her* eyebrows that jump in surprise.

"Actually, this one is just one woman with multiple males, and two of the males have a sexual relationship with each other as well as the woman. But I've read others that have a female in the harem as well, but she's usually just involved with the woman. When the other woman starts becoming involved with the other men, it heads toward the polyamory genre instead."

"Like our Jilly, right? That's what kind of relationship she has." Something I said has her looking thoughtful and a bit surprised, but I'm not sure which part—whether it's because I called her *our* Jilly or if it's because I know what kind of relationship she has or even what polyamory is.

"Jilly is practically a Summers. She's been

working on our family plane for years, and Nana took her under her wing from the very start. She's much like Hope in that regard. Nana likes saving the wounded birdies. Not to mention she's Jonah's sister. I think you met him when you went to the studio with Oliver. As for me knowing what polyamory is, I wanted to be informed when Jilly announced that's the kind of lifestyle she wanted to live." She frowns a little when I admit that, so I quickly continue. "I mean, it makes sense in her profession, but I wanted to make sure she wasn't getting into something that would get her heart broken. It's my protective family instincts at play, I suppose, but I couldn't do any less for her than I would do for Jacinta or Hope." *Or you,* I add in my head, but I don't think she's ready to hear that yet. Not to mention, it could send the wrong message if I refer to her in the same sentence as Jacinta. I do *not* want this woman thinking I could see her as a sister. "But it seems to work for her. She's introduced us to a couple of her partners when we've been overseas, and of course we know James and Chris."

"I can't wait to meet her. Do you think she'll talk to me about it? I'm fascinated. I mean, it's like one of my books in real life. I'd love to know how it all works in reality, but I don't want her to feel like I'm prying."

I chuckle at her enthusiasm, and my dick, which had gone down, roars to life again. Harlow may find herself with firsthand information very soon. "I'm sure she'd be glad to talk to you. She's not shy or embarrassed about it at all."

She bounces on her seat in excitement again, much to my amusement. It's cute seeing her enthusiastic about something. She's always been combative during our interaction, which I know is entirely my fault, but it's nice to see a different side of Harlow. I want to keep seeing this side, so I can't help the teasing that escapes my mouth.

"So, Harlow, you didn't tell me if the sex scenes are hot." That stops her bouncing, and I see her body vibrate before she turns to look at me. I can feel the heat of her stare on my cheek, but I need to keep my eyes on the road, so I don't turn.

"It's so hot, Declan, that I regularly need to use my BOB to relieve the pressure."

Fuck me. I was teasing her, but she just brought the thunder and knocked all the wind out of my sails. My cock is once again hard as fuck. "Much like I needed to take the edge off last night," she tags on.

And slam dunk. Put in my place and there's nothing left to say. Or is there? "Did you moan my name as you came? Because I moaned yours." The tension in the cab is off the charts, and she squirms on her seat like she needs relief. It's all I can do not to pull the truck over, haul her into the sleeper cab, and fuck her brains out. Taking my eyes off the road, they meet her green ones, and I see her look from me to the cab behind, but then she shakes her head. That fog of lust is gone, and a new light enters her eyes.

"I can't really remember what came out of my mouth, but my eyes were rolling back in my head and my toes curled. But then, like most men, the batteries died and I was done for the night. My vibrator did the equivalent of rolling over and going to sleep. Another disappointing experience much like the rest of my sex life, I'm afraid." She looks away, but a cheeky grin crosses her face. "Apart from that one night in college..."

My eyes are back on the road, but a smirk crosses my face along with a twinge of jealousy hitting me in the gut. I ignore it and play the game. *Okay, let's see who can't take the heat first. You won't scare me off that easily, Miss Harlow.*

"Oh, do tell?" I try and keep it light, hoping she'll play along. We have a deadline, and I'm much too professional to fuck with it by pulling over, no matter how badly I want to, but it's kind of fun to keep the sexual tension going. *For research purposes, obviously.*

She must agree because she takes the bait. "Well, I had two friends with benefits in college. I didn't have the time for a relationship, nor did I want all the drama that would come with it when I wasn't able to commit as much time as they wanted, due to my studies. So that kind of arrangement suited me well. But I was a little flustered during exams, and I found out I'd accidentally arranged to meet them both on the same night."

I snort as the story takes an amusing turn. "Oh, I bet they loved that." I can see her shrug out of the corner of my eye, and her smile is one of pure satisfaction.

"At first, they were a little annoyed, but after I invited them both in and made up for my mistake, I can tell you they weren't complaining."

Holy fuck! My foot slips off the accelerator for a moment, and I can't help that my mouth drops open. She giggles next to me, obviously happy with my reaction.

"Damn, Harlow. Knowing what you want and not being afraid to take it. That's sexy as fuck. I love it when a woman doesn't play games with sex. It's annoying as hell when they do." And I mean every word of that. Threesomes are almost a collegiate rite of passage, so I can hardly judge her for that. Honestly, finding out that she'd experimented and enjoyed being shared between multiple partners just makes my dick hard. Definitely ups the possibility that she won't mind being shared between me and my brothers.

"Declan, the one thing you will learn about me is I don't play games about anything. I learned very early on that I didn't want to be anything like my mother, and game playing was the most used weapon in her arsenal. Did you know by the time I was ten she had told me my dad was about twenty different people? I gave up asking after that, and I learned that every promise to tell me his name if only I did whatever new thing she wanted was completely false. So no, one thing I don't do is play games, and I hope that you all will realize that eventually."

And just like that, the sexual tension dissolves as she throws my and my siblings' bad behavior back in my face. I guess we've got a lot of making up to do, but I can't say I don't relish the challenge. Harlow is going to see a completely different side of us and hopefully Jacinta as well. When the Summers go all in, there's no escaping us.

Chapter Six

Harlow

It's hard to hide my internal squirming after having such an intense conversation with Declan. Jesus, my eyes just about popped out of my head when he started asking about my books, and then having a civilized conversation turn dirty... What the fuck has gotten into the man? I needed to add in that reminder of their previous behavior just to catch a break.

What has made his attitude do such a turnaround? Is it because I almost fucked him in the stables last night? Or did it start before that, like when I called him because Princess was having her kittens?

"How's Princess?" I ask him, and a worried frown crosses his face.

"She's good, but I'm a little worried about one

of the kittens. It doesn't seem to be doing as well as the other three. I might take them to the vet when we get back if it hasn't picked up by then."

Fuck! Well, I've been having fun hiding that secret from them all, but it would be irresponsible for me not to say anything now that something is wrong with his babies. No secret is worth compromising their safety. Based on what he shared about his college years, he basically confirmed what I already thought. There's a very short list of who and what Declan Summers passionately cares about. I mean, the man asked his father to buy a house so that he could have his siblings and his *cat* around him because he was lonely. If that doesn't show his priorities, I don't know what does.

"If you want, I can have a look when we get back," I offer.

I laugh internally as he frowns and shoots me a confused look before turning back to the road. "What would you be able to do?"

"Declan, did Nana and Poppy never mention what I studied in college? You all have been so busy assuming that all I do is ride horses for the Bostons. In fact, none of you have really taken any time to ask me anything about myself. All of you jumped on Jacinta's bandwagon, assuming I'm some gold digging whore out for Dad's money." He shakes his head, looking a little embarrassed that I'm calling him out, and I sigh. "I *do* have a real career, you know. I'm a veterinarian, Declan."

The look on his face as it swings toward me again is hilarious. In fact, it's so extreme the truck lurches to the side, a squeal escaping my mouth as I grab the handle above the door. He quickly corrects the truck, but the look of disbelief remains.

"I was hoping to specialize in exotic animals, but I'm not limited to them. The interview I went to the other day was for an internship with a private zoo, but unfortunately, due to your sister's billboard, I am no longer considered a suitable candidate for their program. Something about loose morals not being the image they want to portray." He starts to sputter some kind of response, but I wave them off.

"To be honest, I don't want to work for a place that's so damn judgmental anyway. Back to the actual topic, I'm happy to have a look at the kittens for you. Princess is a first-time mom, so maybe she's just a little confused about what she needs to do. A lot of people assume that it's instinctual for all animals, and for many it is, but it's not unheard of for new animal moms to struggle sometimes just like new human moms do."

Declan's mouth is still open and closing like a damn goldfish. There isn't much I can do about that, so I just settle back and watch the world go by. I have no clue where we are, but the scenery is pretty.

"I'm sorry, Harlow. It seems we were wrong in so many ways." His voice is low and apologetic, and he has the grace to look embarrassed, but I don't plan on letting him off the hook that easily. He deserves to squirm.

"Yes, you were. You all were."

"Aren't you a little younger than normal vet school graduates?" He's moved from being apologetic to curious, so I shrug my shoulders, not opposed to giving him more information now that the secret's out.

"Yeah, I started college courses early and completed a few AP level classes in my junior and senior years that fill some of the basic prerequisites, so I had a head start before I enrolled in college. Once I was there, taking the absolute maximum number of credits every semester, as well as winter and summer courses when they offered something I needed, helped me keep up a competitive pace. I love animals and learning about them, but I was pretty eager to get out in the world and get started, so it wasn't a hardship to finish as quickly as I could. I had every intention of looking for an internship on the East Coast, and I also had a job offer from the local vet that Chuck has used for years. When Mom died, I was kind of in limbo, not having made any decisions, and then I found out about Brad. I also had the option of starting my own practice with Melinda and Chuck's backing, but I thought getting some experience under my belt might be a better idea. Plus, I know that I'll always have them as a safety net, so there was no rush to begin something that I felt I hadn't truly earned, ya know? If I wind up needing their help, I know they'll be there, but I want to try and make my own way before I lean on them."

"So, zoos?' he pushes, not touching the subject of Melinda and Chuck and their money. Smart choice, given how much turmoil there's been thanks to their assumptions about my intentions. If he focused on that part, I think our current peaceful atmosphere would have blown up.

"Yeah, I love exotic animals, but I'm a big cat freak. Tigers especially. I want to be involved with the conservation of such a magnificent and endangered species. And *not* like that crazy online show. I want to help them for real."

There's something both freeing and kind of strange about this moment. Declan now knows more about me than any of the other siblings. How is it that one of the ones who was the most hostile has managed to get all that information out of me? Oh, that's right, he almost gave me an orgasm last night. Maybe I'm feeling just a little bit warmer toward him even though he did deny me in the end. Honestly, if I had put bets on who I'd confide in first, I would've put my money on Kai. But there's something… almost nice about talking to Declan when he's just being a normal human being.

The drive is true to the GPS' estimation, taking about six hours, and we spend the time chatting on and off about different things, only taking breaks for lunch, horse checks, and gassing up. I discover that Declan scuba dives and loves cars. Apparently, a few of the fancier ones in the garage are his. He asks me more about my love of abandoned buildings, and I try to interrogate him about the count's home. Unfortunately, he doesn't seem to know that much. The count had disappeared by the time Brad had adopted him, so he never got to meet him.

The last hour or so of the ride is quiet, with Declan looking like he's deep in thought, so I open my book up again and read the rest of the story. At one stage, I read an entire scandalous scene, constantly looking between the pages and him to make sure he isn't somehow reading over my shoulder. Reading sex scenes in public always makes me feel so fucking shifty, but this time, it's a little different. It might make the scene even hotter, knowing that Declan's right next to me while I'm reading through an orgy.

Finally, the truck starts to slow down, and I look up from my book, literally pages from the end. Damn it, it looks like we're here. Here being a vineyard with a castle on the property. Putting my bookmark back into the book because only heathens dog-ear pages, I throw it into my bag and look around. It's my turn for my eyes to just about bug out of my head. Before me in all its medieval splendor is an honest to goodness castle.

Surrounding the castle is a vineyard, but I can also see trailers and vehicles and tents set up, as well as paddocks of horses.

"The owners of this property rented it to us for the duration of the movie. We've set up all around it, and we make trips to nearby forests to film scenes. Most of the crew are staying in town close by, but we have trailers on site for the stars to use in between filming breaks. It gets quite hot, so they're all air-conditioned."

As we approach the area teeming with people, someone wearing a high-vis vest approaches the truck, gesturing for Declan to wind down the window.

I can only hear Declan's side of the conversation, but soon enough we're moving forward toward paddocks that I can see contain more horses. Just as the truck comes to a full stop and he pulls the brake, a blur is already running toward us. She stops dead in front of the truck, and a squeal of excitement escapes my mouth as I watch her jump up and down, waving her hands, barely visible over the front end of the truck.

Ignoring Declan's questioning look, I open my door and jump down. My knee aches a little when I land, but I ignore that as I run to my best friend.

Max and I collide like long-lost lovers who have been separated by war or something. Both of us babbling, not paying any attention to one another, and by the time we pull apart, I have tears streaming down my face, and she looks pissed off as fuck.

"What the fuck, Harlow Stubbs." She punches

me in the shoulder, enough actual force behind it that I have to wince. "Apparently, you have a whole heap of shit going on, and I have to find out about it from a stranger! Do you know how that makes me feel? You have a fucking stalker and have been in *danger*, and I'm just finding this out now. Mom and Dad are going to kick your ass when they find out. "

I roll my eyes as, once again, Max makes it about herself. I love her, but she's extremely self-involved. "How on earth did you find out?"

"Your new friend Alex has enough common sense to realize that your oldest friend in the world may be a little concerned and gave me a heads up, telling me everything that's happened." She gets distracted, her gaze moving over my shoulder, and I feel someone approach behind me. I'm assuming it's Declan because Max gets a wicked glint in her eye before she looks back at me and punches me in the shoulder again. "And Alex Winters, bitch. Please tell me you are tapping that fine piece of man meat. Girl, he looks like he could give you a *very* good time." She fans her face before acknowledging the person behind me. "Oh hey, Declan, long time no see."

I turn so I can see him. There's a frown on his face, and he looks like he's a little tense. "Declan, do you remember Maxine Boston?"

His frown clears into a smile, his body relaxing a little. "Of course I do. Maxine and Jacinta used to be the terrible twosome for a couple of weeks every summer, but then she stopped coming." A frown crosses his face as if he's just thought of something troubling. "How come you never came with them when they used to visit?" Before I can answer, Max does.

"That bitch of a mother wouldn't let her. Treated her like trash and wouldn't let her have any fun." Like usual, Max's face twists as though she's sucking on a lemon. Yep, my mother tended to have that effect on people. Then it's her turn to get some sudden idea, and she almost does a double take at Declan. Now, her expression has darkened into fury, and I step back as she pushes past me and approaches the unfortunate soul, her finger jabbing into his chest.

"What's this I hear about you and all the others being complete and utter fuckheads to my girl? You guys are idiots for not seeing how lucky you are that she even allows you to breathe the same air as her, let alone want to be friends. And to even think she was after Brad's money is completely ridiculous. My parents have tried to give her shit over the years—a car, a trust fund, her own veterinary practice—but she's refused them every time. All it would have taken is for Jacinta to call me and say hey, what's she like, and I could have cleared up this whole fucking mess, but no, the Summers kids know best." She stops, taking a huge breath after that little spiel, and drops her finger before turning her back to him.

"You guys are fucking lucky that she wants to be part of your life, and if you all want to reject her so badly, just know that my parents will always welcome her back with open arms, knowing how absolutely valuable she is." And with that mic drop she grabs my hand and pulls me away. *Fuck me.*

What the hell is going on with Max? She never, not once, joined in with her snobby friends belittling me, but that doesn't mean she ever really stood up for me either. She supported me at home or when we were on our own, and I never took it to heart or let it hurt the sisterly bond we had between us. I honestly thought she didn't have this much of a backbone in her, but I guess I was wrong. Maybe our time apart, however brief, has hit her differently now that we're adults. There's a real chance that I could make a life here and leave her back in Connecticut. Absence must really make the heart grow fonder and all that shit… If this is the new Max, I will happily take this version of my best friend and pseudo sister who's got my back in fantastic fashion.

"Come on, I'll show you where the horses need to go and then I'll give you a hand unloading them." She drags me away, not realizing I'm speechless at her last little rant.

"Harlow." Declan's voice has us stopping in our tracks, and I turn to face him. His eyes tell me how sorry he is for his behavior. I guess it hurts to be called out, but I'm going to need to hear that apology in words. At this point, his dad, grandparents, me, and my best friend have all had some kind of "come to Jesus" moment with the Summers kids, so they need to either join the party or just leave me alone. "I'm going to find the director and have a chat with him. I'll text you later when it's time to leave?" I nod and he walks away without ever saying anything else. My eyes go to his ass that's lovingly wrapped in his jeans, traveling eagerly to those powerful thighs which I can personally attest to the strength of.

"Oh, girl, you eye fuck him any harder, you're going to give yourself a concussion," Max whispers in my ear, and I whip my head around, guilty that I've been caught. I start to deny it, but she holds up her hand. "Oh no, you don't. Alex has told me *every-thing* that's been going on with those boys. He thought that your two besties should get together and share some information. He's even pulled Hope into our three-way chat now, so quite frankly, you're fucked. But I want to hear the story from your mouth now, and you better not skimp on any dirty details. I want them all."

Breathing out a huge sigh, I roll my shoulders. "Well, hold on to your panties because Alex and Hope don't know the half of it."

So, as she shows me around the movie set and points out the paddock the horses will be in, I tell her everything that has happened from the moment I stepped onto the plane with Nana and Poppy until

I got out of the truck. All the drama with the stalker, the animosity with the siblings, and the sexual tension with each and every one of the damn brothers. By the time I'm finished, I'm exhausted.

Max looks at me incredulously. "Holy fuck. I think I need a cigarette after all that. How is it that you haven't thrown yourself at any of their feet and begged one of them to fuck you?" I scowl, thinking about last night.

"I almost did last night, but they're all about safety first now, and we're not talking condoms. We're talking 'protect Harlow from the psycho who wants to…' Well, who knows what they want to do, actually. They're sending some mixed fucking signals. Max, I'm so fucking confused, and to be honest, I'm scared. Scared of my attraction to all of them, but mostly scared of what this stalker may do. I had every intention of tucking tail and coming home, but Declan has convinced me to stay for Dad's sake. And I'd be lying to myself if I wasn't staying to see what could happen with the guys. It's like something out of one of our books, and my attraction to all of them is just making me even more confused. Hope insists I don't need to choose, but… I just don't know. Could I do this? For real?"

She gapes at me before a determined look crosses her face. "Right, let me introduce you to the grooms who are going to help me with the horses, and then we'll get them unloaded and settled. And *then,* you and I are heading to the bar in town. This calls for copious amounts of alcohol and a bestie night out."

I shake my head. "We didn't plan to stay the night, and I brought nothing with me. Also, I'm not sure what Declan has planned."

She scoffs and drags me in the direction of a couple of men standing around a horse being shoed. "If he knows what's good for him, he'll shut up and just accept the overnight stop. Neighpalm Productions has booked out one of the hotels here for crew, so there are a few rooms available there. You can stay and still be on your way early tomorrow morning."

I don't get another chance to get a word in before she's introducing me to some of the crew and I get caught up with the hustle and bustle of unloading the horses and gear and getting them where they need to be. Max never did like hearing the word no.

Chapter Seven

Harlow

By the time the horses are settled, the sun is setting and I've finally heard from Declan. Apparently, he needs to stay overnight to work out some things with the director Sean anyway, so he went ahead and got us rooms at the hotel. At least that makes my girls' night with Maxine that much easier.

Leaving the truck on site, Max and I catch a ride into town with a couple of members of the crew.

Max pushes open the door to her room and waves me in. "Come on, I'm just going to change my shirt. I've got horse slobber on it." I wander into her room, noticing it's quite nice for a smaller country town, everything looking newish and clean. Max strips off her own top, tosses it into a corner, and digs around in the suitcase on her bed.

"When did you get here?" I ask, frowning. She hasn't even had a chance to unpack.

"Late last night. I flew into San Francisco, and one of the crew picked me up." She pulls a new top over her head as I look down at my own shirt, finding a smudge of something across my left boob. Before I can even ask, a shirt hits me in the face, and when I pull it off, she's smirking at me. "I always got your back."

Throwing the shirt on the bed, I hurry forward and throw my arms around her, hugging her tight. Within seconds, hers are hugging me back. "Fuck, I've missed you," I sigh into her hair.

"As banging as your boobs are, Harlow, I'm not into girls," Max mumbles from where she's squashed against my chest, but I hold on for a little longer. "No, seriously, I'm suffocating here." Rolling my eyes, I let go and pull away.

"Drama queen," I toss back at her as I pull my dirty top over my head before replacing it with her clean one. After I borrow her shower in a can, we're ready to hit the bar.

Leaving my backpack behind, I tuck my ID, phone, and debit card into the back pocket of my jeans, and I'm good to go. Max is in the bathroom, brushing her hair, and I feel around my messy bun. I mean, it's called a messy bun for a reason, isn't it? *It'll be fine.* Though I guess that's a naive thought. I should've remembered that Max is incapable of going out with me and giving up all control. "Oh no, get over here. Let's pull out that damn bun and wear it down for a change."

So, sighing, I once again give myself over to the darkside that is Max. By the time we leave, my hair is down and brushed, and I'm wearing mascara and lip gloss. She really can't help herself.

As we walk from the hotel to the nearby bar, the balmy night comfortable and filled with the sounds of families and young couples, Max hooks her arm through mine. "So, which one are you going to fuck first?" In my surprise, my toe catches on a crack in the pavement, and I stumble, pulling Max along with me. She giggles at my reaction, but I can feel her eyes on my face.

My cheeks heat as I shake my head. "I don't know what I'm doing, Max." I stop and face her. "I'm so confused. You know how I feel about Nana and Poppy, and, well, Dad has wiggled his way into my heart now too. You know I always wanted a parent who gave a fuck, and he fits the bill perfectly. But as for his children..." I sigh, loudly. "I know that I have this totally ridiculous urge to fuck them... all of them... but I don't know what the fuck else to do with them at this point."

Max blinks at me as I suck in air, totally at a loss. Finally, she grabs me by the hand and pulls me through the doors of the nearby bar. "This calls for copious amounts of alcohol."

While we wait for a hostess to seat us, I glance around, taking stock of our spot for the evening. TV screens are scattered through the room as well as sports memorabilia. *Ah, a sports bar.* There are booths down one side of the room with tables scattered between them and the bar, a row of bar stools lining the bar, and the beer taps are glistening with condensation and the little plaques that tell you what each one is.

A cute girl comes over wearing a pair of cut-off denim shorts and a shirt with what I guess is the bar's name on it. "Table for two?" she asks with a bright smile.

"Can we get a booth?" Max asks, and the girl nods and leads us to a vacant one, handing us menus to look over while we wait for our waitress.

"One of the crew was saying that the ribs are really good here, and he also happened to mention that the area over there is for dancing when the dinner rush has finished." Max points out a currently vacant space in the back of the bar. There looks to be a raised platform that would be big enough for a band too.

Once I've decided what I'm going to have, I look around the room, recognizing a couple of guys standing at the bar. Max had introduced me to them earlier, and they both give me a friendly nod. "Huh."

That catches Max attention, and she looks in

the direction I am. "What?" she asks, a frown on her face.

"I can't believe those guys actually remembered me," I tell her, and she snorts with laughter.

"Girl, one, you're hot. And two, you're their boss and pay their bills. Of course they're going to be friendly." My eyes shoot to Max, and it's my turn to be confused.

"What the fuck are you talking about?"

"Harlow, you're a Summers. Your family owns the company making the movie. You employ all these people."

Just then, before I can retort, a different girl approaches us. Unlike the one before with the friendly, sunny disposition, this one doesn't look like she wants to be here. She's wearing the same uniform, but her top is so tight I can see her nipples through the fabric, and her makeup is also dramatic. No shade intended, but the scowl on her face makes her look ugly.

"What can I get you?" she asks, her tone of voice and total inability to make eye contact telegraphing that she has zero interest in waiting on us. I don't even have to look up to know that Max is grinding her teeth together. One thing she hates is being ignored.

"We'll get two margaritas, and I'll have the ribs, fries, and slaw. What will you have, Harlow?"

"I'll have the creamy chicken Alfredo with sun dried tomato, spinach, and bacon."

The girl finally glances up from her order pad and looks me up and down, one eyebrow cocked. "Sure you want the carbs? We do have some nice salads."

"Oh fuck, no, you didn't." Max stands up, but I tug on her arm. The girl's words don't bother me. I know what I look like, and I know the kind of food I can eat. I work too hard to be eating only salads. I'm pretty sure the girl had made up her mind before she came over to us. Some women just see attractive females as competition. My mom did, and like my mom, she's lashing out as a defense mechanism for her insecurity. I know not all women are like that, Hope being my most recent proof, but I don't have a lot of patience for the ones who are.

"Yeah, I'm good. Pasta would be *great*. I had one hell of a workout before I came here. My boyfriend fucked me for hours, and I'm starving."

Looking like she's swallowed a lemon, our waitress turns around, heading back to the kitchen with no further words. Max, on the other hand, dissolves into giggles. "Fuck, Harlow, you always know what to say."

I screw up my face, grumbling, "Yeah, well, my pasta will probably be spat in for my troubles, but I can't stand girls like that. We're supposed to lift each other up, not tear one another down."

"Ignore the bitch! Let's get back to all your boy dramas. Don't think that Alex hasn't told me all about Nana's plans to build you a harem, and I say 'yay, Nana!' Will she find me one too?"

I roll my eyes so hard that I swear I see the back of my brain. Trust Max to blow off all my worries and get straight to the heart of the problem.

The waitress returns with our margaritas, not at all carefully placing them on the table. In fact, she's so rough with mine it sloshes over the sides. We watch as she turns and stomps back to the bar. She and the bartender stand there and watch us. I'm sure the conversation they're having is bitchy, but I just don't have the energy to engage today. So, putting a huge smile on my face, I pull the straw out of the glass and down that sucker in one go. Placing the glass back on the table, I wipe my mouth with the back of my hand and signal to the two watching us for another round.

Max is outright chuckling now, not bothering to hide her amusement. "Look, Harlow, I know you. You haven't ever had a proper relationship. Why don't you take this time and get to know them all individually? If you get to ride their cocks a time or two, bonus. I know you're looking for someone to love and be loved by, but you're so damn scared because of the way your mother treated you, you've never taken that chance before. Leap now, and you may find yourself with not one but six men to love. All the previous shit is just that, shit. What happens from here on in is what matters. Make them work for it because you are *so* fucking worth it."

Tears prickle my eyes, and I'm reminded once more why I keep Max around. Although she can be careless with my emotions sometimes, when it comes down to the crunch, she's got my back. I reach out, grabbing her hand and squeezing it tightly.

The waitress returns with our next round, not giving this one much care either. *Holy fuck, what has crawled up this girl's ass?*

Once she leaves, I pull my hand away and grab my drink. I seem to be using alcohol as a bit of a crutch at the moment, and that realization sends a twinge of worry that I may be just like my mom, but I quickly shake the thought off. I am *nothing* like that woman. I know when to stop, and it's okay for me to treat myself or occasionally overindulge with my bestie.

"Thank you. I needed to hear all that. I guess I just wanted someone to give me permission to like them all, ya know? I'm kind of diving right into the super deep end of dating by even thinking about trying this out." She crosses her arms and raises an eyebrow.

"Oh yeah, but from my three-way chat with Hope and Alex, they've been telling you that the whole time," she says, calling me out on my shit, but I shrug my shoulders.

"Yeah, but they're new friends. With you, I know I'll get the truth whether I like it or not."

"You bet your ass you will."

Just then, our food arrives, and we're both quiet. People watching makes good entertainment while I devour the creamy dish, the tang of the sun dried tomatoes the perfect offset to the rich sauce.

While we're eating, Max's eyes bug out of her head at something over my shoulder, and when I turn around to see what's going on, I find Declan standing at the front of the bar with three men, two who look extremely familiar. His eyes light up, and he points to our booth.

"Can we join you?" he mouths, and I turn to ask Max who has paled slightly.

"Is it alright if they join us?"

"Do you know who that is with Declan?" she whispers quietly, her facial expression moving back and forth between awe and panic.

"I'm assuming Sean Walsh, but I'm not sure about the other two even though they look familiar. Do you know who they are?"

"Oh, for fuck's sake, Harlow. Your damn abandoned videos are limiting your fucking movie veiwing. The hot blond one is Cayden Storm, and the panty melting dark-haired one is Jarred Reed. They're the hottest things in Hollywood as far as male movie stars go." *So that must leave the guy with black hair as the director. He's younger than I'd expected. Maybe early thirties?*

"Huh. Does Neighpalm represent them?" I ask, and she shakes her head.

"No, I don't think so, but they've both had a

falling out with their previous representation, or that's the rumor going around movie sets at the moment. Or it was at the one I'd just left. I overheard Selena Cross gossiping with one of the other actresses about it one day."

I turn back to Declan, and he's still waiting for my response, so I quickly nod my head. With a point at us, the sunny hostess shows them to our booth. Luckily, it's big enough for the six of us, so Max and I squeeze right over.

Declan pushes in next to me, with Sean Walsh on his other side. Jarred and Cayden take a seat on Max's side, and I see her cower in on herself in a way that's totally unlike her. *Hmm, what's with that?* She's usually bubbly and outgoing, not nervous and shy.

We basically have enough time for brief introductions before we're approached by the waitress, and fuck me, this is a completely different woman than we dealt with before. Her eyelashes are fluttering, and she's got a sultry smile on her face.

"What can I get you boys?" she practically purrs, nothing like the surly greeting that Max and I had gotten.

The guys don't order any food, but they do ask for a round of drinks and two more margaritas for me and Max. She leaves, swaying her hips like she's fucking Shakira or something... and the margaritas must have destroyed my filter because I apparently said that out loud if the laughter is anything to go by.

"Whoa, Harlow! I didn't pick you to be catty about other women," Declan teases, and I'm about to put him in his place when Max jumps to my defense.

"That bitch suggested that Harlow should probably watch her carbs when she ordered pasta for dinner and has spilled every one of our drinks. Not catty, deserved."

Both Jarred and Cayden eye the part of my body they can see and snort at Max's words. "Nothing wrong with what I can see," Cayden drawls, and I watch as Max tries to control the shiver down her spine at the sound. Smothering a grin, I thank him.

"It looks to me that you can eat whatever you want, and even then, who's to tell you what you can and can't eat?" Jarred says, his voice just as seductive as Cayden's. I hadn't realized he was English. Max must have been totally unprepared for that one too because she once again fails to hide her reaction. "Are you cold, love?" Jarred asks. "Cayden, shift a little closer so we can keep Max warm." There's a twinkle in his eye and an exchanged glance over her head that she misses, but I don't. Looks like my bestie may have her hands full with these two, but I'm sure she's up for the challenge.

They shift a little closer, both leaning in when Cayden asks her about her stunt riding. The three of them chat quietly, while on Declan's other side, Sean gets up, phone in hand. "I'm just going to head outside and take this. It's quieter." He hurries away, leaving Declan and me alone as I watch the waitress carry a tray toward us again.

"Feel like causing some trouble?" I ask out of the corner of my mouth before she approaches the table. Her shoulders deflate slightly when she sees the other three in deep conversation, not paying any attention to her, but her eyes brighten again when she takes note of Declan. He gives the slightest nod as she places everyone's drinks in front of them.

"Remember I told you my boyfriend fucked me so well I needed to carb load for the next round?" She sneers but nods her head as I snuggle into Declan, forcing him to lift his arm up so that he can pull me close to his side. *God, he smells good.* "Well, I was just trying to convince him he needed to do it again so I could ride him like a cowgirl next time."

Seriously, you could hear a pin drop before everyone bursts into laughter. The girl turns pink and hurries away, no snide glance or remark this time. "I bet we get a new server for the next round," I say, sipping at my drink, the tart taste really hitting the spot.

Chapter Eight

Harlow

few of the tables are moved out the way, making the back dance floor even bigger as a small three-piece band sets up on the stage. The music is catchy, and soon the floor is full of people bumping and grinding.

"Would you like to dance?" Cayden asks Max, and again, she flushes before nodding her head. Cayden takes her by the hand, pulling her out of the booth, and together they walk to the dance floor before disappearing within the crowd. Jarred gets up and follows after them. You'd think in such a small place they'd be swarmed by fans, but the dancers either don't recognize them or they're used to seeing them around since they've been filming here for about three weeks.

Sean still hasn't returned yet so that leaves me

and Declan alone. "So, was I good?" He has a smirk on his face, and I'm momentarily stunned by his good looks and the flow of tequila through my body.

"Huh?"

"When I fucked you so good you needed to carb load for round two?" *Fuck my life.* When I said that to the waitress, I was all in petty bitchy mode, and it hadn't even occurred to me what the consequences might be.

"Sorry," I mumble, but he laughs. "I was just so pissed. How dare she look down at me for being able to eat a decent meal! Both Max and I work freaking hard every day. We deserve to eat well. Or I usually do. I've been slacking since I've come to California, but I guess going for a jog is out of the question until the stalker is found."

His smile turns serious. "I'd probably stick to the gym downstairs for a little while, yes," he agrees and then jumps a little before pulling his cell out of his pocket. He keeps eye contact with me when he answers, not telling me who's on the other end of the call. "Hey, man! How are you feeling today?"

My heart races. It must be Holden on the other end. Aside from checking out directions this morning, I've barely looked at my phone all day. I didn't know what I was going to say to him, and I knew it was only a matter of time until he tried to speak to me. "No, she's right here. No, I don't know where her phone is or why she's not answering it. Okay, yeah, tell Dad I'll make sure she turns it on. Yes, I'll get her to message him." Declan is frowning at me now like I'm a naughty child, and I feel like one too. "Tomorrow…. Yeah, hang on a second."

He holds the phone out to me, and I shake my head. Despite the eye roll, his voice is more patient than expected when he replies, "You need to speak to him."

"What if he hates me, Declan?" I whisper, hoping that Holden doesn't hear. He sighs, looking exasperated.

"He doesn't hate you, Harlow, but you *do* need to speak to him. He's worried about you, and he needs to be resting, not worrying."

Now that he's played with my guilty heart-strings, there's no way I can dispute his reasoning. Taking the phone from his hand, I put it up to my ear. "Harlow! I can hear you breathing. You can't avoid me, you know." Holden's voice does some-thing to me, and I burst into tears. Not those deli-cate tears that slide down your cheeks, sparkling in the light in such a way that authors can make some big romantic scene out of it that eventually ends in some kind of awesome sex. Nope, I'm jumping 10,000 levels ahead of that, straight into ugly crying with a sniffling nose and the world's most pathetic lip wobble. *Fuck. Me.* Declan looks shocked for a moment, and there might just be a hint of panic in his eyes before he gathers me in his arms and pulls me close. His warmth is a much needed comfort in my wave of sorrow.

"Hey now, are you crying?" Holden coos. "Don't be like that, beautiful. I'm okay."

"But it's all my fault, and I'm so sorry," I wail, and the chuckles I receive in response only make me cry harder.

"Shhh, it's not your fault. The only thing I'm upset about is that you're not here to kiss me all better." Well, fuck, that has my tears subsiding as another kind of emotion raises its head. It doesn't help that Declan has me pressed against his chest. "Declan tells me you'll be back tomorrow, and they're releasing me then, so I expect you to come and find me when you get home. The doctor has prescribed lots of cuddles from a sexy woman as the cure to what ails me."

A smile crosses my lips as I wipe my face against Declan's shirt. I can feel his chest shake with amusement, knowing he's likely able to hear Holden considering I'm pressed against him for dear life right now, but I don't look at him. "Hmm, I think maybe you have your prescription wrong."

He chuckles, and this time, the sound sends a wave of heat through me. "No, baby, but I am going to milk it for all it's worth."

Before we hang up and I return Declan's phone, Holden and I talk for a little bit longer with me promising I'm safe and that I'll come see him when we get home tomorrow. Declan doesn't remove his arms from around me, and I look up into his eyes, not understanding what the two of us are to each other right now. Not to mention, it's been a *long* twenty-four hours. "Ready to get out of here?" he asks, and I nod.

"Yeah, just let me write Max a note on a napkin. Will she be alright if I leave her with those guys?" A mysterious smile crosses Declan's face.

"Yeah, she'll be fine. They've just verbally agreed to sign with Neighpalm, and they won't want to jeopardize that, trust me." Well, that's all very cloak and dagger, but I'm too tired to push as to why.

Climbing out of Declan's arms, I head to the bar. I really don't want to talk to the waitress again, so I take my chances with the bartenders. The guy I talk to smiles and quickly hands me a pen and napkin where I write Max a quick note. Passing it back, I thank him and settle out our tab.

When I get back to the table, I stick the note under Max's half-full drink. "Shall we go? Or should we wait until they come back to the table?" Just as I ask that I feel a hand on my waist. Spinning, I find Sean smiling at me.

"Are you off?" he asks, looking between me and Declan. Declan slides out of the booth and sticks out his hand for him.

"Yeah, Harlow and I have a long drive home tomorrow, and we don't want to start too late. Holden's being released in the morning, so we need to get back to see him." Sean grabs Declan's hand, shaking it with a frown on his face. "Horrible thing that's happening to you, Harlow. I'm so sorry. If you ever need any help, please call me. You can get my number from Dec."

"Yeah, thanks. That's kind of you." I smile at him as he squeezes past and sits down. "Can you see that my friend Max gets my note?"

"Where did she get to?"

"She's on the dance floor with the other two." Declan nods in the direction of all the people, and Sean grimaces.

"Well, it doesn't look like they're causing too much chaos, but I'll stay and keep an eye on them."

"Much appreciated. I'm glad you got all those issues ironed out and are back on track for filming. Just know you can call me at any time to talk. Would it be alright if Harlow got a tour of the castle tomorrow before we head home? I know she usually likes her buildings more abandoned than that one, but I'm pretty sure she'd get a kick out of it."

My mouth drops open in shock. *Who is this man?* Be still my beating heart. Talk about racking up brownie points. I look to Sean, eager to see what he has to say.

He smiles, an indulgent look on his face. "Of course she can. We're shooting outside tomorrow, so feel free to wander at your leisure."

Declan thanks him, and I echo mine enthusiastically before he puts his hand on my back, guiding me to the exit.

We pass the waitress on the way out, and I can't resist one last dig. "Time for round two," I tell her with a cheeky wink that makes her red in the face. Declan snorts as we step out into the cool night air.

The temperature has dropped quite considerably, sending a shiver down my spine. "Wow, it got cold," I complain, and Declan immediately grabs me by the hand and tows me down the street.

"Well, come on then. Let's hurry. You can have a warm shower when we get back to our room."

Hello, what?

"Did you say *our* room?" I ask, stumbling slightly to keep up with him. He notices and slows down, but he doesn't meet my eyes.

"Yeah, there was only one left, and I didn't think you'd mind sharing?" I almost run straight into him when he stops unexpectedly, finally making eye contact as he raises a brow. "But if it's a problem, we can go back and wait for Maxine to finish with Cayden and Jarred."

I'm at that stage of my inebriation where I've gone from having fun to being just plain tired, and the thought of going back in there and dealing with the passive aggressive waitress then wading through that crowd of people to find my friend has me shivering, and *not* with desire.

Shaking my head, I push him in the direction of our hotel. "God no. You better not snore," I warn.

When we get to our room, I find out he'd gotten a few essentials together while I was with Max. Both of us have toothbrushes, and there's clean underwear as well. He also has a pair of pajama pants to sleep in, and it looks like I've got the matching shirt. "Sorry. It's not much, but it's all they could come up with on short notice." He looks a little sheepish, but drunk me decides he's earned a kiss on the cheek as I pass him on my way to the bathroom, change of clothes in hand.

A little while after the warm shower he promised, I exit the bathroom, steam billowing out in front of me, to find Declan on the phone once more. It looks like he's on FaceTime with Nana.

"I'm really worried about that one," I can hear him say.

Nana's voice comes through clearly when she asks, "What do you want to do?" A plaintive mewling sounds in the background. *Ah, the kittens.*

I move a little closer and look over his shoulder. "Hi, Nana."

She smiles at me even though she looks tired for the first time since I arrived. Sometimes, it's easy to forget that the woman is not a machine. All this worrying about her family must be getting to her. *I'm going to try to convince Poppy to take her away.* A vacation from all the craziness and a convenient way to keep them out of the line of fire. "Hello, dear, is Declan treating you right?"

"He's being the perfect gentleman," I assure her.

Nana being Nana, she frowns slightly and mutters what I think is "That's a shame." *Hilarious. Maybe Poppy needs to make that a romantic getaway.*

"Nana, can you point the phone at the kitten Declan is worried about for me?"

The screen wobbles as Nana does what I ask, and when the screen stops moving, I can see Princess feeding three little kittens. There's a fourth one off to the side, looking listless. "Nana, can you grab a bit of the kitten's skin at the nape of the neck and pull it away from its body? I want to test it for dehydration."

Her face lights up. "You told him you're a vet? He must be behaving if you're letting him get to know you."

"Yeah, it's not like I could avoid it when he was telling me about that little fellow." Nana gets down next to the enclosure, the movement of the phone making me feel slightly dizzy, but she follows my instructions. Just like I thought, the skin doesn't ping back like it would if the kitten were well hydrated. I turn to Declan. "Do you have any kitten formula and feeding supplies?"

"Yeah, I bought them just in case. They're in the drawer in my walk-in closet." I take a quick and hopefully unnoticeable breath to steady myself. How cute is it that he bought supplies just in case? I know we've got a lot of shit to figure out, but the way he cares about his cat really makes me feel like he's going to be redeemable. Call me naive, but it's always mattered to me how people treat the animals in their lives.

"Nana, if I text you the instructions, do you think you could feed the kitten overnight? Or if you can't, maybe one of the others could." Before she can answer, Declan jumps in.

"Jacinta will do it. Nana, can you keep them company until she gets my message with the instructions? I'll tell her to sleep in my room so she can return the kitten to Princess after each feed."

With a few more instructions, it's all arranged, but even after we hang up, Declan's body language tells me how worried he is. Poor guy loves that cat and her kittens. His head is down, and his shoulders are hunched as he puts his phone down on the bedside table. Not waiting for him to turn around, I step up to him and put my arms around him. It's a little awkward because I've never had the need to initiate this level of comfort for someone other than Max and her mom and dad before. I guess, like anything else, I'll get better at it with practice. For now, he'll get my awkward Harlow hug and like it, damn it.

"Don't worry. Everything will be fine after we get some fluids into it. If it hasn't picked up by the time we get home, we'll take it to the closet clinic." He shudders in my arms, but the tension leaves his body as I rest my head against his back. "Do you know what they are? I never asked you."

"The two seal points are males, and the two chocolate points are females," he tells me, breathing in a huge inhale before stepping out of my arms. Without another word, he steps around me and goes into the bathroom, closing the door behind him. It feels like the distance between us just grew huge again, but I'm not sure why. Even if there isn't a romance between us, surely we can have some kind of relationship? I don't think it needs to be all or nothing. Or at least, I don't want it to be like that now that I've gotten a little closer to knowing who Declan really is.

Grabbing my phone out of the pocket of my jeans, I settle myself on the bed and send Nana a message with a few extra tips on how to feed the kitten. Hopefully, by the time we get home tomorrow, it will be better. I'd hate to think anything else is wrong with it. There was an ultrasound machine in the stable, and my mind starts wondering what other supplies they might have. If they have some sterile saline and syringes, I could set up some subcutaneous fluids when I get back, if it hasn't gotten any better

It's difficult to not run through all the scenarios in my head. Does the kitten have a congenital abnormality? Did it get exposed to a virus? Did it aspirate some milk and get pneumonia? Did that happen because it had a cleft palate and I didn't notice? I shake my head to clear it all away. Poor Declan will be devastated if it has neurological problems or something else, and it's easy to get lost in all the what ifs. Running a hand through my hair, I realize how freaking tired I am, my eyes feeling gritty and heavy. Still slightly drunk Harlow comes to the decision that there's nothing to be gained by worrying Declan further. I won't make him run through all the possibilities with me.

Once I've closed the mental door on that, I shoot Max a quick text, wanting her to message me when she gets back, no matter the time. God only knows when Declan's coming out of the shower, so I turn out one of the lamps, leaving the other lit on his side of the bed. That's right. We only have one bed, but it's huge, so it really doesn't matter. I'm also so freaking tired. Last night's drama combined with the emotional rollercoaster from the last few days has my eyes closing quickly.

I must have fallen asleep because the movement of Declan climbing into bed startles me, but his whispered words and body heat have me drifting off again in no time.

We must have forgotten to close the blinds because the bright sun shining through the windows has me waking even earlier than I'd set my alarm for. Snuggling back into the warm, hard body behind me, I'm tempted to go back to sleep, but then the hand on my stomach moves, and I freeze.

Whoops, looks like Declan and I ended up spooning in the middle of the night and that's *his* morning wood that I'm grinding my ass against.

I hold still, but the hand that's on my stomach starts to creep higher, caressing its way toward my breasts. *Shit, what do I do?* I don't think he's awake yet; he's still relaxed against my back, so I'm pretty sure he's sleep groping me. Do I let him go and enjoy the moment, or should I wake him and stop him? Declan and I still have a few issues between us, the biggest one being his loyalty to his sister.

Biting my lip, my mind whirls with indecision. But before I can make a choice, my alarm blares loudly through the room. Declan's hand stops its ascent instantly, and his body tenses behind me.

"Well, I'd like to say I'm disappointed to wake and find myself groping a sleeping woman, but it would be a lie." His voice is raspy and still sleepy, but it tickles my ear, causing goosebumps to break out over my skin and my nipples to pebble.

Very carefully, he lowers his hand, removing it from under my shirt before rolling away from me and onto his back. "I'm sorry. I need to have an important conversation with my sister before any of this goes further," he says quietly. With that, he climbs off the bed and disappears into the bathroom. There's a weird combination of emotion in his statement, some mix of disappointment and shame, and I don't know what to do. I've got to admire the guy for sticking to his guns no matter the attraction between the two of us, but there's another part of me that's frustrated he can't let it go.

While I'm waiting for him to finish in the shower, I quickly get dressed in my clothes from yesterday and check my messages. I never heard it, but Max messaged that she'd see me on set before we left today.

I still need to grab my backpack from her though. Decision made, I shout through the bathroom door. "Declan, I'm just going to go and get my backpack from Max. I'll be back in a moment."

"Okay," he shouts back, sounding a little strained. I would probably sound the same if I was rocking morning wood that could pound in a nail. Yes, I had paid attention when I ground back into him, but then I had my hand on it the other night too, and Declan is *not* lacking in size.

Grabbing the key card, I let myself out of the room and go in search of Max and my backpack. Hopefully, I'm not walking into anything in her room. At this point, I'm not sure if I'd be more embarrassed or jealous.

Declan

uck. Again, I find myself in the shower with my hand on my dick because of Harlow. I swear I wasn't even this bad in high school when I first discovered girls, but waking up next to her, her warm body snuggled into mine, that plump ass pushing against my cock and the feel of smooth skin under my palm... It almost had me coming in my pants. I had to move away; otherwise, I might have started something again, and until I talk to Jacinta, I don't want to do that.

I can't keep going on like this. When she comforted me after we got off the phone with Nana, I knew I was a goner. This woman who asked me about my cats, who probably saved one of them... This woman is nothing like I thought she was. Nothing like any of us assumed she was. I have to find a way to make my sister see that.

A wave of fury stabs at me as I continue to run my hand up and down my cock. I'm so angry I'm practically choking it, but it's just what I need at the moment.

Harlow's voice through the door has me pausing, but when she tells me she's going to get her backpack from Max, there's a sense of relief. Now I can do this without feeling guilty that she's just on the other side of the door. "Okay," I call back from between gritted teeth.

Why the fuck did my PI not find out about her being a vet? In fact, I haven't heard from him at all which is strange. Something is going on with him, and I need to get to the bottom of this. I've been waiting for weeks for info on Harlow and just recently her mother. Something is fishy. The only reason he would be avoiding me is if someone was paying him to avoid me. The guy's good at his job, but he's shifty as fuck.

My mind floats back to the feeling of the swell of Harlow's breast under my hand when I'd finally realized what I was doing. A few seconds more and I would have had one of those perfect nipples in my hand. My mouth has already been on them, and I'm dying for a repeat. A loud groan leaves my mouth as my cum shoots onto the shower curtain, and after a few more strokes, it's too sensitive to continue. *Fuck, how am I here again?* If I didn't feel like I needed to talk to my sister, that could very well have been Harlow's tight pussy gripping my cock. I swear then and there, that's the last time I use my hand. Next time, I will be doing this with a very willing partner.

Chapter Nine

Oliver

The buzz of the tattoo gun is usually music to my ears while the bite of the needle is a balm that soothes my battered soul, but today, it's just a pain in the ass. Literally.

"Dude, that pony got you good. How have you been sitting, let alone going for a horse ride with your family?" There's genuine amazement in Jonah's voice, which speaks to the absolute demonic nature of Harlow's prized DS. He's outlining the shape of the bruise and teeth marks that I'm convinced will never fully heal. "I know I don't have to tell you this, but I can't color it in until the bruise fades. I'll take a picture so that I get it right later, but for now, you'll have to settle for the outline."

Gritting my teeth, I grunt my agreement. "The damn thing's a menace, but I should know better than to turn my back on a strange animal. I've been taking painkillers and sitting on a cushion as much as possible. The ride the other day was a nightmare, but I wasn't going to miss it when everyone else was going. And then I was glad I hadn't skipped it because Holden got shot." The last bit is said with such an obvious hitch in my tone that neither Jonah nor I can pretend it didn't happen. The gun stops buzzing, and my friend's hand comes to my shoulder in comfort. Jonah knows everything about my and Holden's history, so he's always been a safe and objective person for me to talk to. Talking about your ex is tricky, especially when most of the people you'd want to confide in are both your siblings and his. I'm not really sure there's any way they could all be objective about this, though they try, especially Jacinta.

"How is he?" I turn my head to look at him.

"Really fucking lucky." My eyes close as the memory of how he looked in the hospital flashes into my mind. "I was so fucking scared, but it helped me make a few decisions."

Jonah squeezes my shoulder before his hand drops. "Oh yeah, like what?" he asks as the gun starts up again. He resumes working on the outline, and I give myself a second to revel in the sensation. I don't love the pain that this bite has caused, but there's always been something therapeutic about the feel of getting a tattoo.

"Well, for one, I need to get Harlow to forgive

me. This is part of that. A reminder to never be an ass."

"I still can't believe you didn't warn her," Jonah growls as he presses a little harder than necessary, making me yelp, but he doesn't need to say anything else. He already let me have it the day after it happened. Not only do I have to stop being an ass, I need to be more mindful of who I let influence me. I knew my sister had problems and wouldn't be able to look at Harlow without her past coloring their future. It's people like Jonah, the ones who met her only once but saw the goodness in her, that I should have let whisper in my ear.

"I know! I'm an idiot, but I'm going to do everything I can to make it up to her. I need to reassure her I'm not upset about the car either. Maybe invite her to come and help me pick a new one? And I need to set things straight with Holden. Back when we first got to Dad's, I let my anger and insecurities rule my heart, but I'm not that scared boy anymore and neither is Holden. He's not the boy desperate to fit in, willing to give up everything to avoid rocking the boat. He can see for himself that our family loves him no matter what. I just need him to realize that I still love him as much as I did before we were adopted."

"Holy shit, man. So, full court press, hey." I roll my eyes at Jonah's basketball reference. He doesn't look like he'd know a basketball from a football, but he's a huge sports fan. Hockey especially. The man hails from one of those states that gets more snow than anything else, and the California weather has never been able to melt the love of snow and hockey from his veins.

"Yep, and I won't rest until I make them both mine." I pause for a moment. "Well, maybe Harlow will end up with more than just me, but I want my 1/6th share." Every time I say it, I'm still surprised that I'm not bothered by the idea, but it also makes sense to me in the way that I know I love Holden, yet I think I could grow to love her. If I could love two people in their own ways, who's to say that she shouldn't have the chance to fully embrace her own capacity for love?

"Oh, so it's like that, is it? The Summers boys are fixing to settle down. Got their eye on the prize and heaven help those that get in their way." He chuckles, and I nod with satisfaction. Jonah has always been able to roll with the punches, and it's hard to think of anything I feel like I couldn't tell him. Given he's bisexual and completely open to taking on more than one partner at a time, he's also had his fair share of crazy nights that he's shared with me. He's been one of my closest friends for years, and he's seen all kinds of unconventional, even poly, relationships, so that's not something that would ever give him pause.

With his sister Jilly being our favorite hostess for the family plane, I'd say that all the Summers hold Jonah's family close to our hearts. We don't trust easy, us Summers, but when we find people we care about, we hold on with everything we've got.

"Yes indeed. And we can be ruthless if we need to. Harlow doesn't stand a chance." At least not after we make everything up to her and earn her forgiveness. I'm still not sure how we're all going to make that happen yet, so I change the subject because there's something I've wanted to talk to him about.

"So we've got that new shop opening on the east coast; we still haven't got enough artists to man it yet, and I haven't found anyone I'd trust to manage it. As much as I'd miss you, are you interested in heading up the new store? We'd pay to relocate you and cover your rent for the first six months. If you end up hating it, you can come back, absolutely no hard feelings. Hopefully we'll have found someone we like to run it by then."

Once again, the gun stops buzzing, and the pain in my ass stops. "Are you serious?" he asks quietly from behind me.

"Of course I am. You're like a brother to me. I trust you with my life."

"Then I would be honored, man." I sit up gingerly, and we embrace in the way of the man, all back slaps and not holding on too long. He pulls back, and a cheeky glint hits his eyes. "So if I'm like a brother to you, does that mean I get a share of Harlow too?"

My mouth drops open in surprise, and he bursts into laughter, pushing me back down on the table.

"Dude, your face! God, I'm going to miss that when I leave."

And just like that, I have a manager I trust for my new shop and plans in place to woo my loves.

A couple of hours later, I'm heading for the hospital, cushion under my ass while the pain constantly reminds me of what not to do. I need to be able to tell Harlow about my childhood and how I ended up being adopted by Dad. It's no excuse, but it might help her understand the motivation behind my actions or lack thereof. I just need to figure out what's happening with Holden first because telling my story inevitably ties into his.

I had insisted on picking Holden up, so he can't escape our much needed and long overdue conversation. I'm using the limo today, which means we can talk without me having to concentrate on driving, not to mention *my car was trashed*. I hope I get one good punch in when the stalker is caught. That car was my baby, though it doesn't mean more to me than Harlow's safety.

The limo pulls into the patient pick up at the hospital, and I climb out gingerly. I've been living with pain for days now, so extending it for a few more isn't really a big deal. Hopefully, one day Harlow and I can laugh about it, preferably while we're both naked in bed. Maybe with Holden laying on her other side.

I make my way through the hospital up to the floor where Holden is. When I get to his room, he's flirting with the nurse, but he looks like he's dressed and ready to go. Nana had dropped off clothes yesterday. Clearing my throat, they both look up.

"Ah, it looks like your ride's here." The male nurse smiles at me when I enter the room. Like many of LA's residents, he's unnaturally pretty, and I find myself gritting my teeth with jealousy. But I smile and pretend it doesn't bother me, just like I've been doing since Holden decided we couldn't be together. I'd told Harlow that I preferred pussy to cock, but to be honest, it wasn't that at all. It was this man in front of me. He's the only one I've always wanted. There have been others who stirred my interest, but the real deal has always been him. And now it's Harlow too. Hopefully together.

"Oli?" Holden looks behind me like he expects others to walk in. "Are you on your own?"

"Yeah, Dad's arranging more security for the house, and the others all had meetings they couldn't get out of. Oh, and Jacinta is kitten sitting. One of Princess' kittens isn't well. Nana spoke to Declan last night, and he asked her to bottle feed it, which needs to be done every two hours. So... you're stuck with me."

"That's no hardship," the nurse tries to say under his breath, but I catch it. Holden must too if the scowl he shoots in the nurse's direction is any indication. Good, I want him feeling things. To be honest, anything would be good, but jealousy is a bonus. It would surely beat the apathy he's displayed toward me for years. Never mean or unkind, just indifferent, like he went from loving me, and loving me *hard*, to acting like it never happened. It hurt like a knife through the chest. Holden is one of the reasons why I survived living in the group home. I think if it hadn't been for him, I wouldn't be here. But I think I did the same for him too. Both of us were in really dark places, and one of the first things Nana did for us when we came to live with them was get us into therapy. It took a while, but eventually, I learned that I wasn't to blame for any of the things that had happened to me. I learned to love myself and that I wasn't to blame for the way Holden treated me either. It was his way of dealing with all his issues.

"Well, Holden, you're good to go. Make sure you rest that shoulder for ten days or so, and you'll need to get the stitches removed on day ten. Best to keep it strapped until then so you don't bust the stitches open. And then you're going to need to go to physical therapy to help with movement. I'm sorry, but you're probably going to be uncomfortable for a while to come," the nurse explains, handing him a slip of paper. "Here's a prescription for antibiotics and painkillers. Take the antibiotics twice daily but the pain ones only when needed. Maybe at night for sleeping because they're strong and you don't want to become reliant on them. And if there are any problems or signs of infection, come right back in and we'll take care of you." He pats Holden on the knee and gestures to the wheelchair at the foot of the bed. "Now, if you just climb in here, we'll bust you from this joint."

Holden wrinkles his nose but does as he's told, and that tells me, more than anything, that he's still not 100%. Usually he's stubborn as fuck about doing things himself. The nurse helps him to stand since his right arm is strapped to his chest, immobilizing any shoulder movement.

"You're probably going to need help for a few days while your shoulder is strapped. Don't try and do things that you'd normally do because if you trip and fall, you'll end up breaking the other arm when you can't brace yourself with both." He hands me a pile of paperwork and a spare sling for his arm. "Shower with this on, and you're probably going to need help because we wouldn't want you slipping. Is there someone at home that can help with that?"

Holden looks up at me from the wheelchair before carefully blanking his eyes. "I'm sure someone will be able to," he mutters.

"Yes, we have lots of people that will help him if needed," I tell the nurse, and he looks between us, trying to gauge the mood, but I guess he gives up.

"Great," he says with a blinding smile at Holden. "If not, I work for a temp agency as a second job, and we go out to people's homes to help with that sort of thing. My card is in the paperwork. Don't hesitate to call if you get stuck."

Well, fuck, he just dropped the mic. He pushes Holden out the door and leaves me to follow along behind. The ride down the elevator is quiet and riddled with tension, and as we finally make it to the patient pick up, I breathe a sigh of relief when I see the limo.

Mason, the driver, jumps out and comes around to open the door for us. "Good afternoon, Mr. Summers. Good to see you, sir." Mason smiles at Holden, and Holden returns the sentiment some-what wearily.

"Thanks, Mason, it's good to still be alive."

The nurse sets the brakes on the chair and goes to help him out, but I beat him to it. Handing the paperwork and shit to Mason, I steady Holden as he gets to his feet. His skin is a little clammy under my hand and he feels slightly chilled. Frowning, I help him into the limo and pull a blanket out of one of the hidden compartments, shaking it out and placing it over him. Our eyes meet, and he can't hide the warmth in them anymore. If this moment hadn't been such a long time coming, I might have scoffed at myself for how much joy that sight brings me, but I've been waiting for what feels like forever to see those eyes again.

"Thank you," he tells me with a tired smile. I pat him on the cheek and back out to take the stuff from Mason. I thank the nurse who gives me a tight smile and calls goodbye to Holden, reminding him to call if he needs him, but I quickly climb in and close the door. *Nobody got time for that.*

Once we're all in, the limo moves forward smoothly, leaving the overly friendly nurse behind. Gripping the paperwork like it's a snake, I shuffle through it to find the card and roll down the window without a second thought. Out it goes. And I don't even give a fuck that I just littered.

A deep chuckling has me freezing. Fuck, I forgot he was here. Meeting his eyes, there's amusement in them and no small amount of heat. "Jealousy looks good on you, Oli."

Holden's leaning back into the corner of the limo, the blanket still tucked around him. Not saying anything, because I can't deny that my jealousy and I like that he's alright with it, I place the paperwork on the other seat. I lean back, putting some distance between us so I can fully see him as I say what I need to get off my chest. It's now or never. Steeling my nerves and taking a deep breath, I start to talk.

"I'm sorry," Holden says, stealing the wind from my sails. "God, Oli, getting shot and knowing that it could have been you or Harlow or any one of us, made me realize how stupid I've been for the last ten years. I pushed you away in some misguided bullshit attempt to make everyone happy. I've missed you so much, but I was worried that if I tried to get you back and you rejected me, I might just die. So these last few years, I've just been living in a mess of my own making, and I've been an incredible asshole by forcing you to live in it too."

"So I carried on, smiling on the outside but shriveling up on the inside. Drugs only went so far at numbing the pain. It wasn't until my therapist suggested music that I felt like I could see a glimpse of light again, that, and the fact that at least I could still be close to you despite it not being in the way I wanted. I started to get a little bit of life back, but I think that if I didn't have my music and at least the ghost of you in my life… I wouldn't have survived, Oli."

My heart is breaking yet healing at the same time, and it's the strangest sensation I think I've ever felt. The thought of him being gone... He could've so easily left my life forever… It sends a cold chill through my system, but there's also the little warmth unfurling, some tiny seed of hope. I so desperately want this moment to be going in the way that I'm hoping for.

"I don't want to just survive anymore, with these little bright spots that still can't break through the darkness because I'm missing something. Someone. *You*, Oli. Going forward, I want you in my life, no more shutting you out. If you decide you don't want to try again, then I will accept that, but I'm not giving up on us unless you explicitly tell me that's what you want. I'm sorry it took me so long to see that when Dad adopted us, it was for real. I was just so scared that one wrong move would take this chance of a new life away from us, but I know better now. I know they would never want either of us to deprive ourselves of what we needed or wanted to be happy. I want you in my life, and I want Harlow in my life, and I'm hoping that maybe we can do that together." Over ten years worth of crap has spilled out of Holden's mouth all at once, but all I really hear is that he wants to give us a chance.

There are tears in his beautiful hazel eyes, and he's waiting with baited breath for a response. My heart races, and I have goosebumps all over my skin as my stomach rolls with all the emotions I don't know how to express at the same time. Although I had this long spiel planned, I'm now speechless, so I just lean forward, careful not to knock his arm, and gently place my lips to his. His lips are warm and plump and oh so familiar even though he's no longer the boy I remember. He's very much a man, but that makes no difference. This is like coming home. Once, twice, I kiss him gently before pulling away.

"I was ready to fight for you, so hearing you say that makes it easier to breathe. You said so much that speaks to both of us, and all I can say is that I want to be with you, and I want to be with Harlow, and after that, I'll never be able to ask for anything else because I'll have everything I've ever dreamed of."

I shuffle my body closer to him, and we sit silently all the way home, simply reveling in being next to each other. The feeling of my hand clasped in his is the best thing I've felt in years apart from having Harlow wrapped around me.

Although we've got a long way to go, I'm going to relish taking care of him while he recovers, and maybe we can make plans about how we're going to convince Harlow to give us a chance.

Together.

Chapter Ten

Harlow

Finally finding Max's room, I knock on the door and wait for her to answer. When she does, she looks disheveled, flushed, and only opens it a crack, my bag hanging off her finger. I try to peer around her, but she blocks my view and looks over her shoulder for a moment while a smile crosses my face.

"You go, girl!" I mouth before leaning in and giving her a kiss on the cheek.

"Thanks for last night. I really needed it. I missed you so much," I tell her quietly, and she smiles, nodding.

"Call me anytime. I want to hear about your trip to Hawaii," she says before we wave goodbye and she closes the door. I wonder which one she has in there, but I'm sure I'll be able to get the juicy details from her later. She's never been shy about sharing in the past.

Moving back toward the elevator, I head downstairs in search of the included breakfast, shooting Declan a text on the way. I need coffee before I'm fit to go anywhere.

Excitement prickles in my stomach as well as no small amount of amazement that Declan arranged for me to get a tour of the castle. I can't wait to see what it looks like on the inside, and I won't say no to being a little closer to the horses once more before we leave. I know it's Max's responsibility now, but I still need to reassure myself that they're doing okay.

Feeling relaxed for the first time in days, I quietly enjoy my liquid energy and the delicious food I grabbed from the buffet. I know I shouldn't be on my own, but what are the chances that the stalker followed us? Would they really do anything to me in a crowded restaurant? I can't help but argue with myself that Declan wouldn't have let me wander off if there was any reason to think I was unsafe, and it feels nice to be normal for just a moment.

It's about twenty minutes later when Declan finally joins me. His hair is damp, and he smells good even though he's dressed in yesterday's clothes. There's a smile on his face as he takes the long way over, stopping at the buffet before settling across from me.

"What are you smiling about?" I ask him, and it just gets wider.

"Do I need a reason to smile?" he teases, not answering the question.

"Um, yes. From my experience so far, you do." He looks a little sheepish that I pegged him correctly with that one.

"Touché. But I'm happy because I just spoke to Jacinta and the kitten has improved a bit overnight, so I'm feeling a lot more hopeful than I had been. Also, the company is pretty good too." He takes a bite of his danish and sips at his coffee before sighing. "God, that's good. I needed that."

We eat in a comfortable silence, and it's Declan's phone beeping that interrupts the tranquility. "That's our ride. Ready to go?"

Draining the last bit of my coffee, I stand and gesture for him to lead the way. Once again, he puts his hand in the small of my back and guides me where I need to go. I know a lot of women would hate that, but I like it. Makes me feel special.

"So... all that carb loading last night and we didn't put it to good use," Declan whispers in my ear, and I stumble. He catches my arm and helps steady me, a cheeky grin on his face. *Damn him.*

"Oh well, there's always next time." I pat him on the cheek. "I'm sure I'll do plenty of carb loading when Kai takes me to Hawaii over the weekend." Declan's mouth drops open in surprise while I turn and walk away, high fiving myself internally. Yup, that's right, gotta keep him on his toes.

Out in the front, there's a van full of people waiting, and we take the last two seats. Someone slides the door shut once we're in, and we head out to the vineyard. Everyone is fairly quiet, but I don't think that's because the boss is in the car; more likely, it's because of the early hour. Everyone still looks a little blurry eyed, and one or two look seriously hungover.

When we arrive, Declan and I are the first to climb out. He grabs me by the hand and tows me toward the entrance of the castle. For the next two hours, Delcan and I tour the marvel that is Castello Di Amorosa. We see the armory, torture chamber, the great hall, and the royal apartment. The beautiful furnishings and authentic decor makes me feel like we could be anywhere in the world.

But eventually, we have to stop, parting ways for each of us to take care of our last item of business. I head toward the stables while Declan ventures out to find Sean. Smiling at a few familiar faces, I snatch up a few carrots out of the feed shed and find where my babies are being kept, my heart warming with the way they whinny and peek over the stall doors when they hear me coming. Samson throws his beautiful black head up and down, his mane flying like he's in some kind of shampoo commercial. Silly creature, he is.

I'm just dividing the carrots between the four of

them when Maxine shuffles into the stable. Her eyes don't quite meet mine, and I feel a frown cross my face.

"Are you okay?" I ask, and she shrugs a little.

"Yeah, but can we not talk about it right now?" She cuts off my questions before I've even asked. When she looks up, she's got dark circles under her eyes, and I can tell she's been nibbling on her lip too. She only really does that when she's thinking about something, and I rack my brain, trying to come up with what could be the matter.

"Fine, but don't think I'm going to let this go. You've been there through all my shit, and I can tell something is bothering you. When you're ready to talk about it, I want you to call me." I grab her and give her another hug. Her arms come up around my body, and she squeezes back, so I'm hoping it can't be *that* bad. Max tends to turn off when something really throws her off, so if she's hugging me back, that's a good sign.

"Thank you," she whispers.

"Alright, we need to be going," I tell her, pulling away. "I'll give you a call in a couple of days to see how these guys, and you, are getting on."

"Harlow," she calls as I walk away, so I turn back to look at her. "You need to call Mom and Dad and tell them everything. I've avoided it 'til now, but keeping this secret isn't fair to me, and they deserve to know what's going on. You don't want it to cause a rift between Dad and Brad if they find out from someone else."

"Yeah, I wanted to call Melinda anyway. I miss her, and I need some motherly advice. Well, actually, I just want to hear her voice, but I'll make it seem like I want her advice too. You know how she loves that shit."

Max grins, probably thinking back to the many awkward teenage years where we both suffered through Melinda's well-meaning but highly embarrassing life talks. "Yeah, poor Mom. How did she end up with two kids who are so damn independent? She loves to feel needed."

"I just hope she doesn't judge me when I tell her about the boy situation."

Max scoffs, "Please! She's going to eat that shit up. And you know she and Dad never became snobby like a lot of their rich friends. It's Mom's down to earth poor person influence."

I roll my eyes. "You're a fucking snob. What are you talking about?"

She laughs, finally showing a little more of that regular feistiness in her eyes. "Yeah, but I could be a lot worse."

"Too true!" I throw up a hand in salute and actually leave this time, the sound of Max cooing to Delilah making me smile again.

Heading toward where we parked the truck yesterday, I find Declan leaning against it, all sexy and hot, surrounded by a group of women. A wave of jealousy flows through me as I watch him flirt with them, but when his eyes meet mine, I can see how he really feels. He's smiling, but his eyes tell me he wants nothing to do with any of them. He's good at putting on the friendly act. I guess these people are his employees, so he has to be nice to them, but does he need to be *that* nice? I would much rather see him aiming his cold Mr. Aloof persona at all of these women, the one that says 'I'm fucking off limits to all of you.' The one that I saw so much of in the first few days but haven't really seen since Princess had her kittens. Was that only three days ago? So much has happened since then.

"Ok, ladies, time to move along. We need to get on the road if we're going to make it home today." I shoo them away, getting dirty looks from one or two of them, but I don't give a crap. "I don't know if it's because we're leaving or the fact that I said we were going home together," I murmur as they head off.

The light in Declan's eyes changes as he watches the women drift away, and the tension bleeds out of his body. "Are you okay?" I reach out, putting my hand on his arm.

"Yeah, it's just hard, you know? To be nice when you know all they want from you is some-thing. So much of California's population wants to make it big, the ones in the actual movie industry even more so, even if they're the caterers or the cleaners or whatever. It wears on you after a while when all they want to do is talk about themselves and what movies we're working on. It would be nice if they were interested in me as a person for a change." Between this and our drive here, I'm getting a better feel for who he is, and these little peeks at the real Declan—his hobbies and even some vulnerabilities—is making me really want to learn more and maybe let him learn about me too.

He shakes his head and steps up, opening the door of the truck for me. "Come on, let's get going. I'm ready to see Holden." He moves out the way and goes around to the driver's side as I climb up and into the cab.

Before long, we're leaving the castle and movie set behind us. I watch the scenery go by, not moving to grab my book this time.

"So, have you ever scuba dived in Hawaii?" I remember him mentioning he liked to dive yesterday.

"Yeah, Hawaii is great for diving," he replies enthusiastically. "Why, are you interested in giving it a go?"

"I don't know about scuba diving, but I wouldn't mind trying snorkeling while we're there. I've never done that before."

"I wish I could come with you and show you one of my favorite spots, but I've got a major meeting set for Monday morning, and I don't think you guys will be back by then. I've got a feeling Kai's going to drag it out for as long as possible. I know I would if I had you all to myself. Not to mention Jaxon will want to spend time with you as well."

"Jaxon?" I look at him in surprise, and he frowns.

"Yeah, didn't you hear them say that the other day? Jaxon needs to check on the new hotel, so he's going with you guys."

"I guess I'd forgotten what with everything that happened." He looks at me quickly before his eyes go back to the road.

"Is that going to be a problem? Jaxon has been just as aggressive as I have, but I know he's regretting it now."

I shrug, not really wanting to talk about it. Jaxon is like Oliver. Someone who I thought I'd clicked with, but then he let me down when he assumed the worst of me. He's also the one I've had the least to do with. Even at the offices the other day, despite me helping him out with Raquel, that cold indifferent man made an appearance. He gives me whiplash, and I had hoped for a stalker-free and drama-free relaxing time away with Kai.

"Look, Jaxon and I were assholes. I'm not going to deny it. I know it's harder with the two of us, but look how well you and I are getting along now. This could be you and Jaxon too. I know you guys hit it off when he was out there for the nightclub opening."

I'm a little unsure about opening up to Declan about his brother, but I guess if we're going to attempt any kind of relationship, all cards should be on the table: total transparency.

"See, that's why I'm so wary. We did hit it off, but then he lashed out."

"Yeah, I can't say we don't have our fair share of issues since all of us do. But can you find it in your heart to at least give him a chance? Don't blow him off. If I know him, he's going to be working twice as hard to make it up to you. And I'm going to talk to Jacinta. I know that she was the worst of us all, but I swear, there's such a beautiful person underneath all of that."

It's sweet how determined he is to champion his sister, but I'd rather he focus on his own issues than trying to get in the middle of mine. Jacinta and I need to figure shit out for ourselves if we're ever going to have any type of relationship. A life of stilted silence and cold glares just because she's guilted into begrudging kindness isn't my idea of a real sisterhood. "Declan, you deal with yours and her issues. Don't try to fix mine and hers. We have to do that for ourselves, and until she changes her mind, I'm afraid we're at an impasse. I might not have a lot of relationship experience, but I do know that I want to be with someone, whether it's physically or romantically, who knows for sure that I'm what they want. There is nothing here between us, or even the potential for it, until you can say that, and I think your issues with your sister won't let you do that."

"Okay fine, but just keep an open mind, please!" He sounds so… unlike him. It's almost like he's begging, so I put him out of his misery and nod my head.

"I'm not promising anything, but I'll try," I compromise, and he looks happy with that, relief softening his face and tension. Why he's so determined to fight Jaxon's battles too, I have no idea, but I don't want to upset him and break the peace that's settled between us, so I'll push him on it another time.

For much of the drive, he tells me all about the diving in Hawaii, the types of coral I might see along with the different kinds of fish, and by the time we get home, a buzzing excitement is running through me. Though if I'm being honest, it might be my excitement at the thought of seeing Holden more than the thought of exotic fish.

I mean, it would be no hardship to snuggle up next to him while he was resting. He *did* suggest it, and I would be a bad friend if I didn't give him what he wanted. Especially because I'm the reason he got shot.

Declan and I park the truck back around near the stables, but when we climb out, there's a commotion that stops us in our tracks. Jacinta is saying something, yelling really, and though I can't make out the words, I can clearly hear the emotion there: fear. My heart races. *What if the stalker has struck again?*

"I thought Dad was getting security for here?" I ask Declan.

"He was supposed to. Come on, let's go see what's going on." He grabs my hand and drags me in that direction as I brace myself to face what lies ahead of us.

Chapter Eleven

Harlow

"What's going on?" Declan asks as we jog into utter chaos.

"Oh, Harlow, thank god!" Dad shouts in return, not making either of us feel any better. "Prada's in labor, and something's wrong. The vet's still forty minutes out, and we have no idea what to do right now."

I push my way past the gathered people to peer over the stable door, absently noting that it looks like everyone but Holden is here. Jacinta is inside the stable, sitting at Prada's head and stroking her face, while Josh is at her hind end with a terrified look on his face. Not stopping to talk to anyone else, I head inside, Declan following close behind.

Moving slowly but surely so as not to startle the distressed mare, I make my way to Josh and squat down. Immediately, I can see the problem. There's the telltale sign of a red sack which tells me right away that the placenta is separating before it should. *Shit.*

"I need a pair of scissors or a scalpel and a pair of gloves. I'll make do with hand sanitizer if you can't find the latter. And be quick!" I call to the people outside.

"What the fuck? What the fuck are you going to do to my horse?" Each of Jacinta's words comes out as a gasping sob, and I don't know if it's the late night, the craziness of coming home to this situation, or if I'm just a terrible person, but I'm kind of glad to see that she's not the world's prettiest crier either.

Thomas quickly returns and slowly makes his way into the stable, hands me a pair of gloves which I immediately pull on, and then passes me the scissors from an open suture kit. Jacinta shouts, lunging at me, but Declan is quicker. Luckily for both me and Prada, he manages to catch her before she can get to me. If she managed to knock me out, I have no idea what would become of Prada and her foal.

"Calm down, you're frightening Prada," he scolds, keeping a tight hold on her as I work.

"But what is she doing?" Jacinta stammers.

"Just trust me and focus on calming yourself down. We'll explain when it's over." She narrows her eyes, not happy that there's something she doesn't know while I'm preparing to be intimately close to her horse with scissors, but at least she's not crying anymore.

"How long has she presented like this?" I ask as I carefully slice the placenta open, quickly moving out of the way as the retained fluid comes gushing out. I pass the scalpel to Josh and proceed to insert my hand into Prada to feel for the foal's front legs. Finding them right inside the pelvic canal, I grab hold of them. Now, Josh can be useful; I motion with my head, wanting him to come closer. I'm going to need some extra strength for this. "Help me." He comes forward and puts his hands on my arms from behind. Together, we wrestle with the foal before pulling down toward Prada's hocks, and with a little more effort, the foal slips out with a whole heap more fluid and the ruptured placenta.

"About five minutes," Josh tells me, and a wave of relief flows through me. Maybe it will be all right. "I don't know who's looking out for this horse, but you guys got back here just in time." I start to vigorously rub the foal's chest, hoping to feel a heartbeat and see the rise and fall that will tell me we can be optimistic. Thankfully, it's doing both, and a big sigh escapes my mouth.

"Can someone get me a towel?" I call out to our audience, and I'm quickly handed a towel which I rub all over the foal's body to keep it stimulated. He's a *very* lucky boy. If we had been any later, it could be a completely different situation.

"It's a boy," I announce happily, and when

nobody answers, I look up. Nana, Poppy, Dad, and Declan are all looking on with pride, while the others are slack jawed with disbelief.

"What the fuck was that?" Jacinta demands as Prada struggles to stand up.

Eventually, she succeeds, leaning down to nudge at the baby in my arms once she's upright. I'm not sure how much time has passed before the little foal starts to struggle, but it does, so I stop rubbing it and stand up, helping it to its feet. It makes its wobbly way over to Prada and intuitively starts nursing. *Thank fuck.* I think we've avoided Dummy Foal Syndrome. We'll have to keep a close eye on both of them though, and Prada may need a course of antibiotics.

Now that it's all over, I realize that I'm wet and covered in gunk, up to the shoulders, from reaching into Prada, and it's *not* a nice feeling. Wish I'd thought to grab the overalls too, but there really wasn't any time. And my family is still waiting for an explanation.

"That was what we call a red bag delivery. Unfortunately, Prada's placenta separated from her uterine wall before she was able to give birth to that little guy. This cuts off the oxygen supply to the foal, and basically, they suffocate. By cutting it open and delivering as soon as we could, we managed to lessen the impact. Josh said it was only five minutes, so I'm hoping the foal hasn't suffered any severe side effects. The fact that he's up, breathing on his own, and nursing now are all good signs."

The peanut gallery still looks gobsmacked, and Jacinta waves her hand impatiently.

"Not that…. *That.*" She points from me to Prada and then waves her hand all around again. Still standing too close to her, Declan leans back, which is a smart move considering his sister's almost slapped him in the face twice now. "What did I just see?" Her eyes are wide, and her mouth opens and shuts like a goldfish.

She cannot be serious now. I snark back, "Oh, that? Well, I'm a qualified vet, so that was me performing an emergency procedure on your horse. I'm assuming you didn't want to wait until the other vet got here to deliver a dead foal."

The remaining ignorant siblings burst into sound, talking over each other to the point where I can't make out what's being said, and Dad and my grandparents add to the noise as they argue with them. Jacinta, on the other hand, is a different story. Although she'd been nagging at me a moment ago, now she's just staring at me with tears in her eyes. She shoves at Declan's arms until he lets go. Once she's free, she slowly walks toward me. *Okay, totally have no clue where this is going right now.* Paying no mind to the fact that I'm covered in birthing fluid, she wraps her arms around me and immediately starts sobbing again. *Oh god, I'm not good with criers.* "Thank you. Oh, thank you.

Can you ever find it in your heart to forgive me, please? I was so wrong about you, and I see that now."

Without any thought, my arms come around her, and I rub my soiled clothes all over her, making sure she's as filthy as I am. She snorts with amusement but doesn't pull away. "I think we can probably work something out," I say quietly, finally stopping my antics and returning the hug. And I can't say it's not nice.

"Are you telling me that all this time you've been letting us believe you're a horse trainer, but you're actually a fully qualified vet?" The annoyance seeping from Jaxon's question only triggers my own, and I spin around to face him, crossing my arms and holding back my grimace at the disgusting *squish* that accompanies the movement.

"No, Jaxon, that's what each and every one of you assumed. Not one of you ever thought to take the time to ask about my life, so I think it's entirely your fault that you didn't know the truth about me. You just assumed, and you know what they say about assuming things."

"It makes an ass out of you and me!" Kai chimes in, smiling. He just looks impressed and maybe a little turned on. Glancing down at myself, I shudder at the sight. I'm hoping it's the brains he's attracted to and not the gunk because that would be the second time he's been turned on when I look like shit.

"*They* knew." I point to Nana and Poppy and Dad.

Jaxon turns an accusing eye on Declan who holds up his hand. "Hey, I just found out yesterday when she helped with my kitten."

"That was *you*?" Jacinta gasps. "I thought Nana or you had spoken to a vet on the phone." She looks at Nana accusingly, receiving only a shrug in return.

"Well, I *did* speak to a vet. You just didn't know it was Harlow. What was it that Harlow said about assuming?" Her eyes cast down to the floor, Jacinta nods, appearing sheepish enough that I almost chuckle a little at their expense.

"From now on, how about we actually use words to communicate with one another instead of assumptions; I think we'll all find things go a lot smoother that way," Poppy says, his gentle patience breaking the tension.

"Wow." I glance over to Oliver at the sound, only focusing on him for a moment before I switch over to Thomas. For some reason, he doesn't look surprised at all. I think he's known all along that there was more to me than what everyone thought. But why wouldn't he say anything? No, if he knew for sure, he would have told them. *So what the hell does that look on his face mean?*

Eventually, Prada's vet arrives, praising me for a job well done while simultaneously reminding me that if I'm going to practice in California, I should get licensed for the state. With everything that was going on, I hadn't done it before I applied for the internship. It's at the top of my list when we get back from Hawaii since I'll need a current license ready for the next application.

Needing to do his due diligence, the vet follows the same steps I did, checking that all of the placenta had been delivered then checking over both Prada and the foal for strong vital signs. He also gave both the mare and the foal an antibiotic injection just because it wasn't exactly a sterile field when I stuck my arm into her, and he left behind a couple more just in case. After he got a quick rundown of what had happened, I'd gotten another round of thanks when he recognized my quick thinking. It definitely made me feel accomplished to hear him say that he wasn't sure they would've survived had I not been there.

Everyone else had left after the vet arrived, leaving just Jacinta, Josh, and me to deal with him, and now both horses are resting quietly in a clean, fluid-free stall. We handed their care over to Josh who said he'll move a cot down into the barn tonight and watch them for signs of trouble. Jacinta tried to argue about it, but he insisted. I know it was a long night for her too since she was up and taking care of Declan's kitten, so I'm glad she gave in without too much back and forth.

Finally, Jacinta and I make our way back to the house. It's quiet and dark now, the sun having gone down before the vet arrived, and the walk back is filled with slight tension between us. It's nothing compared to what it had been in the past, but it's still going to take a while for us to move on from everything. The bottom line is that I'll take whatever progress we can make at this point, and I'm willing to meet her halfway if it'll get us to a consistently civil relationship at the least.

We part once we get to the kitchen. I desperately need a shower and hurry to my room to do just that, but as I get there, my door is cracked open again. That's strange. Princess is still in Declan's room in the enclosure. Why would my door be open? Slowly, I put a finger against it and push it open.

"Harlow, listen, I just wanted to—" Jacinta calls from behind me, but the state of my room has her words turning to a buzz in my ears. *Holy shit.*

"Fuck!" Jacinta must be able to see what I'm looking at from behind me. My stomach lodges itself in my throat, and I feel nauseous. My room is trashed. It looks like a herd of rhinos have stampeded through it and massacred a flock of birds at the same time. Red paint and feathers are everywhere, and there isn't a single surface that hasn't been damaged by the knife that is lodged into the wall above where my head would be when I sleep.

A shudder makes its way through my body, and I slump against the doorframe. So much for escaping the stalker. They certainly didn't take the two days off while I was away.

"Yeah, I need you in Harlow's room. Be quick and bring the others. Maybe not Nana and Poppy." Jacinta's words start to come back into focus toward what must be the end of her call to someone, and then her hand is on my shoulder. "Come on, Harlow. There's a room in our wing you can use. I don't think you should be on your own, and there's nothing that you can do here."

She's pulling me away from the doorway as the thudding sound of people running echoes down the hallway. Dad and his sons push past the both of us, but I think I'm still in a little bit of shock. After the high of saving Prada's foal, this is a huge come down, and it's all just too much. I wanted to speak to them, to ask how this had happened, but no words can come out.

I feel Jacinta wrap her arms around my shoulders and guide me away from the mess, the contact an unexpected comfort. The angry voices left behind in our wake are definitely in need of some of that.

"I thought you were getting security?" I hear Declan snap at Dad.

"I did! I had them patrolling the grounds, but

the company was a bit short-staffed for the last few days, something about having a big client who needed a lot of their men. They've been doing the best they can, but there's a lot of ground to cover until the company can send more men tomorrow." Dad sounds shaken too, and my numbness gives way to guilt, my body unconsciously hunching down like a wounded animal. Jacinta whispers soothing words to me, but it's just background noise to the emotions whirling through my mind.

I should go. Run back to Connecticut and stay as far away as I possibly can. I mean, this didn't start until I came here, so it's got to be someone who's upset that I'm here. What's the likelihood they'll follow me home and terrorize me there? But then I'd be putting the Bostons at risk too. Fuck, I need to find a job somewhere far away from any of the people I love. Give up on my zoo dream and take a spot at some country clinic in some backwater town and hide. I can't let it go on like this. What if it had been one of the others instead of just my room?

Not paying attention to my surroundings, I jolt in surprise when the bright lights of a bathroom switch on, my mind coming back to the here and now.

"This is your bathroom in this wing. Have a hot shower while I find you something to wear. You'll feel better after that, I promise," Jacinta reassures me gently, turning the shower on and checking the temperature. Seemingly happy with it, she nods and turns to me, hands on her hips. There's a frown on her face, and she's tapping her foot as she looks at me. *There she is!* I thought she'd been body snatched by aliens, but Miss Bossy has made a reappearance. I can't find it in myself to be upset about it; there's something about this side of her that reminds me of Max, and weirdly, that makes her presence even more comforting. It's like I'm on autopilot though, because under her gaze, I start stripping off my clothes. Nodding her head, pleased that I'm following her instructions, she disappears, trusting me to do as she commands. The bathroom fills with steam as I discard my soiled clothes onto the floor. All of them can go into the trash; there's really no saving them now.

Climbing into the hot shower, I slide my back down the cold tiles until I'm sitting on the floor, dropping my head into my hands atop my raised knees. I can't stop the uncontrollable sobs that escape my mouth, though I don't think I could even pinpoint why I'm crying. The stalker? My destroyed room? Holden being shot? The vandalized car? I mean, take your fucking pick. All of them, none of them, I have no idea. I'm not sure how long I've been crying for, but the door opens before Jacinta steps into the shower, clad in only her underwear. She slides down next to me and wraps her arms around my shoulders, pulling me against her chest. Everything I'm feeling continues to rush to the surface as she rubs my back, holding me without any words passing between us.

This is the first time in my life where anyone has ever done something like this for me. It's not that Melinda or Chuck or Max wouldn't have done this, but I think I've always tried to present myself as strong, as… unflappable. They knew how deeply my mom hurt me, but I think that part of me felt like I might be letting her win if I broke down and showed them just how far those wounds went. Usually, whenever I get to that desperate point, I find myself sobbing with no comfort at all. It's not like I make a habit of crying when others are around. For Jacinta to be giving me this level of comfort actually has the sobs subsiding. My breath hitches, a sob or two still escaping, but all the tension leaves my body. Soon it's just the two of us, me being supported by someone who until recently had resented me with every fiber of her being. It's funny what extreme circumstances will do to people.

Pulling away, I rest my head on her shoulder. "Thank you." She grabs my hand and gives it a squeeze of reassurance.

"What you did for me today… It was every-thing. Prada is my everything. My horses have been there for me throughout the years, loving me unconditionally, wanting nothing more from me than their general care. Today, there was nothing I could do, and I failed them. But you, you were able to give them back to me when I was so close to losing them. Saving her and her foal meant the world to me, and being here for you is the least I can do. Even strong women need to break sometimes, but we always come back better and more resilient than before. We will get this person, Harlow, and when we do, well, let me tell you, they're going to wish they had never fucked with a Summers."

Holy shit. I look at her with shock, but she pretends not to see it. Honestly, it's okay. I think there's probably a limit to how many emotions she's willing to deal with in a day, especially when they have to do with me. We've taken about 1,000 baby steps in the last 72 hours, so I'm fine with giving her some space.

But that doesn't change the fact that she called me a Summers. Will wonders never cease? I can't wait to see where we go from here. I'm sure it won't be fully smooth sailing, but I think the worst is behind us. Or the worst in our relationship anyway. Something tells me the stalker is not going to be happy with the fact that I haven't turned tail and run.

What fresh hell am I going to bring down on us all next?

Thomas

Surveying the destruction that is Harlow's room, I run a hand through my hair in frustration, pulling just a little too hard at the strands. The sting makes me grit my teeth, but at least it helps sharpen my focus for the moment. Fuck, how does this keep happening? Not one single part of this room has escaped the stalker's violence, and they chose the perfect moment to strike. Though who knows if they came here yesterday while Harlow wasn't home or sometime while we were all out at the stable. This bastard is too sneaky, and I'm getting fed up with being a step behind.

God forbid if they had decided to wander into the other wing after trashing Harlow's room. Holden's been here, alone, and they could've taken another crack at him. I'm surprised Oli is still standing at this rate; he was panicked by the sight of Harlow's room, but when the realization hit him that Holden could've been in more danger, my brother nearly had a heart attack. He took off upstairs to check on Holden, and I doubt he's coming back down any time soon.

I take another deep breath and force myself to study her room more closely. Feathers litter all surfaces, most stuck to objects by the red liquid that has been spread across the room. Based on the congealed consistency of the substance, I'm pretty sure it's not paint, but the police will have to run tests to confirm my suspicions. Dec, Jax, and Kai are still arguing with one another, so my eyes go to Dad. The strain this is taking on him is evident in the worry in his eyes and the creases across his forehead.

"What is that smell?" Kai asks, his nose wrinkled. Stepping up to the bed, I grab a broken coat hanger from the floor, using it to push away some of the debris. A suspicious yellow stain is on the surface of the mattress, and I can barely ignore my urge to recoil.

"Is that piss?" Jaxon adds, the disgust in his voice mirroring exactly what I'm feeling right now.

"Well, I don't really want to get down there and sniff it, but I'm going to say yes," I tell them, about to drop the coat hanger on the mess, but then I notice the note. A corner of a piece of paper is sticking out from under what remains of a pillowcase. Using the coat hanger again, I lift the bit of material.

I can get to you anywhere. Don't think hiding behind the Summers makes you safe.

Curses fill the air as I drop the material back on it. I don't want to disturb anything else, so I'll let the police bag it up.

Dad steps out of the room, phone in hand to call the police yet again, while Declan herds Kai and Jaxon back out to the living area since there's nothing they can do right now but get in the way. Kai follows willingly, but Jax pushes back against

Dec, clearing his throat so that I turn to give him my attention once more.

"Can you see if her clothes survived the attack?" Jaxon asks. "I'll take some up to her." *Huh, that was actually thoughtful of him. I guess he really is trying to make amends.* It's not that my brother is an asshole all the time, but he's not really the kind of guy who takes care of the woman he's with. Sure, from what comments I've overheard completely against my will, they seem to think he's great in bed, but he doesn't really put his effort into the "boyfriend" behaviors like making sure his partner has what she needs, going out of his way to take care of things for her, that kind of stuff. Expensive jewelry? Sure. A "loan" to pay off some bill he's gotten swindled into paying? Absolutely. But this seems like he's actually thinking about Harlow's *feelings*, not just some surface situation that he can fix with a little flex of his black American Express. Looks like Harlow's forcing Jax to grow up a bit. I hate to say it because I really don't need more complications, but it makes me like her even more. At heart, I think I believe that shit about how a good partner brings out the good parts of you. With hindsight, I think that's one of the biggest signs that my ex wasn't right for me. God knows the bitch brought something out of me, but it definitely wasn't the best of anything.

He's staring at me expectantly, an annoyed look on his face, so I must've kept him waiting too long.

Shaking my head, I walk over to Harlow's wardrobe with him trailing behind me. *Hopefully the destruction was limited to out here.* But when we get there, we're greeted by an almost identical sight. Harlow's clothes haven't escaped the destruction. No feathers in here, but every single piece has been shredded, shoes included.

"What the fuck?!" Jaxon exclaims, pointing over my shoulder at an open drawer. We both step up closer as I hear him gag behind me.

The drawer is full of Harlow's panties, but there's something spread over all of them. Something any red-blooded man would recognize as instantly as Jaxon obviously did.

"That sick fuck!" The words slip out of my mouth as I take in the semen-covered pile of material.

"How is there so much? He must have jacked off a couple of times." Not a question that I really want to answer, but Jaxon has made a valid point that I'm not sure he's even aware of—when the fuck was this bastard here that he got away with the wreckage in this room and had enough time to leave *that* behind?

"Obviously this guy gets off on what he's doing," I say blandly while everything is churning inside of me. "Come on, she can borrow something of Jacinta's. Even if there was something salvageable in here, I don't want her wearing anything this sick guy might have touched." I herd him out of the room, pulling my phone out of my pocket.

Dad is still on the phone with the police as we exit, looking like they're not offering much, if any, comfort. "Nothing we can do until the police get here," I tell Jaxon, but he stares at me blankly, like he's not understanding what I'm saying.

"How are you not messed up by this? I mean, I know you're trained and everything, but this is affecting our family, Tom! Are you really so cold now that it doesn't bother you?" I know that he's just lashing out, needing a way to let loose the anger that's built up so quickly inside him, but that doesn't mean he hasn't hit me where it really hurts. He's not wrong, and that's exactly why it's a bit of a low blow. I hide a lot of what I do, not wanting to see their judgmental and disappointed eyes. Does this bother me? In some ways, yes, it really does. I care about Harlow even if I'm not able to reconcile in what way yet, and I don't want to see her hurt or threatened or scared. But I've seen things worse than what lies behind Harlow's door… I've been a part of things worse than what lies beyond Harlow's door. But I can't bear for my brother to know that, so I have to put the mask back on.

Keeping my face neutral, I reply, "Of course it bothers me, but there's nothing I can do about it for now, and getting upset isn't helping anything."

He just shakes his head and storms off. Better that I'm left alone anyway. I noticed I had missed a phone call from my contact, but with everything that happened in the last 48 hours, I haven't had a chance to respond.

I make my way through the house and out onto the back deck, phone at my ear, so no one stops me as I pass them in the living area.

Finally, he answers. "Fuck, Summers, where have you been? I've been trying to get a hold of you for days."

Jake Jennings is a full-time agent that works for the same agency I do. We've always gotten on pretty well, so he was my first thought when the situation escalated to the point that I needed to get some investigating done on my own terms. He's been looking into Harlow's background for me since Dec's PI has proved to be completely fucking useless.

"Sorry, man, this stalker kicked things up a bit, and one of my brothers got shot." I explain, hearing a soft hum of acknowledgment in response. "And we've just found that they were able to break into the house and trash Harlow's room."

"I have some shit to tell you. I thought you said that this girl was a horse trainer and worked for her foster parents." He sounds confused, so I guess he must have discovered what we did a few hours ago.

I blow out a huge breath and sit down on one of the chairs outside, readying myself for whatever's coming next. The night air is cold, and the only sounds are insects and the quiet hum of the pool pump. The faintest hint of mumbling comes through from inside the house, but I know that my conversation will remain private so long as I keep my volume down.

"Turns out I was wrong," I mumble, to which he very gracefully snorts. *Yeah, I messed that one up.*

Half an hour later, I have a clearer picture of Harlow and of her mother, but still nothing really to go on.

"The mother's death was definitely on purpose, but they have no leads. That's as far as I've gotten," he tells me, and I'm both confused and disappointed. It doesn't make sense that the same person would've killed her mother and then stalked Harlow. Her mother was a manipulative junkie, so it stands to reason that her untimely end was a direct result of her own poor life choices. Harlow, on the other hand, with her connection to the Bostons and her recently discovered connection to Dad, has a lot more strings attached for this stalker to pull. To what end, I have no fucking clue. It seems like they could benefit more from forcing her to stay with us, finding a way for him to get some kind of payout from our family, but the attack on Holden and the threat to Jacinta say otherwise.

"Damn it! I think we need to start looking further out. Let's investigate the Bostons and the people that work for them. I think we also need to get a clearer picture of what Harlow's mom got up to on a day to day basis and who she spent time with." he agrees to everything easily enough, though I get the feeling that I'm going to owe him one hell of a favor after this. Maybe I can get Dec to pony up tickets to some of the upcoming Neighpalm Productions premieres. It's an easy way to impress a date, and the last time we caught up, he mentioned a new lady friend.

"Oh, and can you check in on a private eye by the name of David Sands? He's been doing some work for Declan, but he seems to be missing in action."

With that, we wrap up the conversation and hang up, my mind running through the information Jake just told me. Leaning back against the chair, I close my eyes. Fuck, Harlow had amazed me with her cool and calm reaction to the incident with Prada. I knew there was more to her than everyone had assumed. I just hadn't realized how much more. Thanks to her, my sister is still whole. It might sound dramatic to say that about a horse, but Jacinta loves her family, her job, and her animals. Really, for as superficial as many people assume she might be, she's a girl with simple tastes, and if you were to take away one of those three pillars, she would just crumble. The only reason her leave of absence from Neighpalm didn't crush her is because she knew that it would eventually end. Harlow will never understand how meaningful her heroics were tonight. She's just… kind of amazing.

Seriously, she's almost enough to change my

mind about no serious relationships and make me jump on board this harem thing my brothers have suggested. Not only is she gorgeous but she has an intelligent mind as well, and that's sexy. I'm just not sure it's worth the risk. Do I trust her and hope she doesn't destroy me like the last one did? Or would it be better for everyone involved if the stalker got what he wanted and chased her away? She and Dad could continue to communicate via the internet, and he could go to her. None of us really need to be involved in that. But then again, am I favoring that option because I'm thinking practically, objectively, and using my training to make that choice? Or is my objectivity being clouded by my desire to avoid another messy relationship?

Fuck all of this. I need to keep my mind on the job and my priorities straight. And that's keeping my family safe, not throwing that sexy temptress up against a wall and showing her what happens when I'm fully unleashed.

Chapter Twelve

Harlow

Jacinta leaves me alone to finish my shower, and when I get out, I find a pair of black yoga pants and a cami laid out on the bed for me. No underwear, but that's okay. Towel drying my hair, I pull on the clothes which fit well despite Jacinta being a little shorter than I am. A quick study of the room makes me realize it's a match to the one in the other wing. A shaky smile crosses my face at the thought that they'd made me up two rooms just in case. Let's face it—the siblings were never going to let me be comfortable on this side when I first arrived, but things feel different now. For the first time, I really think everything is going to be okay.

Hanging the towel back up in the bathroom, I wipe the steam from the mirror and peer at my reflection. Dark rings circle my red eyes, and I look exhausted. Rummaging around in the drawer of the cabinet, I find a hair brush and pull it through my blonde locks, calling it good when it looks neatish.

My stomach rumbles with hunger after the long day, so I decide to go and find some dinner, planning to pass out the second I'm done scarfing down some food. I'm not even going back to my room on the other side of the house. In fact, doing my best impersonation of an ostrich sounds like the perfect choice. I'm going to stick my head in the sand and pretend not to have seen it. Tomorrow is soon enough to deal with it.

When Jacinta first brought me to the room, I wasn't in the right state of mind to pay attention to my surroundings. With my head now a bit clearer and in full ostrich mode, I look around and figure out that I'm on the same floor as Kai, my new room opposite his. *At least I'll know where to run back to once I grab some food. Eating alone sounds perfect.*

But when I get to the kitchen, I find that I'm not going to be able to do that. Everyone is gathered at the table while Mrs. Heyton bustles around, setting out hot dishes.

"Harlow, I spoke to Detective James, and he's sending out the crime scene unit to dust for fingerprints. But I'm afraid everything you own has been destroyed. We will of course replace it all as soon as possible," Dad tells me as soon as I walk into the living area. *Fuck! Everything?* Not wanting to face that just yet, I act as though he hasn't just talked to me. *Head in the sand, Harlow. Get the food and get back to that room.*

"Where's Oliver? And did Holden get home okay?" I ask, looking for anything to distract myself from the reality of the situation.

"Oliver is keeping Holden company upstairs," Nana says. Her eyes are filled with sympathy as she pats the chair next to her. "Come sit down. Have dinner with us. The company will be good for you. Gretchen is going to take a tray up to both of them in a minute."

"Actually, if you don't mind, I think I might take a tray too? I'd like to see Holden. I haven't had a chance to yet, and I really need to apologize."

"You don't need to apologize, Harlow," Dad tries to reassure me, but I just get angry.

"But I do, Dad," I snap at him. "None of this would have happened if I wasn't here. It's all my fault." Dad's eyes are filled with concern, so I ease off on the attitude. "Let me do this, *please.*" While I've managed to push down the frustration, I think that last word reveals entirely too much of a different nature. This time, his eyes soften as he nods in understanding, a barely perceptible sigh escaping with the movement.

"Okay. Just give me a minute and you can go." Dad gets up and leads me into the lounge area, sitting me down then claiming the spot beside me.

The sadness in his eyes does nothing for my currently fragile nerves, sending my heart racing. "Detective James says he doesn't need to talk to you because you haven't even been here, but he did ask me to pass on to you that he spoke to the detective in Hartford. The toxicology report is back, and there's something a little weird about the results. They're running some more tests, but they're going to start investigating your mother's case as a murder instead of an overdose. Things just aren't adding up. They've questioned some of the trailer park residents, and she was overheard arguing with another woman the morning she was found. Apparently, it got quite heated." My stomach lurches as a wave of nausea hits me. "Though he did say her body was ready to be released for burial or cremation, whichever you've chosen."

I can feel everyone's eyes on us, and though I should be able to feel the heat of a blush burning across my cheeks, I'm frozen. My mother was murdered. Sure, she was never a nice person or a good mother, but *murdered*? That's another thing. Why? My mind is reeling, and Dad reaches out to get my attention. "Do you mind if I tell the others? They've all been on edge too, and they've been really concerned about wanting to keep you safe."

"No, that's fine." With a shake of his head, he gets up and goes back to the table. I can hear him murmuring to them, but it's all background noise to the chaos in my mind. What am I supposed to do with this information? Who would she have been arguing with? She didn't have any female friends; she had managed to scare all of them off by flirting with their significant others. Honestly, she didn't have friends, period. They were just all marks she could scam something from.

"Harlow…. Harlow." I look up at Thomas, blinking in surprise. He must have been calling my name for a while.

"Would you like me to deal with your mother's remains? Did you have a preference?"

Blinking again, my mind is a muddle. I haven't thought about any of those details. In fact, I'd forgotten about them completely. Fuck, I'm a bad daughter. Just because she was a shit mom doesn't mean I have to do the same thing.

"Uh, cremation, no service, and I don't need the ashes."

"All right, I'll make those arrangements so you don't have to worry about it. Did she have any other family that might want the ashes or need to know?"

I shake my head. "I don't know, none that she ever mentioned to me. Melinda might know. I was going to call her tomorrow, so I'll ask."

"Okay, well, I'll do that once you let me know what Melinda says," he replies, smiling gently.

"Thank you, Thomas."

"Harlow, if you want to stay home instead of coming to Hawaii with me, I'll understand. There's a lot going on at the moment, and I wouldn't blame you if you'd rather just hunker down here and get a little time away from the world. Once Dad gets the rest of the security here, this place should be a fortress. There won't be a way that asshole will get in here again." And there it is, one of the reasons I need to go. Kai is just so kindhearted, and even though the disappointment in his voice is giving away how he really feels, he's making this offer nonetheless.

"NO!" I blurt out. *Nice, Harlow, scare the man off. Try it with a little less yelling this time.* "No, I just want to get away. I know that seems like I'm running away, but I need the distraction. Please," I plead, looking over at everyone at the table. None of them look like they're judging; in fact, they look like they agree with me.

"Are you okay with me tagging along, Harlow?" Jaxon sounds a little nervous, which is understandable. With everything that's passed between us, I know Dad wouldn't give me a hard time if I said no, but I don't have the urge to do that.

I shrug my shoulders, indifferent either way. And I actually think I really do feel that indifference. It's not even ostrich Harlow making that decision; at this point, things with Jaxon need to either sink or swim, and I'm leaving that outcome in his hands. "It's your plane. Who am I to tell you that you can't come?"

He frowns, yet somehow the man still looks beautiful. It figures that even though I'm in some sort of shock from my room being trashed, my brain still makes the effort to remind me of just how good-looking Jaxon Summers is. "Harlow, it's yours too," he says. "You get as much of a say as any of us." Dad beams at Jaxon like he's won a Nobel peace prize, and I guess to Dad, he has. Them including me in the family is everything he's dreamed of since he found out about me. I can't say it isn't nice, but my feelings toward these men are *not* familial. *That's a whole other mess to figure out.*

"Yeah, I mean, okay, I don't mind if you tag along. I'm not sure about Kai?" When I glance over at him, he's smiling enthusiastically. Okay, that speaks for itself.

"Good, it's settled," Kai says, and the frown on Jaxon's face lessens. He still looks nervous, but the too-attractive almost pout is gone.

"We'll leave about lunch time tomorrow. Not sure how long we'll be away for yet, but at least a couple of nights."

Kai must see the panic that crosses my face. "Don't worry about packing, Harlow. We can shop for anything you may need when we get there."

Just then, Mrs. Heyton bustles through the kitchen door, carrying a tray.

"Just in time, dear. I'm glad you got my message," she says, smoothly handing the tray off to Oliver as he walks into the room. It has two plates on it topped with silver covers. She turns and hurries back into the kitchen, the door swinging widely in her wake, before returning once more with another tray that she hands to me.

"Enough talk now! My food will get cold," she scolds everyone, gesturing to the table. She then shoos her hands at Oliver and me. "Off you both go. Holden needs to build up his strength so don't make him wait. Oh, and one of you will have to help him if he needs it." She gives us a stern look, and Oliver and I exchange a glance before nodding like naughty children.

"Yes, ma'am," he replies, turning and carefully hurrying back the way he came.

"Can you get me a can of soda?" I ask her, wanting to grab a drink before I leave, but she insistently flaps her hands at me again. "Holden's fridge is fully stocked with drinks, like all the fridges in this house." She puts her hands on her hips like she can't believe I would even suggest that she'd forgotten about it.

"Okay, and thank you for this." I lift the tray with an awkward nod to her before turning to my family. "Goodnight, I'll see you in the morning." A chorus of goodnights follow me as I head back the way I'd come. Passing through the cozy shared living area, I make a note to find some time to use the reading nook down here. I want to have a look through the books now that I've almost finished mine. I could read on my phone, but I like the feel of a paperback in my hand and the action of turning the pages.

Climbing up the stairs, my body is weary with exhaustion, but the effort is worth it since it means I get to skip dinner with the group. I have so much going through my mind with the stalker and mom being murdered and everything that has happened. But the only thing playing through my overworked mind is that no one—and by no one, I mean Declan—seemed concerned that I was going to Hawaii with both Jaxon and Kai. In fact, he seemed pleased, if his grin had anything to say about it. Thomas hasn't really shown any interest in me, so his acceptance of the situation isn't a surprise.

In any case, I think I need to voice my concerns to the brothers before any of this goes any further. The air needs to be cleared so that I don't have to be worried every time I'm spending time with one or two of them instead of the entire gang. I want to explain to them that although I want to spend time with each of them, I also want to spend time with the others. That really, I'm being incredibly selfish and don't want to choose. I owe it to myself to take a chance. I'm just starting to think about how to start that conversation without being awkward, mindlessly heading down the hall to my new room at the end, when I hear a shout.

"Mistress!" The word has me stopping and smiling to myself. Turning, I approach the open door and look in.

Sitting in the huge bed is Holden, arm in a sling across his naked chest. Oliver is next to him, and the food tray is set up between them both. He's smiling, and his beautiful hazel eyes are bright. Thankfully, his skin is flushed and healthy, not the pasty gray it was the last time I saw him. Relief has my knees almost buckling, and I lean against the door for support. Both boys frown before Oliver jumps off the bed, hurrying over and taking my tray from me. He puts it down on a desk off to the side then grabs me by the arm, guides me over to the bed, and gently pushes me down into the spot he'd been occupying.

"Are you okay?" Holden sounds concerned, and when my eyes meet his, he has little worry creases in the corners of them. My skin prickles with goosebumps as a feeling of joy flows through me. *He'd been shot because of me, but he still worries. He's almost too good to be true.*

"I'm okay, just pretty tired." I scan up and down his body, and apart from the sling, he looks good. *Really good, damn it.* All that golden flesh on display has me thinking inappropriate thoughts, flashing back to our moment together on the dance floor. Although his arm is strapped across his chest, one nipple is exposed, the bar in it glistening in the light, and I want to lean down and bite it. Punish him for making me worry. *Whoa, where did that thought come from? Am I taking this mistress thing too far?* When I finish my perusal of his body and my eyes meet his again, there's a smirk on his face and a whole heap of desire smoldering in his eyes.

"See something you like… Mistress?" he teases, and I fidget on the bed before leaning in, my breast rubbing against his arm, as I whisper in his ear.

"Oh, I sure do." My mouth goes from his ear to hovering just above his lips, and I can feel it when he gasps in a quick breath of air. But before our lips connect, I pull away and grab a broccoli stalk off his plate, quickly shoving it into my mouth.

"So damn good, and I'm so freaking hungry." I mumble around the mouthful of food.

I finally remember Oliver's in the room when a burst of laughter comes from behind me. "She got you there, Den."

Holden's eyes go from turned on to shocked the moment the nickname comes out of Oliver's mouth, his throat working as he swallows deeply. Okay then, as exhausted as I am, it's time for me to grow a backbone and be assertive. I climb off the bed and gesture for Oliver to retake his spot.

"I have questions, and you guys have the answers." They both look warily at each other before turning back at me. "But I'm freaking starving, so why don't we eat some food and relax before we get into the deep and heavy stuff?"

The two of them look to be a mix of confused and hopeful. We've got some shit to sort out between the three of us, and maybe if we put some of it out there, we'll have time to start bringing up the tension that's tying me up with their brothers too.

We spend the next half hour avoiding the giant elephant in the room while we eat the delicious meal Mrs. Heyton had prepared for us. Oliver tells Holden all about the drama with Prada and how I was like a superhero, revealing that my secret identity saved the day in the nick of time. I can't stop the snort that comes when I see how dumbstruck Holden is, cringing when the soda I'd been drinking bubbles up my nose.

"Well, that's what you dumbasses get for assuming shit. All of you deserve to grovel just a little after the way you treated me. That was just a bit of payback."

Aaaannnd I guess we've come full circle. It's time to face the music.

Chapter Thirteen

Holden

The ache in my shoulder is dull and muted at the moment thanks to the painkillers, but the ache in my soul from Harlow's words can't be so easily numbed. Oliver's brow furrows in a way that only ever means he's determined, and he nods, acknowledging that he knows exactly what I want. What *we* want.

Oliver gets up from where he's sitting next to me. He'd been helping me with the things that I couldn't manage on my own, and we giggled like school kids when at one stage he'd missed my mouth and food landed on my naked chest. I wanted to suggest he lick it off, but I managed to hold my tongue. There's plenty of time for those kinds of games. He grabs both our dishes and Harlow's and puts them back onto the nearby desk before coming around to my side and helping me shuffle over to one side of the bed. With another insistent wave, he motions Harlow into the newly vacant spot then joins us, taking a seat near our feet. I know he'd like to sit on her other side, squishing her between us, but we have to take care of some business first, and as much as I'd like to run with a fun distraction, she deserves better than that.

"We were such idiots, Harlow. Especially me. Can you find it in your heart to forgive me?" Oli begs before I can even get a word out. Wanting to get a feel for where Harlow's at, I keep my mouth shut and watch this play out. He needs to apologize more than me. Oli told me about what happened between the two of them at Neighpalm Ink. I didn't warn her or help her stay out of Jacinta's trap, but I also didn't hook up with her and tattoo her then shatter the trust we'd started to build.

She takes a deep breath and releases it as an audible whoosh of air. "Oliver, what you did hurt me more than what Jacinta did. Her prank was childish and ridiculous, and yeah, I was upset because it was my first public appearance as a part of this family, but that felt like nothing compared to your betrayal." Her piercing green stare doesn't leave him the whole time, and Oli's body droops at that direct hit. I want to comfort him, to take him up in my arms and tell him that we'll figure this out, but I don't dare get in the middle of this. If I want to have the both of them, I need to let this happen whatever way she wants it to.

"I thought you and I had something. And contrary to what you believe, I don't let just anyone throw me up against the wall and ravish me." A confused wrinkle appears on her brow, and she mumbles something else under her breath. Despite trying to keep it to herself, I still manage to catch the words. "Though it seems to have happened more with you and your brothers than it ever has before." She shakes her head and continues, ignoring my smirk.

"I realized you must have known about the billboard because after you received that text, you closed yourself off. Instead of going 'Hey Harlow, Jacinta's going to fuck you up tonight,' you shut down. Your inaction hurt way more than Declan, Jaxon, and Jacinta's verbal attacks, and way, way more than Holden and Thomas' indifference. You were the first to open up to me, and I feel like it was just convenient to use me at the time. I helped you get rid of the clingy artist, but then I wasn't needed for anything else, so you stepped back and allowed Jacinta to play her games."

A tear trickles down Oli's cheek, and I'm honestly a little surprised. I know that we both want her in our lives, but I guess I wasn't really understanding how deeply he was feeling. Oli doesn't cry for just anyone; as far as relationships go, the last person that I know he shed a tear for was me.

"I'm so sorry. The moment it happened, I knew I'd done the wrong thing. I knew it was wrong, and I can't deny that, but there's still that part of me that tries to do everything it can to avoid causing waves in the family that chose to love me. I know that you didn't have the easiest upbringing either, so I hope I'm not assuming too much by saying that I think you understand just how precious it is to find someone who wants you after others have decided you're utterly not worth it." He sighs, his gaze coming up to meet mine before moving back to Harlow's. I didn't force his hand or make him let Jacinta take the lead, but I played my own part in breaking Oli. His last comment wasn't meant to be a jab, but it hurts me anyway. I'll always regret that I ever made him feel unwanted.

"You know that Holden and I were adopted later than the others. We were almost seventeen by the time Dad brought us home. He and I had been living in a group home for about eight months by then. His story is his." When Harlow turns to me, I close my eyes and nod, knowing that when he's finished, it's time I share my own past. "Mine is not one I like to talk about or even remember, but I want you to know me, to understand why I made the wrong choice so that maybe you'll consider giving me a second chance. My parents were very much like yours, but not only did they do drugs, they cooked and sold them as well. They couldn't always pay for the materials they needed to make them, so they started using me as currency." Oli's gaze is on his lap. He won't look up at us until he's done sharing; even though I've heard it before and know him more intimately than most, he still has difficulty talking with me about this. I know how great his shame is, and the fact that I can't physically comfort him at the moment frustrates the hell out of me.

"One of their suppliers, a fucking creepy guy, had a taste for boys. Thankfully, he didn't like them too young, so I was safe for a while, but by the time I was fourteen, they were giving me ecstasy and then passing me to this man. He would use my body, and because of the X, I liked it. Begged for more, in fact, so it became a regular thing. Since I didn't fight them on it, they didn't even bother to make sure they had enough to pay him with. They knew that no matter their lack of funds, they could just pay him off with me. Until one day, my parents pissed off the wrong person. Both were killed in a home invasion along with the guy they'd been selling me to." Oliver's eyes cloud as he gets lost in the memory, his breathing increasing to the point that I'm almost ready to say fuck it. If he gets worse than this, I'm pulling him over to me. It might be clumsy, and it might be awkward for Harlow, but he needs to be held so that he knows he's not back there anymore, that he's not alone anymore.

"He was fucking me when it happened. His heavy body pinned me to the ground, and—" He shudders, a sob escaping his mouth before it sets in a firm line. "I can still feel his hot blood covering my face as he bled out. The home invaders took exception to pedophiles. Murderers with morals, who knew? One of them freed me, but the damage was already done. There's something about that spray of hot blood hitting you… feeling a weight hold you down when you know that you can't help yourself… I was already a goner at that point. I went into the system since there was no family to take me in, but after two foster homes returning me because of my screaming nightmares, I stayed in the group home. I was assigned a shrink, and it helped somewhat, but it wasn't until Holden came to stay that things started to get better for me."

Harlow's face is covered in horror, and a tear trickles down her cheek. She jumps up from where she is and crawls down the bed, her delectable ass just barely distracting me as she wraps her arms around Oliver's shoulders and hugs him tightly. He sobs quietly, but neither of us speak, just letting him be for now. I'm so freaking proud of him for telling her. It's not something he *ever* talks about. His shrink encouraged him to talk about it, but apart from me, Jacinta is the one person he opened up to about it. I don't know what she said and I'm not sure I ever will, but afterward, it was like he was so much lighter. Like by opening up about his demons, he'd managed to purge them. That sharing between the two of them was a huge moment for him in terms of feeling like the Summers were truly his family. He's never been as whipped by her as Declan and Jaxon, but there's definitely a soft spot that he's had for our sister ever since he let her share some of his burden.

He pushes away from her, wiping his eyes and looking determined as he keeps hold of her hand. "Anyway, Jacinta was the one person I talked to about it all, and because of her, I learned not to be ashamed of my sexuality and liking boys. She helped me start believing that not everyone was going to break my heart if I let them in. People could love me and have it be real. Them getting close to me didn't mean that they were just using me." His gaze turns to mine, and I shudder at the hurt in them. I guess it's almost my turn to tell my tale. "And that's why I didn't go against Jacinta and tell you." He runs a hand through his blue hair and shakes his head. "There are still a lot of things that are a hot fucking mess in my life… *I'm* a hot fucking mess, but I know with certainty that I won't hurt you like that again, and I'll do whatever it takes to make it up to you. I hope you can find it in your heart to forgive me."

I can tell by the look in her eyes that she already has. Harlow is now seeing the broken boys we were, the skeletons in our closets that created the foundations of who we are now. Sure, thanks to Dad and the advantages he gave us, we've been successful. But success can't cure all the pain and insecurities that others never see. It might give us the resources to mask those things, to make the world see only the facades we want it to, but it doesn't wipe away the darkness that fundamentally shaped how we view the world and people around us.

"Oliver, I'm sorry too. I see the seven of you having this amazing life with Dad and Nana and Poppy, and it's too easy to forget there was a reason you all ended up here. I can't say that I've made the same mistakes that you or any of the others have, but I've had my own moments of weaknesses where the ghosts of my past haunted my present. I want to have a place in this family, whatever form that takes, and I can't promise that I can forget about the hurt you caused. However, I know that I can grow and move past it, and I think I'd like to do that. With you... " She places a hand on his cheek, and something inside me clenches with the tiniest bit of jealousy, though it's not because I want to take either of their places. Instead, I want to be by their sides, my own body thrown into the mix instead of watching from the head of the bed with my arm slung across my chest.

"Let's give a fresh start a try?" She places a gentle kiss on his lips before pulling away and looking at me, a flush of guilt on her face. But I just smile, showing her that I'm not upset in the least.

"Well, I guess it's my turn for storytime." I pat the bed next to me, unable to resist the desire for their company. "Both of you come up here, and let's get comfortable. I want to snuggle… well, as much as I can while I tell you." Harlow crawls back up the bed followed by a much lighter Oliver, though he winces in a way that causes me no small amount of amusement. His painkillers will have worn off, and his new tattoo must be giving him some grief.

"Harlow, before you get comfortable, can you get Oli's aftercare cream out of the bathroom? It's on the sink." Oli's eyes widen with panic as she climbs off the bed and goes in search of it. By the time she comes back, that panic has darkened into a promise for revenge, though I can definitely say I'm not intimidated in the least.

"You got a new tattoo?" she asks, walking up to his side.

Before he can answer, I jump in. "Yeah, and he can't see it, so can you rub some of the cream in?" I ask, biting my lip to stop from laughing.

"Of course. Where is it?" When we got back from the hospital, Oli had gotten me set up and comfortable on my bed, then he'd taken a quick shower. When he came back out of my bathroom, he was wearing a tank and a loose pair of pajama pants, forgoing any boxers to lessen the pressure against his new tattoo.

Rolling his eyes, he turns over and gestures to his ass. Harlow's eyebrows jump in surprise, and her eyes widen before she looks at me, eyes narrowing. "Problem… Mistress?"

"Oh, don't you Mistress me, buddy. You are *very* quickly tallying up infractions. Punishment will be swift and severe when it comes." Holy fuck, my dick gets hard just thinking about all the ways she could punish me. I will sub for this woman any fucking day. Thank god the bed sheet is over my lap, but it's not saving much of my dignity since Oli's face wound up close to my lap when he rolled over. He's got an up close view of what I'm dealing with now, and though there's a snarky smirk on his face this time, there's also an echo of the heat that I'm feeling. I don't know if he'd join Harlow in giving me directions or if he'd be aching to sub for her too, but I'd love to take him in any way I can.

She pulls down his pants, exposing his tasty butt cheeks. I got to give it to DS; she does have good taste. I'd like to take a bite out of them myself. And from the look in Harlow's eyes when she glances up again, I don't doubt she's thinking the same thing. I can see her nipples pebble beneath her cami, and she swipes her tongue across her lip.

"Holy shit. Did you tattoo DS's bite mark? Dude, you're not supposed to tattoo over bruises." She sounds horrified, but there's a touch of awe mixed in there too, like she can't help but be impressed.

He turns his head to look at her. "I wanted a reminder of one of the stupidest things I did in my life to make sure I never do anything as idiotic again."

I don't know how, but he's apparently just said the magic words. Harlow practically melts into a puddle of goo, a blinding smile on her face, and I'm holding back an eye roll. I cannot believe that worked. He turns back to me and winks at my shock. *Ass.*

She gently rubs the cream into the tattoo, but I'm pretty sure she takes longer than needed and cops a feel of his tight backside at the same time. Not that Oli looks at all upset. When she pulls up his pants and gestures for him to move over, his pants are tenting as badly as mine did, but unlike me, he does nothing to hide it.

She sees it as he moves so she can climb in between us, but she simply responds with a roll of her eyes, trying to hide the smile that I know wants to break out across her face.

"Okay, time for serious stuff part two," I announce, and that stops their smiles instantly. "Oh, no, mine isn't as bad as Oli's," I try to reassure her. "It's more the stuff afterward that I'm ashamed about and wish I could take back." My gaze flits between the two of them, hoping that Oli understands what I'm trying to say.

I tuck Harlow into my side, my good arm wrapped around her, and Oli lays his head on her lap so that we're all touching. Something about this feels so comfortable, so right. Oli's always been home to me, and that feeling just expanded when we were found by our family. Now, sitting here with the two of them, I know there's space in that home for Harlow too. In fact, I'm starting to feel more complete than I ever have.

I hate to disrupt the warmth of this moment, but I know it needs to be done. It's now or never, and if I don't say it now, I know I'll be losing out on the chance to really create a connection between the three of us. Sighing, I start my story.

"I guess I need to start by telling you that I came from quite a religious upbringing, and when I found myself attracted to men as well as women, well, that didn't fly with the family. My parents were ashamed, and they kicked me out of our home. I spent some time on the streets, but CPS eventually caught up with me, so I ended up in the system as well.

By then I was fifteen and well and truly out of the closet. I knew I liked boys and girls, and I wasn't going to pretend otherwise to appease anyone. My first foster family was nice, and they even had a son about my age. Tyler and I would hang out at home all the time, but when we were at school, he pretended not to know me. I was okay with it; I had my own friends. But it soon became more than hanging out. It started with a quick kiss... Tyler surprised me when we were wrestling on his bed one day." Oliver's hand comes up to pat me on the leg, giving me support and much needed comfort. The same way that I know his past, he knows mine. We might have had this painful distance between us for the last few years, completely of my own making, but no one knows me like Oli.

"After that, it slowly grew. Kisses became caresses which became hand jobs which developed to blow jobs. Eventually, we lost our virginity to one another, but Tyler was so firmly in the closet that he threatened me. If I ever told anyone, he would make sure his mom and dad kicked me out. So I kept quiet. At school, I was open about my bisexuality, and I hung out with a very artsy crowd. The music and drama kids were so accepting of that sort of thing, so it was no big deal, but Tyler and his asshole jock friends were always slinging shade our way. No matter how many nasty words were thrown at me, I just kept my mouth shut. I wanted to believe that one day he'd wake up. I needed to believe, I think, that he would realize someday that we were meant to be with one another."

Oli's grip on my leg grows tighter as I come to the next part of the story, knowing what's coming. "One weekend, Tyler's parents were out and he had come into my room as soon as they left. Neither of us realized that they had forgotten something and returned. When they walked into my room, I was on my knees with Tyler's cock down my throat. His mother screamed, and his dad yelled, and Tyler pushed me to the ground and claimed I had forced him. How I could force him to let me blow him, I have no idea, but the parents believed him, of course. Within hours, CPS was picking me up.

They were smart enough to realize it was consensual and that Tyler was making shit up to hide the fact he was into boys from his parents, but by then the damage had been done. The loving, kind family I had been taken in by had turned on me in an instant, and I promised myself that I would never let that happen again. No matter how much it seems like someone could love you or care about you, they can turn on you if you crossed the right line. Or at least that's what I started to believe after what happened with my foster family."

When I finally look at Harlow, having avoided doing it during that part of the story, her eyes shimmer with sympathy. "Oh, Holden, I'm so sorry. But that doesn't explain this. How did you go from losing that faith in people to giving Oliver a chance?"

"Well, when Oli and I met in the home, we sort of gravitated to one another. Although I think it was an instant attraction on both our behalves, both of us were wary. Oli, because he was always high on ecstasy when he'd had sex, and it wasn't exactly consensual. Me, because Tyler had hurt me so badly. I really thought that he would at least admit to us being involved prior to getting caught together, but he didn't. He was willing to let his parents, two adults I had trusted and respected, think the worst of me. He wanted them to think I was a *rapist* rather than confront a completely normal truth about himself. At that point, I was just having a lot of trouble seeing myself as having any value..."

Oli sits up and takes over the story. "When I had first been picked up by CPS, I sort of went a little crazy after I was placed with the first family. They had a daughter, and I seduced just about every one of her friends in an attempt to prove that I wasn't into guys. That it was only the drugs that had fooled me into enjoying the experience, that had kept me from screaming to the world that I was being raped. Needless to say, things didn't end well with that family, so then I was sent to the group home and met Holden. Even though I wasn't sure about my sexuality, I realized I was attracted to him, and the fact that I felt that attraction while sober made me want to at least try it. So we kissed. I knew then and there that I liked guys and it wasn't just the X that had caused my reaction, so we dated. We did things that couples did, and it was amazing." His eyes are glassy as he remembers back to that time, bringing a heavy dose of guilt.

I clear my throat, ready to take up the story again because it really is my burden to share what happened next.

"Then Brad came along. We didn't hide that we were a couple, thinking there was no way that he would adopt one of us, let alone both, but when the news came that he would, I guess I had a little mental breakdown. My thoughts went back to my first family and how disgusted they were that I was caught with my foster brother, and I decided I wouldn't jeopardize the adoption for either of us, so I broke up with him. He begged and pleaded, but I basically ignored him. We both went a little crazy those first few years, living so close to one another and not being together, and we both acted out. Drugs, fights, sex. When I look back, I guess *that* probably did more to jeopardize our new family than anything, but Dad and Nana and Poppy never gave up. Oliver got into his drawing and me music, and things got better."

"But now?" Harlow pushes.

"Well, being shot has woken me up to how freaking stupid I've been, and now I don't want to let my life pass by thinking what if."

Chapter Fourteen

Harlow

My heart aches for these two who have been through just as much shit as I have, but I have another question which is incredibly selfish. I promised myself I'd ask all the hard ones, so even if I feel a little awkward about putting them on the spot after they've both bared parts of their souls, I need to follow through with this.

"So where does that leave us?" I wave between us all, not sure whether I really want to hear the answer. I'm happy that they're making their way back to one another, and I guess I shouldn't be greedy, but I can't help feeling disappointed.

"Well, hopefully, it leads to you sandwiched between the two of us," Oliver mumbles into my lap before turning his face to look at me, a cheeky grin covering it.

"Really?" I ask, looking between the two of them while trying to stifle the smile that threatens to break through. I don't want to broadcast how excited I am about the thought of this happening. Sure, I'm ready to start anew with Oliver, and Holden and I have this whole situation between us, but I don't know if I'm ready for them to see just how into this idea I am.

"Yes, Harlow, I think we both agree that if we couldn't have you as well, both of us would be devastated. I mean, we would be happy with one another, but you just seem to be the missing link. There's never really been a time where either of us were invested in getting to know someone new, and for us to both have that now *and* for it to be the same person, well, it just makes us feel like this is something we can't afford to lose. Like *you're* someone we can't afford to lose. We want a chance at this, the three of us."

"Okay." I slowly draw out the word, not sure what to say next, but I try to fumble through it anyway. "But what about if I'm with some of your other brothers too?"

Oliver sits up and crawls over my body until I'm squished, carefully, between the two. Their body heat radiates, warming my skin and curling my toes. My heart skips a beat, and my core throbs.

"As long as you give us equal time, we don't

care. In fact, Nana has been whispering in my ear about what a good idea it would be. As long as it's only our brothers, neither of us has a problem with it." Oliver's mouth is inches from mine now, and I can feel his breath on my lips.

"Nope, we think keeping you happy and well loved is the best thing, and if they can help out with that, then we're all for it." Holden's breath brushes along the shell of my ear, and my nipples ache with how hard they are. Just as I'm about to lunge for Oliver's mouth, he pushes away.

Moving into the bathroom, he comes back shaking out two pain pills and hands them to Holden followed by a glass of water. Holden throws them back and then returns the water to him.

"But for now, I think we need sleep. You're off to Hawaii with Kai and Jaxon tomorrow, and you need your rest, as does Holden. Now give him a kiss goodnight. He has to sleep on his own because of his shoulder."

As I turn to Holden, I don't miss the disappointed look on his face, and neither does Oliver. "Oh, don't worry, there will be plenty of time to make up for it, but if your arm heals wrong, there goes your music, not to mention it will make it difficult to do all the things you want to do to Harlow."

I giggle as he quickly loses the sad look and gently scoots down under the covers. When he's ready, he lifts his head, mouth puckered. I love seeing this cute side of him. Leaning in, I place a gentle kiss on his mouth that turns into more. Although he gave me an orgasm on the dance floor, I hadn't been able to taste his mouth. A groan escapes me as he deepens the kiss, his tongue tangling with mine, but hands on my hips pull me away all too soon.

"Now, now, remember what I said! Don't want to damage that arm," Oliver teases.

"It's not my arm that's aching," grumbles Holden, and I wink at him.

"Told you I would get my punishment." His eyes light up, and he bows his head. "Yes, Mistress." Oh, that's so much fun. Oliver must think so too if the groan behind me is anything to go by.

Climbing off the bed, I go to take my tray with me until Oliver waves me off. "Leave it, I'll deal with it in the morning when I get his breakfast."

"Are you going to bed?"

"I'm going to sleep in the arm chair in case Holden needs something in the middle of the night. My bedroom is down a floor, so I wouldn't be able to hear him."

"Oli, I have two legs, you know," Holden grumbles sleepily.

"Yeah, but I wouldn't want you to stumble or something on the way to the bathroom," Oliver scolds him.

"That can't be comfortable. Just come and sleep in my bed. It's right next door, and we can leave both doors open. I'm sure we'll hear him if he needs us."

Oliver frowns skeptically, but Holden perks up. "Go, Oli, she's right. I'll call out if I need you, but you're not going to get any sleep in that chair, as comfy as it is. Please."

Oliver relents, and I watch as he leans in and kisses Holden too. *Holy shit!* That was hot. The threesomes I've had in the past, the guys hadn't touched each other, so I had no idea what a turn on that would be. Now I just want to climb back into bed with them both. That Chris Isaak song is screaming in my head, a soundtrack to my thoughts. *Baby did a bad, bad thing.* I want to do really bad things with both of them. Like now.

A throat clearing has me jumping with guilt, and I feel my cheeks blush with embarrassment. They're both looking at me like they know what I was thinking. "Were you just humming Chris Isaak?" At least Holden sounds amused. Well, shit, I must have been humming out loud.

"Goodnight!" I shout, turning and running in the direction of my room. Their chuckles follow me, but I stop, my eyes scanning the door to see if anything looks wrong. Hands on my waist have me jumping as Oliver comes up next to me.

"Go on, open it. I very much doubt anyone has been able to get in; the house has been filled with people all evening. Not to mention they would have had to pass Holden's door to get to yours. He would have seen them."

I turn to him. "I know I didn't want to hear any details earlier, but was there anything on the surveillance cameras?"

"No, they were wiped remotely." Oliver huffs in frustration and annoyance. "Someone hacked into our security system and wiped them from the external system. Dad's got a security expert coming in while you're in Hawaii to do a full assessment of our security needs. No more messing around until this asshole is caught. You may even find yourself with a bodyguard."

I start to argue with him, but he puts a finger over my lip, hushing me. Just as I'm about to bite the damn finger off, he takes it away. "You can argue with Dad about it when it happens. Let's go to bed, shall we?" He grabs the handle and pushes it open as I brace myself, but my shoulders relax when the door reveals the tidy, empty room just how I had left it before dinner.

"Come on. It's been a long day, and you must be exhausted." Oliver pushes past me and pulls me into the room, leaving the door open behind us. He climbs into the bed while I hold an inner debate whether to leave my yoga pants on or not, but then I remember I'm not wearing any underwear. I climb in after him, not missing the heated look in Oliver's eyes, but he doesn't say anything. Reaching up to the switch above the bed, he flicks it off, plunging us into darkness. There's some space between us, sure, but I can still feel his body heat, so I toss and turn, trying to get comfortable. I'm not used to sleeping with someone in the bed; having Oliver next to me is making me restless.

Suddenly, a big hand grabs me around the waist, and I'm pulled toward him. He wraps his body around me, big spoon to my little, and grumbles, "Damn it, Harlow, how am I supposed to sleep with you wriggling like a worm?" He snuggles into the back of my neck, and in barely more than a minute, my whole body relaxes. *Whoa, I wasn't expecting that to work.* Before I can even track the passing of time, I feel myself drifting off to sleep, more comfortable than I've felt in years.

Waking up the next morning, Oliver's body heat is still against my back. Sometime while we were sleeping, his palm had crept under my cami and is now cupping one of my breasts. As my mind starts to focus on other things, I realize that Holden hadn't woken us in the middle of the night, or if he had, I hadn't heard him. My heart races in panic at the thought of him falling into a coma or something, and my body tenses. Oliver must feel it because he snuggles into my neck, his hand doing more than just cupping my breast now.

"Mmmm, best way to wake up ever," he mumbles sleepily while grinding his morning glory into my ass. Because of course he has one, just like his brother did yesterday morning. Slapping at his leg, I try to untangle myself.

"Damn it, Oli, Holden didn't call us. What if he's not okay?" He stops his groping but doesn't move.

"It's okay, baby girl. I got up and checked on him. Helped him to the toilet and gave him some more painkillers. You were so sound asleep I didn't want to wake you." My whole body relaxes at his words, and I breathe out a sigh of relief.

"Oh good, I was really worried." Rolling over, I put myself face to face with Oliver, pulling the sheet over my mouth to hide my morning breath. "Hi," I whisper through the sheet, not quite sure how to proceed with this gorgeous blue-haired man. Does he want to only be with me if Holden is too, or are we going to have something of our own as well?

He pulls the sheet away from my mouth. "None of that crap." He leans in and gives me a quick kiss on the lips, not a care in the world that the door is still open and anyone could walk in.

I guess I'm going to have to ask. I want as few mixed signals as possible, because if we're doing this for real, it's going to be complicated enough on its own. "Oliver, should we be doing that without Holden? I guess what I mean is, are we going to have individual things, or is it just going to be a me, you, and him thing, so when the other isn't around, we shouldn't touch each other?" With a smirk, he pulls me closer so my chest is now pressed against his. He lifts my leg to wrap around his hip so that his cock is now rubbing against my clit. I can't regret or be embarrassed by the groan that escapes my lips. I want him. God, I want him.

"Now what would be the fun in that?" This time he slants his mouth over mine and kisses the life out of me while rubbing against me. Dry humping one another, I'm panting and close to coming within minutes. His hand leaves the back of my head and creeps beneath my top again. Pinching my nipple, it's just the right thing to set me off. I pull away from his mouth, trying to muffle my moans against his chest so that anyone else who's around doesn't hear what's happening with the open door.

Oliver grunts, and I feel even more wetness on my yoga pants as it seeps through his pajama pants. We're both going to need a shower before we go anywhere.

As our breathing settles, he kisses me slowly once more. "Now, *that's* what I call a fantastic way to start the morning." He smiles at me, and I can't help but agree.

"I'll say." A voice in the doorway has us both looking up. Leaning against the frame, a very obvious tent in his pants, is Holden.

A frown crosses Oliver's face, which I'm sure

matches the one on mine, and he pulls away, sitting up.

"What are you doing out of bed? You could have fallen." Holden rolls his eyes and walks toward us, carefully climbing onto the bottom of the bed.

"Oliver, I was shot, not paralyzed. I'm fine. But I heard some interesting noises, and I wanted to investigate. If you want to give me a hand with something, you can help me with this." He points with his good hand to the tent in his pants.

Oh yes freaking please. Oliver looks at me to check if I'm okay with it, and I swear if I nod any harder, my head might pop off. They both laugh, but Oliver gets up to close the door.

"Why don't you lay down in my spot?" he suggests to Holden, who carefully does what he says. I lock my eyes on Oli as he climbs back onto the bed, prowling toward Holden with lust burning in his eyes. And when I look down, there's no hiding that he's hard again.

"Harlow, don't you think that Holden has been a naughty boy again?" *Oh, Jesus save me.* I think I'm going to self-combust. I wriggle where I am in the bed, my core tingling, ready for more.

"*Very* bad. He needs to be punished," I say sternly, playing along. Oliver slowly pulls down Holden's pajama pants, and his cock springs back, long and thick and mouth watering as Oliver throws his pants to the side. Glistening at the end is a piercing. *So Oli's not the only one who has one.*

Not wanting to be left out, I wiggle down so I'm level with Holden, and together we watch as Oliver runs his tongue up his length. Holden and I both groan our delight. "Fuck, Oli, don't tease me," Holden begs, but I think that's exactly what he needs.

"No, Oli, do tease him. Lick it up and down like it's your favorite lollipop," I order, and Holden groans again. Oliver does what I ask, and I move a little further down to run my tongue over Holden's nipple, taking the bar I saw last night and giving it a tug with my teeth before laving my tongue over it again and again. Soon enough, Holden is squirming on the bed, his cock glistening in the light, and he reaches out his good hand to me.

"Please, Mistress," he begs. "It hurts so good." Not wanting Holden to do any damage, I nod for Oliver to go ahead. He uses his tongue once more around the head of Holden's dick then takes it deep into his throat, cheeks hollowing as he sucks. A shout leaves Holden's mouth, and I'm squirming just as much as he is, finding myself unable to look away from Oli's bobbing head. *Holy fuck, that's sexy as hell.* I want to join him and see if he tastes as good as it looks. Oli must see the want in my eyes because he pulls off and leans back.

"You want a taste?" The sound escaping from Holden and the twitch of his cock make his opinion of that option quite clear.

"I won't last if she does," he warns, not looking

at either of us. I crawl down the bed, still a little unsure, but Oliver grabs me and kisses me senseless, erasing all my fears.

"Taste him, Harlow. Lash him with your tongue and punish him for his transgression." I'm almost a little giddy at the thought of Oli joining in on this little dynamic Holden and I have going on, and all worries disappear in the anticipation of the pleasure I'm going to give our partner.

"Please, Mistress," Holden begs as I lean over and run my tongue along his hard length. Oliver gets down next to me and we kiss again, but this time Holden's cock is caught in the middle. The power I'm feeling right now, knowing that Holden is at our combined mercy, is a heavy kind of rush.

"Holy fuck!" he shouts, his hips thrusting up. I keep licking as Oliver takes the tip into his mouth, hollowing his cheeks. It's messy and chaotic, but god, it's revving my engines higher than they've ever been before. If it's this good when we're teaming up on Holden, I can't wait until we do more. My mouth leaves his dick, and I use one hand to caress his balls while my other creeps into my yoga pants. My core is throbbing so much it's getting uncomfortable. Sliding my fingers through my folds, I gather some wetness and then slide my two fingers across my clit.

Oliver's mouth leaves Holden's dick for a moment, and his fingers follow the trail mine just made until he too is running his fingers through the mess in my pants. Pulling them back out, Oli's hand goes underneath where I'm playing with Holden's balls, and I smile, knowing what he's doing. Sure enough, Holden is shouting and thrusting hard within seconds. Oliver takes it like a champion and swallows down everything he has to offer. While Holden's still lost in his release, I'm coming too, my core clenching around nothing. Though I needed the release, the empty orgasms are never quite as satisfying as one with penetration. I hear both guys groan again and look up to see that their eyes are on my hand in my pants.

"Fuck, that was hot. I need a cigarette," Holden mutters as Oli grabs Holden's pants off the floor and helps him back into them.

When he's done, Oli flops down on the bed next to me, kissing me deeply once more, and I can taste Holden on his tongue. Pulling back, he looks me in the eye. "Everything okay?"

I think it's sweet he's checking that I'm alright after that, and his care for me makes me feel even more comfortable about admitting what I'm thinking. "Oli, I've got to say that's the hottest thing I've ever fucking seen. I can't wait to play with both of you some more when Holden's shoulder heals."

"Stupid fucking stalker. I swear, when I get my hands on him..." Holden mutters, disgust tainting the satisfaction that was painted on his face a moment ago. "Cutting into time with my man and my woman."

A rush of warmth runs through me at his words, and I can tell by the pleased look on Oliver's face that he feels the same way too.

"I don't know about you guys, but I need a shower," Oliver says. "Holden, if you give me twenty minutes, I'll give you a sponge bath."

"Is that code for something that I don't want to miss out on?" I joke, possibly a little too eagerly. They both laugh as I sit up and raise an expectant eyebrow, needing an answer to the question.

"No, he's not allowed to get it wet so showers are out for now," Oliver explains.

"Alright, I'll leave you to it then. Holden, just stay here instead of going back to your bed. Oliver, you go use his shower while I have mine."

"But we would save water if we shower together," he teases, but as tempted as I am, I don't want to rush this.

"Tempting for sure, but I need to get ready to go. Kai will come looking for me soon." Thankfully, Oli doesn't look too disappointed, so I kiss them both and hurry through a shower. I don't regret anything that just happened between the three of us, but that doesn't mean I'm ready for Kai to walk into the middle of it. *Yet.*

Chapter Fifteen

Harlow

Once I'm showered and wrapped in a towel, I realize I haven't actually got anything to put on, so I wander out to my room. Oliver and Holden are still snuggled up on the bed together, the sight filling me with those fluttery little butterflies that I totally have to ignore for now.

Neither of them have noticed me yet, so I take a moment to just watch them, and it's so stinking cute seeing them like this. On their own, each of them is a different kind of irresistible, but seeing them together, even in a snuggly intertwined knot, well, that's deadly. They're tentative, a bit shy and still not entirely sure with one another despite the earlier sexy times. I guess having me there might have made things easier. Now they need to work out themselves without me involved. Hopefully they'll have it sorted out by the time I'm back from Hawaii; they deserve to be happy now that they're sort of finding each other again.

Holden leans in to kiss Oliver, and a groan leaves my mouth at the sight. *Fucking sexy.* But it also stops them since they turn to look at me. My groan of desire turns into a huff of disappointment, but they only snicker at me. *Assholes.*

Moving over, I sit at the end of the bed, out of reach of both of them, so I won't be tempted to touch.

"Hey, Oli, was there anything in my wardrobe that was salvageable? Something that I could at least wear on the plane today?"

They exchange a worried look, and I sigh. "Just tell me. I'm not fragile, you know. I *can* cope with whatever it is you're not telling me."

"Harlow, we know one thing for sure now. The stalker is male."

I can feel my face wrinkle in confusion. "How?"

"He marked his territory," Oliver says quietly.

"What? He *pissed* on my clothes? But how do you know that the stalker's male then? Granted, that would be harder for a female."

They exchange another glance, and Holden grimaces while Oliver runs a hand through his blue hair. "No, Harlow, he masturbated all over your underwear and then shredded everything else."

I freeze in horror, unable to comprehend what

Oliver just said to me. Gaping at them both, a tear trickles down my face at the violation.

They both look horrified at the sight of my tears, and at least that makes me snort a little in amusement. How one tear can terrify two men, one who has just been shot, I don't know, but they both look terrified.

Before I can say anything, Holden elbows Oli with his good arm. "Go and hug her, you idiot. I can't. Man, we're the worst boyfriends ever." Startled, Oliver throws himself at me, jostling all of us and causing Holden to wince in pain. That's enough to kick me out of my pity party.

"Be careful!" I smack the idiot as he wraps his arms around me, but I give in and snuggle into the safety of his chest, breathing a sigh of relief.

Holden smiles once he sees me relax. "And this might be a good thing. He obviously wasn't thinking clearly when he did that because now they have a DNA sample to compare." Hope flares that this might be coming to an end soon, but Oliver kills it.

"Unless he's not in the system." And I stiffen again, starting to get a bit scared at what he might resort to next. If he's marking my clothes as his territory, what else does he think is his? What would he do if he managed to get me alone?

"Fuck, you're an idiot," Holden mutters. "Even if he's not, when they find a suspect, it'll be easy enough to cross them off or to confirm they're the guilty party now."

Oliver places a kiss on top of my head and moves away before helping me to my feet. I'm left clutching at my towel to keep it wrapped around my body. Luckily, it's one of those big sheet towels so I don't have to worry about flashing too much.

They both chuckle as they watch me wrestle with it, neither of the *gentlemen* offering a hand. Though I guess Holden only having one is a good enough excuse. "Come on, let's go down and see if Jacinta has got anything else you can borrow. I'll grab you some breakfast too, Holden."

A look of disgust crosses Holden's face, and he carefully climbs out of bed. "Fuck no! I'm not spending another day in bed." Oliver starts to argue, but Holden holds up a hand. "I am coming down to eat and spend the morning with whoever is around, even if it's just Mrs. Heyton, and then when I get tired, I will come back upstairs to rest. I'm sure you're not going to let me out of your sight, so I will be completely fine. I refuse to stay in that bed one more day, Oli, and I need to call Hope too. I've got two meetings this weekend that I need to reschedule for next week, not to mention that band from the other night is coming in to sign their contracts, but I'll push them all back. Know this, I *will* be going in next week even if you don't like it."

Oliver blanches at that, his nose crinkling and that hand running through his slightly faded locks again. "I've got interviews all week with artists at the shop. I can't come with you."

I can see by the stubborn set to Holden's face and the worried one on Oliver's that this is about to lead to an argument. So, walking over to Holden, I tuck his good arm under mine and start leading him downstairs, Oliver following behind like an obedient puppy. "Look, if you make them for Wednesday or later, then I should be back from Hawaii, and I'll go with you. You're not going to be able to drive or write or anything, so you'll need some help for a few days."

"My secretary can help with that," he whines, and it's my turn to cut him off.

"Yeah, no, I didn't like the way she looked at me. It was all kinds of territorial, and if we're going to do this," I say firmly, gesturing to the three of us, "'bitches are going to have to learn you're off limits. If that means I need to stake my claim on you or any of the others, even in a public space, that's what I'm going to do."

Well, fuck. Yep, just declared that out loud. Shit, we haven't really established any rules, and I'm already going cavewoman here. Are we out in the open about this? Maybe we'll need to hide it so that the media doesn't get wind of it? Do I want to be considered their dirty little secret? So many thoughts run through my mind as I start to panic, my breathing increasing and the boys exchanging another worried glance. Poor bastards are really getting the brunt of all my emotions this morning.

Let's just toss them right into the deep end of boyfriend duty.

"Harlow, what's wrong?" Holden asks, squeezing my arm where we're connected.

"Is this something we're going to hide? I mean, I know I haven't talked to Kai, and I'm not even sure if Declan is fully on board or aware either? But are we going to hide the fact that I'm in a relationship with one of you, let alone most of you? Is this going to be a huge scandal and bad for Neighpalm Industries? What's Dad going to think?"

Shit, I hadn't even considered Dad in this. I am a terrible daughter. I know Nana and Poppy will be fine with it. In fact, I bet Nana will get all smug and shit and say it was her idea all along. But what about Dad? How is he going to feel about his daughter dating most of his sons? Surely, the media will make it into something dirty. Is that going to damage the company? I'm shaking by the time all these thoughts run the gauntlet of my mind, and Holden keeps me close even though I try to pull away. Instead of giving me space, he pushes me up against the hallway wall and crowds in, Oliver next to him, until all I'm breathing in is sexy intoxicating maleness. My brain misfires with the feel of their bodies against mine, and all I can do is blink up at them above me.

"Shhhh, calm down," Oliver soothes, stroking my hair as Holden takes one of my hands with his good one, putting it to his lips and placing a gentle kiss in the middle of it.

"No, we haven't worked out all the details, and yes, we will have a conversation with Dad before we go public with it so he's not blindsided, but he's not stupid. He knows Kai invited you to go to Hawaii with him, and I'm pretty sure he's aware it's not a brother/sister bonding trip. And no, we are definitely *not* going to hide this, Harlow." Holden's voice is gentle but firm, like he's reassuring a scared animal, and… I guess that's what I kind of am.

"No way are we going to hide it. I want everyone to know that you're my woman, making sure the men know that you're off the market," Oliver grunts, all caveman-like, and I just scoff. *Yeah, because I had so many offers previously. But at least I'm not the only one feeling a little possessive.*

"For now, enjoy your trip. Talk to Kai and see if he's on the same page as us. We'll talk to Dad, and we will let you know what he said when you get home. Go and enjoy yourself drama free, and hopefully by the time you return, they will have caught the guy responsible for all your stress."

Both kiss me, turning me into a puddle of goo again before they pull away, Holden tucking me under his good arm before we make our way downstairs. I'm still in a little bit of a daze when we stop at a door on the second floor, Oli knocking on it since Holden refuses to let me go.

"Come in," a muffled voice calls through the

door, and Oliver pushes it open. The fragrance that hits my nose as the door opens is pure Jacinta. I remember Hope telling me it's her own signature perfume that some designer had made her. Her eyes widen slightly as the three of us step into her room, and I can certainly imagine why. Both boys are still in only pajama pants, and then here's me wrapped in a towel. Oh well, she's going to have to get used to it if we're going to do this relationship thing. Maybe they need to have a talk with her too after they've talked to Dad. Make sure that I'm not on the receiving end of her vengeance again.

Before any of us can say something, she registers the towel wrapped around me. "Oh, Harlow, you haven't got anything to wear. I'm sorry." She somehow extricates me from Holden's arm and drags me in the direction of what must be her closet. My mouth drops open when the automatic light comes on as we enter, this space even more strongly filled with her signature scent.

Holy shit! In front of me is a wardrobe to rival the one at Neighpalm Couture. My wide eyes track Jacinta's movement to pick up a remote, and with the click of a button, the racks start to whirl. I'm too scared to blink as clothes rush past, afraid I might miss something.

"I forgot all about it last night, so I meant to bring you something to wear this morning. Dad had Cecelia go and buy you some clothes to replace what you lost. She was going to use the helicopter to bring them out here last night and then stay over, but I put a stop to that." We exchange a conspiratorial glance. At least we're on the same page concerning Cecelia. There's just something about her that rubs me the wrong way.

"I told them you could just borrow mine until it was time for your flight. She can meet you at the airport to give them to you. Anyway, take your pick..." She waves at the mountain of clothes in front of us, but I'm still frozen in a bit of shock, albeit for a different reason now. Who is this person? I mean, I know we called somewhat of a truce last night, but wow.

"If I know Kai, he'll be on the go all the time. Grab a pair of shorts and a cami again. I haven't got a bra that will fit you because your boobs are bigger than mine, but there are a few with built-in shelf bras that'll be tight enough to hold you in." She opens a nearby drawer and pulls out a brand new five-pack of panties. "Here. I'm not sure if Dad will have remembered to ask her to get you some, and she's just spiteful enough to 'forget,' so take these in case."

With another click of the remote, this time aimed at a blank wall, it starts rotating. Racks of shoes are lined up according to what looks like style. She goes over and pulls out a pair of flip flops. "Not sure what shoe size you need, but this should keep you going until you stop somewhere to buy a pair." She holds out a black pair with a couple of crystals in the straps. As I go to grab them, she snatches up my hand with her free one. Not expecting the contact, I look up, and when I meet her eyes, the lightness from before has gone, replaced with something I recognize all too well—guilt.

"I just wanted to say to you again that I was wrong, and for what it's worth, I am so sorry. If I could wind back time and stop it, I would, and it's not because I've been well and truly spanked by Nana and Dad. It's because you saved the one being who has loved me unconditionally. Why would you do that if you were some self-serving bitch? Holding back or "accidentally" messing up would've been the perfect way for you to repay me for the billboard and for humiliating you." She lets go and turns around, but not before I see a tear drip down her face. "I know I started to tell you some of this earlier, but I have to get it all out. Don't get me wrong, I know my family loves me, and I am so very thankful for that, but Prada, well, she doesn't know or care that I'm a fuck-up. She doesn't judge or look disappointed or anything, and she listens. I tell her everything, things I don't want to talk to my brothers about, and she relies on me. Well, and Josh, but as long as I'm here, I feed her and brush and care for her. She needs me as much as I need her, and to be honest, I don't think my family is the same. None of them need me. I'm just the one they need to take care of, and I hate being a burden. Maybe…

you and I can figure out some ways that we could possibly need each other? I've never had a sister before."

And there it is. It's like looking in a mirror. Both of us given up without a fight by mothers who didn't give enough of a shit to even stick around long enough to teach us how to be loved. To teach us that we are worthy of love and that there are going to be people in our lives that we can rely on and trust to do just that.

When she turns back to face me, tears are streaming down her face, and I let go of that last lingering bit of doubt and resentment. Something settles inside me as I decide that Prada is not going to be the only one that needs Jacinta. I'm going to make sure that she knows I need her too. *Fuck it. I guess I'm going all in here.*

I step forward and put my arms out, needing her to make the final step so I know this is really what she wants. And with a hitched breath, she does. Before I know it, we're both sobbing in each other's arms.

"Hey, what are you girls doing in here?" Oliver calls out, his voice coming closer. Poor bastard doesn't know what he's about to step into. "We need to—Oh fuck. Is everything okay here?" he asks very carefully, making me snort. My snort sets off Jacinta, and the tears turn into uncontrollable giggles.We're lost in this strange mix of gasping giggles that nearly knock us off our feet, and we need to hold each other up, each of us clutching at my towel to keep it in place. Thank god it's so big.

"What the fuck?" Oliver swears in confusion.

When I get myself under control, I can finally spare a moment to check in on him. He's frozen in place, wearing the most adorable scrunched up expression that has me bursting into laughter again. Eventually, we get ourselves under control.

"It's okay, Oliver. Why don't you help Holden down to breakfast? Jacinta and I'll be there in a minute."

Still wearing that tentative male look that says he thinks we've lost our minds, he disappears.Once the bedroom door closes, I drop my towel and pull my clothes on. Jacinta's eyebrows raise in surprise, but she smirks once she's recovered.

"Not shy, are you?"

"Nope, I'm really not, but I also figure we're going to be sisters. Isn't that the kind of shit sisters do? I've only had Max for practice, but I feel like you're going to be a whole different story."

"Who the fuck knows? I've only had pain in the ass brothers. I guess we'll have to learn together."

And as far as learning together, I guess a good place to start is with transparency. I feel like if we're going to go forward and grow and develop a rela-tionship, I need to clue her in on my feelings for her brothers. I don't want to get her back up if she finds out from someone else or walks in on something. I don't think the family would survive that kind of implosion.

"Speaking of your pain in the ass brothers... in honor of our new sisterly relationship." I stop and grab a hair brush off of a cabinet in the middle of the room and start to pull it through the tangles of my hair. "Just so we have full disclosure, I think I'm going to try some kind of relationship with them."

Her mouth drops open at my candor. "Oh yeah, which one?" she asks, playing along with an impressively calm demeanor.

"Probably at least four of them, possibly five, and to be honest, I'm not a hundred percent sure on the sixth."

"Thomas the hold out?" she asks, crossing her arms, and this time it's my turn for my eyebrows to jump in surprise. Not the reaction I was expecting, but okay.

"Yeah, actually," I admit, returning the brush and stealing a band to pull my hair up into my favorite messy bun.

"Yeah, he's pretty messed up from the ex, but I have faith in you."

"So you don't care? I'm going to be a straight shooter with you here. I'm being sincere when I say that I think you and I can become sisters to each other. You put me through hell, I'm not going to sugarcoat that to spare you any guilty feelings, but I've been learning a lot about this family and what brought you all together, and I think that I can rise above our past. In order to do that, I need to know, sincerely and without anything held back, do you have any lingering issues with me being a part of this family in whatever way it all pans out?" I lean against the cabinet and finally hold her eyes. I'd been avoiding it, but I can't if I want to be genuine. This moment between us *needs* to be real if Jacinta and I are going to have a future, if I'm going to risk giving her a piece of my heart and letting her in to really become a sister to me.

"If you are serious and don't play one against the other and they are all aware of the situation, then who am I to stop you? God knows they've made horrendous choices in the past, but maybe, just maybe, this time they may be making the right one. I appreciate you checking in with me first, but I don't control my brothers." Hmm, I beg to differ on that one, but hey, I don't want to argue, so I let it go.

"If they want this like I'm starting to think they do, nothing I could have said or done would have stopped them, but I promise I'll play nice if any of them talk to me about it. The holdouts are probably worried I'll freak out and plan another billboard if they get too close to you." Grabbing my hand, she drags me out of the wardrobe. "Come on, let's get breakfast. You've got a long weekend ahead, and I'm sure Kai's freaking out and thinking you've decided to cancel on him. He's surprisingly vulnerable, that one." She stops with a cheeky grin on her face. "But make sure you make Jaxon work for it, as a favor for me. Stupid boy always has women throwing themselves at his feet, and I'd like to see him grovel, even just a little bit."

With a laugh, she pulls open the door and drags me downstairs, but a cracked door and Declan's deep voice have me stopping. "You go ahead. I just want to check on the kitten before I leave," I tell her, and she smiles before disappearing down the stairs and leaving me behind. Now it's my turn to get a little payback. A smile on my face, I barge into his bedroom.

Chapter Sixteen

Harlow

Slamming the door open without a second thought, I'm not prepared for the sight that reaches my eyes. *Holy fuck*. Declan is on his bed, clad in only his boxers briefs, with a little chocolate point kitten on his nicely defined chest, syringing food into its mouth, all the while cooing to it. Fuck me, I think my ovaries spontaneously combusted. I mean, I know it's an animal, but hey, I'm a vet. Not to mention the seriously important question of how he stays so tan when he works in an office building all the time. I can't wait to unravel the mystery that is the Summers brothers, but I need to tread carefully with this one. Still not really sure where he stands.

He hasn't even flinched though I know he's seen me. Finally lifting his head, he casually raises one eyebrow at me. "Yes?" His voice is low and gravelly so as not to scare the kitten. Taking it all in, I feel a little sheepish now.

"Ah, yeah, I was trying to get a little payback," I explain as I move across to the bed.

"Harlow, if you want to see me naked, you only have to ask." He smirks at me. "Preferably on your knees."

"Keep dreaming, asshole," I scoff, but the idea of how that could go is in my head now, ready to cause all kinds of problems for my panties. Thankfully, I manage to school my face and change the subject to what I'm really here for instead. "Is this little one doing better now?" I ask, reaching over and taking the kitten from Declan's chest, and yes, my fingers might have brushed against his skin by accident.

I examine the kitten all over, and its tiny plaintive squeaks are loud and enthusiastic, as is his squirming. His skin has the full spring back you would expect from a well-hydrated kitten. "Have you seen him on Princess yet?" I ask, looking around the room for the enclosure. He climbs off the bed, syringe in hand, and gestures to his closet. Walking into it, I'm hit in the face with that exotic scent that is all Declan. I have no clue what it is, but it makes my nipples pucker under my cami. It really is mouthwatering, and I have no idea how our brief time alone together has me as thoroughly trained as Pavlov's dog.

On the floor in a quiet corner is the cat enclosure. Looking in, I can see Princess with her other three kittens where she looks up at me with a meow. Unzipping the mesh lid, I place the other kitten back with its siblings and watch as it nuzzles instinctively, finding what it needs, and starts feeding. "I think you can be happy now that this one is back to normal," I tell Declan, standing back up. "You can do away with the feeds now, and it should survive on what Princess can provide. Also, leave the enclosure open. The kittens won't go anywhere, but Princess might need to stretch her legs or just get away for a little bit. She'll return."

I feel a heat at my back, so I spin and find Declan inches from me. "Good morning, Harlow. Sleep well?" His words are so suggestive that I start to blush, and his eyebrows raise in surprise. "Oh, what does *that* blush mean?" He leans in and whispers in my ear, the stubble on his chin brushing across my cheek, "Could it be that one of my brothers made sure you had a good night?" I push at him, my blush deepening, to get him out of my space.

His chest is a solid wall of muscle, but he easily moves out of my way with a laugh, and I push past him, not wanting to be trapped in a confined space while we still have issues between us. I'm not sure I wouldn't jump his bones if we'd stayed there any longer.

Once I get back out into the wide space of his

bedroom and can breathe easier, I whirl around to face him, hands on my hips. Time to ask the hard questions again. "Would that be a problem?"

He raises his eyebrows as I step toward him slowly. "Would it bother you if I spent the night with one of your other brothers worshipping my body?" I push as I run my hands over my curves, his eyes locked to their path. He can't hide his reaction, and I see his cock harden under the thin fabric of his briefs, watching his chest quickly rise and fall as his heart rate increases.

"No, surprisingly it doesn't. Anyone else, I'd be jealous as fuck, but strangely enough, it makes me happy thinking about you and my brothers. As long as you're willing to throw a little sugar my way as well."

His hands slide to my hips and he pulls me even closer, his eyes twinkling playfully. I like this side of Declan; it's such a contrast to what I've seen previously.

"So..." I reply, my voice low, getting on my tiptoes so we're even closer now. "Did you have that little chat with Jacinta?" I ask, not letting him in on the fact that I've already spoken to her about my feelings. Nope, he needs to make his feelings clear as well.

"Not yet," he says as he leans in to claim my lips, but I quickly dodge them and duck out of his hold, hurrying for the door before I do anything stupid like climb him like a tree.

"Well, let me know when you get that done. I know how badly you wanted to do that before we started something," I taunt, a small smile on my lips as he groans in frustration and runs a hand through his silky strands.

"What the fuck was I thinking?" he mutters, but it's loud enough to hear, spreading a huge grin across my face. This is so much fun and a kind of payback all on its own.

As I run downstairs, I'm happy that my knee doesn't seem to be giving me any more pain. I'm looking forward to the weekend, and I can't wait to see what Kai has planned. *And Jaxon,* that thirsty little voice in my head whispers despite me being unsure whether he's earned his own time with me yet.

Jaxon

I was nervous as fuck all night. thinking about our upcoming trip to Hawaii with Harlow, so I eventually gave up on trying to sleep. Instead, I swam laps in the pool. The early morning air was fresh, and it had the smell that it got when the seasons were starting to change. Late summer was leading into autumn, and although there isn't a huge change in California, you can still tell that it's coming. The water was cool and refreshing on my restless body, and I don't know how long I lapped back and forth, but by the time I was done, the sun was poking its way over the horizon, lighting the sky a pale blue in what looked like another cloudless sunny day.

Breathing hard, I lean against the tiled wall, pushing my dripping hair back off my face

and trying to get some of my breath back. And while the swim has succeeded in wearing my body out, my mind hasn't stopped racing. My thoughts are stuck on every moment I've spent with Harlow and how things have changed since she appeared, beginning with that night I first met her at the club.

I was an idiot to let Jacinta get into my head when Dad had announced to us all that a biological daughter had come forward. Of course all seven of us were skeptical since we've all had our fair share of people trying to form relationships with us because of our money and success. Some of us have been burnt more than others; Thomas is about as closed off as anyone could be when it comes to women. But Jacinta was the worst of us. When mom betrayed her again the second time, she broke something in my sister, something that I'm not entirely sure can be fixed.

But Mom didn't just break something in Jacinta, she damaged something inside of me. I have a nearly terminal weakness for damsels in distress—a hero complex some might suggest—and time and time again, I have fallen for a sob story. Fallen for women who "needed" my help, usually with money, only to be used and cast aside, or more often they were chased away by my sister. I always figured if she was able to chase them away, they weren't with me for the right reasons. Just once, it would be nice to be wanted for me. I think that's why I was so angry about Harlow. When we had met at the club, she seemed to be strong and independent, not the kind of woman who'd turn around and only ask about what I could do for her. It was like a breath of fresh air, a real chance that maybe I could have something for myself.

And then I fucked it all up, was a giant ass, and Jacinta did her usual. Well, actually, she might have done her worst; most of the girls never got quite as much of a public shaming as Harlow did. But lo and behold, she didn't run away. Sure, she tucked tail for a little bit to get some of her fight back, but she's still fucking here, and if that isn't proof enough that she's truly here for Dad and not some-one's bank account, then I don't know what is. Why else would she be willing to suffer the way Jacinta and the rest of us treated her? She could get money from the Bostons and put up with far less bullshit.

Of course, I realize all of this *after* I've dealt myself a serious disadvantage. Story of my fucking life.

So I made a decision as soon as I invited myself along on Kai's trip to Hawaii that I was going to sit down with Jacinta and have a chat with her. I love her, but I won't let her get in the way of me, or any of us now, pursuing a relationship of some kind with Harlow. Although it seems my sister has done a bit of soul searching herself, and probably a call to her shrink has helped, but she seems to be softening her stance. Especially after Harlow helped save Prada yesterday. And what the fuck is with that? Harlow's a vet? I'm sure we talked about careers that first night, but when I think back I asked about her calluses on her hands, and she told me about horse training. I guess I just made the assumption there.

Between that situation and the way she dealt with Raquel the other day, Harlow has more than proved that she'll never be anyone's damsel. Even the martyr-driven attempt to leave us behind at the hospital showed her for what she truly is, a white knight. A slightly misguided white knight with defi-nitely questionable survival skills, but a white knight nonetheless. I don't get the feeling that she needs me at all, but for the first time, *I* might need some-one, and I think she could be the person who saves me from my worst enemy of all: myself.

A bang on a window startles me into looking up. It must be later than I thought because my sister is standing at the glass doors to the patio with a coffee mug in hand, waving at me.

She pushes one of them open, a big smile across her face. I haven't seen her look that happy in a long time. What she's up to? "Hey, come and have some breakfast. I made you a cup of coffee," she calls, and I give her the thumbs up.

Exiting the pool via the steps, I try to think of a way to make up for all my bad behavior with Harlow. I've already arranged to have a gift basket of sex toys waiting in her room at the new hotel as an apology for my ungrateful overreaction in my office. I didn't want to presume anything, so I reserved three separate rooms, but they all have interconnecting doors, just in case.

Grabbing a towel from the nearby storage seat, I rub at my hair to stop the dripping water before drying my body and wrapping it around my waist. The pace of my steps starts to pick up as I head inside, eager for that coffee and some food after all that exercise.

Jacinta is already at the breakfast table, talking softly with Mrs. Heyton as she lays out a basket of toast and big platters of meats, cheeses, and spreads. Looks like we're having German-style breakfast today. Yum.

Leaning down and giving my sister a kiss on the head, I take the seat next to her. Her fingers are flying across the screen of her phone as she fires off a message. "What are you doing?" I ask, curious because the frown on her face is practically stormy.

"Bloody Lindy has sent me an update from the office. She says she misses me and hopes I'm enjoying my time off and the creative juices are flowing, but not to worry if they're not because the new designer is amazing. All capitals AMAZING. And I wanted to know why she had already started since they were supposed to be starting next week."

"Who's that, dear?" Nana asks as she walks into the living area. Jacinta turns her attention to Nana, not wiping the frown off her face.

"The new designer. Rochelle or something. Why has she started already? And when are you going to stop punishing me? I know I did wrong. I'm working on it. I even apologized to Harlow, and I think we're going to be okay." By the end, her voice has dropped, sounding more like that small insecure child she used to be. Fuck, that tugs at my heartstrings, and I know this is no act. Putting my arm around her, I give her a quick sideways hug and another kiss on the head as Nana examines her before her eyes soften.

Sitting down across from us, she sighs. "Jacinta, it was never really about punishing you. We just needed you to see your behavior for what it was: destructive. One day you would have done that to the wrong person, and it could very well end with you losing the business completely because we would be sued for all it's worth. Not to mention it was never your place to decide about Harlow. Poppy and I have known this woman since she was a little girl; our trust in her should have been enough of an assurance for all of you. You should have trusted our judgment and known that we would never bring anyone into the family that we didn't fully believe in."

Jacinta nods, and I can see her bottom lip waver with a mix of disappointment and frustration. Her estrangement with Dad has hurt her the most, but she's always had her own special connection with our grandparents too. She wants to be cherished by Dad, but she wants to make Nana proud, and it's become very clear that Nana's pride in her has taken a hit. "But saying that, I think you've learned your lesson, and now that you realize what a good and kind and wonderful person Harlow is, she'll get to see the same thing about you. You will see that you have so much more in common than you have ever realized. And I think you will find she will be a wonderful addition to this family and sister to you. In whatever capacity that may be." Nana's comment has me remembering what I wanted to say to my sister, but before I can, she keeps going. "I think you can start back at the company next week. Jace will be back and ready to start then, so you can work out how the three of you are going to work together. It will bring a new dynamic to our design lines, and I'm excited to see what happens. This is the beginning of something great, Jacinta, not the end of your leadership in the company. Hopefully this time, you'll trust me."

Despite being pleased about returning to the company, she's no doubt put out by the idea of the new designers. It doesn't look like she has much of a choice at the moment, so I guess she'll learn to deal with it. At least she'll have another outlet for her grumpiness besides Harlow.

"Actually, I need to say something as well before we get surrounded with people." I turn in my chair so that I'm facing her. She looks a little startled but recovers quickly while Nana leans in, an interested glint in her eyes. "You know I love you, don't you? And how I always will?" She smiles and nods.

"Of course, doofus, I love you too."

"Well, I wanted to let you know that I'm interested in Harlow, and I want to see where a relationship between us might go."

With a roll of her eyes, she pats me on the knee. "Yeah, okay, because *that* wasn't obvious." She turns back to her coffee and leaves me gaping at her.

"*And?*"

"Dude, go for it, she's hot. If I was into girls, I'd be wanting a piece of that too." And just like that, Jacinta blows all my worries out of the water. Nana snorts on the other side of the table as I open and close my mouth like the idiot I apparently am.

"But... but, you don't like her."

"Oh, Jaxon, that was *so* last week," Jacinta says, adopting a valley girl tone. "Keep up, please."

"But..." She sighs loudly at my stammering, and I'm rewarded with another eye roll. *What the fuck?*

"Look, I know what I did was wrong, but seriously, after last night there's no way I can continue being a bitch. So from now on, I will do my best to make it up to her, and what better way than gifting her all my brothers?"

Nana is just about rolling off her chair with laughter as Jacinta reaches over and closes my gaping mouth. "Heads up though, bro, those other boys have gotten a head start. You've got some catching up to do. Time to put on your big boy pants if you want to get back in the running."

"What do you mean, they've got a head start?" Her words have brought me out of my shocked state, and I feel my eyes narrow as her comment really sinks in.

"Well, Kai was never an asshole, so he's totally been in the top spot since day one. Clever boy. Plus, he's Kai, so he's got that big smile and upbeat thing down pat. The rest of you are kind of broody, to be honest. Now, Holden was shot, and that rockets him straight into second spot, and Oliver was pretty cozy with the both of them this morning, so I'm pretty sure he and Holden are working out their issues, and they've got you beaten there because some man on man action is hot."

Looking toward Nana, I'm stunned to see her nodding her head. "Oh, I'm so glad they could sort things out. I was hoping this was the wake-up call they needed." She has a slight glimmer of tears in her eyes, but that's just typical Nana. The woman could always be a shark in the boardroom, but she's got a huge soft spot for her family. With every new grandchild, her heart just continued to grow bigger, and she's always been straightforward about wanting nothing more than for each of us to be happy. "And she's not wrong about man on man action. If only your Poppy was so adventurous..."

That last comment is said with such a wistful sigh that I cringe, unable to hide my reaction. *Eww, Nana, that's an image I didn't need.*

"And Declan spent two whole days with her when they went up north with the horses. Plus, with the whole vet revelation? I'm sure his obsession with Princess is going to earn him points. I mean, a hot guy with a kitten is a winner to a normal girl, but a vet? Oof, you're screwed. Thomas isn't even in the running 'cause his head is too far up his ass, so that leaves you in last spot, buddy. But don't worry, I've got an idea."

Jacinta has her scheming face on again, but I'm not concerned if it's going to help me with Harlow.

"You need to get her what she wants the most," she tells me.

"But what is that? In the past, every woman I've dated has been happy with me throwing expensive gifts at them, but I don't think that's going to work this time."

Nana shakes her head, agreeing with me. "No, he's right. Harlow isn't into that kind of thing. She never was, not even as a little girl."

Jacinta grins, eyes bright and more excited than she's been in days. "But she's into abandoned houses, and she's dying to see that one across the road. Get Emma's number from Dad and call her! Maybe you can get her in to tour it. Make sure you're the one who goes with her. She can't go on her own until this asshole is found, so it's perfect. That might at least get you ahead of Declan."

Fuck me! Jacinta may actually be onto something. Before I can say anything else, Holden and Oliver arrive for breakfast, and both Nana and Jacinta throw their effort into fussing over Holden. But that's okay. I have a plan now, and I just have to put it into motion.

Chapter Seventeen

Harlow

When I get down to breakfast, I find that everyone but Declan and I are already there and eating. Dad is over by the glass doors overlooking the pool, having a quiet conversation on the phone with someone. He's obviously got some good news because he's grinning widely, and as I scan the table for somewhere to sit, my eyes suddenly stop on Jaxon. His hair is damp and tousled, and he doesn't have a shirt on. Did he come to breakfast straight out of the shower? I know I felt his body against me that night, which feels so long ago now, but seeing it for the first time... *holy hell.* What I thought were just forearm tattoos are actually sleeves, and he has one that comes down and over his shoulder and chest and wraps around his side. I don't want to make it obvious that I'm staring, so I try not to focus on figuring out what it is, but when I meet his aqua-marine eyes, they're sparkling with amusement. Damn him and his naked chest of mass distraction.

"Jaxon, go and put a shirt on so Harlow doesn't poke her eye out with a fork while eating breakfast." Nana shoos him away as the rest of the table cracks up. Feeling my cheeks heat, I shrug. Now that I've been caught, I unabashedly watch him as he walks by with a towel wrapped around his waist, my breath catching when it starts to fall to the ground. Damn it, he's wearing swim trunks. When my eyes drift back up, he stops and winks at me before picking the towel up. Bastard knew what he was doing.

Shaking my head, I sit down at one of the vacant spots next to Poppy and give him a kiss on the cheek as I do. "Alright, Hally my love?" Poppy asks, putting down the paper he had been reading, and I give him a smile and a nod in reply. Satisfied with my answer, he goes back to reading the paper. I've always loved his easy acceptance; Nana is the pusher in their relationship, while Poppy is just so easygoing that he's the perfect balance.

Conversation continues around the table, and I help myself to a piece of toast as Dad says goodbye to whoever he's talking to. Shoving his phone in his pocket, he comes over to the table, kissing Nana, Jacinta, and me on the top of the head before he sits down in another vacant spot, a grin still across his face.

"Was that Cecelia?" I ask, pointing my knife in the direction of his phone. "Is she going to meet us at the airport so I can get some clothes? As much as I appreciate Jacinta letting me wear hers, I'm going to need to replace mine eventually."

"What? Oh no, that wasn't Cecelia. But if you message her when you're on your way, she'll meet you there. I had a message from her this morning saying she had you sorted."

I look to Kai to make sure he has my back. "Have you got her number?"

"Yep, I'll let her know when we're going to be there."

"Maybe tell her a little early so that she isn't late," Jacinta suggests, giving him a look.

Since he nods, Kai must comprehend whatever it is she means by that look. "I'll tell her half an hour earlier than planned. That way we won't miss her."

Dad frowns, his brow creasing in adorably naive confusion. "She's usually very punctual and reliable."

"Yes, for *you*, Dad," Thomas, who's been quietly minding his own business until now, chimes in.

"Who's usually reliable and punctual for Dad?" Declan asks as he makes his way to the table. Thankfully, he's dressed, but unfortunately for my ovaries, he's wearing one of those suits. I don't think

I can survive shirtless kitten daddy Declan *and* boardroom Declan in the same morning. How much can one girl take?

"You're staring," Poppy whispers, and I quickly shut my eyes. When I open them again, Declan's taking the vacant seat directly across from me and the bastard winks, his trademark smirk in place. Fuck, I think I want him to go back to Mr. Cool.

My head thunks down on the table in front of me. I'm not sure I can survive these men now that they've all but declared war on my lady garden.

Conversation continues around me as I try to compose myself, everyone acting like my resignation is just a totally normal part of their breakfast routine. Maybe I should sneak into my room and see if the stalker managed to find my vibrator. Surely, that could be salvaged? I'm definitely not asking Cecelia to grab a replacement for that.

Oliver brings us back to the question. "Dad was saying Cecelia is usually so punctual and reliable."

Declan snorts. "Only because she wants into his pants, or should I say bank account."

Dad's lips purse in surprise as he looks around the table. "Do you all feel like this?" he asks.

"Fuck yes."

"Absolutely." Jaxon has come back into the room just in time to throw his two cents in, now wearing a shirt and a fresh pair of shorts.

"Can't stand the bitch." Snort! That's Jacinta, of course. Poor Dad, his eyes get wider and his lips thinner as all of his children add their own opinions and even Nana and Poppy give him an affirmative answer.

"She couldn't even be bothered to learn my name," I chime in, not wanting to be left out of this family bonding moment.

"Brad, dear, you are a brilliant businessman but terrible with the ladies. Harlow's mother did a number on you, and much like your sons, you have been afraid to commit to anyone ever since. Not to mention that with your complete lack of social skills, you miss all the cues women throw at you. Cecelia makes herself indispensable so that you need to spend more time with her than most people do with their PAs." Nana sighs like she doesn't want to hurt Dad's feelings. "And since the subject has been broached, as an employee, she makes herself entirely too comfortable out here, and her having access to the security codes and access codes for here *and* all the businesses makes me nervous."

"Do you really think so?" Dad asks, a stunned expression on his face.

"No one in the past has had as much access as she has. Frankly, I'm not even sure you realize how much you have given her. Thankfully, you still require that you must sign everything so she can't approve anything in your place," Poppy expresses, folding his newspaper and putting it on the table next to his plate.

"She's like the sphinx guarding your inner sanctuary. You may have noticed we don't stop by without warning anymore?" Jaxon grumbles, and Dad nods his head. "She told us we needed to have an appointment to see you or we weren't going to be allowed through the office door." Dad's eyes widen, and the faintest flush starts to appear on his cheeks. His eyes dart quickly around the table, though I'm not sure if he's inspecting everyone's expressions or just so embarrassed that he can't decide who's safest to make eye contact with.

"Did you know I sent you an invite to my latest showing at Paris Fashion Week?" Jacinta asks quietly, looking down at her plate. This time, he furiously shakes his head, the splotches on his cheeks growing darker.

"No, I just thought you were too busy to sit with me. Why didn't I get it…" His voice trails off as he puts two and two together.

I wonder if I should tell him about when she threatened me but decide from the look on his face that he doesn't need anything else added to his disappointment.

It's quiet as we watch Dad think about everything Nana and Poppy have said. "Why haven't either of you ever said anything?" He sounds hurt, and Nana and Poppy exchange carefully guarded glances.

"Neither of us had really thought about it in the past, but with this stalker we have been looking very closely at the people that can come and go so freely on our property, and the current situation has brought to our attention that maybe extras shouldn't have access to everything."

"You're not suggesting that Cecelia is responsible for stalking Harlow?" Dad practically gasps, looking surprised and concerned. I'm not even sure how I feel about the suggestion. Do I think she likes competition for Dad's attention? Fuck no. Am I willing to believe that she'd go so far as to *shoot* one of Dad's kids to get more spotlight for herself? I have no idea, but I hope not. She'd have to be seriously deranged to think she could get away with that once the family had their full resources dedicated to finding the perpetrator. I just don't understand how it would benefit her in the long run.

"No, not at all, but this has got us all very worried, and I don't think it would be a bad idea to restrict access to just the family for now. I've spoken to Chuck, and we're going to ship all the horses to him for the time being."

Oh fuck, Chuck knows? Poppy must hear my gasp because he reaches out and pats my hand. "He and Melinda are expecting a phone call first thing this morning. I'm sorry, but I couldn't hide it from him."

I nod, my heart thundering at the thought of that upcoming conversation. I had planned to call them anyway since Max and I had our talk, but I've just found myself a bit overwhelmed with the Prada emergency and then getting wrapped up in Oli and Holden.

"Josh is going to go with them, so that will be one less thing we need to worry about."

"What about Prada and Coco?" Jacinta asks, looking worried. "Are they alright to travel?"

Everyone turns to look at me. Oh, how the tables have turned. "Well, to be honest, no. Coco isn't steady on his feet yet. If it was a short journey, I'd probably okay it, but it's cross country and on a plane. I think it would be better if they stayed behind. I'm sure between all of us, we can manage. I'll check him over before we leave, and you just need to remember to give him his antibiotic injections." Everyone quickly agrees to help, trusting my word, and a bit of pride swells in my chest. It feels nice to be valued, to be recognized as capable and have my opinion respected. This is what I've been waiting for.

Poppy adds, "I've asked Gretchen to take some vacation time, and she's heading back to Germany to visit her sister for a little while, and the two housekeepers are taking paid leave. That leaves it so the only people who should be on the estate are us."

"I need you to allow Hope access too, please," Holden demands, albeit politely, a stubborn set to his jaw. "She needs to update me on things I've missed over the last few days. She's been acting as vice-president of Neighpalm Records while I've been gone, and I think we've known her long enough that we don't doubt she's trustworthy."

"I don't know why you haven't just made it

permanent," Oliver mutters around a piece of toast. "The girl knows just as much about it as you do."

Holden grumbles, "Because she won't let me. She likes being in charge of the PR department and says it keeps her busy. She's agreed to consider being my VP once she decides she wants to slow down a bit."

"She needs a partner," Nana declares, turning to Poppy. "Add Hope to our list of people to fix up, please." Her grandchildren all chuckle as Poppy rolls his eyes.

"Yes, dear."

"Of course, I will let the guards at the front gate know," Dad assures him. "I've also got someone coming in to check out the surveillance security. Try to make it more difficult for someone to hack into our system. No damn point in having security cameras when someone can wipe the drive."

"Anyway, back to Cecelia," Nana says, bringing the conversation around. "No more coming out here with documents, no more using her as an escort for functions, and *definitely* no more sleep-overs. We will clear out her room and have her belongings returned to her. Just inform her that these restrictions will be in place until further notice as a matter of security. If she doesn't like it, well, then I'm sure she will find herself another position. But somehow I doubt it."

And like the matriarch she is, Nana has just laid

down the law. Poppy nods his head in full agreement with Nana, and Dad just looks resigned, if not a little concerned. His brow is creased, and he's biting his lip in what looks like a nervous habit. *Why would he be worried?* Before I can ask him, Poppy takes over.

"Now, one last thing. Our annual Neighpalm Charity Ball is coming soon. It was supposed to be a masquerade this year, but due to the circumstances, I think we should scrap that. Usually, we would have it here, but with the security risk I suggest we also have a change of venue. It will be held at the ballroom at the Neighpalm Hotel in downtown LA, and the guest list will be thoroughly vetted before invitations are sent. I'm pretty sure whatever is going on is personal and not business-related, so I'm relatively confident it will be fine, but we're better playing it safe," Poppy decides, and the children groan just like... children. I snort, but Kai narrows his eyes at me.

"No, Harlow, don't laugh. Just wait, you'll find out what it's like to be propositioned by the people you'd least expect. The wealthy are bored and vicious, and they like to play. And dude, some of the things they'll say and offer are fucked up." Kai shudders, and all of his brothers follow suit. Even Jacinta looks slightly pale.

"You will all be required to attend. Preferably with dates, but if you can't find one, I will find one for you," Nana informs them... and me? We're all currently receiving a cringeworthy staredown, and I'm mentally running through the list of every man I've ever talked to in case it'll get me out of ever being faced with that look again.

"Dibs on Harlow!" Declan calls out.

"What the fuck!"

"Damn it!"

"Hey, no fair!" The chorus of complaints has me almost speechless.

"You dibs her?" Jacinta's quiet voice has the boys quickly shutting up. "Whatever happened to asking a girl if she would like to be your date? What if she doesn't want to go with you? She's good friends with Shane Silvers *and* Alexander Winters. Maybe she wants to go with one of them. Lord knows they can probably dance better than the lot of you." Jacinta looks a little ill at the suggestion, but I guess she's taking this whole sister thing to heart. I may have to put her out of her misery, but then again, it won't hurt for her to sweat just a little longer.

"Don't forget her new friend Jace," Nana calls out cheekily.

"Well, there you go." Jacinta gestures broadly, her voice getting louder. "Harlow has lots of options, so how about instead of dibsing her, you show her some proper respect and ask her." She holds up her hand as mouths start to open. "Not *now.* Now you've just looked like a bunch of asses. I suggest you give it a while for it to fade in her memory."

Ha! I think I like being on Jacinta's good side; it's fun watching her put them all in their place. Almost in unison, the guys cringe, though Dad gives her a wink. Jacinta practically preens at his approval, and I have to desperately hold my laughter in. This family is so much fun now that they're not all anti-Harlow.

Thomas clears his throat. "Dad, Poppy, and I need to go and inspect the headquarters of the NW European Airline we bought. I think it would be a good idea for all of you to take some time and come too, or Harlow at the very least. You can stay on the yacht at Cannes, or I have a place in Ireland where you could stay too," he offers quietly, and everyone looks surprised. Huh, I'm right there with them. He's willing to be with me alone if the others decide not to come; he was friendly enough in the stable the other day, but I didn't think we were on 'alone together' kind of terms.

"When did you buy a place in Ireland?" Declan asks.

"Just after the Clarissa fiasco. I wanted a place I could go and be anonymous, and it works well there," he tells him, a firm note in his voice sending the message that he doesn't want to go into any greater detail right now.

"I think that's an excellent idea," Dad tells Thomas. "Let's make it a week from Monday. That gives Holden's shoulder a chance to rest, and he can see the physical therapist as well. It also gives you all time to get your leadership teams up to speed on what needs to be done while we're gone." No one argues, so I guess that's supposed to be that. But then Dad looks at me. "Is that alright with you, Harlow?"

"Oh yeah, sure. I haven't got a passport though. Will I be able to get one in time?"

Everyone looks at Thomas with concern. "I can take care of that for you while you're in Hawaii," he says, and the room collectively exhales. Huh, another thing I'm going to have to ask about. I'm not an educated world traveler since I really haven't even traveled around the US, but it seems to me that it might be kind of hard to get a passport for someone who isn't you. What is it about Thomas that makes him so confident he can get this done? Not only him, but everyone else. Clearly, they believe he's able to get this done. Not to mention he's familiar with a gun, was trusted to guard the stables alone after that dummy Jacinta set up, and there are all these little looks that just hint at secret after secret to uncover. I'm dying to ask about all of this, but I know it's not the time.

In the silence that follows, Kai stands up. "Okay, if everyone is done with updates, I'm going to finish my packing." He gives Nana a kiss on the head on the way past. "Harlow, I'll be back, and we'll leave soon, okay?"

"Sure," I reply, smiling as the butterflies in my stomach start to flutter. Holden has started to look tired, so Oliver convinces him to return to bed, whispering something in his ear that causes Holden's eyes to light up and those damn butterflies to flutter even faster. Before the two of them head out from the kitchen, they have a quick word with Dad, asking to speak with him privately, then get a head start to his office to wait for him. Instead of immediately following them, Dad comes over to me. "Be careful but have some fun. I worry that everything has been so stressful for you since you've been here. I'm so sorry, Harlow. I'm almost afraid that you'll leave when this is over and not want to come back."

He sounds so guilty, which in turn makes me feel sad and guilty myself. Needing to do something to make the both of us feel a tiny bit better, I stand up and open my arms for a hug. There's a little hint of surprise in his gaze, not having expected me to offer the little bit of affection, and it makes me that much more confident that I made the right decision. I want to connect with my dad, and I need him to know that I'm happy to have this chance with him despite the drama.

"Dad, none of this is your fault, and I am so glad I'm here and getting to know you. You've done everything in your power now to make sure we are safe, and that's all I could ever ask for. Stop worrying." I give him a kiss on the cheek, and the tension leaves his body before he blows out a sigh of relief and pulls back, making his way after the other two.

Once Dad leaves, Thomas gets up, muttering something about making a phone call as he disappears. Poppy picks up his newspaper and stands up. "Come on, dear, I want to go into the office and start to make those changes regarding Cecelia's access. I know you want to go and check on Couture, don't you?"

Nana quickly agrees, and they both say their goodbyes, wishing me a fun and safe trip.

"I'm going out to check on Prada!" Jacinta says almost too excitedly, standing up and practically sprinting for the door.

"I'll come with you. I want to talk to you about something before I go to the office," Declan tells her, his eyes not leaving mine. A small smile crosses my lips, and I wink in his direction.

"I'm just going to finish my coffee, and I'll be out to check them over," I assure her when I see her looking at me hopefully. I have to give Declan a chance to talk to her on his own; he doesn't need any help from me.

That leaves me and Jaxon.

"Looking forward to the trip?" I ask him.

"You have no idea," he replies, his voice low and gravelly, and I feel my toes curl in anticipation. Wicked ideas try to bombard me of how this trip could turn out for us, but first I need to speak to both him and Kai about the others, and what better place to do it than 20,000 ft in the air? Jaxon hasn't tried to make amends as much as the others have, so if there's going to be any chance of a future for us, we need to work some shit out. Might as well do it when there's no way for him to escape.

Chapter Eighteen

Jaxon

I give my excuses to Harlow, telling her I'm going to grab my bag from my room, because I want to talk to Dad about something, so I search for him in his office. When I get there, the door is closed. A quiet jiggle of the handle lets me know it's unlocked, which is enough of a signal for me. Cecelia's latest interference notwithstanding, Dad has always made as much time for his children as possible. Knocking, I enter without waiting to be called and find Dad with Holden and Oliver in a threeway embrace. They all look kind of emotional, and when Dad pulls away, Holden and Oliver continue to hold hands.

"About time you got that shit sorted. I mean, over ten years is a long time to play hard to get, Holden," I joke, hoping to break the emotional atmosphere, and it works somewhat. Oliver snorts and Holden gives me a relieved smile, but Dad just raises an eyebrow.

"Take a seat, Jaxon; I want to know how you feel about this crazy plan of Mom's. Holden and Oliver have just been sharing with me how they both feel about Harlow and that maybe some of you other boys feel the same. And that Nana suggested that maybe you could *share* her. I want to believe the best in all of my children and look out for all of you, Harlow included, so I need you guys to sell me on this idea. Especially considering your less than warm reception of her. If this is a game in any way, it will not be tolerated." Dad doesn't seem angry, just curious and definitely protective. I can't say I blame him.

Closing the door behind me, I take a seat on one of the chairs while Oliver and Holden share the sofa. Dad sits down behind his desk, his business face on.

"Part of the reason I was so taken aback—" I start, but Dad interrupts.

"Is that what we're calling it now?"

"Okay, let's call it hostile," I admit, and Dad nods, gesturing for me to go on. "Is because I had already met her on my trip to the East Coast for that new club opening in Hartford. She and I had clicked, and if it wasn't for an emergency phone call asking her to return home, things would have gone... somewhere." Dad's wince and the quick way he glances down are a clear enough indicator that he's getting the gist. I don't want to make either of us more uncomfortable by spelling it all out. "I wasn't thinking clearly after that, and I let Jacinta get into my head, so when I saw her in our living room, I guess I overreacted."

"You think?" Dad asks dryly.

"But I misjudged her. And I'm not the only one. I want to make it up to her, Dad. I want to get to know her, and I want to see where it might go."

Dad crosses his arms and looks at me intently. "And if your brothers are interested as well? Would you be happy sharing her? Not to mention this is all on the chance that she gives her full consent to dealing with all of you. She might not be ready to handle all of that. Now, or ever. God knows I'm still hoping she'll forgive all of you, let alone date you."

I shrug, the motion relaxing some of the tension in my body. This question is much easier to answer. "We've all talked about it, and I don't have any problems with it. Surprisingly, I don't feel jealous at all. Just happy for both them and her. Let's be honest, I haven't really had much relationship success myself. I don't think I'm really in a position to judge or decide what kind of relationship she should have or who would be best for her."

Dad rubs a hand across his chin and sighs. "Who am I to get in the way of your possible happiness?" A sigh of relief leaves my lips at his words, but he holds up a hand. "But let me emphasize, and you make sure that the others know this, you better not break her heart. No cheating, lying, or sneaking around, and if I find out you have, Jacinta's punishment will look like a walk in the park compared to what I will do to you all." Dad's growl holds a threatening promise that has us all assuring him before he's even finished his sentence.

"Actually, Dad, I was hoping you could help me with something?" I change the subject slightly after he accepts how serious we are, wanting to get this ironed out with him before we leave for Hawaii. "I'm kind of in last place, or so Jacinta and Nana inform me anyway." Oliver and Holden snicker like twelve-year-old boys, so I flip them off. *Assholes.* "I want to do something special with her, and I was wondering if I could get Emma's number off you. I thought Harlow might like a tour of the house across the road, so I'm hoping I can convince Emma to let us in. Figured our Hawaii trip would give me a couple days to win both of them over. Gotta get Emma on board and make sure Harlow's okay with being alone with me..."

The assholes stop suddenly. *Yeah, not so funny now, is it, boys?* I look at them and wink.

"Well played, brother, well played." Oliver nods his head, while Holden scowls.

Dad smiles at our bantering, but that's no surprise. So long as we don't hit below the belt, he's always found the little snipes amusing. "Emma is coming for dinner tonight. You can ask her then if you want. But I'm sure that Harlow will be thrilled with that. I think she was worried she wasn't going to be able to do it with the stalker around, but I don't have any problem with it if you go with her."

"So Emma's coming for dinner again?" Holden asks, smirking at Dad.

"Yes, she's bringing her girlfriend. Apparently, the two of them get a little lonely in the caretaker's cottage so far from the city. I thought it would be nice to invite them over."

Damn, she has a girlfriend. I was hoping Dad might be in with a chance there. I know he's happy, but it would be nice for him to have a lady in his life. It certainly hasn't been easy for him. Not many people wanted a man with seven adopted, some-what troubled teenagers, but we're all adults now. He's still young, and it would be nice to see him find someone to spend the rest of his life with. Look at Nana and Poppy.

"But, Dad, I won't be here for dinner. We're leaving as soon as Kai gets done packing." I watch my brothers get calculated looks. "Oh no, you fuckers aren't jumping the gun on this one. Please, Dad," I ask him, practically begging.

"I'll ask her for you, Jaxon. Let's make it Thursday next week if she's available. You all should be back from Hawaii by then."

I shoot the other two a triumphant look, and it's their turn to flip me off. "Look at that, you two are already doing coupley things again." Oliver moves to get up to thump me, but Holden pats him on the chest.

"Ignore him, just think about our morning and know that he is most *definitely* in last place." That has Oliver settling, and the smirks they exchange make my victory wither a bit. *What the fuck are they talking about?*

"I better get going. Kai wants to leave soon," I tell them, standing up. Dad follows suit and comes around the desk to give me a hug.

"Make sure you and Kai look after her," he tells me, sounding worried. "You don't need to make a big production out of it. I want Harlow to be able to relax if at all possible, so some subtle eyes on her would probably be best. Unless she's locked in her room, she shouldn't be left alone, but maybe you guys can come up with some little reasons to check in with her, keep her company when you're not out and about."

"I will," I promise, pulling away.

"And Jaxon," Dad calls as I open the door, "make sure you spoil her. She deserves it."

A smile crosses my face at the thought. "She does and we will." Waving goodbye to my brothers, I hurry to my room to grab my bags and get back to the front before Kai starts bellowing at me, or worse, leaves without me.

Harlow

While everyone disappears, leaving me alone at the breakfast table, I decide to bite the bullet and make the call I've been dreading. I head out the large glass doors and sit down on one of the recliners facing the pool, pretending I'm ready for what I need to face now. Grabbing my phone out of my ever-present backpack, I open my contacts and hit the number I need.

It rings once before it's answered. "Harlow Stubbs, you have got some explaining to do." Jesus, Melinda must have had Chuck's phone in her hand or something. I don't get to say a word, just sitting and listening to her rant as tears well in my eyes. God, I've missed her. I've been so bad, but in my defense, it feels like I haven't stopped to really breathe.

Eventually, she runs out of air, and I wipe the few tears that escaped from my cheeks.

"Are you okay, Harlow?" Chuck's deep voice comes out of the phone, and an all too loud sigh sneaks out of me at the question. Melinda must have put it on speaker.

"Yeah, I am. It's been a bit rough, and I'm all over the place, but things are looking better, crazy stalker aside."

"You make sure you have one of Brad's boys with you *every time* you go somewhere," he orders firmly. I can hear Melinda muttering, but I can't quite make out the words. I want to speak to her one on one, but I have things I need to tell them both first.

"The horses were all delivered safely, and I saw Max," I tell them.

"Of course they were. I never had any doubt," Chuck replies, but then I hear a commotion. It sounds like they're fighting over the phone, but Melinda must have won, as per usual, since it's her voice that speaks next.

"How was Max? Did she seem funny to you? I spoke to her last night, and she just seemed a little off."

"She was fine when I saw her last. Making new friends." I manage to keep my voice even because I don't want to tell them what kind of friends or who. That's none of my business, nor do I know for sure.

"Hmm." Melinda doesn't sound too sure, but she doesn't push the point. *Mental note: call Max once we get to Hawaii.*

"Look, I just wanted to reassure you I'm okay. I really am sorry I didn't call you sooner. I promise I will do better."

"We wanted to come out and visit, but we're short staffed, and I can't leave at the moment," Chuck tells me, sounding disgruntled.

Short staffed? "What do you mean, short staffed? Didn't Luke come back?" Where could he have gotten to?

"No, he's back, but the same day he came back, Peter quit. No reason given, just up and left. So with no you or Max and only Luke, who, let's face it, isn't that much help, we're flat out." A small prick of guilt stabs at me, but I quickly shake it off. I know that's not why he's telling me.

"Well, Josh is coming with all of the horses from here, and I'm sure he won't mind helping. In fact, I think he'll get a kick out of it."

"Yes, thank god for that," Chuck replies, sounding really tired. They've always been hands on owners instead of hiring people to do everything. But it's more than a one man job, and without Max and I there to pick up Luke's slack, I guess it's becoming too much.

We finish the phone call, Melinda and Chuck telling me they love me and me them. I hang up, not a hundred percent happy, but I wasn't willing to talk to Melinda about the guys with Chuck standing right there. With all the stalker business, I don't think Chuck would've believed that I had "girl stuff" to talk to just Melinda about. Normally, he's pretty easy going, but I can tell that he was super rattled.

Just as I'm hanging up, Dad appears from his office. The guys are nowhere to be seen, so I guess they must have finished talking to him about whatever.

"Hey, honey, do you mind if I come out to the barn with you to check over Prada and Coco? What kind of name is Coco for a colt? He should be called Givenchy or Saint Laurent if she wants to go with fashion names. Both of those are *strong* names. I mean, she could have called him Calvin. Anything would be better than *Coco*." His grumbling continues as we head out across the patio and past the pool toward the stables, but I just listen in with amusement. Poor Dad, he's had a trying day already on top of all the other stress.

He falls silent, but then another heavy sigh leaves his mouth before he pulls me to a stop. "I cannot believe I am about to have this conversation with you, and forgive me if I am overstepping any boundaries...." He chews on his lip again, and my pulse speeds up. *Is this where he's going to tell me that he'd like me to leave?*

"Mom and Dad raised me to be very open about sex and relationships; nothing was ever hidden in this house," he starts, screwing up his nose in long-remembered disgust. After a pause, he mutters, "Unfortunately." I don't hide my snort in response, and he only starts to look more pained.

"And I passed that on to my children. You know about Oliver and Holden now, but I want to assure you none of us made them give that up; that was a decision Holden made, and only he could come to the realization that it didn't matter to us. It's such a shame that it took so long, but I'm happy they're working on it now. Unluckily for me, that wasn't the only thing they wanted to talk to me about. Apparently, my sons are really putting this old man to the test today."

He runs a hand through his hair, his eyes searching the landscape behind me. "They all seem to be interested in you too and have informed me that they intend to pursue you. I want you to know that they have my blessing, but that's only if it's what you want." He grabs both my hands, his eyes imploring me to understand. "If you don't, I can tell them to leave you alone, that a friendship is all they will ever have with you. You are my priority at the moment, and they can just get over it. My sons are great men when they don't sabotage themselves, but I don't think I could ever deny that you'd have your hands full. They might not be easy men to love, but they're worth the effort. You are too, no matter who you are and aren't interested in dating."

Holy shit, this man! A sob leaves my mouth, and I throw myself into his arms, ignoring the embarrassment I should be feeling at talking about a multi-partner relationship with my dad.

"Harlow, are you okay? Did I mess something up?" He hugs me, but it's like he's at a loss for words. "Does this mean I need to kill them already?" My body is shaking with emotion, and I pull away, wiping my hands over my face and shaking my head.

"No, Dad. This is about the fact that I love you and wish I had grown up with you because you are everything a girl could want in a father."

He looks stunned for a moment, then a grin splits his face before he pulls me back in for another hug. "God, I wish the same thing."

"As for your sons...." I can't look him in the eye, so I focus on a spot on his chest. "I'm okay with whatever they're planning, but I will let you know if I change my mind. Are you sure you're okay with it?" This time, my eyes do meet his. I want to see for sure that he is. While I'm his priority at the moment, he's also mine. I want a real relationship with my dad, and if the cost of having that chance is to look at the Summers men as only my brothers, I'll do it. I might need to buy stock in Energizer, but I'll do it if that's what he needs.

"Harlow, I always knew that you guys weren't going to be brothers and sister, and if they decide to go the route of dating one woman, which is something I still need to wrap my head around, then I am thrilled that they picked you."

I can't see any insincerity in his expression, so I accept it at face value.

"Hey, what's taking so long?" Jacinta calls, and when we turn, she's waving her hand out of the stables. "Come on, you need to leave shortly. Kai will freak out if you're not ready. The dude's usually pretty laid back, but he's *really* excited about this trip."

She disappears, and Dad and I exchange an amused glance as he continues on to the stables.

"I didn't get a chance to tell you how impressed

I was last night with your quick thinking. Without you, Coco wouldn't have made it." He grumbles the word Coco again, and I snort.

"Just call him CC if you can't deal with Coco," I suggest, and he looks pleased with the suggestion though I bet it will piss Jacinta off.

"If—when—we sort out the stalker situation and you want to stay, we can look at setting you up a practice. I can also put some feelers out if you want to stick with an internship first. Dad did say that the zoo you interviewed with was in some financial difficulties. Maybe we can buy them out."

Well, he definitely got that attitude from Nana. I can't fault the man for wanting to do right by his children, but it's definitely easy to see how the Summers kids might have gotten just the tiniest bit spoiled.

"We'll see," I tell him noncommittally. "At the moment, I'm just enjoying getting to know you and hoping the stalker loses interest."

By this point, we're outside the stables, and I can hear Jacinta cooing to the horses, promising them that I'm going to take care of them. A small smile grows as I think about what I've got ahead of me. Starting the day with Holden and Oli, getting in a little time with the horses, and then my first trip to Hawaii. Maybe I can be foolish for a second and just tell myself that things are turning around. Or at least they will be if I get moving.

"Thanks, Dad. Love you." I leave him blushing

with joy and step into the stable with an impatient Jacinta.

We are driven to the airport by the limo because the helicopter was needed to take Dad, Declan, Nana, and Poppy to the office. Holden and Oliver were spending another day at home, but I think Hope was going out to update Holden and who knows where Thomas was. Off doing mysterious things probably.

Like the return trip from dropping off the horses with Declan, this one was filled with us getting to know each other. A rowdy game of 20 questions was played, nothing too serious, favorite color and animals, that kind of thing.

When we arrive at the airport, we pull up in front of a smaller plane than the last one we were on. Kai must see my disappointed face.

"What's wrong, Harlow?" he asks, helping me out of the limo.

"Oh nothing, I was just looking forward to seeing James and Chris," I explain, shaking my head. "They were really kind to me on my flight out, but Poppy told me they fly the big one."

"If the big one isn't being used, one of them will fly this one," Jaxon interjects, pulling his and Kai's bags out of the trunk of the limo. "Not sure who was scheduled to fly today. Normally, Kai would do his own flying, but he wanted to sit back and enjoy the flight with you. "

"You have your pilot's license too?" I ask him in surprise. Declan was the only one I'd seen fly.

"Yeah, both helicopter and plane. It fits well with my adrenaline junkie nature." He winks, a full body chuckle erupting from his mouth. I can feel myself growing lighter the more time I spend with Kai; there's just something about his contagious joy that makes me love being around him.

Before I can say anything, the door to the nearby office opens. Cecelia storms out, a scowl on her face and a rolling bag being haphazardly dragged behind her.

"You're late. I've been waiting for fifteen minutes," she complains as she gets to us. *Hmm, I thought she was told to be half an hour earlier than us.* Seems they were right about her trying to miss us. Bitch. "Here are your damn clothes. I don't work for *you*, so don't ask me to do anything again," she spits, eyeing me up and down. "You don't even work for Neighpalm, and I will not run around and do errands for you. Find someone else, or better yet, do them yourself."

She turns and walks away, leaving both Jaxon and Kai gobsmacked that she would speak like that in front of them. Or that's what I'm assuming anyway. Me, I don't care. The woman means less than nothing to me. She can say what she wants.

"I'd say Nana was on the right track with that

one. Man, is she going to be pissed when she finds out that her access has been reduced," Kai says, shaking his head.

"I'd like to be a fly on that wall when they tell her," Jaxon agrees, and they both snigger childishly.

Rolling my eyes at them, I start toward the small jet, pulling the case behind me, but they both catch up, Kai with their two bags over his shoulder and Jaxon taking the one out of my hand. They allow me to walk up the stairs first, and when I get up there, I'm thrilled to see a familiar face.

"Good morning, Harlow, nice to see you again," James greets me cheerfully.

"Hey, James. How are you?" I ask, giving him a hug. He was the first person to be kind to me on this adventure, and I'm grateful to him.

"Really good," he replies, smiling broadly.

Pulling away, I move so that Kai and Jaxon can board the plane. They both shake hands with James before passing, and there's something honestly genuine about their words when they check in on how he's doing.

"So the flight is about five and half hours. You asked for no hostess, but there's a platter of food and drinks in the galley as requested. Just help your-self to it when you want it," James tells us as the jet fires up its engines. I must look confused because he laughs. "Chris is on the flight too. Kai asked us if we wanted to spend some days in Hawaii together instead of flying home, and Jaxon put us up at the hotel. So of course we couldn't say no."

I look at them both, and they shrug. "Nana mentioned that you liked them both and they made you feel comfortable, so I asked them to fly. It also doesn't make sense for them to return when nobody else needs the plane." I throw my arms around Kai at his explanation, kissing him on the cheek.

Jaxon grumbles about giving them their accommodation, so I roll my eyes but give him a hug and a kiss on the cheek too. Need to make some baby steps if I'm going all in here.

We settle in for our flight, and before long, we're high in the air, winging our way to the tropical island.

Chapter Nineteen

Harlow

We're just finishing up our meal when I decide to broach the topic of *us!* I've had a couple of glasses of wine, so my filter is a lot thinner than normal. Normally, I'd agonize over this a bit more and work out like ten different ways to get to the point, but the wine has decided I'm just going to blurt it out.

"So I had a little chat with Holden and Oliver last night, and I think it's time I had the same chat with you two." They exchange a glance, but Jaxon gestures for me to keep going. "I find myself attracted to, well, all of you despite your past behavior. I'm not really sure what it says about me as a person, but it would be dishonest of me to deny it. I'm not going to play games with any of you, so even though I probably should hang some of you out to dry, I'm not going to hide or lie about what I feel." I look at Jaxon when I say this because, let's face it, Kai has been perfect.

"When I originally agreed to come to Hawaii, I was thrilled to be able to spend time with you." This I say to Kai, but I can't read him. Though he's normally so expressive and full of energy, he's got one hell of a poker face right now. "And don't get me wrong, I still am. I can't wait to get to know you better, but I feel the same way about Holden and Oliver and possibly even Jaxon and Declan." I'm glad they're letting me talk, but at the same time, I didn't drink enough wine to help me painlessly power through this with no idea how they're feeling. I stand up so I don't have to look at them, beginning to pace up and down the aisle. "I originally felt horribly guilty about this. That I couldn't just pick one of you, but I've since come to a conclusion: why should I? Why should I have to choose? Why couldn't I see where things went with all of you? Unconventional relationships are trendy these days, and after talking to Holden and Oli, they kind of made it clear that you guys wouldn't be opposed to trying it either."

Whirling around, I collapse into a chair across from the two of them. I want to be able to see both their faces, though that's still absolutely no help. My breathing increases with worry, and I chew at my lip as they exchange another damn glance.

Kai is the one to respond first, taking mercy on

me in my obviously impending freak out. "Harlow, as much as I would like to hog you all to myself, I can't do that to you or my brothers. I can see your interest in them and vice versa, even though they all tried to hide it, and I would be doing you all a disservice if I opposed it. To be honest, I'm not all that jealous. I love my brothers, and I think that you're what they all need. With this kind of arrangement, you will never feel neglected or second best because there will always be at least one or two of us around. I want this to be real and for it to last, and as much as I want you in my life, I don't think I could do justice to one woman by myself." Kai doesn't sound disappointed or sad; in fact, he sounds pleased that I've brought the subject out into the open.

"I'll just be happy to get a second chance after I was such an ass," Jaxon tells me, his eyes focused on his lap before he manages to look up at the end of the sentence. "I really am sorry for the way I behaved. I let Jacinta get into my head, and I was a complete asshole. Please say you forgive me and are willing to see where things might take us. I spoke to Jacinta and told her I was all in and to leave me out of her problems, but I have a feeling that maybe all of that is over now." He's twisting his hands in this strangely vulnerable way, not what I expected from him, and I think that's one of the things that tugs at my heartstrings. Sure, he's been a major asshole, but what Hope told me about his and Jacinta's history just keeps repeating in my mind, filling the silence.

Looking down and noticing his nervous tic, he stops before staring me dead in the eye. There's a sincerity there that I haven't seen since the first moment we met as two strangers just passing by one another in a bar, and that's my undoing. Plus, he's got to mean this if he actually spoke to Jacinta. I know, with more certainty than anything, how much he prizes his relationship with his sister.

"Forgiving takes time, Jaxon, but we are well on the way to it being a thing." Fuck, now I feel incredibly awkward and can't meet either of their eyes. "So yeah, we're all on the same page. Good. That's totally… good."

"You didn't mention Thomas," Kai probes carefully, and I shrug, looking anywhere but at them. "Harlow," Kai growls, and my nipples pucker. Fuck, I am a needy bitch.

"Look, it's not a lack of interest on my behalf, but apart from a couple of intense looks, he and I haven't really had anything to do with each other. At least with Jaxon, I know our chemistry is off the charts as long as his attitude doesn't get in the way. Even Declan has warmed up to me, and we had a good time when we dropped the horses off. But Thomas… I just dont think he's interested in me. I've been told a couple of times that he has an extreme dislike of the female persuasion. I don't know what I can do to convince him that I'm not like his ex, nor do I even know if I want to or not. I know next to nothing about the guy, and I feel like I need to know for certain before I try to get involved with his emotions. I would hate to convince him to give me a chance and then realize that maybe I don't even want it in the first place."

"Ok, but don't count him out," Kai pleads, and I shrug, shivering slightly. I'm not sure if it's because of the cool temperature of the plane or thinking about Thomas.

Jaxon must assume it's the former because he stands up and grabs hold of me, dragging me over to sit between the two of them on the couch.

"With Thomas, *you* need to decide. He won't pursue you, so you're going to have to be the aggressive one. But if you can convince him, you will find him to be the most devoted of us proba-bly." With each passing word, Jaxon incrementally moves closer so I can feel their body heat. My nipples throb as my panties get damp.

"Yeah, he worshipped the ground Clarissa walked on. He was attentive and loving and gener-ous, and she wanted for nothing. But like I said, he's a busy man and she had no interest in being faithful or loyal. It's why he was so devastated when she did what she did. She could have had every-thing he has, including half an airline company, but she just couldn't see that. She wanted more."

Kai looks at Jaxon, who gestures for him to keep going.

"She tried to seduce a couple of us, but we shot her down. We tried to tell him, but he refused to see it. It wasn't until she finally betrayed him and the country by selling military plane plans that it finally hit him in the face. He was broken by it. There's honestly no other word to describe it. It set him back *years*, regressing him into the person he was when we were younger. We had worked so hard on getting him out of his shell helping him overcome the bullying from his asshole classmates, and Clarissa stole that confidence from him. He could never figure out what was so wrong with him, so lacking in him as a person and a partner, that would make her so desperate to hurt him. He went to great lengths to make sure she paid for her betrayal, but some of the things he's done for that company were at a great cost to him. Maybe you can help fix some of that. I know that it's not fair to throw a project at you when you're opening yourself up for a relationship, but we just know that Thomas is worth it. He just needs someone to remind him that he's better than his past, better than his ex ever thought he was, and that he's enough, just as he is."

Okay, now this is more like it. We're getting to the bottom of the mystery that is Thomas Summers. I sit up straighter, warmed by them both now. "You guys keep acting all mysterious about him. Is there something I should know? What company are you referring to, surely not Neighpalm Airlines? Dad doesn't seem like he'd ever make any of you guys do something that would hurt you. Unless I'm completely wrong about him?"

Again, they exchange another glance over my head, and nerves start ratcheting up again. Did I get this wrong? Is there something about Dad that I need to know? "I swear, if you two don't stop it with the weird Jedi mindmeld shit, I'm going to kick you both… *hard*," I threaten, and they both crack wide grins like I'm cute or something.

"I guess we can tell you. We haven't been very careful about keeping it a secret around you, and now that you're a part of the family, they'll probably vet you anyway. No one apart from Hope and the family knows about this, so you will need to keep it to yourself, no telling Max," Jaxon warns me.

Any of the levity in their gazes is completely gone now. They've both pulled slightly away, stealing some of that warmth, so that they can look me in the eyes.

"When Clarissa betrayed us, Thomas teamed up with the Federal Department Of Counterterrorism to help bring her and the people involved to justice. They were so impressed with his contributions, they wanted to cultivate some kind of relationship with him. He couldn't be convinced to leave Neighpalm, but he did complete the field agent training and still works for them occasionally as a sort of independent contractor, I guess. I'm not really completely sure what to call him, but anyway… He can get into elite parties and social events, and considering who he is, no one ever looks twice. I'm pretty sure they've had him do some fairly unsavory things too, but he never talks about that." Kai says that last bit quietly, and I can tell that he's worried about his brother.

"So, that's also the long explanation as to why he's getting your passport for you. He's got government connections," Jaxon says, standing up. "Who wants another drink? I need one after all that serious talk." For the first time, he makes some kind of ridiculous grimace, the expression totally exaggerated, and I'm so startled to see it that it drags a laugh out of me.

"Not for me. I've got to drive the rental when we get to Hawaii," Kai tells him, but I nod my head.

"Yeah, I wouldn't mind another glass of wine, please." Jaxon heads to the front of the plane where the little galley is located between the cabin and the cockpit.

Still not ready to change the subject, Kai turns in his seat even more and grabs my hand. "Keep on trying with Thomas. I'm afraid if we all have you and he doesn't, he'll drift further away from us than he already has. And don't be afraid if he's nasty or aggressive. It's a defense mechanism, and it's just his default mode since Clarissa. You're going to have to give back as good as you get, and we will have your back. Promise me you'll try?"

"I don't know him well enough to make any promises, but I'll put in some effort and see where it gets us." Seemingly satisfied with my answer, Kai leans back in his seat again.

I shiver again, but I'm not sure if it's from missing Jaxon's body heat or the information they just told me about Thomas. There's something so sad about the idea of him keeping apart from his siblings. Even when I was cursing them all, I wouldn't have been able to deny that they've got a strong bond between them. He must be so lonely.

"Why don't you see if Cecelia packed you a sweater?" Kai suggests, getting up and retrieving my suitcase from where he stowed it. When he gets back, he places it at my feet, leaving it for me to check its contents. I'd rather have him wrapped around me than a sweater, but I lean forward and open it anyway. When it falls open, I can do nothing but stare in horror. Inside the case is about a hundred post-it notes with *fuck you* written on each one and what looks like clothes a two-bit 80s hooker would pick up at the Good Will like sequined boob tubes and micro mini skirts. Dear god. There's even a leopard print bodysuit. They're all stained and smell like smoke, booze, and body odor. On top, there's a handwritten note.

This is payback for not letting me through at the hospital. Don't mess with me. You'll regret it. It's not signed, but it's obvious it's from Cecelia. The handwriting is very different to the one the nurse had delivered to me, and I'm feeling a weird sense of disappointment. I had been leaning toward Cecelia being the stalker, but I guess I was wrong. It would've been nice to be able to get rid of two problems at once. The longer I stare at the note, the more my mind whirls with questions. *If it's not Cecelia, then who?* Each question brings that anger rising quicker, until I can't help but let it out.

"Fucking bitch." The growl that escapes my mouth is loud and feral, bringing Jaxon rushing back from the galley.

"What's wrong?"

"Cecelia didn't do her job getting Harlow's clothes, and now she has nothing," Kai snaps, showing him the contents of my suitcase while I stew in my anger. Now I'm glad she's losing all her access to the house and companies.

"I don't get it. Does she really think she's so safe in her position that this won't impact her job position if I tell Dad?"

Kai's brow is creased in thought as he tries to puzzle it out. "Do you think that maybe she actually has something on Dad?"

"What, like blackmail?" Jaxon's frowning now too, but he doesn't look like he's understanding this any better than us.

"Yeah. I mean, she gets away with a lot. Some of the things she does, there's no way Dad would allow anyone else to get away with. And we know he's not sleeping with her, so it can't be because of that," Kai muses. My heart starts to race in worry. Is Dad being scammed? What could she possibly be holding over his head?

"Fuck, you may be right. I think we need to ask Declan's PI to look into Cecelia's background a little more," Jaxon suggests, and Kai snorts.

"No, I think Declan's PI is as dodgy as fuck too. He's been waiting on that information about—" He breaks off and looks at me guiltily, but I roll my eyes.

"Look, I don't doubt he had me investigated. I would be disappointed if he hadn't. But he mustn't have done a very good job because Declan didn't know about me being a vet either," I tell them, waving off the guilt.

"That's the thing... The PI never got back to him about you at all. He's been stalling, but we don't know why. It's time for Declan to find us a new PI, I think. Thomas has some leeway to check people out with his connections, but he can't abuse that." Kai leans forward, resting his arms on his legs. "I'll call him as soon as we land."

"And I'll take you shopping to find some proper clothes." Jaxon closes the case and puts it to the side. "I'm good at shopping for women." A frown crosses my face, and Kai groans.

"Dude, really?"

"Because of Jacinta is what I mean! She used to

make me go shopping with her all the time." The jealousy I felt at his words eases away. Of course he would be with Jacinta. The idea of him trudging along after her, carrying piles of bags, is actually kind of adorable. I don't mind him standing by his sister when he's not supporting her in trying to label me a gold digger.

"Okay so how about this—It will be dinner time by the time we get to Oahu. How about I book us dinner somewhere and then we can go shopping afterward? The stores are open later in the evening, and we should be able to get you at least the essentials if not everything you need," Kai suggests, pulling out his phone and scrolling for some ideas. I look down at my outfit.

"Can we make it somewhere casual? I'm not dressed for anything fancy, nor do I have anything to get changed into," I grumble, still pissed at that bitch.

"Of course, I know this cool little beachfront café that has amazing food. We'll go there."

That sounds good enough to me, so I nod in agreement before stretching my arms above my head and letting out the yawn I've been fighting. "Harlow, you look tired, and we're still a couple hours away. Why don't you have a nap? " Jaxon points in the direction of the back of the plane. "There's a bathroom back there if you need it, and those seats recline flat." He points at the seats opposite the sofa. "There are blankets, pillows, and other things up here." He stands up and opens the cubby storage above the seats then pulls out a laptop bag.

"I've got some work I need to do. I'm scouting some new locations for clubs so we can expand our network. We don't have much in Europe, and there's a rundown resort on one of the Greek Islands that we're looking at buying." He opens the bag and pulls out his laptop, putting it down on the table in front of the sofa. "There's also a cruise line that we're looking at to expand the Neighpalm brand."

The draw of a nap is almost too alluring, but the idea of getting to know more about the two of them gives me a jolt of energy that keeps me in my seat. "That's exciting. Are you guys always looking to expand your businesses? What about you, Kai?"

"Well, we're actually looking at purchasing an ice hockey team. The team is in a bad way financially, so they're looking for a buyer. I love ice hockey, and it would be a great way to broaden our investments. The energy drink side of the business practically runs itself, so I don't have much to do with that on a daily basis. I have a great team who deals with manufacture and distribution, and I have another that deals with the extreme sports side of it. With all of that help, I'm not kept as busy as all of my brothers, so I'm looking for more of a challenge."

"Hockey?" I bounce on my chair in excitement. "Oh, which team? I love hockey."

"The Colorado Grizzlies." He gives me a little side eye, probably thinking that won't mean anything to me.

I wince when he tells me. "Oh yeah, they're having a *dismal* season. They really need some new blood, and from what I heard their coach is an asshole and a drunk, not to mention those rumors regarding the owner's son."

I wink, completely delighted by the look of total surprise on Kai's face. "Chuck and Melinda had me on skates and horses almost as soon as I could walk. They were huge fans of keeping little girls busy and giving us the chance to develop some active habits at a young age. I won't claim to be as big of an adrenaline junkie as you, but I definitely grew up loving that feeling of flying down the ice or on the back of a horse. I haven't had a chance to get back on the ice much since I was so busy with school, but I'd love to get out there again."

Kai's eyes light up with excitement. "That's awesome! We'll have to hit the ice when we get back for a little one on one."

That does sound like fun, but I'm hit with another yawn and decide it's time to take the opportunity to nap. Standing up, I stretch again before reaching for the blankets and pillow that Jaxon pointed out. I can feel their eyes on me, and when I turn around, both of them are staring at my ass. They both jump when I clear my throat, sheepish grins on their faces as they realize they've been caught.

"Can you pass me the other laptop bag?" Kai asks, running his hand through his hair, a cheeky grin on his face. His request means I have to turn around and stretch up again to reach it, but I'm sure that's a *total* coincidence. Despite the roll of my eyes the moment I turn around, I'm smiling.

"Don't think I don't know what you're doing," I growl playfully, and they both chuckle. Passing him the bag, I take a seat on the chair and Kai shows me which button to press so it lays out. It's surprisingly comfy, and I put a pillow under my head while he throws a blanket over my body.

As my eyes close, he leans in and gives me a kiss on my cheek, bringing a smile to my lips.

"Next time tell my brothers to let you sleep in a little longer instead of waking you up so early," Kai whispers in my ear before brushing my hair back and returning to his chair. I crack an eye open and find he's watching me. When he sees me look, he winks and grins before looking back down at his laptop.

Shit, Kai must have heard us this morning. I wasn't really thinking about who else might be around, but of course, his room is directly across from mine. He doesn't seem upset, so I'm not going to let it worry me. *But hang on, since when did I back down so easily?*

"Maybe next time you can come and join us," I

mumble back, watching him closely. His head shoots up, and he looks at me wide eyed. This time, I wink, and just before I roll over and put my back to both of them, I catch him adjusting the bulge that has appeared in his pants. Yeah, that's what you get for teasing me.

Chapter Twenty

Kai

The rest of the flight is quiet. Harlow naps while Jaxon and I do some work. I set up appointments with the agents of the two surfers I want to check out and book us a snorkeling tour to do once all of the business is out of the way. Hawaii is one of my favorite places to go, and with how little of the world she's gotten to see, I want to make sure she loves it too.

"Do you want to come snorkeling with us?" I ask Jaxon before I make the booking.

He looks up from his laptop. "I've got meetings with contractors for the next two days. I wanted to squeeze in as much as possible so I could get at least one day with our girl."

I smile as a feeling of warmth flows through me at his words. Yeah, *our* girl. I like the sound of that.

"Ok, well, we're going to head to the North Shore tomorrow, so I can check out these two surfers I'm interested in. I wanted to take her along to see them with me because I thought she'd get a kick out of watching them surf the famous Pipeline. After that, we're heading to Waikiki for a longboard lesson. The next day, I'm going to take her to one of the waterfalls and maybe have a picnic and a swim, and then I've chartered a helicopter for the afternoon to do some sightseeing by air."

Okay, part of me knows that I might be overdoing this, but I can't do what the others can. I'm not as suave as they are, and I don't have Thomas' 007 thing going on, or Oli and Holden's… whatever the hell it is they have. But I can show Harlow that she's special, giving her experiences she's never had and stealing her away from the bad parts of the world for a while. I want her to know the real me, and the guy that can do those things is definitely a huge part of who I am, but soon, I'm going to have to share the rest of me with her. I think that I just want to show her that I'm worth it before I throw my baggage on her shoulders.

"Dude, that sounds awesome." My brother sounds a little envious, but I'm not going to feel guilty. If I'm going to share Harlow with them, then I'm going to make the most of the time I get to spend with her. He'll find his own way to have some special time with her. If I know Jaxon, he's already got something underway.

"How about that last day, we do a snorkeling tour in the morning? We can take her to the Honolulu Zoo in the afternoon. I overheard Nana and Poppy talking, and they said she loves exotic animals. I guess she wants to do an internship at a zoo, and even had an interview before Holden got shot, but she didn't get the position because of the crap with the billboard." Jaxon's eyes tighten, and his mouth purses. I know that he feels more guilty about it now, which is good. That can't get Harlow's opportunity back, but Jaxon is a fierce person to have by your side, almost as bad as Jacinta, so maybe we can all work together to try and fix this.

"God, I should have stopped Jacinta." He runs a frustrated hand through his hair until it sticks out like he's touched an electric fence. "Between my own fuck-ups and not stopping Jacinta from making her own, I have so much to make up for." He blows out a defeated sigh.

"I have faith in you, man. How about you have tomorrow evening with her alone since I get her during the day? If you get your meetings finished, you can come on the helicopter tour as well. We could take her out somewhere special on that last night before we leave. If we're all in this, then it's not some kind of competition. Would I love to have more time alone with her? Yeah. Do I want to share some time so that you can make things right and we can make her happier in the long run? Fuck yeah.

We're brothers, and if we get this relationship situation off the ground, we're a team."

"Good plan," he tells me, looking happier. "Make it fancy and I'll make sure she has something nice to wear for it."

"Okay, will do. We'll have to bring her back again for a longer stay so she can do all the other things, but for a short trip I think she's going to love everything we've got in store for her." With that, the two of us go silent, each lost in their own thoughts or work, and my mind flashes back to Harlow's whisper.

When she suggested that maybe next time I should join them, my cock got so hard in my pants it was uncomfortable. Each of us is as kinky as the next, and joining in really wouldn't have bothered me. Not with Oliver and Holden, I'm not inclined that way, but I would have liked to help please Harlow. For the two of them, their prior relationship trumps a brotherly one, but they're strictly in the family category for the rest of us.

But maybe you'll get your chance on this trip, whispers through my mind, and I unabashedly adjust myself again. I already know there's a gift basket waiting in her room, packed with all kinds of toys, as Jaxon's first attempt at an apology. If nothing else, she'll be able to have some fun on her own while I lay in my suite and dream about all the things I'd like to be doing to her. I'm not totally sure what Harlow's into, but I have a feeling she'll adapt. She's potentially tying herself to six men who all have less than vanilla tastes in the bedroom, so I guess we'll find out pretty quickly.

I, for one, am beyond ready to find out. It's my opinion that she'd look beautiful tied up, but I'm willing to go slow. She's worth it.

The sun is setting on the horizon once we eventually land in Honolulu. Harlow slept until about ten minutes before we landed, though that's no surprise. We went straight from the airport to our dinner reservation, snagging a seat on an open balcony with magnificent views. The ocean in front of us was glassy and still, and the view over the bay was spectacular. The colors of the setting sun reflected off the ocean, creating a magical effect. The meal was filled with easy questions, and Jaxon and I were locked onto Harlow's lips the entire time, transfixed with her stories about why she loved exotic animals and the career she was hoping to establish.

An hour or so later, I'm still fondly thinking about our dinner as I pull the Jeep into the parking lot of the shopping complex Jaxon directed me to. The reason that we're here pops back into my head, and I realize I should update the others. Plus, that'll give Jaxon a little time to work on his one on one time with our girl. Staying where I am, I pull out my cell phone. "You guys go ahead. I'm going to make a call and find out how Holden is doing, and I want to talk to Declan about those things we discussed."

As they wave goodbye and disappear into the nearest shop, I make my call to my oldest brother, hoping that he may have a few ideas regarding the whole situation.

"Hey, how's paradise?" Declan's deep voice answers after the second ring. "I can't believe I had to stay here and deal with these meetings. I would have loved to do some snorkeling with Harlow." I smirk at how disgruntled he sounds.

"So I take it you've changed your mind?" I tease, even though I'd had no doubt about it.

"Fully committed. I've even told Jacinta. Of course she just said 'duh' and 'of course you are.' Then she proceeded to lecture me on the best ways to woo a woman. Fucking hell, Kai, when she started giving me tips on the best way to go down on one, I ran. Like... what the fuck? I'm not some fucking horny teenager." Declan sounds disgusted, but I'm laughing so much I have tears running down my face. Jacinta likes to fuck with us all, but because he's normally the responsible straight and narrow one, he gives her the best reactions.

After I calm down, I ask him about Holden and Dec reports that he's doing well and that he and Oliver are acting like a couple of lovestruck teenagers, neither wanting to let the other out of their sight for too long. "We'll let them get away with it for a week or so since the shooting really shook us all up, but they'll need to go back to work eventually. Hope came out to talk Neighpalm Records with Holden, and while she was here, Oliver made some calls about the East Coast shop, but he still needs to interview a few artists for it. At least they were all amenable to coming out here for the interview. It also helps that Jonah's going to be around to see them too." Declan rambles on about a few more business things, but eventually, I get a chance to tell him about the suitcase debacle and my theory. He was livid that she would have the audacity to do something like that. Getting a new PI and having them dig into Cecelia is on the top of his list.

Neighpalm Industries does extensive background checks, especially for employees in positions like Cecelia's, but that only guarantees that she was clean at the time she was hired. We don't routinely conduct follow up checks once someone is formally working with us, so who knows what shady shit she could be into now. Though if she checks out clean again, that might be worse. All it would do is point a bigger arrow at the theory that she has something on Dad.

The biggest thing we disagree on is whether or not we should confront Dad or talk to Nana and Poppy yet. I'm a bigger fan of just getting this out in the open, but Dec is of the opinion that confronting

Dad could just lead to an even more complicated problem and that talking with Nana and Poppy might stress them out too much. I hate to admit it, because I want this settled, but he's got a point. If Cecelia really has something on Dad, something bad, then we need a plan of attack before there's any chance she knows we're onto her. Otherwise, it could be catastrophic for Dad as well as Neighpalm Industries.

Once that matter's settled, I let him go, knowing he's itching to get started. I expect Jaxon and Harlow to be a little while longer, so I decide to head inside one of the shops on my own to kill some of the wait. By the time I leave, not only do I have a spring suit that's hopefully in her size, thanks to Jacinta's advice, but I also have an extra special surprise. A silver anklet from one of the displays caught my eye, the delicate chain decorated with charms in the shape of a dolphin, fish, and sea turtle. Maybe this could be the start of a new tradition for us, adding something to represent the experiences that we plan to give her and all the adventures ahead of us. With a final check of my phone, I finish up and tuck the small bag with the anklet into my pocket before rushing back to the car. I want it to be just my secret for now, so I can maybe plan some special way to give it to her. Now I just have to come up with an idea...

Chapter Twenty-One

Harlow

Shopping with Jaxon is fun. He's flirty and attentive but not overbearing. It helps that he's hot and all the sales assistants are extremely helpful… *overly* helpful if you ask me.

I'm trying on a dress in the dressing rooms with Jaxon waiting just outside when I overhear one of them approaching.

"Is your sister okay? It's so cute that you take your sister shopping," the girl coos, fawning all over him. Seriously... his *sister*. Yeah, nope! I never knew that I would be the jealous type, but I've definitely got some feelings right now.

I step out wearing the dress I'd grabbed off one of the racks. It's a strapless body con that fits me like a glove and would definitely get two thumbs up from Max. It has a typical Hawaiian floral print, and it sits somewhere between my knees and thighs. "I don't know. I think this one fits pretty good. What do you think, not my brother Jaxon?" The sales girl's face wrinkles as she tries to figure out what I just said, but I'm watching Jaxon and his reaction. His eyes bulge, and he swallows as he runs his gaze the length of my body. "Do you think this will be suitable for a dinner with you and not my brother Kai?"

He finally snorts at what I've just said and stands up, walking over and wrapping an arm around my waist. "Well, not my sister Harlow, I say you look good enough to eat, so maybe instead of dinner *with* me and Kai, you can be dinner *for* us." He swoops in and fuses his mouth to mine, and the fawning sales girl is immediately forgotten about. There's no hesitation on his behalf, and as his scent surrounds me and everything else falls away, I'm dropped back into the memory of us and the night-club and all the things he had done to my senses. By the time he pulls away, I'm breathing heavy and thanking god that I kept my underwear on under the dress.

Calling over his shoulder, he says to the sales girl, "I'll take all of them like this in this size."

"But there are like ten different designs, and they're three hundred dollars apiece!" Obviously, she doesn't recognize Jaxon.

He pulls away from me and digs around in the pocket of his shorts, pulling out his wallet and then a black credit card. Without looking at her, he hands it over his shoulder, his gaze still fixed on mine. He watches me as I run a finger over my lips, savoring the still-present tingle, and smirks, winking before he turns around.

"We'll take everything she tried on, and she'll need some shoes too. I'll have a look while she's getting changed," he instructs, and the sales girl stands there a little speechless until she finally comes to her senses. She quickly rushes in and grabs everything I've already tried on, leaving the booth empty other than my clothes and the dress I'm still wearing. She bundles it all up, grabs the card, and disappears with it, leaving just me and Jaxon in the dressing area. He stalks toward me, and I back up until I'm in the booth and have nowhere left to go. Crowding in close to me, he pulls the door closed behind him. He runs his nose up one side of my neck, inhaling before he groans.

"God, I've had the smell of you in my mind since that day, and getting the taste back in my mouth makes me want to drop to my knees and see what you taste like elsewhere."

Fuck me! I want that too, but he must see the hesitation in my eyes that my libido wants to ignore. He places a couple of kisses on my neck, each light touch having enough suction that I'm pretty sure he's going to leave a mark. "But I know I have to make up for my mistakes before I can get my reward, so I'm going to back out of this booth and let you get dressed before I try and convince you to change your mind." He kisses me hard once more and then turns, leaving me a panting, quivering mess. My knees buckle before I collapse onto the bench in the dressing room, my hands clenched in fists as I try to calm myself.

Jaxon is so fucking addictive. When he's not being a douche, he is so magnetic, and just like the first time, I find myself drawn to him. It took everything in me not to just push him down to his knees, but we're not there yet. I'm both glad and incredibly disappointed that I was able to use some of my very thin self-control to not cave to my lusty self.

When my breathing gets back to normal, I peel off the dress, my belly button ring glinting in the rooms lighting. A smile crosses my face as I remember Alex and me deciding we were going to get something pierced during the few days of Summers-fueled rage after the premiere. Probably not my smartest decision, and I have vague memories of Shane trying to stop the both of us, but Alex insisted he get something in solidarity with me. Or maybe it was the other way around. Who knows?

Though the memory of Alex and my decision is one that makes me laugh, the event that led to it doesn't have such pleasant feelings attached to it. *Better to keep moving forward for now.* I grab the clothes Jacinta lent me and hurriedly get dressed, eyeing the pile of new clothes. Not only have I got the dresses, but I've found shorts, shirts, a sweater, and a comfy pair of jeans. I also need to grab a bra, some panties, and a pair of sneakers as well.

Picking up the dress and throwing it over my arm, I head back out the front. The sales girl is half draped over the counter, still trying to flirt with Jaxon, but his gaze is on his phone in his hand. He looks up as I approach, and a grin crosses his face.

"All good, not my sister Harlow?" I chuckle and try to place the dress on the counter, settling for placing it on top of some overstuffed bags.

"Just let me grab some more underwear," I tell him, heading to the rack where those are. "And I need some shoes."

"I grabbed these, but I wasn't sure what size." He holds up a sexy pair of silver and black heels which will go with all the dresses that he liked. Wow, he has great taste. I smile back at him, but I try not to let it grow too big. The man's already got a big enough ego. *Though maybe he's earned a little bit of it.*

"Oh, I like them! Size nine, please." He smiles, thrilled with my response, and turns to the sales girl, just barely missing the disgruntled look that took over her face while he couldn't see her.

She scurries away to get the right size, but as she passes me, I pick up a pair of nearby sneakers. "Can I also get these in a nine too, please?" She nods, not meeting my eyes, and continues on her way.

Jaxon's phone beeps again. "That's Kai. He's waiting for us at the fountain in the middle of the mall," he tells me, so I quickly pick out the underwear I need and add it to the pile at the counter. He eyes it with interest but doesn't say anything. I may or may not have picked out a few strappy and lacy pairs. I'm not entirely sure where this trip might take me, take us, but a girl's gotta be prepared for any circumstance.

Finally, we are all rung up and the clothes are packed into carry bags. I swear the sales girl deliberately took her time getting my shoes, but it's not like it scored her any extra time with Jaxon. The two of us spent the time quietly talking back and forth, just sharing pleasant small talk while we waited.

As she hands Jaxon back his card, her number written on the freaking receipt, I see red. Leaning in, I wrap my arms around his neck and kiss him hard, and if I accidentally throw in a little groping, well, that's my secret. When I pull away, he looks a little dazed, so I pluck the receipt from his hand with a smug smile. I look up, making sure to meet the sales girl's eyes, then slowly rip the receipt in half. She doesn't deserve any more of my energy. With that, I pick up my bags and exit the store, Jaxon right behind me chuckling under his breath.

"Jesus, did you just channel Jacinta? She would've approved of you putting that girl in her place." Turning, I wink at him.

"I don't know about that, but no one likes a woman hitting on the person they're with whether they're involved or not. It's just rude. But Jacinta is a gorgeous, confident woman, so I'm sure she wouldn't put up with that shit either."

We hurry down an escalator that isn't too crowded, and I see Kai across the mall, sitting on a bench in front of the fountain. Perched next to him, swinging his legs back and forth, is a small boy. Possibly six or seven. The two of them look to be having an animated conversation.

When we get closer, I can see that the boy is wearing a Scooby Doo t-shirt, and it seems they're having a conversation about their favorite episodes.

"Shaggy and Scooby are my favorite," I hear the little boy tell Kai. "I always wanted a dog, but my parents won't let me have one. They say I'm not responsible enough. Mom says I eat as much as Shaggy and she's not sure she could afford to have both me and a dog who eat that much." He's grinning as he tells Kai this, so I'm assuming it's a running joke between him and his mom.

Kai looks up as we approach. "See, here's my brother and our girlfriend Harlow. Hey, guys, this is Sam."

Sam waves at us in the confident way some children have. "Do you really have two boyfriends?" he asks innocently. Not looking at either of the two 'boyfriends,' I nod my head.

"Yup, sure do." *Not even going to tell him I have five.* His eyes go wide in that adorably naive way that only little kids are capable of.

"Wow, my mom should have two boyfriends.

She's so busy working three jobs that she doesn't have time for anything else, but if she had two boyfriends, she could have more time to spend with me and they could look after her too!"

Gah, the innocence of children. My heart breaks for the child in front of us as a harassed-looking young woman rushes up to us. She doesn't look like she's much older than early twenties. She's wearing a faded pair of jeans and a shirt that's seen better days. Tears streak her face, and her hair is messy like she's been pulling at it. Poor girl is frantic.

"Sam, there you are. I couldn't find you, and I was so worried." She throws her arms around him and pulls him against her chest. He hugs her back but then untangles himself a moment later.

"I found the fountain like you told me to if I ever got lost," he declares proudly.

"You did great," she praises, calming slightly now that she's found her precious child.

"This is my friend Kai and his girlfriend and her other boyfriend," Sam tells his mom, pointing to all of us.

She smiles at us, but it's that wary smile you give to strangers, especially strangers talking to your child. "Hi, I'm sorry if he was any trouble."

"No trouble, I was just keeping him company until you showed up. He was sure you would so he wasn't upset at all," Kai tries to reassure her.

I watch them as he tries to ease her worries, easily seeing that she's exhausted; the dark circles under the eyes give it away immediately. The clothes she's wearing are a little too big on her small frame, and she sways like she hasn't had a good meal in a long time. Poor girl is run ragged, and Sam said she works three jobs. No wonder she's ready to collapse.

Jaxon must be able to see the same thing I can. He grabs out his wallet, pulls a business card out of it, and hands it to the girl. "I don't mean to pry, but Sam mentioned that you worked three jobs. That can't be easy, and it mustn't leave much time to spend with him."

She folds her arms defensively, practically bristling at his words. "I do what I have to to keep a roof over our head and meals on the table," she snaps, and he holds up his hands.

"No, of course you do. I mean no judgement. I'm interviewing staff for the new hotel I'm opening soon. Why don't you come down and interview? I'm sure we can find you a full-time, well-paying job with medical. That way you'll have more time to spend with your boy here."

"Neighpalm Industries?" she asks, looking down at the card in her hand. "That's that new hotel on the beachfront that people claim is a sex hotel." She doesn't sound disgusted, just curious, and when I look at Sam, I can see that Kai has distracted him again. Excited snippets about Spiderman and the Avengers reach my ears, but I focus back on Jaxon's conversation before I can really figure out what they're saying.

"Well, kind of?" Jaxon says, looking a little sheepish. "Come in tomorrow at eleven and I'll show you around so you can judge for yourself. Then, if you're still interested, we'll find you something. Neighpalm has no problems with their employees learning on the job."

The woman looks like she wants to, but there's still a little bit of suspicion in her eyes.

"Look them up online," I tell her. "It will prove to you that it's all above board. None of the employees will be expected to have sex with the customers. It's not like that," I assure the woman, and Jaxon looks horrified.

"God, no. Did you think it was a brothel?" he asks her, dumbfounded, and she shrugs.

"I never trusted local rumors, but they *do* gossip."

"No, definitely not a brothel, and you will *not* be required to have sex with the guests. But the hotel is about helping the guests meet their fantasies, so you may be asked to procure them things that are not necessarily available in the local mall. As long as you're open-minded, it shouldn't be a problem. Like I said, I'll give you a run down when you come in for an interview. There's no obligation, just come and check it out."

She agrees, and when we finally leave the mall, Sam's mom Kara looks almost excited for tomorrow. I hope that Jaxon can help her out. Then Sam won't have to grow up with an absent parent. Unlike mine, she seems to care about him, and it's not through lack of wanting to spend time with him but her circumstances. It will be awesome if we can at least do something to lessen that burden.

Harlow

After a quick stop at a nearby supermarket to grab the other things I need to replace, we finally make it to the hotel. Because it isn't open to the public yet, there's no concierge to greet us or valet to park the car when we arrive, so Kai drives straight into the underground parking once Jaxon opens the gate for us. Grabbing out our luggage, including my empty suitcase and all the shopping bags, we take the elevator up to the foyer using Jaxon's all-access master pass.

When the doors open to the foyer, we step out into the polished movie set of *The Great Gatsby*. Lots of reds and golds and brass. A magnificent chandelier hangs as a centerpiece to the foyer, and red velvet drapes cover some of the white walls. The furnishings are all draped with plastic, so I can't get a good look at those, but the bare walls have paintings on them that are all a little naughty in nature... only if you look too closely at them. In big vases, large feathers are used instead of floral decorations, and an actual gramophone is set in the corner, all of it bringing to mind guests walking the lobby wearing silk and fringe and drinking champagne. Altogether, it's a rather sensual feast for the eyes that sets the tone for the hotel perfectly.

"Wow, Jaxon. This looks amazing," I tell him as he leads us to the check-in desk and walks round behind it. It's a little weird to be the only people here, no staff around, but I kind of like it too. I always wanted to be locked in a department store after hours as a kid, and this feels a little like that.

"Yeah, the designer did an impeccable job," he tells us, looking pleased. "She's a new one that I decided to take a risk on, and I think she knocked it out of the park."

"I'll say!" Kai exclaims, picking a feather out of the vase on the counter and trying to tickle me with it. Giggling, I knock it away. "You should get her to redo some of the older properties."

"That was my plan. A couple of them really need a face lift." He fiddles with something behind the counter, handing us both plastic cards when he comes back around to us. "I wanted to go with old-fashioned keys for all the rooms, but the team decided that it just wasn't a good idea for security or convenience, so we went with the cards," he tells us as he picks up his bag and a few of mine then leads us back to the elevator.

"How long until the hotel is ready?" I ask him as he pushes the button for the third floor.

The three of us stand close, not uncomfortably so, but my nerves are already tingling from the almost contact as the doors whoosh closed and the elevator starts to move.

"Most of the rooms are finished. It's just the dungeon and the penthouse that need to be completed in the main structure now, then some of the villas on the grounds."

Dungeon?

"The underground space isn't all parking. There's a dungeon room that's modeled off an old castle torture chamber, but it has some fun sexual aids in it. It's also completely windowless so it helps with that sense of sensory deprivation. Our goal was to provide a safe place to set the mood and let everyone indulge in their fantasies."

The elevator comes to a stop and he leads us out, turning left and walking down the hall. "The penthouse is a fun suite. We've designed it so there are four hidden rooms. There's of course the red room of pain from that movie, along with a role play room featuring a huge wardrobe of costumes. The last two are theme rooms; one is a library with couches and a rolling ladder along the shelves. It's for that ultimate *Beauty and the Beast* fantasy or those clients who prefer school girl/teacher. That one has costumes too. The other one is set up like a bedouin tent for the harem girl/guy fantasy. By keeping those spaces hidden, it gives that extra feeling of naughtiness to the act as well as a sense of fun when they have to find them. We don't tell them how; they've got to look for them."

I feel my panties starting to flood with desire. I wouldn't mind staying in the penthouse the next time we come here. Thank goodness both of the guys are slightly in front of me; otherwise, I'm sure they would see my pupils dilated with lust. But as we continue to walk down the hall, I watch Kai subtly adjust himself. *I guess he's thinking along the same lines as me.*

Jaxon stops at a door, giving that guy nod that seems to mean a thousand different things. "This is yours, Harlow. Kai and I are on either side of you." As he speaks, he slides the card through the reader then takes a step back after pushing the door open. "A lot of the rooms have different themes. There's the jungle room, the caveman room, the 80s porn room, rock and roll room, medieval room, and the ice room, just to name a few. Some are themed to a certain country, like Egypt or Morocco, and we have a lot of movie-themed rooms as well. There are also suites for people with fetish kinks like furries and ponyplay, so we really are hoping to make this an inclusive spot for all kinds of clients. I wasn't sure what might be your interest, and I didn't want to presume anything, so I gave you one of our completed unthemed suites."

Stepping inside, I look around the gorgeous room. Done in muted but sensuous colors, it's a masterpiece. A humongous bed is the centerpiece, the size guaranteeing it must be custom-made. There's enough room for five people, possibly more if they don't mind cuddling up with one another. The bed itself is a platform style that has been designed to look like it's floating, and there's lighting underneath it to accentuate that.

Stepping up to it, I run my hand across the light gray velvet cover that looks inviting and sexy before my eyes go to the matching button-tufted upholstered headboard behind the bed. This one is a much darker gray that shimmers slightly in the low light. A mountain of pillows is piled high on the bed, and I barely resist the urge to launch myself into them. Instead, I flick the switch on the funky black lamp shades sitting on the mirrored bedside tables. Plopping down on the bed, my eyes roam the room, the excited thrill humming across my skin with the thoughts of all the naughty things we can do in here.

In front of the bed, running along the wall, is a long low chest of drawers and cabinets, and sitting above that is a mirror that practically spans the length of the room. Beyond the bed is a seating area with a couple of plush couches and a coffee table, gray velvet drapes behind that setup which must cover a window.

"Wow, this is gorgeous, Jaxon. People are going to love this place! It's such a fun idea." I go back to the entrance and grab my suitcase and all the shopping bags I can carry, putting them on the chest of drawers. Jaxon strolls into the room and picks a binder up off the bedside table.

"And not only will we offer a room service menu, we'll offer a pleasure menu too. We have the whole range of Sugar and Spice products available for purchase, plus each room comes with free condoms and lube. In case we're lacking something, our pleasure concierge will be available to get clients anything they want. For example, if one of our guests wants to indulge in sploshing, the concierge will procure whatever food they require and bring out a plastic cover to protect the surfaces of the room they wish to use."

"How does one go about keeping everything... How do I put this delicately... sanitary?" It's something I've always wondered about. While I haven't had much hands on experience outside of those college threesomes, even women watch porn. We have needs too.

"We have two sets of all costumes and props; the ones that have been used will be removed and taken down to our laundry for cleaning. We have a number of processes depending on the material. All surfaces get sanitized, and each of the beds has a protective layer of plastic between the mattress and the bedding. It's extremely thin, and we put a thick fabric mattress protector between it and the sheets so you can't feel it." He goes over to the bed and untucks a corner, lifting it up to show me. "It gets changed each time the room is vacated and cleaned. In fact, I think you'll find our process is better than a lot of the five-star hotels in the world. It's almost as good as sleeping on a brand new mattress every day."

"Well, that's good to know."

"So the three of us are the only people here."

"But didn't Chris and James say they were staying here?" I interrupt, and he smiles.

"I put them up at the other Neighpalm property this time round and promised they could indulge here on their next trip. I want them to get the full experience, and we're not quite ready for that yet," Jaxon explains before continuing. "None of the employees are working overnight since we don't have any guests, but they're here during the day as they continue to set up the hotel and figure out how to best streamline our services. That means room service is unavailable," he adds apologetically, "but the chef will be here early in the morning, and he's making some test dishes for us to try out. We still haven't finalized the menu, so this will be a great way to make some decisions."

Kai's been quiet while Jaxon has been telling us all about his hotel, but he steps forward now.

"Tomorrow morning I've got an appointment to meet with two guys who I'm hoping to add to my new extreme team. If you're up to it, I'd like it if you came with me to meet with them. I thought you and I would head to Waikiki beach afterward, rent a malibu, and I'll give you a surf lesson and catch some waves of our own."

A thrill of excitement runs through me, both at the thought of spending the day with Kai and having a surf lesson. I'd always marveled whenever I saw someone surfing with the elegance and determination required to conquer the forces of nature like that. Surfing wasn't something that I ever got to experience since I'd grown up in Connecticut and couldn't travel without my mom's permission, but I've seen competitions online and on tv. I'd never thought about ever taking a lesson, thinking it was something you just grew up doing, so to have a chance to give it a go is thrilling, and I can't help but give Kai brownie points for thinking about it. Might not be as many as Declan for the castle tour, but who am I kidding? Kai was probably in the lead anyway.

"I've got to work all day tomorrow, so you guys are on your own. I'm hoping to join you in the afternoon the following day, but you're definitely mine for dinner that night. If that's okay?" Jaxon asks me. The little note of uncertainty in his voice makes me smile. I like this side of him that actually leaves wiggle room to adjust based on what I do and don't want, instead of making assumptions and deciding things for me.

"Yeah, that sounds good. I can't wait to spend time with both of you." They look pleased with my answer, and a sense of warm desire flows through me. It feels good to be wanted.

After talking a little bit more about what they have planned, they both say goodnight with much too quick hugs. It's all I can do to give each of them a kiss on the cheek and pull myself back so that they can head into their rooms on either side of me.

Closing the door behind me, I give in to my urges and take a running leap onto the bed, rolling around in excitement. God, the bed feels like I'm laying on a cloud, enveloping my body in such a way that I don't know how I'll climb out in the morning. Grabbing a pillow, I shove it over my head and scream, letting out all of the nerves and emotions that I've been bottling up all day. In fact, for weeks now. This is the first time I've really been alone in days, and I needed that.

Breathing heavily, I let the pillow fall to the side. As all the tension leaves my body, I pick up the plea-sure menu and have a read through it. Wow, the variety of things offered has me sitting up. There are pages and pages. It's not even a menu, really, but a book. Mind boggled from all the options and their descriptions, I drop it onto the bed and climb off it, not sure what to do with myself next, but when I glance around the room, something catches my eye. Over on the coffee table there's a gift basket, and I actually get to be excited this time. Recent surprises have *not* been good ones, but I'm feeling comfortable and safe with Jaxon and Kai, and my heart doesn't immediately leap into my throat at the unexpected sight. The cellophane wrapping crinkles loudly in the silence of the room as I untie the bow around the top.

Pulling back the wrapper, I pick up the note nestled in the offerings.

Harlow, I'm sorry I was such an ass when you asked about samples that day in my office. I was so out of line. Please take this basket as a token of my apology. Jaxon

Smiling, I place the note on the table and start digging through my surprise gift. Firstly, I pull out a bottle of expensive champagne and a gorgeous glass to drink it with. Then there's a selection of chocolate-covered strawberries. *Very nice indeed.* Putting them both to the side, I keep searching, but once I see the other items, I feel my cheeks heat. I squirm at the thought that Jaxon may have picked these items specifically for me. The first thing I pull out is a bottle of lube, followed by a large silicone dildo. It's probably seven inches, so a good size. There are also handcuffs, nipple clamps, and a flogger, but the thing that catches my eye is one of those weird-looking clitoral stimulators. I've seen hilarious reviews about these and been curious but had never done anything about it. Further under the toys are a couple of books, a new note placed atop them.

Harlow, Jacinta told me that you're really into RH books. These are a couple she said she had read and would recommend. Xoxo

Grabbing out the books, the lube, and the clit toy, I throw them on my bed and head to the bathroom for a shower. I'd like some background noise, so I pick up the remote from the table and start pressing buttons, hoping something will turn on. But as I hit a big green button, a whirring noise sounds and down from the roof drops a large screen tv. With another click, it turns on, and imagine my surprise when a menu of porn streaming sites pops down. There's also Netflix and other movie streaming channels, but the majority is porn. There's even a couple of hentai sites. Looking between the tv and the door, I wonder how sound-proof the rooms are. *Maybe I'll just wait until I've had my shower.*

Throwing the remote on the bed with the other things, I enter the bathroom. Like every-thing else, it's beautifully designed, with dark grays and black marble. A large bath is the focal point of the room, with a door leading to a separate toilet. There's a vanity with a large mirror, and the shower is a glassed masterpiece tucked around another marble tiled wall. You need to press buttons to get it to work, and when it does, a rain-fall of water pours from the ceiling. Getting undressed, I make the most of the amazing shower without worrying about how much hot water I use, unlike my little one back home in the stables.

My mind blanking of everything, I feel the tension leave my body. I'm truly relaxed for the first time in weeks. It's been nice not constantly looking over my shoulder today, worrying about when the stalker may strike next, and my mind drifts to my two companions and all the things we could get up to over the next couple of days. I'm hoping I can convince Jaxon to give me a tour of the hotel since there are no guests at this stage. It might not be the most glamorous way to spend our time, but I want to appreciate every chance that I have to hang out with him. It's an investment in building something, I hope.

Climbing out and drying off, I wipe some of the condensation off the mirror and really look at myself. Do I look any different after all that has happened in such a short period of time? Cleaning my teeth, I think back over the last couple of weeks. I've made new friends, and I'm pretty sure they're going to be solid and reliable friends, not just the type that flit in and out of your life. I've made huge inroads into developing a solid and loving relationship with the man I had wished so hard for all my life. And I've opened my mind to relationships of a more intimate nature than I've ever had before. Based on all of that, I almost feel like I should be unrecognizable. But as I study myself, I still see that unsure girl who got onto the plane what feels so long ago even though I no longer feel the same.

A self-satisfied grin crosses my mouth as I finish my teeth. Blowing that girl in the mirror a kiss, I walk naked back out to the bedroom, throwing myself down on the bed. Flicking through the porn menu, I make sure the volume level isn't too loud just in case the walls are thin. A sigh escapes as I settle back into a comfortable position, ready to take care of some of the sexual frustration that has been building up for weeks. Oliver's fingers helped this morning, but it only took the edge off, so let's see if I can help a little more.

Chapter Twenty-Three

Harlow

The following morning, I'm up early, having slept like a log thanks to that godly mattress. I'd been concerned that I wouldn't, having slept with Declan one night and then Oliver the next, but I guess knowing I'm thousands of miles away from the stalker made it that much easier. And maybe the self-care helped just a little as well.

After showering, I change into a pair of denim shorts, a cute yellow tank top with a hibiscus on it, and my new sneakers. I shove my swimsuit into my backpack, along with some sandals, and head downstairs, ready to check out the breakfast tasting menu.

Well placed signs show me the way and I find them both in the empty dining room at a large table covered in delicious-looking dishes, I give them both a kiss on the cheek before sitting myself in a seat in between them.

"Sleep well, Harlow?" Kai asks innocently enough, and when I glance between the two of them, they don't look like they're insinuating anything.

"Yeah, slept like a baby for the first time since this thing with the stalker all started." Then a thought occurs to me, and I add, as casually as I can, "Hey, Jaxon, are all the rooms soundproof?" I got pretty loud last night while caring for myself, and I swear that clit toy almost made me pass out. Now, whether I'm hoping they heard me or not, I'm undecided. I like this slow easing into things situation we've got going on, but I also wouldn't mind teasing the fuck out of them.

"Oh yeah, completely soundproof except for the couple of voyeuristic rooms. It's a set of three rooms that all have two-way mirrors for walls. They have the ability to turn it on and off as needed, and there are also speakers for the sound. Some people are into that kind of thing and get off on strangers watching them."

A small sigh escapes my mouth when he says this, and of course it doesn't go unnoticed. I'm finding that outside of their initial gold digger assumptions, the Summers men seem to pay too much attention to me. Kai shoots me a cheeky wink but doesn't say anything. Turning back to Jaxon, I take advantage of his excitement to tell us about this new venture of his.

"So, tell me more about your great aunt and the Sugar and Spice empire. I mean, I know about the sex toy stores, but tell me about the other thing," I ask while I dish myself some food. It looks like a frittata of some kind with mini tomatoes, spanish sausage, and layers of potato.

"The Sugar and Spice club in Vegas is basically a high-end sex club and brothel. They also provide high-end escorts for important people who want eye candy on their arm for important events. They get all the newsworthy press of a beautiful companion without the stress and pressure of a relationship." Jaxon leans back in his chair and takes a sip of his coffee, not in the least shying away from the topic. "Aunt Merideth's girls and guys are sexy and intelligent, and you would never guess they were paid to be there. Aunt Merideth has always been ahead of her time, so of course, she saw a niche market and decided to fill it. The fact that she was a woman getting involved in the sex industry shocked a lot of people, which is stupid because there have been women madams around for a very long time. She just made it into more. And you know what people are like, the more exclusive and secretive it is, the more rich, bored people flock to it. Although her member list is top secret, I've seen some *very* famous people making use of her facilities with my own two eyes."

Unwilling to sit back, Kai finishes his pastry and jumps into the conversation. "And her staff are extremely discreet. They all sign NDAs and are aware that she has the money and power behind her to have them enforced, not that it's ever been a concern. She looks after them, so none of them would betray her. Not to mention, she vets every single one of them beforehand to avoid any issues with mental or emotional instability. All of her sex workers are there because they like sex, not because they haven't got any other option. Same with the strippers and other staff. They love working for her, and even if it's only a job while they attend college, they're well paid and don't want for anything. The only rule she has is no committed relationships while working for her. Boyfriends and girlfriends can become extreme complications."

"The chain of stores is a relatively new venture, but let's face it, sex sells, and people are a lot more adventurous these days. It's mostly online sales, and she has a huge warehouse and a team of packers, but the couple of high-end stores do a roaring trade as well. She even has a design and technology team that create their own sex toys, and they're also working on virtual technology which is where they think the future of everything is going."

By the time I'm finished trying everything, I'm worried I'm not going to be able to get myself into the Jeep, but at least I can say that both food and conversation were fantastic. Saying goodbye to Jaxon, we make our way downstairs.

Kai snorts with laughter as I haul myself into the passenger seat and strap myself in while groaning and rubbing my stomach. Still chuckling, he starts up the car and pulls out of the underground parking. He's put the top down today, so as we start moving my hair blows around and into my face. But when we emerge out into the open, the sun is shining, there's no wind, and it just seems like a perfect start to the day.

"That chef of Jaxon's was a food master, wasn't he?" Kai teases as he heads away from Waikiki Beach.

"God yes, I'd gain a thousand pounds if I ate that kind of breakfast every day," I groan, wincing at the thought of everything I'd shoveled into my mouth.

"Somehow I doubt that very much," Kai comments, giving my figure a quick heated glance. "So the drive out to the North Shore takes about an hour. We're going to sit and watch the surfers at Pipeline for a little while, and then we're going to meet the two guys at a restaurant not far from there to talk to them."

"Tell me about your extreme sports teams. Are they pro surfers?"

"Yes, in the past I've used individuals to promote Neighpalm Energy Drink, but this time around, I want to create teams that travel together, live together, *and* play together. I think it will create a more cohesive dynamic. It's easy with the winter sports guys because the events they compete in usually include a range of sports, but the summer sports are a little trickier. Surfers stick to surf competitions, and mountain bikers and motocross guys stick to their own comps. So I wanted to put together a team of guys who were comfortable competing in all sports. I'm not necessarily looking for pros, more like adrenaline junkies that will try anything. They won't be competing so much as traveling and trying things all over the world. I think these two are going to fit my summer team perfectly. They're a set of brothers, twins actually, and they come from a wealthy enough background that they don't need to work." He looks at me to see my reaction, his eyes darting back to the road a moment later. I guess my expression gave me away.

"I know what you're thinking because I thought the same thing before I researched their back-ground. But they're actually not privileged assholes. When they're not taking part in death-defying sports, they do a lot of volunteer work in whatever country they happen to be in. They also give a lot to their local community and have established a youth rec center in their hometown, giving bored kids the chance to get out of the house and off the streets. It has mini golf, laser tag, archery, tram-polining, and there's even an American Ninja-style course. They offer martial arts lessons, and there's also an arts and crafts center, as well as a kitchen where children can learn to cook. All the food cooked in their lessons is donated to homeless people in the nearby area."

"Wow, that's amazing! More places need to run these kinds of programs. Have you ever thought about sponsoring them or partnering with them to make this a more country-wide initiative?" I ask, though his broad smile answers that question.

"I'm already ahead of you. That's one of things I want to discuss with them during the meeting today." He sounds excited and pleased, though I'm not sure which part is causing each reaction. Is he more excited about the possibility or the fact that I'm genuinely interested in his plans?

Before I know it, the drive is over and Kai is pulling the Jeep into an empty parking space close to the famous surf break. Jumping out, he gestures to my backpack. "Bring that. I can't lock the car without the roof on, so it's best not to leave anything in it." He reaches into the backseat and grabs out a few towels, a tube of sunscreen, and a couple of bottles of water for us both. "Can you throw these in your backpack?" he asks, passing everything over. He places a set of binoculars around his neck so that they rest over the Neigh-palm Energy Drink logo on the shirt he's wearing today. With a firm grasp of my hand, he starts leading me toward the beach.

When we get down on the sand, it's picture

perfect. The waves are gently rolling in, and the sky has held up for a clear blue extending into what feels like eternity. I don't know much about surfing, but the waves look to be forming nicely, and the surfers out on the water seem to catch them easily enough, riding for a little while before peeling backward.

Kai finds a spot he's happy with then puts the towels down and tugs me onto one. He places us so I'm sitting in front of him, his legs to either side of my hips. Placing his binoculars next to us, he pulls me back against his chest and leans his chin on my shoulder. Much like the day in the back of the truck, Kai makes me feel safe and secure and slightly turned on with his easy affection. I could definitely get used to this.

From here, the dozen or so surfers look so calm and relaxed as they bob in the ocean, waiting for a wave. "Pipeline is actually one of the most deadly surf breaks even though it looks so calm on the surface," Kai murmurs close to my ear. "It's a reef break, so it creates amazing waves that range in height up to 20 feet. The waves suck out a lot of the water, so when they wipe out, surfers can be thrown against the jagged reef. Countless people get injured each year, and some even die."

His words cause a shiver to run down my spine, and he rubs his hands up and down my bare arms. He picks up his binoculars and peers through them at the surfers out on the waves. "Did I tell you the guys I'm here to see are twins? Identical ones. Lucky for me, Tristan has longer hair at the moment so I can tell them apart, but they usually like fucking with people." He points at a surfer that's paddling toward the wave. "That's Tristan." We watch as he makes it onto the wave and is lifted by the powerful force. As it propels him forward, he effortlessly pops to his feet and rides the wave, disappearing into the short barrel before popping out on the other end where he then cuts backward off the wave.

We sit and watch for a little while longer. Occasionally, Kai will tell me something about the history of the surf break, but we watch in comfortable silence for the most part. His breath is warm on my neck as he occasionally leans closer, placing kisses on my exposed shoulder.

"I'm really glad you came with us, Harlow," Kai whispers quietly. "I really like you, and I'm enjoying having you all to myself." His words make me want to squeal and do a happy dance, but I take a deep breath and shove it down before turning and looking him in his gorgeous brown eyes.

"I'm really enjoying having you all to myself too, no interruptions, no stalker drama, just us." I lean in and press my mouth to his, taking a leap. He seems a little taken aback, like he wasn't expecting it, but he quickly recovers. Putting one hand on the back of my head and deepening the kiss, he sweeps his tongue along my lips. I gladly allow his gentle request, and he lovingly worships my mouth as his hand tightens in my hair, pulling just a little. That bite of pain is a perfect counterpoint to the delicious things his kiss is doing to the rest of my body.

Just when I'm thinking about taking this a step further, movement out of the corner of my eye has me pulling back. Kai turns to see who it is, and his eyes light up before he untangles himself from me and jumps up.

"Kai, my man! I thought it was you. Imagine my surprise seeing you with a hottie." The blond surfer has his dripping wetsuit pulled down to his waist and his surfboard under one arm, but Kai still gives him one of those man hugs, the two of them slapping each other on the back.

"Justin Owens, ready to join the winning team yet?" Kai asks, smiling widely before turning to me. "This is my girlfriend, Harlow. Justin is currently sponsored by Redbull. I keep trying to convince him to defect, but he's not interested."

Justin holds out a hand to me, and I shake it, smiling. "Nice to meet you," I say, looking up at him while shading my eyes with my free hand.

He gives me a blindingly white toothy smile. "You too. I've never seen Kai with a woman before, so you must be a pretty special lady." He turns to Kai, looking him up and down. "So, why are you here? Obviously not to surf since you've got no gear."

Kai turns back to the waves and points out the

brothers. "Here to have a chat with those two, see if they're interested in joining one of my teams."

Justin holds a hand up to his eyes, shading them, as he squints in the direction Kai pointed. "Oh, the Blaze brothers. Good choice, man. Not only are they wicked athletes, they've got good hearts too. Going to be a smart partnership for both parties. Smart, *very* smart."

They chat a little longer about mutual friends before Justin says, "Hey, I'm having a party up at the house tonight if you want to come." He points at a house not far away. "Some of the old crew will be there, and I know they'd love to see you." Kai looks at me, gauging my interest, but I just shrug and smile.

"Whatever you want to do, I'm easy. I don't think we had plans tonight, did we?"

"We might come, but I'm giving Harlow her first surf lesson back at Waikiki this afternoon. We'll see if she still feels that way afterward or if she's too sore and tired by this evening," Kai tells him, laughing.

"That's wicked, man. Good luck, Harlow, I hope you love it. Well, keep it in mind," Justin says before they do another one of those man slapping hug things. That done, he takes off down the beach.

Kai holds out a hand to me, and when I grab hold, he pulls me to my feet. "Justin is a three-time world champion and the youngest person to win the Pipeline Masters. He's also a super nice dude. We could easily be rivals because he works for the other huge energy drink on the market, but he's not like that."

After one last look, he picks up the towels and his binoculars and we head back up the beach. As we get to the top, I turn around, spying a couple of surfers making their way back to the shore.

"Come on, I know you're probably still full from breakfast, but they do some amazing açai and granola bowls at this place as well as smoothies," Kai offers as we get back to the car and climb in.

"I could eat," I tell him, and it's to the sound of his laughter that we pull back into traffic and head to his meeting.

Chapter Twenty-Four

Harlow

With a firm agreement from the Blaze twins, Kai's meeting was a success, with promises to send over contracts that would be signed the following week when they returned to LA. My surf lesson was so much fun. Kai had bought me a wetsuit to use, and we rented a large board from one of the places along the beach. We spent hours splashing around in the small surf, and by the time we had finished, I'd managed to stand up a couple of times.

By the time we make it back to the hotel and finish dinner, another variety of test dishes for the hotel's eventual menu, I'm ready to collapse, but the promise of Justin's party and Kai's excitement about it are too much to resist. Honestly, I'm just enjoying spending time with them, so I'll fight against the exhaustion and make the best of every moment I can. I'll probably be asleep on my feet by the time Jaxon has his turn tomorrow, but I have the feeling it'll be worth it. Surfing and a party today, then a luau tomorrow? This kind of stuff happens in the books I read, not real life, but I'll happily accept this fantasy for a little while longer.

By the time Jaxon drops Kai and me at a house that sits just back from the beach, it's lit up and full of people. Music is pumping out through the doors and carrying down the beach on the breeze. Holding my hand again, Kai steps through into the chaos, taking me with him. He's greeted by what feels like every second person as he makes his way through the crowd, but he doesn't stop to chat like so many of them want. Instead, he keeps going until he finds the kitchen and a whole boatload of tubs filled with ice and bottled drinks. Pulling out a beer, he raises his eyebrow at me. At my nod, he flips the top off with a bottle opener left on the bench and passes it to me before he takes another for himself. Grabbing my hand, he tows me out onto an open balcony where Justin is standing, his arms around a pretty Hawaiian girl.

Justin's face lights up when he sees Kai, and the girl in his arms squeals before launching herself at him. On instinct, he drops my hand, catching her and whirling her around in a hug before she pulls away. A prick of jealousy sits in my stomach, but she quickly moves back into Justin's arms.

"Justin didn't tell me you were coming!" she complains to him, smacking Justin on the arm.

"Erica, this is my girlfriend Harlow. Harlow, this is my distant cousin Erica. Her mom and mine were second cousins or something, but we grew up in the same neighborhood until…" He breaks off, and both Justin and Erica's faces dim, their smiles looking more unsure as sympathy creeps into their eyes. "Well, I haven't told you that story yet, but I promise I will," he assures me.

"Your *girlfriend?*" Erica gasps in surprise. "Holy shit, now I've got to hear this story!" Before he can get into it though, another group of guys approaches Justin and Kai. I step away, giving them some space to catch up, and move to a little corner of the balcony. The wind off the ocean is cold, and I'm wearing a pair of jeans I'd paired with a nice cami in a raspberry pink color, but I'd forgotten to bring a sweater. Before I have a chance to regret it, Kai joins me, sidling close to my body and angling his to block the wind.

"We won't stay too long. Just give me an hour to say hello to a few people and then we'll get going," he promises, looking down at me. He's suddenly shoved out the way as Erica pushes in, grabbing my available hand.

"Come on, it's freezing out here. I'll grab you one of my sweaters, and we'll go downstairs to huddle around the fire pit." She drags me away while Kai watches on hopelessly, unable to stop the hurricane that is his cousin. Not sure what else I can do, I wave and smile so he knows I'm okay, and the look of relief on his face is the last thing I see before she pulls me into the crowd.

After a brief stop at the kitchen to dump our empties and grab more beer, she leads me through a closed door and down a corridor. "We keep the bedrooms and things off limits during parties. Everyone knows the deal; there are two bathrooms down on the bottom level, so there's no reason for anyone to be in here."

She pushes open the door to what must be the master suite. A large bed surrounded by a white mosquito net takes up the most space in the room, with beach-inspired decor surrounding it. She ducks into a walk-in closet, swiftly coming back with a thick hoodie "We don't need these very often in Hawaii, but when Justin has to go to the mainland for things, I usually bring one," she explains, handing it to me. "Okay, now we're ready to sit by the pit while the boys talk waves and whatever."

I t's more than an hour later when Kai catches up to me, but I don't mind. Erica has kept me company the whole time, and she is seriously a nice person. She also introduced me to Justin's sister Madeline, a photographer who was visiting while in between shoots, and hearing about all the places she's been has me jonesing for some international travel. When we exhaust that topic, it's Erica's turn to grill me about how I came to know Kai. They're both fascinated and horrified by the whole story, but by the end, they were intrigued and curious as fuck about my potential six-way relationship. It's weird how comfortable I felt confiding in these two girls about such a personal matter, but I'm not going to examine the feeling too closely. I've never had that close circle of friends, but I think that Alex, Hope, and Shane are starting to teach me that I should be open to making new connections when the opportunity arises.

Kai gives Maddy a quick hug and a kiss on the cheek in hello before crouching down in front of where I'm sitting on the comfy sofa. It's positioned the perfect distance from the fire pit—close enough not to be cold but far enough not to overheat. In any case, Erica, Maddy, and I had moved from beers to shots halfway through my story, so I'm feeling no pain. I'm not hammered, but I am mellow and chilled.

"I'm so sorry." He looks so sheepish and adorable that I can't find it in me to even pretend that I'm annoyed with him. Normally, I'd totally take the chance to tease him a bit, but he's just so damn cute.

"It's fine, babe." I wave him off, and his eyes widen slightly in surprise, maybe at my sudden use of a pet name, but then a pleased smirk covers his face. "The girls have been hearing all about the shit storm that has been my life for the past few weeks." His smirk drops, and instantly, I feel bad. "No, don't do that." I scramble to sit up properly and wrap my arms around him, pulling his face to my chest. "I told them you're my absolute favorite part of the whole thing." His body starts to shake, and I pull back just enough to try and see his face. "Are you okay?"

"Sweetheart, I have never been better," he says, his voice muffled by my cleavage. "I could die a happy man right now." I pull further back as he starts chuckling. I guess I did try and smother him with my boobs.

"Oops, sorry." My cheeks start to heat with embarrassment, but he quickly shakes his head.

"Nope, don't you dare apologize! I'm glad the girls have been looking after you. Since we stayed later than expected, I had Jaxon call a car service to pick us up, and I just got a text telling me it's here. I'm sorry I haven't had a chance to catch up with you this time," he says to Erica, a frown on his face. "But we'll be back for the grand opening of Jaxon's new hotel, and I'll get him to send you an invite and a couple of complementary nights. We can catch up then."

Erica's had more to drink than me, so she starts to tilt just a little too much as she eagerly bounces up and down on the sofa. "The sex hotel!" she squeals, and Kai rolls his eyes with an exasperated sigh.

"Poor Jaxon, that's going to drive him nuts."

I giggle. "But that's what it is, and I don't think it will. He's super proud of that hotel and so he should be."

Kai hauls me to my feet, his strong grip helping to counteract the little woosh of dizziness that accompanies my quick switch to being upright. "Come on, chuckles, we need to move it. Otherwise, the driver is likely to leave without us."

Taking off my borrowed hoodie, I return it to Erica before we say our goodbyes to the two girls, heading out the front without making any stops along the way. Sitting on the road is a black limo, and Kai drags me straight to it, the driver already waiting by the open door. I slide across the seat, my teeth already chattering by the time the driver closes the door again. It's not long before we're moving back toward the other end of the island, and at this time of the night there isn't much traffic on the road.

"God, I hadn't realized it gets so cold here," I tell Kai, rubbing my arms.

He searches through the hidden cabinets until he finds a blanket before scooting over toward me, placing it over my legs, and hauling me into his arms. I snuggle in close, the warmth of his body going a long way to help. "It's the cold wind off the ocean at night and the fact that we're heading into autumn. Although it doesn't change as dramatically as the mainland, it does still cool down. It's definitely a shock after such warm days."

I practically try to burrow into his chest to steal the warmth, and by the time I'm comfortable, I'm basically sitting on his lap, causing a pained groan to leave his mouth. "Harlow, how drunk are you?" he asks through gritted teeth.

Shaking my head against his chest, I pull back and look at him, loving the heat in his eyes. My toes curl, and I squirm a little more. "Not so drunk that I don't know what I'm doing."

The words have barely left my mouth before his descends on my lips. He lays me down across the seat, his body on top of mine, and we spend the rest of the trip home making out like teenagers. Which is okay because I never did this when I was a teenager. Hands and lips roam, but clothes stay on because I don't want to start anything else here in the limo. As turned on as I am, and I can feel he is too, it's almost like a mutual agreement that we wait until we get back to the hotel.

When the limo comes to a stop, both of us scramble to get out of it, and we end up rolling off the seat, our limbs tangled in the blanket. Righting ourselves, we exit the limo, our laughter filling the silence of the night around us. Kai whips out his access card and gets the main doors open for us quicker than I can track the movements right now. Grabbing my hand, he drags me across the foyer to the elevators, still chuckling, but when the elevators open and we step inside, he puts distance between us. My bottom lip pushes out in a pout when I realize he's on the completely opposite side of the elevator, and I know I look so ridiculous that there's no way he's missing my reaction. "Babe, if I touch you now, or you touch me, there's a good chance that we won't get to your room. I'm sure it wouldn't be the last time that Jaxon's elevator was christened, but maybe we should hold off on that for now."

My eyes go to the elevator buttons, wondering if there's a pause one somewhere amongst them, but Kai immediately knows what I'm doing. Wouldn't that be a rush, going up and down in the elevator with Kai fucking me against one of the walls, and maybe, just maybe, Jaxon would find us. A groan leaves my mouth at the thought, and it's like a switch is flipped in Kai.

"Babe, you're killing me."

Unfortunately, the elevator ride is short, so none of that gets to happen, but I don't stop staring him down, letting him see my desire written plainly on my face.

"Fuck it," he growls, lunging for me, but the elevator doors woosh open. He sweeps me up into his arms and strides down the corridor. "Yours or mine?"

"Don't care." I'm basically panting now. I just want him to get to a room, any room. Fuck, Jaxon is one of the only people even in this hotel right now. Maybe the hallway is good enough?

He's practically jogging down the corridor with me in his arms, and my impatient lips travel to his neck and start to nibble. A hard bite has him stumbling and just about dropping me. "Fuck, babe, you got to stop, or I'll throw you down here."

Another giggle leaves my mouth. It's intoxicating making this man react like this, almost more than the alcohol was.

Finally, we're at my room, and he loosens his grip just enough that I can wriggle around to get my access key out of my back pocket. It's his turn to distract me now, his arms around my body and his mouth on my neck as I fumble with the card. "Kai," I whine playfully. "If you don't stop, I won't be able to open the door." He pulls away reluctantly, and I manage to swipe the card and push the door open.

The room is exactly how I left it this morning. There are no housekeeping staff working at the moment, so the bed is unmade and the toys I used last night are on the bedside table. A moment of embarrassment hits me, but I quickly shake it away. I don't care if they know I was taking care of myself last night. It's not like we aren't about to take care of each other right now.

The door slamming closed behind me has me whirling around, watching with wide eyes and excitement thrumming through my veins as Kai stalks toward me. I back up until my legs hit the bed, falling back with an oomph escaping my mouth, but the sight in front of me has me captivated. Kai pulls his shirt over his head to expose all those golden rippling muscles that I need my hands on right now. His chest is a sculpted masterpiece, and now I can check out the tribal tattoos that I hadn't paid close attention to last time he'd gotten semi-naked with me. Maybe the shadowed lighting around the spa had hidden them, but now they stand out in contrast. Over one shoulder and across the chest, the tribal swirls and dips scroll beautifully across his defined body.

"Careful, babe, you got a little drool." He smirks and points to the corner of his mouth.

"And I'm not even slightly ashamed," I tell him, though I do wipe at where he pointed. *Just in case.*

Watching as he toes off his shoes, his jeans are the next thing to go, exposing more rippling muscles and that delicious as fuck v that points like an arrow to the treasure. His skin-tight boxer briefs do nothing to hide his *very* prominent erection. *Thank god I warmed myself up last night.*

Palming himself, he stalks closer, stopping at the foot of the bed. "Now one of us is wearing a few too many clothes," he says as he unbuttons my jeans and peels them down my legs and over my feet. My hands fist the sheets as he alternates between each leg, placing kisses all the way back up. When he gets to my panties, he runs his nose over the front of them, inhaling deeply. "God, you smell amazing, and I bet you taste the same." He pushes them to the side before swiping his tongue through my folds. My thighs just about crush his head in reflex to the delicious sensation, but they slowly relax, giving him plenty of room to move.

Sitting back, he peels the panties down my legs, tossing them away to the side before going back to his task. Licking and sucking, I'm slightly embarrassed by all the noise he's making, but then he groans again, and I just let the sensations wash over me. I thought I would be more nervous, but this feels right. His genuine acceptance of me from the start and his continued support, not to mention getting to know him better over the last few days just makes this whole experience… more. More than any one night stand or friend with benefits arrangements could give me. There's a deeper level of connection, not just physical but a real emotional connection that I hadn't realised until this moment had been missing.

His tongue flicks across my clit, and I swear it's like he lit the detonator for dynamite. As he does it again, the pleasure builds at a rapid pace that has my noises joining his. Plunging two fingers into my wet channel, he curves his fingers until he hits the right spot inside of me, then that rapid pace grows even faster. I'm a panting, writhing mess when he seals his lips over my clit and sucks hard. My vision is filled with stars, and my whole body spasms as my orgasm ignites. A scream I can't control leaves my mouth, and a distant part of me is praising Jaxon for his forethought in having these rooms sound-proofed. I have the feeling that any other time I wouldn't mind Jaxon watching or even joining in, but I'm enjoying this chance to have a moment with just Kai. His fingers continue to pound into me through it all, my pussy walls doing their best to trap them in place as my back bows off the bed in pleasure.

Breathing heavy, the pleasure starts to ebb as Kai's mouth relaxes its attention on my clit. Placing kisses on my stomach, he crawls his way up the bed, removing his fingers from my channel with a slurping sound that normally would have made me cringe, but I'm too far gone to complain and he just looks too damn pleased with himself. I won't ruin this moment by getting self-conscious over things that he seems quite happy about. He sticks his fingers into his mouth, licking all the juices off them and turning me on all over again. A huge smile crosses his lips. "Fuck, Harlow, that was hot." He travels further up my body to fuse his mouth to mine, and I can taste myself on his tongue as he kisses me furiously, like he never wants our mouths to be apart. A warmth that's not from my orgasm starts to flow through my body. This guy is slowly worming his way into my heart with his honest affection and the light in his eyes that says he sees me as something special.

Breaking away from my mouth, he peppers my chest with kisses, laving attention on both nipples until I'm writhing on the bed once more, the sheets twisting up underneath my feverish body. So far I've done nothing but lay here and take it, so I push him away and rasp out, "I want a taste of you." But he silences me with another kiss.

"Baby, I promise that I will let you next time, but if I don't get inside you soon, things are going to get embarrassing for me." His eyes crinkle with his smile, but his good humor can't mask the desire that's threatening to end our evening a little too early.

He settles himself between my thighs, reaching down to line himself up. Before he thrusts, I put a hand on his arm. "It's been a while, go slow." I can't quite meet his eyes, a little embarrassed to admit that, but a finger lifts my chin, making it impossible to avoid looking into his gorgeous brown eyes.

Giving me a soft smile, he leans in and gently kisses me again. "I'll take care of you, Harlow." With my nod, he notches himself at my entrance and slowly pushes in. It's a tight squeeze, but as he works his hips back and forth, I feel myself open up to him. He's rolling his hips in a way that feels fucking amazing, and before I know it, his hips are flush with mine. I'm panting with the feeling of fullness, and he groans out loud. "Harlow, god, fuck me. Your pussy is so hot and tight, and it squeezes me *so* good."

My core throbs with his dirty talk, and he groans again. His forehead against mine, those beautiful eyes on me, he starts this smooth thrust that has my eyes just about rolling back into my head. Pulling away, he leans down and grabs one of my nipples in his mouth, alternating between sucking and nibbling.

My arms come up and my nails dig into his back as his pace increases, and he hitches one of my legs over his hip, giving him a better angle that hits exactly where I need him. Before I know it, that tingling feeling is back and my toes curl in anticipation. His pacing speeds up again, our sweat-flecked bodies sliding desperately against one another.

"Kai, I'm close." The gasp leaves my mouth between moans that only grow louder when his hand slips between us to tease me.

"Give it to me, Harlow," he demands, rubbing circles around my clit, and my orgasm explodes out of me, this one even harder than the first. My core clamps down on him as he thrusts a couple more times before stilling, his orgasm riding his body. I shout what must be nonsense because Kai starts to chuckle in between his groans of pleasure.

"Oh, Harlow, if I'm some kind of mutant sex god, then I'm pretty sure that makes you a goddess." He continues to chuckle as he leans in and kisses me while I ride the rest of my orgasm, the spasm slowly easing, though it's still sending small pulses through my entire being.

I tangle my hands in his hair and kiss him back with enthusiasm, but as he rolls off of me, he stills. "Fuck! I forgot to use a condom. Fuck, I am so sorry." I've never seen a man go from post-orgasm bliss to full blown panic so quickly. It might be the tiniest bit funny if he didn't seriously look like he was about to have a heart attack. "I promise I'm clean. I've never had sex without one, and we can go and get the Plan B pill first thing tomorrow." He runs his hands through his damp hair in agitation, and I reach out to still them.

"Kai, it's okay. I'm okay. *We're* okay. I'm on the pill, and I'm clean too, but I can get tested if you need me to. Look, whatever happened tonight, for better or worse, was thanks to choices that we mutually made. I'm a big girl who can speak up for herself, and I would have told you if there was a problem." Yes, we both got a little carried away in the moment, but I would have never let myself get that close to him if I hadn't been protected.

He grabs hold of both hands and brings them up to his lips. "No, it's okay. I trust you." Sighing with relief, he collapses back to the bed, and I snuggle against his chest, his hands running up and down my naked back as we finish catching our breath. Suddenly, the absurdity of the situation hits me, and I start to giggle uncontrollably.

"What?" he asks me, his hands stilling as his curiosity wins out. Sitting up so I can look at him, I wave my hand around.

"Just think it's funny that in a hotel designed specifically for sex, with a whole drawer full of condoms in every room, we both completely forgot about them. Now, *that's* some god-level mad sex skills."

A smile curls his lips before he grabs me and pulls me back down onto his chest. His body relaxes under me, and he starts to chuckle and tickle me. Wriggling, I gasp as he flips me over. "I'll show you some mad sex skills." His mouth descends, and that's the last chance I get to say anything for a long while. The man has some *serious* stamina.

Chapter Twenty-Five

Harlow

A knock on the door the following morning has me waking suddenly and stumbling out of bed, pulling the sheet with me as my only covering. Kai rolls over and grumbles but doesn't move apart from that. The knock sounds again, and I rub a hand over my face to wake myself up before gingerly making my way to the door. My legs and other bits are aching after all of Kai's attention last night. It can't be anyone other than Jaxon, so I brace myself for his reaction.

When I open it and peer out, he's wearing his trademark smirk and snorts after his eyes rake over me. 'Well, I was just coming to ask if you had seen Kai this morning, but I can tell by your well-fucked hairstyle that you may have done more than see him." He sounds a little bit envious, but it's nothing that strikes me as nasty. After my wave, he smugly saunters in, kissing me on the cheek on the way past, but when I close the door behind him and turn to follow, I smack directly into his back.

"Aw, fuck, that's not the sight I wanted first thing in the morning." Peering over his shoulder, it's my turn to snort and chuckle. Kai's now a starfish in the middle of the bed with a *very* prominent morning erection.

His hand comes up, middle finger extended, as he grabs a pillow and puts it over his cock. "Dude, no comments since you're clearly interrupting what would have been an amazing wake-up call," he grumbles from under his other hand. He's covering his face, either hiding from his brother or the morning, though both efforts would be futile.

I push Jaxon to get him moving again, and he throws himself down on the sofa, putting his feet up on the coffee table.

"I came to see if Harlow would like a tour of some of the rooms in the hotel before you go and do whatever it is you have planned this morning." His bottom lip drops in a pout that has me threatening to puddle out of my sheet toga. "While I slave away here… all by my lonesome… with no one to talk to."

He looks so pitiful, and I'm feeling so damn good after all of Kai's attention last night that I decide he needs something to cheer him up. Instead of getting back on the bed like I was going to, I change direction and head toward him. His eyebrows raise, and he scrambles to remove his feet from the table just in time for me to secure the sheet more tightly around my body and plonk myself down on his lap. "Good morning," I mutter as I wrap my arms around him, giving him a hug and snuggling into his chest. This will be a good little test for him. He knows that he can smolder and get a rise out of me, but I want to see that he can be comfortable with those little moments of quiet intimacy. The sexy shit is fun and appealing and sets my body on fire, but if we're doing this, I want it all.

He's slow to react, then carefully, like he doesn't want to startle me, he returns the hug, a rumble of approval sounding in his chest. Based on what I've heard about his relationship history, I honestly don't know if he's used to this kind of contact. I don't plan to ask him about this right now, because what a mood killer that would be, but I'm curious about the last time he just existed and… cuddled with someone when there was no sex involved. "Well now, if this is the welcome I get after my brother gives you a good dicking, then he can have at it any time." He chuckles as I smack his arm, an entirely unrepentant smile on his face.

"I would have given you a kiss too, but one, you made that comment, and two, morning breath," I grumble sleepily to him. He's warm and cozy, and I really didn't get a lot of sleep last night. But before I can get too comfortable, he lifts my head so that I'm looking into his aquamarine eyes that look so much like the beautiful waters of Hawaii.

"Sweetheart, morning breath is my jam," he mutters before fusing his mouth to mine. I try not to allow him entrance, not wanting him to be grossed out, but he bites down, I gasp in reflex, and he's in. And just like that, the familiar taste of him sets my senses on fire. Jaxon isn't gentle or kind as he dominates my mouth, and it makes me think about how he would dominate me in bed too. Having Holden submit to me is a rush, but I'm thinking I'd have no problem switching into the role of someone's submissive. If I trust someone, I'm more than okay with them taking total control. I snap back into the moment when I feel the sting of a gentle nip to my bottom lip, but then he pulls away.

I am left a completely unapologetic, squirming mess on his lap, a pair of jeans and a sheet the only things between me and the thick cock that I can feel beneath me.

"Dude, not fair," I hear Kai complain, and when I look toward him, he's sitting up in bed, having dragged the discarded comforter over his lap. "You're stealing all my morning sugar."

"Well, we can't have that," Jaxon declares, carefully standing up while holding me in his arms then walking me back to the bed. Kai quickly shuffles over to the opposite side, and Jaxon dumps me in the middle before climbing up next to me.

Instantly, Kai's mouth is on me while Jaxon's

hands caress my body. He's staying above the sheet, his touch light, as though he just wants me to know he's there too. There's something relaxed and completely unhurried about his technique, letting me know that we have time to stoke the fire between us. A moment and one nearly bruising kiss later, Kai pulls away with a satisfied grin on his face. "That's better."

Phew. I wave a hand to cool myself down. I'm no longer feeling sleepy. In fact, I think a cold shower is what I need before we go anywhere.

Kai and Jaxon chuckle, and I realize I said that out loud. Kai nuzzles into my neck, nipping and sucking in a way that will probably leave marks. "We don't have to go anywhere, you know. We can stay in and play all day if you want."

A grunt leaves Jaxon's mouth, and when I turn, his eyes are narrowed with jealousy, so I put a hand up to his cheek. "Don't be sad. I want to see the island, and not even his big dick can convince me to miss out."

"Hey!" Kai complains as Jaxon blinks in surprise before breaking out into a chuckle. Leaning forward, he rubs his still hard cock against my hip.

"What about *my* big dick?"

Pushing them both away, I struggle to get out of bed with the sheet wrapped around me. The two big oafs are laying on it, looking entirely too proud of themselves. Shrugging, I give up my struggle and let the sheet fall away before crawling to the end of the bed. Two large groans echo out behind me, bringing a smile to my face, and I face them as soon as I climb off the bed. Hands are on my hips with absolutely no shame in my game. Kai already licked most of me the night before, and if Jaxon keeps up with this non-asshole version of himself, I'm sure we'll just naturally have our turn together soon.

"Don't distract me, either of you. I want to see Hawaii, and we have plenty of time to do whatever *this* is." I wave a hand between us, but I don't think either of them hears anything I'm saying, their eyes too focused on my naked body. Throwing my hands up in exasperation, I turn and head for the bathroom to the soundtrack of their groans. At least that's a nice ego boost for me this time. Rolling my eyes in amusement, I close the door and force myself to have a cold shower; otherwise, there's a very good chance I could turn around and rejoin them in bed.

When I've showered and dressed, I find Jaxon and Kai lounging on the sofas. Kai is dressed and his hair is wet, so he must have returned to his room while I was getting ready.

Going over to my backpack, I pull out my phone and turn it on, already cringing as I think about the last time I went far too long without checking my messages. I switched it to silent when we had gone out last night and forgot to turn it back on when we got back.

I groan when I see all the missed calls and messages on the screen. "Crap." Not knowing where to start, I scroll through my inbox.

"What's wrong?" Jaxon probes, and when I look up, they're both wearing curious faces. I go over and join them in the seating area, holding out my phone.

"I've apparently been neglectful." On the screen there are messages from Dad, Nana, Max, Declan, Alex, Oliver, and even Jacinta. How long has it been since this many people cared about where I was or what I was doing? Honestly, I'm not sure this many people ever have.

"I'm not used to having so many people caring about me. Max, yeah, and Melinda and Chuck, but that's kind of it. I've never had friends like Alex and Shane, nor family, who gave a crap. It was always just Mom and me, and she didn't care where I was unless she needed more money for a fix." They're both silent after that, sympathetic looks on their faces that tread the line between showing they care about me and pushing into pity that would make me angry.

Nana: *Harlow, dear, how's Hawaii? Are the boys treating you well? ;)*

Oh, dear god, Nana broke out the emojis. It's too early for this one.

Dad: *Hi, honey, hope you're having a great time. Loved the photo Kai sent me. Can't believe you didn't fall off the surfboard!*

He did? What a sweetheart. He must have taken that when I wasn't looking.

Jacinta: *Bitch, now that we're friends and maybe sisters, you're not allowed to just disappear without a word. I want details, woman, all the details…*

Jacinta: *Except the sex ones, those I don't need to know.*

Someone else sounds a little friend needy too. Now looking over my shoulder, the boys chuckle when I scroll through Jacinta's messages, and Jaxon sighs, the sound fully relaxed. I didn't realize how much it would mean to him just to have Jacinta call a ceasefire on me, but there was a lot of weight lifted in that noise.

Now, Oliver… *Oliver*…. What has Oliver sent me? I open up the picture and… oh, dick pic.

Kai grimaces, turning his head to nuzzle into my hair instead of keeping his eyes on the screen any longer. "Nope! Too early."

"Hah, see? That's what I said about you!" Jaxon exclaims triumphantly.

"Do you two really need to be reading over my shoulders?" I ask dryly. Ignoring them, I keep flicking through the messages. If they don't want to see dick, they don't need to read my messages.

Maxine: *Call me bitch…. I need some advice.*

Hmm, now I'm worried. There was no joke from Max about sex or the guys or anything, and that's *not* like her. Max will be my first call when I get five minutes, but for now I tap out a quick text saying I'll call ASAP.

Alex: *Harlow love, we're back!! I have so much to tell you. Call me.*

Alex: *We picked the car up from your dad's. Jacinta was looking mighty fine. Nana introduced her to Jace, and the sexual tension in the air was delicious. I hear the two of you are besties now. I need all the deets. Call me.*

Alex: *Bitch, you're not ignoring me are you?*

Alex: *Harloowwwww*

Alex. *You better be getting ravished. That's the only excuse I will accept for ignoring me.*

Alex: *Fine!*

Now, I'm cackling. Alex makes my soul happy. I so needed another friend, and he is perfect. Before I can reply to him, the phone is plucked from my hand, and both of the guys are staring at me with hints of annoyance.

"Is there anything going on with you and Alex?" Kai asks quietly, his voice full of enough undisguised jealousy that I'm not sure he really wants to hear the answer. I cock my head at him in that universal signal for an explanation. I think I already know where this is going, but these boys are going to need to work on their communication.

"Because I'm happy sharing you with my brothers, but not anyone else," Jaxon growls before Kai can answer. Unable to help it, I snort, the sound escalating into a giggle when they just start to look more exasperated.

"Yeah, no, that's absolutely not a thing and never will be, because they have the biggest crush on your sister." His immediate reaction is one of relaxed happiness, but then I think the rest of my statement registers.

"Jacinta? And two guys?" he asks, looking kind of ill.

"Possibly three!" I reply helpfully. "And don't be a hypocrite. You want me to have five."

"Not five, six," Kai corrects just as helpfully, all smiles again now that Jaxon's the only one feeling uncomfortable.

I ignore the six comment because I really think they're off the mark with Thomas. Not ready to dive down that rabbit hole before I've even had breakfast, I stand up, shoving my phone into my pocket. I'll read Declan's text and respond to the others later. I'm sick of the nosy peanut gallery.

"Can I get that tour of the hotel now?" I ask Jaxon, hoping to distract him from all the information running through his brain, and it works.

"Sure can. Let's go." He holds out his hand, looking excited.

"Are you coming?" I ask Kai as I accept Jaxon's offer, but he shakes his head.

"No, I've got to get a few things ready for our morning, and I need to make a call to the office to ready those contracts for the guys. Go have fun with Jax. I'll see you at breakfast."

All three of us exit my room, and while Kai goes to his, Jaxon and I head toward the elevator.

"I thought we'd go down to the bottom so I can show you the dungeon and a couple of the themed rooms, then we can head upstairs to the penthouse."

"Sounds like a plan," I tell him.

We make our way through the hotel, and I'm even more impressed with each room I see. They all show off an incredible attention to detail and confirm that no expense has been spared.

I mean, really—how many hotels can you think of that have an entirely ice-themed room? I don't even want to know how the maintenance on that works, and I don't care. All I know is that the temperature drops to subzero, the bed frame is carved from ice, and the mattress is covered in furs and feather quilts thick enough to keep you warm. And did I mention it's been made to look like it's inside an ice cave? Some of the "frozen" blocks are fake, but the actual ice never wholly melts because of the temps in the room. There are drains in the floor because body heat does warm the room up. I honestly don't know how comfortable the whole setup sounds, but if I had some hardcore Elsa fantasies, I would be in heaven.

Leaving behind the frozen playroom, we continue our ascent to the penthouse, and when

Jaxon pushes open the door to the suite, I follow him inside without reservation. You can tell that this room hasn't been finished yet because there's plastic wrapping on furniture and everything is sort of dumped in the room. There are a couple of big boxes sitting on the kitchen countertop with the Sugar and Spice logo on them, waiting to be unpacked. Looking around, I can envision how beautiful this area is going to be. This suite has gone with the traditional Hawaiian theme, all light and breezy fabrics, potted plants, natural woods and fibers. There are expansive glass doors that lead out onto a large balcony area, also filled with foliage, and I can see it has amazing views over the ocean, so it must be forward facing.

"There are three bedrooms and three bathrooms in this suite as well as the hidden rooms. In theory, it can sleep a lot of people, so we'll advertise it for groups, but we've also made the price reasonable enough for a honeymoon couple to indulge."

On one side of the living area is a small bookcase. He walks toward it, taking me with him, and stops just in front of it with an excited smile. "Now, *this* is where the fun starts." He waves at the bookcase. "Do you want to have a go?"

Looking at the bookcase, I can see lots of the options are mysteries and thrillers, even a Steven King or two, but the one that stands out is the *Kama Sutra*. Reaching out to grab it, I try, but it feels stuck. I yank harder, determined that this has to be the one, and hear a click. With a gasp, I turn back to Jaxon just as the bookcase swings open. "I really didn't think that would work. It just seemed to stand out amongst all the others."

An impressed smile covers his face. "Got it first go." We step through the small door, and it swings shut behind us. When I turn around, there's no opening to be seen.

"How do you get out?" I ask. There isn't even a seam to indicate where the door had been, and Jaxon's smile grows more and more pleased by my curiosity.

"There's a switch on the table," Jaxon tells me. Still not able to see it, I decide to check out the rest of the room instead. "We made the room as sound-proof as we could. You could be sitting on the other side and not know anyone was in here."

The shelves are lined with book after book with a few curios thrown in here or there. There's one of those sliding book ladders that I can imagine would be fun not only to slide back and forth on, but I'm sure it also puts you at a conve-nient height for other activities too. I try not to squirm too much at that thought. There's a coffee table and a sofa as well as a couple of leather wingback chairs that are each paired with side tables and lamps. On one side of the room, the bookcases make way for a fireplace that has a plush-looking rug sitting in front of it. Being windowless, it's only lit up by the lamps on the side tables, creating a stately but cozy feel to the space.

"This is incredible!" I tell him, wandering over to the ladder and sliding it back and forth. Curious, I run my finger over the spines of the books. They all seem to be romance novels, erotica, and porn if any of the titles are to be believed. *The Virgin and the Beast. Sounds fun. I wonder if I can slip a book or two into my bag.*

"Go on, have a slide," Jaxon encourages me from behind. "I can tell you want to. We've all done it. You should have seen the girls when they were stocking the shelves. The wheels were already squeaky by the time they were finished. They're freshly oiled now, so you could really go flying."

A thrill of excitement flows through my body as I carefully step onto the ladder then push off like I'm on a skateboard. It slides smoothly away from Jaxon toward the other end of the shelves, and a glee-filled squeal escapes my mouth. Climbing up a little further, I use the shelves to push myself back again.

"Yup, there it is! That's the noise the girls made too." Stepping forward, he catches the ladder when I get to him, and I almost lose my breath when our eyes meet. Gone is playful and fun Jax, and in his place is a sinful, smoldering god. He steps even closer, his mouth in line with my core. All he has to do is lift up my knee-length sundress and slip my underwear to the side and he would have access to my dripping center.

He leans right in and inhales deeply, groaning as his knuckles turn white from clenching the ladder. When he leans his head against me, I can feel him breathing heavily. "You have two choices, sweetheart. Climb down off that ladder and hit the red switch on the lamp on that side table so we can scurry out of this room and head downstairs to breakfast... *Or* you can lift that skirt and let me have you as my morning meal."

I don't know how I feel about this. On one hand, I'm not sure we're really at the place where we can be intimate. Should I push him a little more to make up for his misdeeds? But on the other hand, I think one of us has to take a leap. For us to see what we could be, I think I need to show him that I'm willing to give him a chance, that I think he could be worth taking a chance on. For all of his bluster and venom, he needs to take as big of a leap as I do. Maybe we can just leap together and try to trust each other?

Of their own devices, my hands move off the ladder and to the base of my skirt, hiking it up slowly.

"Thank you, Jesus," Jaxon mutters reverently. His hands leave the ladder to run up my legs, caressing and massaging until he gets to the top of my thighs. My breath hitches as he slowly lowers my panties then removes them, lifting one leg at a time, before putting them in the pocket of his jeans.

Not wasting any time, he leans in, his tongue flicking gently against my clit until a spasm rocks my body from just that light touch. It's not what I expected from Jaxon, this gentleness.

But just as that thought crosses my mind, he lifts my right leg, drapes it over his shoulder, and shuffles in closer before devouring my pussy with his mouth. His tongue licks and lunges as he sucks and slurps, and my eyes roll back into my head. The whole time, he growls and grunts like an animal while I struggle to stay upright against the ladder, my knees buckling with all the sensations seering my nerve endings. He slides two fingers into my tight channel, and another groan escapes my mouth. "You're so fucking sexy when you moan for me," he mutters before continuing the onslaught.

Within minutes, I find myself on the edge of a climax, barely able to take a full breath before I tip over the edge. My orgasm rolls through me, flowing out like a shockwave, and a wailing screech leaves my mouth. "Fuck!" I pant and breathe my way through it as he gently licks at my clit while he continues to plunge his two fingers into my channel, my body still clenching around him.

As the spasm subsides, he groans and pulls away, removing his fingers before shoving them into his mouth, his eyes not leaving mine as he licks and sucks the evidence of my orgasm off them.

"Now *that's* what I call breakfast."

He removes my leg off his shoulder and then, wrapping both hands around my waist, he lifts me off the ladder and slides me down his body. When my mouth reaches his, he kisses me fiercely. I can taste myself on his tongue, but it doesn't bother me. He lets me slide the rest of the way to the ground before removing his mouth from mine. Making sure I'm steady on my feet, he moves to the coffee table and grabs a couple of tissues out of a box before returning to me and helping me clean up. *Okay, still a bit of a gentleman. Who knew?* To my complete surprise, he takes my panties out of his pocket and helps me step back into them. A tiny part of me is a little disappointed; I didn't realize it was something I'd like, but I was kind of hoping to spend the day knowing he had them tucked away in his pocket while I walked around without them.

"Thank you for giving me that. I know I don't really deserve it yet, but I've wanted it since the moment I set eyes on you in that club." He runs his fingers over my tattoos on my arms. "All this sexy ink and that dress that hugged all your curves. It was mouthwatering." His words have me shuddering again, but I'm still struggling to pull my mind together.

He smiles gently. "Come on, I'll show you the rest of the room, and we can go down for breakfast after that. Kai's going to be a hangry beast by the time we get back there." He leans down and flicks a button on one of the lamps on the side table, and with a click, the door opens. Wrapping one arm around me, he guides me out, but before we allow the door to close behind us, I stop him.

"Can we stay in this room the next time we come back?" My mind has finally recovered, and I want more of what I just experienced. He just smirks and nods, so I pull him to me and lay a kiss on him. He didn't even expect me to return the favor or anything. Pulling away, I lean in to whisper in his ear, "But next time, it's *you* on that ladder." Pulling back, I wander away, leaving him standing there wide eyed, his hand on his dick like he's trying to relieve the pressure.

"You're evil," he calls out, but I just laugh. *Yeah, I am.*

Chapter Twenty-Six

Harlow

After he shows me the rest of the penthouse, I'm determined to return here and play in all the rooms. God, my libido is off the charts by the time the elevator opens, letting us out at the ground floor. We find Kai in the dining room, and the moment he looks up at us, he starts to chuckle.

"Oh, so *that's* how the tour went." Frowning, I raise an eyebrow and stare him down until he points to my hair. "If that's not sex hair, I dont know what is, not to mention the post-orgasm glow."

With an eye roll, I rush over to the mirror on the wall to check myself out. He's not wrong; my hair is coming out of my ponytail, and I do have that well-fucked look. Straightening my ponytail, I shrug. There's nothing else I can do about the rest of it, but I'm not ashamed. "What better way to start the day than with an orgasm?" With that, I join them at the table, an easy smile on my face.

"Wouldn't know," Kai mutters, and I have to say that like all of his other looks, cheeky suits him. *Attractive asshole.*

"Me either," grumbles Jaxon.

Snorting with amusement, I take a sip of my coffee and sigh. "Well, I do, and it's awesome. So what are we doing today?" Kai's face lights up with the change of subject, all pretense of playful grumpiness disappearing.

"I asked the chef to prepare us a picnic, which he has, and we're going to hike to one of my favorite waterfalls and have lunch. Afterward, we're going on a helicopter sightseeing flight." He's practically bubbling with enthusiasm.

"We're on for the luau tonight, and then tomorrow we've scheduled a snorkeling tour and a visit to the Honolulu zoo before a late flight home," Jaxon chips in as he reaches for a decadent-looking pastry. When he catches me watching, he takes a big bite. After he finishes chewing, he winks and says, "Not as sweet as my first offering, but it'll do."

I knew he was going to say something ridiculous like that, but Kai hadn't been paying attention until that point, zoning out into his drink. Coffee flies out of his nose, and he coughs and splutters before getting himself together, using a napkin to clean up his face and mess.

"Damn it, Jax, not while a guy's drinking, will you!"

My eyes go back and forth between the two of them. There's not a single sign of animosity or jealousy to be seen. They truly are okay with the fact that I've been intimate with both of them in the last twenty-four hours, and my heart starts to race a little at the thought. All along I thought they were humoring me and they'd make me pick one, but that really doesn't seem to be the case. All of a sudden, this feels very... real.

"Eat up, Harlow," Kai says, knocking me out of my musings. "The hike isn't too long or hard, but having a decent breakfast will make it easier."

So, while we chat amongst ourselves about the hotel and all the different rooms Jax had shown me, I stuff myself with another delicious breakfast. I'm all for not being spoiled, but I could totally get used to this.

The breath wheezes out of me a little faster than I would have expected as we make our way up the trail. I've been slacking, and my fitness level has dropped since I came to California. I need to make a big effort to use the gym and the pools at home if I want to get it back to what I want it to be. The humidity doesn't help either. The day is slightly overcast, and it has that thick wet feeling of potential rain, but I'm hoping it will hold off. I don't want to miss our helicopter ride or dinner with Jaxon tonight. Suddenly, Kai stops walking, so I take a moment to try and catch my breath, slapping at a mosquito who's decided he's all too fond of me.

"You okay, baby?" A small thrill flows through me at the pet name as I look up to see him watching me with concern.

"Yeah, just feeling a bit out of breath, but I'll be okay," I tell him, waving him on.

He must take me at my word because he turns and continues. "It's just over this hill," he shouts back to me as I follow him up the path. Soon, he's further away, leaving just me and the surrounding nature, the bird calls and the whisper of the breeze rustling the surrounding foliage. If I stop and stand there, breathing in the atmosphere, I could pretend I've landed in Jurassic Park.

Kai's shout makes my daydreams disappear, and I hurry to catch up with him. As I crest the peak, I find an awesome sight—a rock face with water cascading over it to pool at the bottom. It's not a furious pounding of water like I had expected, more a sinuous flow over the rocks, but it looks magical and we seem to be the only people around. Kai's found a smooth table-like rock to dump the backpack and rug on, and he's already in the process of taking off his shirt.

"Come on, let's go for a swim. The water will be refreshing, and then we'll have something to eat," he says as I approach. I drop my own trusty backpack on the rock next to his and look around the area.

"I didn't bring a swimsuit," I reply, disappointment coming through clearly, but he just offers me a grin.

"I know. I deliberately didn't tell you."

I raise my eyebrows at him as he strips off his shorts, leaving him in his briefs, and my eyes are immediately drawn to where his fingers are tucked into their waistband. "Oh really?" I stammer as he strips down and throws them on the ground with the rest of his stuff. I can't look away as his cock starts to harden, taking it for the compliment it is. I'm still fully dressed, yet it's clear how much he and his body want me.

"I dare you!" he challenges before turning and walking toward the water, my eyes locked to that ass. Oh, that ass. I just want to take a bite out of it.

Throwing caution to the wind, I shuck off my dress and underwear, toeing off my shoes and removing my socks. I hurry after him but stop as soon as my feet hit the water.

"Holy fuck, that's cold!" Looking up, I see Kai emerge from the water, almost in slow motion, like Aquaman coming to drag me down to the depths.

As the water drips down his face, he curves a come hither finger at me.

"Come on, Harlow. I'll keep you warm." *Ah, fuck it.* I run to him as fast as I can, probably looking like a spastic sea cow or something, and by the time I get to him, I'm drenched so I just throw myself into his arms. The warmth of his body against mine causes me to let out a groan. I wrap my arms around his waist and grab hold of his hair, angling his head so my mouth can take his.

His thick cock rubs against my pussy as our tongues stroke one another, the friction both a tease and a promise at the same time, but before we can go any further, a shout echoes out around the surrounding area.

"Shit, it looks like we're about to have company," Kai grumbles. Squealing, I push out of his arms and start to swim back to the edge before standing and running the rest of the way. I can hear Kai chuckling behind me, but I'm already out and running for the backpack which better have a damn towel in it or somebody is in trouble.

"Hang on," Kai calls as he exits the water. When he gets to me, he lifts the blanket to reveal two towels wrapped inside it. He hands me one as he takes the other and starts to dry his body.

"Damn it, just when it was starting to get good," he jokes before placing a kiss on the tip of my nose as I wrestle my damp body back into my under-things and pull my dress over my head. Kai is a lot more relaxed but still manages to cover himself before our company descends on the pool.

"Let's just move over there a little bit so that we can have lunch," Kai suggests, pointing to another flat boulder a little further away. "Then we shouldn't be disturbed by the people swimming."

Gathering our things, we move away as the people we had heard arrive in the clearing. Kai shakes out the blanket, gesturing for me to have a seat while he unpacks the basket. As he does that I study the people who have just arrived. It looks like a couple of family groups with teenage kids who're acting like they'd rather be anywhere but here until they spot the pool. With a holler, the boys quickly strip off their shirts and race to the water. The couple of girls are less enthusiastic, but they strip down to bathing suits and follow nonetheless. Their squeals and shouts echo as they hit the cold water while the parents take a seat on the boulder we had just vacated, looking ready for a break.

"Here." Kai passes me a plate of food, bringing my attention back to him. There's cold chicken and salad, along with some crusty buttered bread. He passes me a can of soda to go with it.

"Yum, this looks delicious," I tell him as we dig in.

We've been eating for a while when I finally get the guts to ask the question that's been rolling around in my mind since last night.

"Kai, will you tell me how you came to be with

Brad? What happened to your family?" A shutter comes down over his eyes, and I see him withdraw into himself. It's the first time this fun, charming man has looked so… sad. In fact, he looks *so* sad, so unlike the happy, enthusiastic guy I know, that I try to backtrack until he cuts me off.

"I'll tell you, but it's not a pretty story. My mom and dad weren't childhood sweethearts or anything. They hooked up, and my mother got pregnant. My dad was thrilled; he had always wanted children, and he asked her to marry him. She said yes, but because it was demanded of her by her parents. She was an only child, and her mother and father were her only family as well. They wanted her to provide her child with stability, and they were firm believers in the idea that if she was adult enough to have unprotected sex, she was adult enough to be some-one's wife. Mom was seventeen and my father twenty. He was an only child too, but his parents had died the previous year, so he had no one. Mom and I were an instant family for him, and he couldn't have been happier about not being alone any longer."

He looks up at me, his eyes glistening with tears that are just so out of place, and my heart lurches. I feel like now that he's started, he needs to finish. Telling me this will open up a door between us, and I want that to happen, but at the same time, I'm ready to make any promise in the world to ensure that he never has this look in his eyes again. Swallowing hard, he lets a shuddered breath out. I can tell this story is about to go bad, so I reach out a hand and grab hold of his.

"He was a great dad. We played ball, he taught me to surf, and he was my best friend. He worked hard to provide for us, but he wasn't raking in big bucks, so we had a comfortable life, or that's what I remember. But my mother wasn't happy. In fact, she became increasingly unhappy as time went on. Dad was going to work and coming home to look after me while my mother was going out and 'finding herself.' Turns out Mom was sick of the ball and chain that was me and Dad, and she was doing drugs and sleeping around."

His eyes drop away while he tells me all this, focusing on a spot on the ground. "It was late one night; Dad had put me to bed after reading me a story, but something woke me. Hearing shouting, I stumbled out of bed and wandered out to the kitchen, realizing it was my parents screaming at each other. Dad just kept asking her why until she screamed, 'Because I hate you and I hate that fucking kid.' There was a thud, more of my dad's shouting, and then there was a gunshot." He takes a deep breath, his shoulders shaking with the force of the subsequent exhale.

"I was afraid and didn't know what to do, so I ran and hid in a closet. I heard the kitchen door open, and she started wandering through the house, calling my name, but I didn't answer. When the cops found me, I was curled up asleep under a pile of clothes. A lady was with them, and she picked me up and carried me out of the house, but not before I looked through the open kitchen door and saw the blood all over the floor. When she carried me outside, there were all these flashing lights and an ambulance. My mother was hand-cuffed next to a police car, screaming at everyone, but Dad was nowhere to be seen." His now haunted eyes meet mine, and one of those tears slides down his face as I feel one of my own on my cheek.

"Turns out Mom was hopped up on something, and she shot him dead. They said it was a lucky shot, there was no way she should have been able to hit him in the chest in her state, but by the time the neighbors had called the police, they only arrived in time to find him dead on the floor. He died, bleeding out on the floor all alone, because I was a coward and hid."

I gasp at his words and scoot myself toward him, pushing aside the picnic stuff so I can wrap my arms around him.

"No, Kai, not a coward. You were a kid," I try to reassure him. I know how it feels to take on a responsibility that isn't yours to shoulder. For so long, I thought that I had played a part in my mom's behavior, but I can look back at that now and know that she was fucked up all on her own. It wasn't that scared little boy's job to stop his deranged mother, and I'll tell him that however many times he needs until he starts to believe it.

"The social worker told me that I probably would have been next if I hadn't hid. That's why my mom was calling my name; she wanted to make sure that she got rid of both of us. Anyway, she's serving a life sentence in the women's prison, and I haven't seen her since. With no immediate family to speak of, I ended up in the foster system. The foster family I was placed with knew Brad through working in the original Neighpalm Hotel here in Hawaii, and they heard he was looking to adopt, so they approached him when he was here for a meeting. They were lovely people, and I think I could have had a nice life with them, but they thought that I would be a better fit for Brad. The rest is history."

Pulling his head around, I rest my forehead against his and force him to look at me. I lean in slowly enough that he has time to pull back if he's not in the mood for this type of comfort, but when he remains still, I place a kiss to his soft lips. "Thank you for sharing your pain with me." His body relaxes as I kiss him, his eyes open but finally filled with relief, and after a moment, he lunges for me, wrapping my body in a tight embrace.

"Woohooo, get it, man!" one of the teenagers yells, lightening the atmosphere. Kai and I pull apart, and when we look over, the boys are giving him a thumbs up. The parents, on the other hand, look mortified as they call out their apologies. Kai waves them off but stands up and starts to pack our things away, the mood lighter and more peaceful now.

Helping him, it's not long before we're hiking contentedly back down the trail toward our car. The drive back to the hotel doesn't take long, and I'm looking forward to having a shower to wash off the sweat I accumulated on the walk home. We're just pulling into the underground parking garage when Kai grunts.

"What's wrong?" I ask, a little concerned as he pumps his foot up and down on the brake.

"Fuck, the brakes aren't working!" he shouts as he takes a corner too fast. The downhill slope of the underground garage has us steadily speeding up. The tires squeal as he tries to turn, but the car is moving wildly without the brakes to balance us out.

"Fuck, Harlow!" he shouts. "Brace yourself!" He tries to slow the car down by weaving back and forth; thank god there aren't many other cars down here. His adrenaline junkie habits must have included some kind of crazy driving classes because so far, he's managed to miss them more smoothly than I could've imagined. Unfortunately, any relief is extremely short lived because we're approaching the wall much, *much* too fast.

With another chorus of murmured curses, he pulls the hand brake, but it's too late. My body is thrown forward, and there's a huge crash as the airbags explode around us when the wall suddenly stops our forward momentum. As the front of the Jeep crumples on impact, my seatbelt slams me in place, knocking the wind out of me and exerting a bruising pressure on my body that I know I'll feel later.

Dazed and confused, the smoke from the airbags causes me to choke. I look over to the side to find Kai's got a cut on his forehead. There's blood trickling down his face, and he looks a little dazed but otherwise alright.

His gaze meets mine, his eyes darting around like he's having a little trouble focusing. "Are you okay?" he groans.

"Yeah, I think so," I tell him, trying to assess how I feel. There's a ringing in my ears, but I can hear a shout over it. Before I can work out the noise, my door is wrenched open and Jaxon is there. Frantic with worry, there's fear written all over his face.

"What the fuck happened? We all felt that upstairs." Kai's door is wrenched open as well, but from my vantage point, I can't see who's there. I struggle to move again, but Jaxon holds me in place.

"Just wait, Harlow. An ambulance and search and rescue team is on its way. We need to let them get you out and have a look at you. I wouldn't forgive myself if I hurt you because we acted too hastily."

I lean back with a sigh, knowing he's right but

finding that common sense is not my best friend right now. As I try to quiet my racing heart and find some semblance of calm, one thought brings that panic surging back.

How the fuck did our brakes fail?

Chapter Twenty-Seven

Harlow

The next few hours are a blur of policemen, medics, and a hovering Jaxon who shows more mother hen qualities than I would have ever thought possible, but eventually, we're allowed to leave. Both Kai and I were checked over; he had the cut on his head looked at, but they deemed it to not need anything. We were both sore from the airbags and the seatbelts, but apart from that, we came out relatively unscathed. He had managed to lessen our speed with the weaving and pulling the hand brake, and although I think the paramedics are trying to make us feel better, I definitely don't feel lucky when they continue to assure us that it could have been much worse. *How is reminding someone that they could've died supposed to be uplifting?*

We decide to skip the helicopter tour, Kai being in no state to fly us, and make use of the hot tub facilities, ordering in Uber Eats instead of going to the luau. The kisses and assurances of a rain check go a long way toward making me less pouty. We all sleep in my room since Jaxon is in full overprotective nurse mode, refusing to let either of us out of his sight. It's cute as fuck, but my body hurts too much to laugh. After essentially tucking us in, he finds us a non-porn channel to watch, and we put on a movie, but I don't think we watch much of it. Nestled between the brothers, my eyes become heavier and heavier until the last thing I remember is the both of them leaning down and giving me a kiss on the head.

The following morning, I groan as I wake up, but it's not in delight at having two gorgeous men keeping me warm all night. My body has been battered and bruised, and it wants to make sure I know that. Stretching as I wake hurts, so I'm not looking forward to moving. As I open my eyes and look around, I realize both boys are missing, but I hear a toilet flush before a very disheveled Kai walks out of the bathroom, grimacing.

"Did you get the license plate of the truck that hit us?" he grumbles, running his hand through his hair when he sees I'm awake.

"No, and I didn't catch it when he reversed it either," I reply, bringing a smile to his mouth.

He pads over to the bed and gingerly climbs

back on with a wince. "Good morning, baby," he whispers as he leans in and gives me a gentle kiss on the lips. "Jaxon has gone to get us breakfast and will bring it back up here. I wanted to know if you think we should cancel the snorkeling trip."

I sit up too fast at his words and groan, avoiding the urge to shake my head. "No! I'll be okay once I have a shower and take some painkillers. Please don't cancel! We already missed things yesterday," I beg, reaching out a hand to grasp his wrist.

He lifts my hand off his arm and places a kiss on the back of it. "Okay, as long as you feel up to it." There's definitely some concern in his eyes, but he seems willing to let my decision be the final one. I breathe out a sigh of relief as the door opens, Jaxon walking in with a room service cart.

"Room service," he calls with a thick French accent. "I am here to service you." Between the absolutely terrible accent and the accompanying eyebrow wiggle, both Kai and I are smiling and I'm about ready to fall over in surprise. Where has this silly Jaxon been this whole time? He comes to a stop and winks flirtatiously at us, but his phone rings before I can find out what's coming next. Frowning, he pulls it out of his pocket, heading out to the balcony after he checks who's calling.

Kai and I look at each other before climbing out and heading over to the abandoned cart. Lifting the couple of lids, I find omelettes and platters of bacon, breakfast sausages, hashbrowns, and pancakes.

"Yum," I moan and start filling a plate for myself.

"Hey, save some for us," Kai jokes, doing the same. We each take a seat on the sofas, resting our plates on the coffee table, and start devouring the food.

Jaxon's frowning when he returns, and he grabs a bottle of medication off the cart and shakes some pills into his hands. "Here, you each need to take two of these." He hands them to us before pouring us both a coffee from the pot and handing those to us as well.

"Who was on the phone?" Kai asks, taking his pills before washing them down with his coffee.

"That was the police from yesterday." Jaxon fills himself a plate and joins us. "They were calling to say they spoke to the rental place and found out the car had just been serviced, so they checked the brake line. It had been cut. Not all the way through but enough for the brake fluid to slowly bleed out on the drive back from the waterfall."

I drop my knife and fork onto my plate as my stomach fills with dread, my food almost threatening to return.

"Oh god." I place a hand over my mouth in shock, not knowing what I should do. My body is filling with adrenaline, the energy telling me that I need to burst out of my seat and do something, but I have no idea what that something is.

"Fuck." Kai's expletive is loud in the quiet room.

"Yeah, I think maybe we call James and get him to file an earlier flight plan and head home," Jaxon tells us cautiously. Tears start to burn in my eyes with the thought that once again the stalker has fucked up my life. What the fuck do they want? Why don't they just come out with it? How can I possibly fix whatever I did, give them what it is they want, if I'm laid up in a hospital bed… or dead?

The guys must see the tears threatening to escape because Kai goes into panic mode. "I promised Harlow we would snorkel," he blurts out at Jaxon before looking at me, the words coming out awkwardly loudly, like that will convince his brother not to disagree.

"What about making it a private tour then?" Jaxon suggests, but he still looks unsure about the idea.

"Every time the stalker has struck, he had a window of anonymity. Oliver's car had the broken lights, the stable was empty, the shooting was far away, and my room was trashed while the whole family was occupied. I don't think they would risk attacking us in a group environment. It doesn't follow the pattern. The brake lines were another direct attempt to hurt someone, but even that was… quiet. He's doing things that are all kind of distanced from us," I point out to them both quickly. "If we take a tour that's packed with other people, he probably would be too scared. We could do a check on the car before and after the tour just to make sure that we don't have another brake incident."

I don't know if I'm actually making a great argument or if he just hears the desperation in my voice, but Jaxon's looking resigned by the end of my plea. "Fine, but we leave from there, going straight to the airport so we can head home. It may be time to follow through on getting you a bodyguard until this person can be found."

Shakily, I agree to their requests, and when breakfast is finished, I pack my things while Jaxon returns the cart. As the two of them pack up their own things, I stay in my room, trying to very gently stretch muscles that are stiffening uncomfortably fast.

Jaxon's talking to his general manager in the lobby when Kai and I join them to hand in our keys, Kai only lasting through a few moments of small talk before he interrupts. "Come on, man, you can call him later if you've forgotten anything." He follows the statement with a wink, softening the obvious annoyance on Jaxon's face, then gives his grumpy brother a nudge until he agrees to move on.

When we go out to the car, one of the hotel security guards is standing next to it. Jaxon called him to come in this morning and watch that no one could tamper with the car after it had been delivered. As we climb into the car, something occurs to me. "Did that woman come in for an interview? The one with the kid from the mall," I add as he climbs into the driver's seat, leaving me and Kai snuggled together in the back.

His eyes meet mine in the rearview mirror. "She sure did. She's going to do somewhat of an internship with us. She'll work in all the different departments, learning the ropes, and I'm going to make her assistant manager when she completes them. I also gave her one of the staff apartments that are in the back of the resort beyond the bungalows. There's a two-bedroom place perfect for her and her son, and because the public areas of the hotel are fairly PG, the kid shouldn't run into anything inappropriate. There are underground access tunnels from those apartments to the hotel, so he shouldn't accidentally run into any bungalow guests either."

"That's awesome," I tell him, and his eyes crinkle like he's smiling at my praise.

"Yeah, I love helping people out, especially hardworking single mothers. Anything to make their lives easier than it was for my mom." His eyes cloud at that and he breaks our stare, his gaze going back to the road.

"I spoke to James, and the plane is fueled and ready to go." With Kai's change of subject, the awkward atmosphere disappears. "I also updated

Dad on what happened. I've asked him to have all our vehicles checked over just in case, and he's sending the limo to pick us up once we get home. He's already on the same page as Jaxon, so he's looking into candidates for a bodyguard."

I shudder at the thought of a stranger being with me twenty-four seven. Kai feels it where I'm snuggled against him despite our bruises, but I need the comfort after this morning's revelations.

"What's wrong, babe?" he asks, kissing me on the head and rubbing his hand up and down my arm.

"Just the thought of being shadowed all the time. We don't even know what this person wants. It just seems like they want to terrify us more than anything. Like, what's the motive behind it all?"

Kai squeezes me on reflex. "No matter what it is, you're not going anywhere."

"I agree with Kai. I know you're both banged up, but at least you're both alive and in fairly okay condition. We learned something from this experience, and we're going to make sure that we take more precautions next time. Distance doesn't seem to be enough, so we know this person has some kind of resources, and that gives us even more reason to keep you with us and just make better use of our own. With Thomas' connections and our ability to take you to Europe, we can keep any danger away from Nana, Poppy, Melinda, Max, and Chuck, and we'll get backup to help keep the rest of us safe."

Jaxon eyes are pleading in the mirror as they meet mine once more. "Don't go, please. None of us would be able to cope if you left, nevermind how Dad will react. And Jacinta has decided you're one of us. If you break her heart, she may not survive it again."

Fuck, he's laying on the guilt a bit thick… but it's working. "Dude, not cool." Even Kai's scowling at him, getting the same vibe I am.

"I'm not going to apologize." I hear the stubbornness in his voice even though he won't meet my eyes anymore. "I'll use whatever dirty tactics I need to get her to stay. You should be supporting me," he growls unapologetically at his brother, who looks at me, a flush of shame crossing his face as he shrugs.

"He's not wrong."

Before we can argue about it anymore, Jaxon pulls the car into the marina and enters a monitored parking lot. Winding down the window, he chats with the guy in the booth, asking him to watch our car and report if anyone pays a little too much attention to it. I watch as he slips him a couple hundred dollar bills, the incentive quickly disappearing into the man's pocket before he waves us through.

We grab our gear for the tour, my muscles screaming in protest despite the painkillers I took this morning, but I'm determined not to let it dampen my enthusiasm. I'm sure the aches will ease away once I'm in the water anyway.

Boarding the boat, we're welcomed by a tour guide as we take our seat amongst the people already waiting. The boat is big enough that there are twenty of us onboard, and we seem to be the last to arrive because not long after we get on, the boat pushes away from the dock. As we make our way out of the harbor toward our destination, a crew member gives us a safety talk and then passes out equipment to everyone. Once I have my flippers, mask, snorkel, I also decide to take a pool noodle to float on. Better safe than sorry, and this way I can just float if I get too tired.

It's a beautiful sunny morning. The rain that threatened yesterday has disappeared, leaving the sun shining and the ocean calm. A shout from the front of the boat has us all turning in that direction to find a pod of dolphins is swimming nearby, riding the wake of the bow as they jump, twist, and turn, playing in the wash.

The three of us are sitting on a bench seat, and I've got the two guys on either side of me. A contented sigh leaves my mouth. "This is nice. I can practically feel the tension easing." But as I say that another shout sounds out, a quad of jet skis blasting past us a little too close to the boat, making it bounce more than is comfortable. I can see the crew member flipping them off, but they don't seem to care. One in particular slows down, staring at the boat like he's studying us. They're wearing long wetsuits and have scuba tanks on the back of their jet skis. With their hats and sunglasses, it's impossible to make out any defining features, but I can practically feel the one's eyes boring into me. A moment later, just long enough for me to grow uncomfortable, they take off, whooping and hollering.

"What a bunch of assholes," Kai mutters, but neither he nor Jaxon seem overly concerned.

It doesn't take us too long to reach our destination. The crew drops anchor, giving us a safety speech that includes the warning to stay within the boundaries marked by the four red buoys. It's apparently a system that any passerby will know, so other watercraft will avoid that space. Before long, the three of us are pushing off the submerged back board on the boat. Jaxon and Kai helped me put on my mask and snorkel, so, after putting the noodle under my belly, I enter the water. Initially, the temperature is a shock, but my wetsuit soon makes it bearable, and with Kai leading the way and Jaxon bringing up the rear, we swim toward the coral reef, looking at everything below us. It's teeming with beautiful-colored fish and amazing coral that's unlike anything I've ever seen.

The aches and pains soon become forgotten as I marvel at the wildlife. This was exactly what I needed to get back into myself and shake off some of the nerves from yesterday's accident. Kai points, and when I follow his finger, a sea turtle lazily swims by, unfazed by the people in his environment. A flash of movement out of the corner of my eye has me turning, and I watch, my heart racing just a little, as a small reef shark shoots away from the group in the opposite direction. Growing more confident as my interest in the animals outweighs the newness of snorkeling, I swim away from Jaxon and Kai when a school of yellow fish catches my attention. *Can't resist a new animal to study.* A vibration through the water has me stopping and looking around, thinking maybe the engine of our boat has started, but I can't see anything so I put my head down to chase after my yellow fish again. The little buggers keep swimming further away, forcing me to kick faster to keep up with them. A glint of something out of the corner of my eye has me stopping though. I can see something shiny down on the bottom of the ocean. It's not very deep here, maybe ten feet, but I'm not confident enough to dive down and have a look, so I pop my head up to look for one of the guys.

It's only then that I realize I've passed quite far out of the designated area.

"Harlow!" a horrified voice shouts, and I turn to look at Kai. "Watch out!" he screams, eyes focused beyond me. As I swing around to see what he's looking at, my thoughts instantly go to shark. *Fuck, this is it. I'm dead.* To my surprise, it's a jet ski bearing down on me.

I whip the noodle out from under me and wave it in the air, hoping that they'll see it and go around me, but the jet ski doesn't stop. It bears down on me, speeding closer and closer as I frantically start to swim back toward the buoys.

Of course, following along with the luck I've had so far, my efforts are futile. I feel it hit me, my head exploding in agony.

My throat burns as I choke on the water forcing its way into my mouth and lungs. There are bursts of sound all around me, splashing, a motor, and someone's frantic screams.

And then there's nothing.

Thank you for reading!
I hope you enjoyed the book. It would be super awesome if you could leave a review wherever you bought it, because I love to hear what you thought of the story.

**Want more of Harlow and the gang?
Pre order Book Four here**
Wanted Girl

Want to keep up to date with new books coming soon? Sign up to my newsletter here
Newsletter

Another way to do that is to join me Facebook group. I drop teasers and giveaways in there all the time. Here's the link
Lexie's Ladygarden

Visit my webpage and check out reading orders and what else I've written.
www.lexiewinston.com

Acknowledgments

Thank you to all the normal crew this book wouldn't be possible without you all.

Michelle for your invaluable editing.

Emma for all the late night and early morning chats.

Infinity Book Designs for the cover

My beta team for being super awesome as usual.

Grace and Hope for being my rocks, long live the throttle.

Thank you Claire Bosman, Amber Leigh Abbott, and Joy Bromfield for your name suggestions, Cayden, Jared Reed and Coco respectively.

Thanks to all the members of Lexie's Ladygarden
you guys are the reason I continue to do this. Love
you all.

Lexie

Check out something else by me. This one is coming mid 2021. A Sci-Fi reverse harem romance.

Apprentice

Galaxy Circus 1

PLEASE BE AWARE THIS IS UNEDITED AND SUBJECT TO CHANGE. PLEASE DON'T COMPLAIN TO AMAZON IF YOU FIND ERRORS AS THEY WILL BE FIXED BEFORE BEING PUBLISHED.

Chapter One

"Miss Jenson, thank you for responding to our letter so quickly," Mr Ryding, the weaselly looking lawyer says to me from behind the large walnut desk. He's fidgeting with the papers in front of him; stacking them, picking them up, tapping them, and then placing them back on the table in front of himself. He's done it half a dozen times. While I sit there waiting for him to say more, he straightens the pens in the holder to the right of him on the desk. It seems like he's doing everything in his power to avoid making eye contact with my very confused self.

"I'm sorry I'm not sure I understand you. I received a letter from your office saying I have been bequeathed something and that I must present myself in person to sign some papers to receive it. Now, you are also telling me, it was from a grandfather I didn't even know existed, and obviously didn't want me, as I spent the first eighteen years of my life in foster homes"

He looked up, briefly pausing his fidgeting. "Yes that's correct. Though it's grandfather's plural."

Plural? I puzzle internally, never mind, I'll come back to that.

"John, William and Eric Adams are your paternal grandfathers and it wasn't that they didn't want you." His shifty eyes soften briefly, "They weren't able to find you. Your parents were estranged from them and they were not notified immediately when your parents had their accident. When you were placed in foster care, they weren't in the States at the time." He shuffles his papers again. "When they did eventually find out, John rushed back, but by then you'd been placed in the system and your name changed by request of your parents will. You'd disappeared and were well hidden. Due to the nature of their business, they decided that maybe you were better off. Their job was constantly traveling, never settling in one place for very long. No place to raise a child or so they thought. They believed you were safe and loved." I scoff out loud. "Otherwise they would have claimed you immediately." He assures me.

"So why am I finding out about this now? I'm assuming they're all dead? Why leave it until I have no chance of getting to know them or of finding out about where I'm from?" I struggle to understand. "Why did they leave it until it was too late?"

The shifty look in his eyes is back and the fidgeting obviously isn't cutting it as he gets up from his desk and starts to pace behind it. Marching back and forth in front of the big picture window which holds the view of the river, his office backs onto. He stops, takes a deep breath and turns to look at me.

"Well actually that's not quite true. The Mr Adams's have not passed on, they've decided to retire, and the family business must pass down to a family member only, and you're the one that was chosen. They contracted our firm to find you. It has taken quite a while, I can assure you."

"Excuse me?" I gasp, "Are you saying my grandfathers are alive and want to meet me?" As a little girl I would have dreams of a family member swooping in to rescue me from the never-ending cycle of foster homes. I finally gave up around the age of thirteen. I wasn't one of those kids who were beaten or abused in care, I just never seemed to fit in. Never really included or felt like I was one of the family. It would've been nice to know there was someone out there who wanted me. Of course my very sceptical nature decides this is too good to be true.

"Why the fuck am I dealing with a lawyer and not them directly?' my surprise turns to anger. "Can they not even be bother or are they too fucking chicken to face me themselves." I can practically feel the steam escaping from my ears. My Ryding swallows nervously and brings a finger up to try and loosen his collar slightly.

"Ah… but… They're…" He stammers my anger taking him by surprise obviously.

Taking a deep breath I try and calm down. Don't take it out on the lawyer Lila he's just the messenger

"Why me? I'm assuming there are other family members they could turn too?" I rub my eyes, I can feel a headache brewing. They have been steadily getting more frequent and this meeting is not doing me any favors.

"Yes, well no. There are other family members but not directly. You are their only grandchild, and they've decided that it's time you join the family legacy and that you get first option. All the details are in the package." he sits back down at the desk and gestures to the stack of papers he'd been fidgeting with. "You're required to spend twelve months with the business, learning all the ins and outs. If, at the end of the twelve-month period, you're unwilling to continue, the business and the role of CEO and all it entails will pass on to the next eligible family member and you will carry on with life as if the previous twelve months had never really happened."

I stare at the package like it's a snake that's going to bite me. I just don't know what to think. Do I ignore it, sign it over now and wash my hands of the whole debacle? Or do I take a leap of faith and at least meet the men that could be the best or the worse thing to happen to me.

"Can I have some time to think about this" I ask, "It's quite a decision I need to make."

Mr Ryding shakes his head, "I'm sorry but this decision needs to be made now. Our firm has been looking for you for a while and I'm afraid we're out of time. You need to be on a plane to London in two days time. We're going to need an answer now."

It's my turn to start pacing. Jumping out of the chair I've been sitting in, I start stalking back and forth across the room, the pounding behind my eyes has intensified and I rub my temples in an attempt to alleviate it. What to do? It's not like I have anything keeping me here. I don't have many friends, mainly acquaintances. My best friend and roomie is head over heels in love with her partner, she'd be ok if I left. I have a dead-end job in a bar that pays crappy, but keeps me busy. I guess there is nothing specifically stopping me from going. I've always dreamed of adventures, sure that there must be something better in life than what I have been living.

"All right," I tell him, making the decision, "I'm in, show me where to sign."

He goes to the stack of papers on the table and pulls some out. "You need to sign here, here, and here. One of them is a non-disclosure form. No matter what happens, from here on, you are bound by a confidentiality clause. Even if at the end of twelve months you change your mind, everything you see and do will be confidential. A plane ticket is also in the pack, in your name with the details of your flight in two days' time. You'll be met at the airport and a driver will take you to where you need to be. For your peace of mind, you can tell people where you are going and why, but there is to be no sharing of any other details. It's actually a good thing that you don't have a huge circle of friends." I feel a bit insulted at this comment and surprised that he knows that.

"We've been looking for you for a while, we know everything about you" He replies to my look, a little defensively

"Yeah ok, because that's not creepy or rude" I reply sarcastically.

I busy myself signing papers, and by the time I'm finished my hand aches and my head throbs incessantly. Gathering them all together, I shove them in my hand bag; I'll read it all when I get home. "So what business have I just signed my life away too?" I ask Mr Ryding, thinking this is probably something I should have asked before signing. Fuck I'm an idiot, why didn't I ask that first? I mentally slap my impulsive self.

"Have you heard of the Galaxy Circus?" He asks, slightly distracted with gathering all his copies of the paperwork.

"Oh yes, isn't that, that spectacular circus that claims it has aliens as its performers. It pops up randomly throughout the globe and is always sold out." I nod enthusiastically, "People have been trying to debunk them for years. I remember reading that PETA were trying to gain access to prove that their animals are mistreated. They have some special dispensation that allows them to have circus animals, as they claim their animals are shifters, so therefore not really animals." I laugh loudly, "It really is a clever gimmick, and they're lucky that people are gullible enough to believe that rubbish."

He looks at me, a strange glint in his eye. "Are they gullible or just looking to be entertained?" He questions me. "Well whether they're gullible or not is besides the point, it still attracts huge crowds when it does tour. It is one of the most popular circuses' around, even out selling *Cirque du Soleil*, with less shows each year."

"Well what has that got to do with my grandfathers and the business I just signed on to learn the ropes to.

My Ryding looks at me and smiles an oily looking grin. I think it's the first time I've seen him smile since I walked in the door. "Well Miss Jenson with the papers you signed, you just joined the circus."

I flop back into my chair in shock. Guess I should have read all the paperwork first.

"Well Fuck"

PRE ORDER IT NOW